Hayduke Lives!

A NOVEL BY

Edward Abbey

Little, Brown and Company

Boston · Toronto · London

FIRST EDITION

This is a work of fiction. Names, characters, places, and
incidents are either the product of the author's imagination or,
if real, are used fictitiously. Any similarity to real persons,
living or dead, is coincidental and not intended by the author.

Library of Congress Cataloging-in-Publication Data
Abbey, Edward, 1927–1989
Hayduke lives!: a novel/by Edward Abbey.—1st ed.
p. cm.
ISBN 0-316-00411-1
I. Title.
PS3551.B2H39 1989
813'.54—dc20   89-39725
                      CIP

10 9 8 7 6 5 4 3 2 1

Design by Virginia Evans

HC

Published simultaneously in Canada
by Little, Brown & Company (Canada) Limited

Printed in the United States of America

If friendship is equivalent to wealth and good fortune, then I have been a rich and lucky man throughout my life. Therefore, thinking each new book may be my last (for who knows?—and one does grow weary anyway of this infernal scribbling), I hereby dedicate *Hayduke Lives!* to my loyal friends who have so enriched the Late Middle Ages of my slothful and careless even reckless existence, i.e., viz., and to wit:

To Clarke Cartwright, my lover, comrade and wife for the last ten years, indispensable solace and delight to her husband and full-time mother to our children;

to Joshua, Aaron, Susie, Becky and Ben, my five beautiful children, the loves of my life;

to Jack Loeffler, jazz trumpeter, musicologist, river rat, irrepressible wellspring of laughter and good cheer who has dragged me back, many a time, from the fatal luxury of melancholy;

to John DePuy, landscape painter, desert wanderer and fellow misanthrope, who shares with me a wholesome contempt for the wretched human race (considered as one among the other animal species);

to Douglas Peacock, grizzly bear man, adventurer and eco-warrior, Ken Sleight, wilderness explorer, Ken Sanders, publisher, and to Dave Foreman and Bart Kohler and Mike Roselle and Howie Wolke, founders of EF! and true American heroes;

to Bill Hoy, Jim Carrico and Jim Stiles, fellow park rangers in the days when it was still an honor to be a ranger;

to Pam and Clair Quist, Bob Quist, Richard Quist, Mark Jensen, Amil Quale and Bartley Royal Henderson IV, white-water boatmen and Vikings all;

to Dave Petersen, Bill Eastlake, Barry Lopez, Chuck Bowden, Byrd Baylor, Alan Harrington and Edward Hoagland, fellow writers;

to Steve Prescott, Brendan Phibbs and Ian Macgregor, medical men, who yanked me back, more than once, albeit reluctantly, from the edge of the grave;

to Bob Greenspan, Ingrid Eisenstadter, Karilyn and Marilyn McElhenny, Lisa and Laurel and Colin Peacock, Peter and Marian and Katy and Sarah Gierlach, Don Spaulding, D. K. and Sue Adams, Vic Williams, Anne Spaulding, Dan O'Sullivan, Dusty Teal, Tommy Thompson, Jane Woodruff, Susan Prescott, Tom and Carolyn Cartwright, Jane Sleight, Kathy and Celestia Loeffler, Nancy Morton, Leli Sudler, Bill Broyles, Terry and Suzi Moore, Geoffrey Platts, Ann Woodin, Carolyn Petersen, Mary Sojourner, Alice Quevas, Caroline Hogue, Tom Arnold, Owen Severence, Linelle Wagner, Ernest and Nanette von Bulow, Malcolm Brown, Jon Soderlund, Pat Conley, Amador Martinez, Ralph Newcomb, Bill McReynolds, Kevin Briggs, Jim Ferrigan, Katie Lee, Dick Kirkpatrick, "Mitch"

Mitchell, Robert Crumb, Roger Grette, Wally Mulligan, Hendrik von Oss, Gregory McNamee, Bob Lippman (lawyer!), Bob Redford (an actor), Mark Richards (gunman), Donn and Carol Rawlings, Ed Twining, Tom Gross, Brian Walker, Dave West (secret agent), Tom Austin (police chief), Cliff Wood (rancher) and his family, and Drummond Hadley (rancher-cowboy-poet), to all of these my gratitude for the affection and good times and adventures in the world that we shared, that I will never forget, that can never be lost.

E.A.

O pardon me, thou bleeding
piece of earth,
That I am meek and gentle
with these butchers.
—William Shakespeare

Getting even is not the best revenge.
It is the only revenge.
—George W. Hayduke

We stand for what we stand on.
—Bonnie Abbzug

Down with Empire! Up with Spring!
—Doc Sarvis

CONTENTS

Hayduke Lives!

1
Burial

Old man turtle ambles along the deerpath, seeking breakfast. A strand of wild ricegrass dangles from his pincer-like beak. His small wise droll redrimmed eyes look from side to side, bright and wary and shrewd. He walks on long leathery legs, fully extended from the walnut-colored hump of shell, the ventral skid-plate clear of the sand. His shell is big as a cowboy's skillet, a gardener's spade, a Tommy's helmet. He is 145 years old — middleaged. He has fathered many children and will beget more. Maybe.

A desert tortoise. Tortoise, turtle, what's the difference? There is none. The ancient Greeks thought the tortoise a kind of demon. So much for the Greeks. An ignorant people.

This old man follows his regular route, seldom wandering more than a hundred yards from his base camp. Like all desert turtles, he knows his home, loves it, stays there, guards it. Above his head grow shrubs of silvergray sagebrush, taller than trees to him. Above the sage, aligned with the course of a ravine where clear water flows over ledges of rosy sandstone, stand huge fat free-form cottonwoods. Their bright green leaves tremble in the faintest breeze. To the turtle the treetops seem remote as the clouds. Where a buzzard sails, tipping sideways.

Where a small airplane drones through the air on its linear, tedious, single-minded course.

The world tips eastward, a molten sun bulges above the eastern canyon wall. Sun the size of a demon's fist. (Appearance *is* reality, said a wise man, Epicurus.) Wall pink like sliced watermelon, right-angled verticality, rising one hundred feet above the graygreen talus of broken rock, scrub juniper, blackbrush, scarlet gilia, purple penstemon, golden prince's plume. It is the season of spring in the mile-high tablelands of the canyon country. In America the still Beautiful.

Old man turtle keeps to the shade. By the time the sun has flooded the canyon floor with light and heat he will have returned to his cool dark den deep in the ground.

He pauses to clip a stem of grass from its base, folds the green blade into his toothless jaws. Grass getting harder to find these days; his desert infested with a novel enemy, the domestic beef cow. He ambles on.

He stops again to sniff at a nut-brown dropping, the size and shape of a chocolate-covered almond, resting on the sand. Pack rat? Elk? River toad? None of these — but rather the dung of another turtle, a stranger and a female. Old man turtle lifts his head and peers about, wise ancient humorous eyes now a shade brighter than before, alert, their twinkling beads of carmine light set in a mass of leather wrinkles.

Where is she?

Head aloft, he sniffs the air. But the air currents come from his rear, bearing not the sweet fragrance of female turtle in estrus but an odor of something rank, vile, poisonous, of a thing hot and burning, an entity not alive but nevertheless in motion, approaching him from a vast but not incomprehensible distance. The smell is totally new in the nostrils and nerves of old man turtle, totally different from anything known in his fourteen and a half decades of experience. It is a stink even worse than that of cow and cow's dung. Rigid with attention, beak up and neck extended to its full three inches, the old turtle searches memory and the collective unconscious of the tortoise race.

No clue.

The wind changes direction by a few degrees, the dark smell abates, fades off. At once he forgets it.

The turtle lowers his head, steps forward nose to the ground, tracing the spoor of a lovely stranger. A pink plastic ribbon flutters from the head of a stake in the ground, catching his eye. Again the old man stops.

He feels a dim vibration in the crust of the earth. The ground trembles. Again the wind veers, again he smells the harsh violent odor of something unknown and alien to his world. He feels, he smells, and now he hears that thing's approach: a metallic clatter growing loud and louder, a sound as queer and unprecedented as the odor.

Old turtle cranes his neck to look backward but sees only the familiar sprigs of sagebrush with their miniature purple bloom, the red sand, the dried-out cow-burnt clumps of bunch grass, the invading thickets of cheatweed. Above the sage, beyond the cloudy trees, he sees what might be a veil of dust rising slowly toward the blue.

Running cattle? The desert turtle consults his memory file. Perhaps it is cattle. But the stench of cattle, though foul indeed, is nothing like what he smells now. Nor do their cloven devils' hooves create the shrill hard screeching clamor that he hears this time.

The alien. An alien monster, unimaginable, unforeseeable, coming closer, moment by moment.

The turtle lowers his head and hurries forward, feeling pursued. Feeling fear. Aware finally of a new and definite mortal danger. Perhaps he should turn aside, hunt for shelter under the ledges of the creek or among the junipers on the talus slope, but such a plan does not occur to the elementary brain of old turtle. From custom and obeying the homeward instinct, he sticks to the familiar path, bound for his deep and sheltering burrow in the ground.

Too late.

Something huge and yellow, blunt-nosed glass-eyed grill-faced, with a mandible of shining steel, belching black jolts of smoke from a single nostril of seared metal, looms suddenly gigantically behind the old desert turtle.

The monster bellows in his rear, gaining fast, rumbling forward on an endless track of linked and clanging iron feet, shoving before it as it comes a rolling wave of sand, earth, rocks, small trees and mangled sagebrush.

Old turtle looks back again as he trots forward on his little clawed feet, sees the unknown unknowable thing closing upon him yard by yard, hears the grunt and moan then scream of triumph as it uproots a tree, pushing the tree aside to die from its wounds, scraping the ground bare of every living thing, piling a great furrow of ruin into the flowing stream. Ten feet behind the turtle, the monster roars in fury, jetting oily smoke into the air, and clatters forward.

Too late the turtle turns aside from the ancient path. Too late he searches for the sanctuary of overhanging ledge. Glancing back over his shell one last time, the old turtle sees the billow of advancing earth, the flat blunt snout of yellow steel blotting half the sky. Too late —

Turtle drops flat to the sand. Quickly he pulls in head, tail and all four legs as the wave of matter towers above then thunders down upon his brittle shell. His world goes black, all light extinguished. Buried, he feels like Atlas, the weight of earth upon his back. It is a terrible weight, an overwhelming weight, followed at once by a vibrating mass of advancing pressure one thousand times greater. . . .

Above, in the light and the dust, the tractor clatters on, unaware of and indifferent to any living creatures beneath its tread. The shining bulldozer blade pushes another mound of dirt to this side, to that side, over the grass, into the streambed and the clear water. The blade rises, the tractor backs and turns a few degrees, rumbles forward again. A dim anthropomorph, helmeted, masked and goggled, fixed in place under a canopy of steel, attached by gloved forelimbs to a pair of levers, moves jerkily half-blindly inside the fog of dust, one small component of a great machine. . . .

The tractor moves on, down the canyon, guided by a line of pink ribbons twitching on stakes of pale thin lathing. Trailed by its dust and its ten-foot-wide track of barren ground, the yellow machine dwindles with distance, its howl of engine fading off, the tin-can clacking of its plates and sprocket-wheels becoming faint, fainter, dying away to a petty irritation on the air.

Old man turtle is gone. Buried alive. Packed beneath compacted soil, his monument the broad straight imprinted treadmarks of the forty-ton machine, the old desert tortoise dwells now in darkness, silence, a firm and perfect stasis. Not a drop of blood nor a splinter of bone, not even the shadow of his footprints, remains to trace his ephemeral passage upon and through the little world of sunlight and sand, gopher hole and gopher snake, ant lion, sidewinder, solpugid and vinegaroon, green ephedra and Indian paintbrush and prickly pear and Gambel oak and dagger-bladed flowering yucca. They too are gone, down under, overturned and smothered under dirt.

The silence might seem complete, the destruction sufficient. Not so. Miles behind the bulldozer, as yet inaudible, visible from the turtle's grave merely as a pallid box-like structure with upthrust arms, comes the real machine, the true monster, the mega-machine advancing down canyon through its own permanent self-generated shroud of smog. Its engine housing is 120 feet wide, seven stories tall. The top of its main boom is twenty-two stories high, overreaching the canyon walls, longer than a football field. The excavating bucket that hangs from the point of the boom has a capacity of 220 cubic yards — big enough to hold two railroad cars, eight bulldozers, twelve automobiles, or a battalion of soldiers stacked three men deep in firm military formation. The complete machine (with empty bucket) weighs 27 million pounds, or 13,500 tons.

What is this thing? What shall we call this creature, dimly seen within its veil of dust and smoke? It is the Giant Earth Mover, GOLIATH the *G.E.M. of Arizona,* the Super-G.E.M., a Bucyrus-Erie walking dragline, world's largest mobile land machine.

Mobile? Yes, it moves. It does not roll on wheels or track on endless treads but it moves, it walks on a pair of steel shoes mounted — one on each side — above the circular tub that forms the base, or bottom, or mono-buttock, of GOLIATH. The shoes, each 130 feet long, are hoisted in unison, cambered forward, downward and back, raising the base 80 inches off the ground and moving it ahead by fourteen feet at each rotation. Maximum walking speed is 90 feet per hour. A slow but steady pace, sustainable forever — or until the power fails. Very slow indeed; but GOLIATH is a patient monster.

Only a turtle, not the largest but the longest-living of any land animal, could be more patient. As it waits, six feet under, for the coming of the beast.

2

Doc and Bonnie at Home

Pardon me, thou bleeding piece of earth, that I am meek and gentle with these butchers.

Who said that? Shakespeare said that. Well, Mark Antony. So, Shakespeare said it through one of his characters. So what?

He parked his bicycle in a corner of the garage, between the car and the wall. At once, as it usually did, the bicycle folded its front wheel inward and slid to the cement floor. Usually? Always. Never could park his bicycle straight. But what the hell, it's only a piece of tubular alloy from Yokohama. With wheels and attachments — hardly a true Zen machine — but not the one attachment he needed, a parking stand. Didn't Bonnie promise him one for his birthday? her birthday? Reuben's?

He unstrapped and removed the packages from the kiddie's seat mounted over the rear wheel of the bicycle. Nothing broken, luckily, the bottle of Bombay gin intact, that was for him, and the bottle of Mondavi, hers. And the essential can of soda pop for the boy.

La vie domestique, a farcical role for a philosopher, perhaps, but he accepted it. He liked it. At times he loved it. Even the few hours he spent daily downtown at the trauma factory were often a few too many. He missed his little boy. He missed his wife. Every working day.

Avoiding the front door, where the tricycle waited, the treacherous toy trucks, backhoes and front-end loaders spread like a field of mines across the tiles, he took the walkway through the yard gate, past the always dangerous swimming pool — a child can drown in three minutes — and entered by the French doors on the terrace.

"Anybody home?" he bellowed, as he always did on entrance, noting the aroma of marinated chicken on the kitchen air, a trace of forsythia from the open windows by the garden. After all these years and all that gin and bourbon, he still had a good, handsome and functional nose. Other organs might falter from time to time but his steadfast stalwart nose, rubicund but integrated, carried on like a trooper.

He heard a muffled response from the kitchen, peeked in over the half-door, and saw Bonnie bending at the oven, poking something with a fork. As she often did in hot weather, she wore an apron — and nothing else. Tied as it was in back, he loved he adored he worshipped the fetching manner in which the loose ends of the bow, cunningly centered, dangled in the cleavage of her rear décolletage. He froze in the doorway, staring like a horned and desperate teenager.

"Stop leering at me," she said, "and fix the drinks."

Smiling, he untracked himself and did as commanded. Finished, he seated himself on a chair. Fork in hand, she straddled his thighs and kissed him. They touched again in crystal: her wineglass of rose against his tumbler full of ice and gin.

"Where's Reuben?"

"At the Finleys'. They're bringing him home at six."

He took a deep draft of his martini. "Then we've just got time for a quickie."

She snuggled close and licked his ear. "You and who else, old man? You for a quickie? Takes you five minutes to remember where you put it."

The boy came storming in as scheduled, filling half the house with his noisy joy. Doc had barely time to redo his suspender clips before Reuben climbed a chair and hurled himself into the old man's arms: "Daddy!"

That's me, he thought, I guess. If not me who? Whom? And does it matter? It does not. He hugged the squirming animal in his arms, kissed him and set him down, on demand. Reuben was three years old, a bit short for his age (like his mother), but quick and vivid and supple as a squirrel. Also like his mother. He had her dark wavy copper-tinted hair, her large grayblue eyes, the rosy cheeks. So where are the Sarvis genes? he thought again. Where else but in the nose, that proud prominent proboscis like an eagle's beak that leads the soul of man to ever higher braver nobler adventures. My boy. A bit of the old Semitic curve to the nostril, of course, that's her touch again. Gives the lad the look of a young Arabian prince. About to mount his horse.

> The Assyrians came down like a wolf on the fold,
> Their cohorts all gleaming in purple and gold, eh?

Yes.

Bonnie came down from the master bedroom, dressed in red and green and gold, gold blouse, green slacks, a red sash around her still slender waist. In Doc's eyes, in any man's eyes, she was a vision of delight. The years and a little too much desert sun had added wrinkles around her eyes, bleached out somewhat the rich deep mahogany of her hair, perhaps toughened the skin at the base of the throat. How many times had he urged her to wear a scarf around her neck? Reminding her of the holes in the ozone, the greenhouse effect, the dangers of skin cancer? To what avail? She was beautiful. She did as she pleased.

Young Reuben met her halfway on the stairs, shouting again. She squatted to embrace him, picked him up wriggling like a cat, carried him down and into the kitchen, where Doc set the rugged pine table with plates and flatware, wineglass and beermug and an unbreakable synthetic cup for the child, filled with milk. Milk of cow. Bonnie's breasts looked bountiful as ever but she had weaned the boy over a year before; the liebfraumilch secreted there she was saving for the next. The next? Why yes, Bonnie Abbzug was pregnant again. First trimester. For the second, final and forever last time, she swore. But no doubt about it, Bonnie had been stuffed. One on the floor, one in the oven.

Her personal pollinator, *el viejo verde,* her green old man, Alexander K. Sarvis, M.D., F.A.C.S., Professor of Pediatrics at the College of Medicine of the University of Utah, Salt Lake City, poured himself a Bud and sat down at the table. "Hungry," he said, "let's eat. Feel like somebody took me for a run around the block in double time."

"You wanted a quickie," she said, "you got the best in town."

"A succubus from Heaven," he agreed. "I have a notion, though, the whole thing was planned. Whenever I see you wearing that apron I know I'm in for trouble and hard work."

"Hard work!" She laughed. "I did the work."

"But I'm the one that's tired."

"Mutter," said the boy, "what is Daddy talking about?"

"He doesn't know what he's talking about, do you, Daddy?"

"That's right and I don't care and if you really want to find out, old Reube my shrimp, I'll read you a book. When you're ready for bed, that is."

"What book?"

"Well, how about Rapunzel? Snow White? Cinderella?"

"No mushy stuff," the boy said. "I want action."

Doc grinned at Bonnie as she set the casserole of baked chicken on the table. "See what I mean? Little boys really are different from little girls."

"Cultural conditioning, cultural conditioning."

"And the bigger they get the bigger the difference."

"It's all a matter of cultural conditioning."

"At the age of three?"

"At any age."

Doc smiled, tying a bib around Reuben's neck. They'd been going around and around on this topic for years. A circular argument. Finite but boundless. Like many other differences of opinion between — or among — the various American sexes. Us white men, he thought, sole source of all evil, and *them*, the others, those many and various Official Minorities. Which included, of course, the female sex. Only in America could women demand to be considered an official minority group with all the special privileges pertaining thereunto. Smiling, he carved his potato, cut Reuben's chicken into safe bite-size pieces.

"What are you smirking about now?"

"Who, me?"

"Yeah, you."

Reuben pulled the bib free over his head and tossed it casually to the floor. He attacked his meat with a fierce fork.

Replying to his wife off the topside of his mind, the good doctor thought, below, on a more serious, masculine level, Yes it's true, true, takes patience to appreciate domestic bliss.

"Oink," she said, "oink oink."

But at least we're not arguing with George. Anything's better than trying to reason with George Washington Hayduke.

"You're not really answering my question, wise guy."

Answering her question with another flip evasion, he thought,

What would George do if he heard about Radium Canyon? About Lost Eden Canyon?

"What's Daddy talking about, Mutter?"

"He doesn't know what he's talking about, darling. Does he, Daddy?"

"Gender, sweetheart, gender. How to render the gender . . . tender." What would he do if he heard about GOLIATH?

In bed. The silent tube confronted them, bland blond Mormon faces blathering about the weather, basketball, the rising Salt Lake, something or other, whatever. With the volume turned to zero Doc and Bonnie looked at the perfectly hairdressed heads perched like puppets behind a curvilinear plastic barrier or desk or counter of some kind, chipper smiles and empty eyes facing the red eye of the camera. TV, like a child, should be seen not heard.

Doc held the remote-control device in his hand. The one good invention of the television age. "Why am I so tired?" he complained. "Turn it off?"

"You take your patients too seriously."

"They're dying. Most of them. Or else there's nothing wrong with them at all, only their mothers with too much money and too little to do. Anyhow I'm tired. Maybe I'm getting old."

"You old but you not dead." She patted her belly. "Feel it."

He felt it, his big smooth clever hand spread half across the slight but discernible bulge. "What shall we call this one?"

"Deborah."

"Suppose it's a boy?"

"It's a girl. We'll call her Deborah. After my Aunt Sally."

"Your Aunt Sally's name is Sally."

"Her mother was Deborah."

"I see. But I'll bet it's a boy. Another Reuben."

"What's wrong with Reuben?"

"Good name for a sandwich."

"What's wrong with Reuben?"

"Nothing's wrong with Reuben. Who said there's anything wrong with Reuben? He's a little short, that's all."

"He's your son."

"My short son. What makes you so sure this next one's a girl?"

"Not the next one. The last one. Because I know she's a girl."

"But how do you know?"

"I just know." She stared at the TV. The cheerful heads had disappeared for a moment, succeeded by a confused picture of young men and women trying to climb a barbed-wire fence. Demonstrators. As in demonic? Troublemakers. "Just know," she murmured.

"Intuition," he said. He knew better than to pursue this line of inquiry. But he could not restrain himself. "Your intuition tells you."

"Of course."

"Your dream analysis."

"That also. Of course."

"Your magic crystals."

Some tall sexbomb with long black wild hair was waving a flag at the TV cameras. She wore cut-off Levis, shamefully short, and a snug white T-shirt. Both T-shirt and flag bore the same mysterious device: a green fist in a red circle on a field of white. Latin colors.

"Crystals?" she said, with irritation. "I threw those silly things away a year ago. Look at that slut. What's she doing?"

"Good firm legs," he said. "Well-developed mammaries. Genetically sound facial structure. A healthy specimen of the breed, in reproductive prime. You never told me."

"Never told you what? Look at her. Look at them. What are they doing?"

"Never told me about throwing away your crystals. Shall I turn it off?"

"Wait," said Bonnie.

The picture changed. Two men were arguing at a microphone, a crowd of people seated, some standing, beyond them. Some of the faces in the background, out of focus, appeared to be distorted by anger. Contempt? Derision? Both men looked familiar. Distantly familiar, like intimations of a remote preincarnation.

"Doc," she said. "Look. It's Seldom. Isn't it?"

Doc gaped at the murky screen. The camera was being joggled or jostled by unprofessional hands. But he saw, he thought he could see, the angular bony face, the brown skin with pale forehead (where the hatline lay), the tousled tangled straw-colored hair, the basically unsheveled dress — crooked necktie, too-large collar, wrinkled and rumpled jacket — of that one and only same old Smith. That Seldom Seen Smith. Old Seldom Hisself. Always talking, always getting into arguments with somebody.

"And look," Bonnie cried, voice rising with excitement, "that other man. The big fat one in the rancher hat. The one chewing on that rock. Laughing. Don't we know him? Isn't that — ?"

Doctor Sarvis pressed the Off button. The picture collapsed upon itself, sucked into the black hole of electronic innerspace. Extinguished once now and forever. No, he thought, we don't know them. "Tired," he muttered, "very tired . . ."

"Doc!" She snatched the black-button gadget from his hand, switched the picture on again. Slowly, with some reluctance among the dancing whirling unitarily unpredictable quanta of subatomic particles — subnuclear waves? — transcendental subhypothetical wavicles? — a picture coalesced, reassembled itself, assumed color and form and a trivial semblance of human animation.

Four. The four smug smart heads sat there again, grinning through their well-groomed teeth, hairdos constructed in the precise vicious perfection of wigs in a wig shop, shuffling papers with their sanitary hands, their crisp clean polished pure fingernails.

Bonnie cut the picture. Silence. Darkness.

"Doc," she said, "that was Seldom. It was."

"Who?"

"You heard me. Seldom Seen. He's up to something."

"Never heard tell of Seldom Seen. Go to sleep, my love."

She fell quiet for a minute, trying. She stirred. "I can't," she said.

"Can't what?"

"Can't sleep."

"Sure you can, honey." He stroked her shoulder, caressed her plump little belly. Feigning an enormous yawn. "Tired, tired," he murmured, "oh so tired. . . ."

Bonnie lay silent, staring at the dim ceiling. For two minutes. "Doc . . . ?"

A gentle snoring at her side.

"Doc — you asleep?"

He twitched. Turned. Sighed. "Hey . . . ? Huh . . . ?"

"You think Reuben is all right?"

"Who?"

"Reuben."

"You were talking about Seldom."

"Well now I'm talking about Reuben. Do you think he's all right?"

"What's wrong with him?"

"That's not what I asked you. There's nothing wrong with him. I said, Do you think he's all right?"

Doc pondered the question. Linear thinking, he thought. Must get over this linear thinking. Learn to get my right brain into gear. Or is it the left? Get my crystals organized. Tap the old spinal intuition, pump out some extrasensory perception.

"Well . . . ?"

"I think he's fine," he said. "A little small, maybe, for his age-group, but otherwise just fine. Active, bright, in perfect health." There was a pause. Peace, he thought.

"Who is?"

"What?" Please. Let us have peace.

"That's what I'm asking you, for godsake. Who?"

"I thought we were talking about Reuben. Didn't you ask me about Reuben, for the love of Christ?"

"What if I did? It's Seldom I'm wondering about. And don't swear at me in bed."

"Sorry." He rolled to his side, striving for sleep. "Tired," he muttered.

"What do you suppose is going on?" she said. "You think Seldom's in trouble?"

"He's fine. A little short, sure, but . . ."

"What would George do if he were here?"

"George?" Alarm bells jangled in his heart.

"George, I said, who else? What would he do?"

"George is gone," he said. And thank God for that. The very thought of Hayduke loosened something fundamental in his bowels.

"I know. But suppose he's not. Suppose he came back."

"He's gone. You'll never see him again. He's gone."

"But just suppose . . . ?"

"Suppose we go to sleep, sweetheart." He closed his eyes tightly, hoping to shut out inner vision. Difficult. "I love you, honey," he mumbled, faking sleep.

"Love you too . . ."

Eyes shut, stiff as a stone, Doc lay wide awake. Doc was terrified. Yes, it was time for their long-postponed postnuptial honeymoon trip to — Italy? The isles of Greece? Provence? Majorca? Liverpool, Hamburg, Volgagrad, anywhere!

3
The Hearing

The hearing room was jammed. Packed. Packed and jampacked with the Bishop's courtiers, his employees, his menial minions and their families and their relations. All Mormons. And every decent Mormon couple is expected to breed at least twelve children. An unwritten rule of the Church, the one true church here below in the Land of Deseret.

At the long table on the dais, facing the crowd, sat the Suits. That is, the important men in the dark sober business suits who always preside over these affairs: the commissioners of Landfill County; the representatives of the BLM (Bureau of Livestock and Mining), of the NPS (National Parking-lot Service), of the USFS (United States Forest Swine), of the DOE (Department of Entropy), and of the State DG&F (Department of Game & Fishiness); and the spokesmen for private industry, in this case two Denver-based gentlemen presenting the views of Nuclear Syn-Fuels Ltd., a multinational combine with its general headquarters in Brussels and its hindquarters spread all over the globe.

Our globe.

The Suits had long before finished their presentations. Glancing at wristwatches — one of the Denver men wore six of them, three per wrist, each set to a different time zone — and then at the TV cameras, trapped by the high-intensity klieg lights, the sometimes unavoidable public exposure, they waited, bald heads gleaming, for termination of the unsolicited testimony from the common citizens. These, the un-invited and unwanted, would be cut off sharp at 5 P.M., finished or not. Together with the mediums from the media, those minor irritants.

There was also J. Dudley Love, commissioner from a neighboring county, a Bishop in the Church, owner of the state's largest fleet of ore haulers, part-time cattle rancher, night-time pot robber from ancient Indian tombs, important mine-owner and mining-claims speculator with holdings throughout the Four Corners region (Utah, Colorado, New Mexico, Arizona), motel owner, restaurant owner, charter air-line owner, member of the BLM Advisory Board and of the DOE's Advisory Board, aspirant to the U.S. Congress, to the Governor's mansion, to the U.S. Senate, to the Divine Kingdom, father of eleven children (only eleven — a sore point), and former poor boy who got his start as a mucker in Charlie Steen's Mi Vida uranium mine. The big one. Love was also a heavy investor in GOLIATH, the first Giant Earth Mover and walking dragline machine ever to be welded, bolted and slapped together in the Inter-Mountain West. He took great pride in each of these achievements but most pride, perhaps, in his bold and rejuvenated heart. There had been a time, yes, only a few years ago, when, under the influence of a quack heart surgeon and his brazen Jewish big-breasted sexpot of a concubine, Love's heart had softened, nearly failed, began to bleed for things like juniper trees and kit foxes and purple asters and desert turtles. A bad weak shameful period — menstrual, climacteric, you might say — in his life. But with help from the Church, from his fellow Rotarians, from his boys on the Search & Rescue Team, from prayer and God and Jesus, he had gotten over that malaise, had reformed, been reborn again with tough and vulcanized heart to become, once again, the biggest man in the whole damned goddamned canyon country. The new Love. The real Love. The ul-timate Love.

This particular Love was scheduled to testify at 4:45. His would be the last voice and the final face that the sound recorders, Nikons, microphones and the TV cameras would bear away, on videotape, for the viewing public. Such had been his private request to the hearing officer (J. Marvin Pratt, fellow commissioner) and it had been granted as a matter of course.

Meanwhile an hour of tedium remained. One by one members of the audience arose, as names were called from a list, and shuffled shyly forward to say their few and humble words. Dentists, lawyers, mine operators, a local newspaper publisher, cattle ranchers, the county sheriff, truckstop owners, storekeepers, construction contractors, school administrators, highway officials, officials of the state and county Chambers of Commerce, a Congressman, two state legislators — the dignitaries, as customary, had all been heard from first, in order of rank. Now, in the final hour, came a few actual miners, a few actual truckdrivers, even a dude wrangler and one registered nurse, to speak their piece. Each was allotted two minutes. All but two echoed the words and endorsed the wisdom of their betters. Yes, they agreed, these here new uranium mines will create jobs. The new mill means more jobs. Yes, we need industry here so our kids don't have to go to California or Salt Lake City (one near as wicked and Godless a place as the other) to find work. Yes, we need the tax base. Yes, we want to grow. Grow? Yes, GROW! Like that there big machine they got, that GOLIATH, we want GROWTH in our county too. We been neglected too long. Let them wilderness lovers go somewheres else, they got the whole Grand Canyon to get lost in and it serves them right.

Cheers! The joy of unanimity!

The R.N. was called, one Mrs. Kathy Smith. A stout redfaced woman, mother of two, wearing shiny maroon Dacron pants too tight for her large butt, hair done up in a bleach-blond apiary, she clutched the microphone and glared at the crowd, silent, too angry for words.

"Sit down," a man shouted from the back rows.

"Sit down and shut up," suggested another.

Cheers! Applause!

The woman eyed her hecklers. "Shame on you, Duane Bundy. Shame on you too, Eldon Stump. Where's your manners? You had your say, now it's my turn. And I say — "

"We heard it before."

"I say uranium is poison. Deadly poison. It gets in the air, it gets in the water, it gets in the ground — "

"Gets in your hair!" (*Laughter.*)

" — gets in your hair, gets in our children's bones. Strontium causes acute leukemia, ruins the bone marrow, makes people die. Especially children and young people, they almost always — "

"If God didn't want us to mine that uranium why'd He put it in the ground?"

" — almost always fatal for young people. What? God? If God wanted us to mine uranium, why'd He hide it four hundred feet *under* the ground? Like it was something He was ashamed of? [*Boos. Jeers.*] That stripmine will be half a mile wide. The tailings dump will be five hundred feet high. Nothing will ever be able to grow there, this Belgian corporation will dig out the uranium, process it here in our backyard, haul away a few thousand pounds of concentrate and leave us with a million tons of radioactive waste and a slime pit big as ten football fields full of radon gas. Radon gas — "

The hearings officer interrupted. "The right name for stripmine, Mrs. Smith, is surface mine. Not stripmine. This is open cast mining we're talking about, not strip mining. Strip mining is something they do to get coal back in Ohio. Watch your language, please. Stick to the facts and try not to get emotional. Also, your two minutes is up. Now let's see, who's next . . ."

"Wait a minute, I'm only started. About radon — "

"Your time is up, Mrs. Smith." Consulting his list of names. "Next: Joseph F. Smith." Looking out at the crowd. "Smith — you here?"

"I'll finish my say, J. Marvin, whether you like it or not." The nurse hung on to the mike. "And what I want to say is this: you can't cook with radon gas. Radon gas cooks you. You just think about my words, folks, and when this last uranium boom is over we can all talk about it in the nursing home. [*Coarse laughter.*] Inside our oxygen tents. Sure do thank you nice people for all the polite attention."

Engulfed in a storm of boos, jeers, catcalls and laughter, Kathy Smith searched for her open-back chair in the third row, found the chairseat taken by the big booted feet of a grinning rancher seated behind it. He did not remove his feet. The sharp pointed toes of the boots were thrust directly upward, like a pair of spearheads. Mrs. Smith pushed them apart and down, sideways, and planted her broad heavy bottom on the man's feet. He was caught like a skunk in a Number Two varmint trap.

"Smith!" yelled the hearing officer. "Last chance."

A gangling middleaged awkward fellow in rumpled jacket, oversize shirt collar with necktie askew, approached the microphone. His mop of sandy hair, plastered down with water and carefully combed only hours before, had fallen into disorder again: the forelock dangled over his eyebrow, a tuft of hair stood straight up on the back of his head like a sprig of snakeweed.

He adjusted the microphone, raising it about a foot, and introduced himself. "My name is Smith," he said. (*Vigorous boos.*) He grinned. "I guess you already know me. For any as don't, out there in TV land, my name is Seldom Seen Smith. I am a native Utahn and a good jack

Mormon and I make my living in the tourist business. I'm a dude wrangler."

"You're an anti-nuke puke," said a voice from the crowd.

"Bet your life. This uranium industry has damn near ruined southern Utah. Now they want to tear up the Arizona strip. I'm agin it. I'm — "

"You're an aginner, Seldom. You're agin everything."

"Damn near." Grinning, bobbing his head, brushing the forelock out of his eye, Smith continued. "This goldang nucular industry moves into our country, tears up the land with open pit mines, blasts roads everywhere, fouls up the trout streams, poisons the ground water supply, dries up the springs, drives out the wildlife, leaves garbage, junk, mineshafts, tailings dumps and radioactive mills all over the place, takes their profits back to New York and London and Tokyo and Gay Paree and leaves us nothing but miners with lung cancer and a ten-billion-dollar cleanup job which our kids are gonna have to pay for. We're stealing a decent life from our children to buy Lake Foul cabin cruisers and California mobile homes for ourselves."

"Our kids need jobs," shouted the heckler.

"Stop having so many kids," replied Smith.

A moment of shocked silence. Then a chorus of protest: "What? What's that? Genocide? You're agin children too? You want us to shoot 'em? How many kids you got, Smith?"

"Seven," he admitted. "Seven of the little devils. But I got three wives. That comes to two point two kids per wife."

Laughter. Jeers. Impatient applause.

The chairman banged his gavel. "Quiet. Let's have some order here. Not so much emotionalism. Smith, you try stickin' to the issue. The issue here today is a mine-mill permit for Syn-Fuels Limited and jobs for working people. Try not to get emotional, Smith. Stick to the facts and don't interrupt your neighbors when they ask you a question, please. All right. Your two minutes is up and it's time for the final testimony of the day." J. Marvin Pratt raised his head, looking about for his old buddy Bishop J. Dudley Love.

"Okay, but I'm gonna say one thing more," Smith concluded. "And that is I agree one hundred and fifty percent with my wife Kathy." He pointed to the large proud stubborn woman sitting on the sulky cowman's pigeon-toed and pinioned feet. "When she says uranium is dangerous for children and all other kinds of life she knows what she's talking about. Why, if I was one half as smart as that woman of mine I'd be twice as smart as — " Grinning. " — yonder Bishop Love."

Cheers. Jeers. Restrained, sitting ovation. Pointed remarks: "That ol' Smith he hain't as dumb as he looks." "Nobody could be that dumb." "Two point two kids per wife?" "That makes six regular and one six-tenths of a kid." "That must be the one that looks like Daddy. . . ."

Still grinning, grimly, Seldom fumbled his way toward his wife through a shouting crowd now risen to its feet, hands clapping like a panic of penguins, as the impressive figure of Bishop Love marched toward the podium.

The two men passed each other en route. "Smith," muttered the Bishop, smiling his crocodile smile, "I'm gonna core you like an apple."

"What?" said Smith, confused by the hubbub.

The Bishop reached the microphone. He gripped it like the neck of a chicken, yanked it another foot higher. A strangled squawk burst from the speakers. Love surveyed the hearing room, the cheering applauding crowd still on its feet, the attentive video cameras, the alert reporters, the complacent and satisfied faces of the Suits ranged behind the long table at his side. At last, one of their own had regained the floor.

The Bishop's suit, naturally, was a little different from the others. They wore business suits, some with vests; he wore a Western stockman's suit of silvergray gabardine, with leather buttons and a yoke back, the lapels high and sharp, the pockets outlined in red piping. Instead of a standard necktie he sported what was called a "bolo" tie: a string of braided leather passing around the shirt collar and through a clasp on the underside of a brooch. The brooch — or bolo — consisted, in this instance, of a wedge of clear plastic containing a dead scorpion, mounted to an arrow-shaped base of polished black pitchblende (U-235). The free ends of the tie, dangling, were each encased in sterling silver. His shirt and cuffs were fastened with pearl snap buttons. His Tony Lama high-heeled boots, hand-tooled, were made from the skin of a Komodo lizard. (Rare and endangered.) On his large silver-haired pot-shaped head he wore (disdaining to remove it) a silvergray XXX Stetson with three-inch brim, shaped — like his suit, like his paunch, like his gait — in the stockgrower's roll.

Love:

Love, Love, Love, thought Smith, observing this absurd manifestation of reticulated vanity, how come you're everywhere? Bishop Love, J. Dudley Love, you make the grass turn gray, Bishop Love.

He and his wife edged toward the door. They knew what Love

would say. They'd heard it many times before, from Love, from a thousand men like Love, from the papers, from the radio and TV, from the weekly magazines, from the Halls of Congress and the Commerce Chambers, from the lips of little children bearing home from school the teacher's lesson for the day:

Growth. We got to grow. We got to go and grow, forever grow, onward upward forward for-everward, growing with GOLIATH, for God for Country and for Love. . . .

"Folks," bellowed the Bishop, raising both hands for order and quiet, "good folks of southern Utah and the Arizona Strip, listen to me, I'll only take a minute, just like everybody else I'll speak my little piece and let you go. [*Crowd resumes seats.*] Thank you. Now we heard a lot today, especially in the last ten minutes, from those good neighbors of ourn, Mr. and Mrs. Kathy Smith [*laughter*] about how dangerous this nucular industry is. Uranium is poison, they say. Well I want to tell you folks something different: that uranium smells like money to me. [*Cheers!*] It smells like jobs to me. [*More cheers!*] Hundreds of jobs right here in Hardrock and Landfill County and just across the line in northern Arizona. Hundreds? I mean thousands of jobs. [*Thunderous applause!*] Now ol' Smith he says he got seven kids. Seven kids by three wives. [*Laughter.*] Well folks, you know and I know that ain't nothing. I know half you good men got a dozen kids. [*Shouts of A-men!*] Why I got eleven myself and me and the missus — " He winks. " — we're workin' on number twelve. [*Laughter. Cheers.*] Right. And that's why this Syn-Fuels mine smells good to me. Smells like jobs to me. Smells like money to me. I don't mind telling you, folks, I like that smell. [*Cheers!*] Yessir, I like the smell of money. We don't need more so-called wilderness; only attracts more environmentalists. Like a dead horse draws blowflies. Round here we eat them environmen-talists, ain't that right, boys? [*Shouts of agreement.*] Cause there ain't much else to eat, right? [*Right!*] Poison, they say? Cancer? Leukemia? Listen, folks, I'm here to tell you there's one man don't fear the smell of uranium, don't fear the smell of radon. Because I lived here all my life and I worked in the first uranium mines and I'm still here and I don't glow in the dark — [*Laughter*] — and by all heck and tarnation I'm happy as a hog in hog heaven. [*He pats the vial of digitalis in his inside jacket pocket, near his heart.*] Some of us just don't buy this scare talk about cancer and radiation. In fact I'm here to tell you folks, what most of you already know: radiation is good for you. [*Murmur of happy voices.*] That's right, and I'll say it again, radiation is really good for you. What'd you think the sunshine is? Radiation. What's that old sun hisself. One big old nucular power plant boiling away, shooting out all those rays of golden radiation that makes the grass grow, the flowers bloom, the pigs happy and the clouds fill up with rain. Yessiree bob, radiation is good for everything. What does that Seldom Seen Smith know? Nothing, that's what. He's the kind of guy can fall in a barrel of tits and come out suckin' his thumb. An ignorant man! [*Applause.*] And his wife, well that Kathy, she's a good woman, she's a good nurse, but I'm sorry to say she has been sadly misinformed about radiation. Because she's got it all backwards. And I aim to prove it to you. Right here and now. Let me show you something. . . ."

Bishop Love reached inside his suitcoat and pulled a small chunk of carnotite — a friable, yellowish, highly radioactive uranium ore — from an inside pocket. He held it up where all could see it.

"That's carnotite, folks. That's what we got south of here in those big canyons off the Grand Canyon. Now you know and I know the uranium industry is in a slump these days, the American nucular business is shot to hell, the doggone environmentalists are shutting down the nuke plants, but this ore is so rich, my friends, such high-grade ore, that even with yellowcake down to seventeen dollars a pound this stuff is worth mining. Let the price go down to ten a pound this carnotite will still pay. Europe wants it if we don't. And Japan, Brazil, them places. This is pay dirt, men. Radioactive gold."

Murmurs of approval. Love pointed to one of his crew in the front row. The fellow handed him a portable Geiger counter, battery-powered, with probe and cord. Love set the black box-like device on the table, in full view of the audience, switched it on, held up the attached chrome-plated probe in one hand and the lump of sulfur-colored rock in the other. A loud clicking noise began immediately.

"All right, folks, now listen to that music. This high grade or ain't it?" He touched the probe to the ore. At once all present heard the radiation count rise in crescendo to the frantic buzzing of an infuriated rattlesnake. "Hear that? You people out there in TV land hear that? That's high-intensity radiation. That's one mad buzzworm in there. Pure U-238. Yessiree bob, this little yeller rock is hot as a pistol, folks, hot as my Aunt Minnie's old-timey radium wristwatch. . . ."

Murmurs of admiring approval from the audience.

"Yessir," Love went on, "this here is one hot little piece of power. And am I afraid of it? Am I one little teeny-weeny itsy-bitsy scared of it? Watch this."

Love lowered the probe. Holding the rock high in one hand, he turned to face the TV cameras and the glaring lights, the important men behind the table, the crowd in the folding chairs. "Watch me now." Head up, in profile to the cameras, he opened his mouth and placed the carnotite in his teeth, bit off a piece. Chewing vigorously, grinning at everybody and everything, he masticated his tidbit thoroughly, then — swallowed it. Mrs. Smith covered her eyes.

Laughter. Cheers. The assembly began to stand again.

"Yes!" Love bellowed, "radiation is good for you! [*Growing applause*.] Uranium is good for you! Uranium is good for Utah and Arizona! The nucular industry is good for America!"

The audience rose to its feet, clapping like geese, bawling like sheep, roaring with love for Love and heartful joy in its own brave common sense. Holding both hands aloft like a triumphant fighter, Bishop Love shouted his benediction. "And now, folks, now everybody, I want to invite you all to come across the street with me to Mom's Café. I'm gonna buy a Pepsi for every man in the house!"

Seldom Seen Smith — face flushed with anger — struggled toward the microphone, going the wrong way against the current of the surging, laughing, cheering, merry throng. The cameras watched. J. Marvin Pratt, chairman and hearings officer, reached behind his chair and unplugged the microphone, then departed with the other Suits, all smiling, through a rear exit.

4
GOLIATH the Super-G.E.M.

The lonesome juniper, nine-tenths dead, thrust its bare burnished gray claw toward the blue. A brown towhee crept beneath the juniper's one live branch, picking at the turquoise berries and the bugs that crawled within the clutch of surviving green. High on the rosy canyon wall a wren sang out, flute notes falling in a bright cascade of quicksilver semiquavers. A pair of ravens watched and listened. On the rimrock, in dark silhouette against the sky, a horse and rider waited, watching, listening. Above them all, high in the vault of heaven, one black buzzard sailed in lazy circles, waiting for something, somebody, anybody, anything incarnate and animal, to die. Where there's life there's hope.

The flat treadmarks of the tractor lay stamped upon the desert turtle's grave, implacable and mute, final, permanent, perfect. Nearby, in the half-dammed streambed, a funnel of muddy water poured around the encroachment of the spoilbanks of overturned earth, broken and jumbled sandstone slabs, torn sagebrush, mutilated and slowly dying trees — Gambel's oak, stripling cottonwoods, sapling willow, box elder, singleleaf ash, pinyon pine, juniper.

On the far side of the stream appeared a similar, almost identical broad highway of progress, improvement and development: the earth scraped bare of vegetation, the rocks and trees and brush bulldozed aside and piled in ragged heaps beyond the lifeless track. The tread-marks of the iron tractor led both ways — down canyon toward whatever lay concealed around the next bend, up the canyon toward the natural springs that formed the source of the stream. Beyond were high rolling tablelands of red cliffs, sandstone domes, grassy swales, forests of sage and juniper and pinyon pine.

In that direction, beyond and within its self-generated pall of smog and dust, laboring forward but with many miles to go, came the machine. The mega-machine. The red and yellow *G.E.M. of Arizona*, the Super-G.E.M., high as a hotel and taller than a grain elevator, heavier than 150 Boeing 727 jet-liners, wide as a railroad barn or wider than six Caterpillar D-9 tractors lined end-to-end, with enough power to supply electricity for a city of 100,000 —!

"From Bucyrus-Erie. An international business. Flood control. Canals. Underground utilities. Pipeline construction. Dam construction. Road construction. Mining metals. Mining non-metallics. Mining phosphate — soil food. Mining energy. The multibillion-dollar U.S. coal and uranium industry and a larger electric power industry continue to grow each year, here and abroad. B-E machines lead in surface mining — worldwide. Energy needs and energy mining. On the increase. Everywhere. With new regard for mining's legacy. Reclamation. Improved, more useful land — the legacy of open cast mining. The ultimate step. In the cities. In the country. In the remotest regions. Bucyrus-Erie is there. Here. Everywhere. Essential ingredient . . . people. Skilled. Well-equipped. Conscientious. Trained. Motivated. Dedicated to precision and accuracy. Experienced management. Worldwide manufacturing. Tradition of excellence. Commitment to quality. Leadership. Advanced designs. On Nature. On Life. On YOU! . . . Bucyrus-Erie."

The 4250-W Walking Dragline.

GOLIATH.

One hundred feet above the buried turtle, the near-dead juniper, the flattened-out canyon floor, the man on the horse sat quietly in the saddle and watched, listened, waited.

The horse was a large old castrated stallion with dangling mottled cock eighteen inches long, like a length of rotten salami, staling with some difficulty on the hard stone of the canyon rim. Prostate trouble. The horse, off-white in color, had mangy patches on flank and shoulder, feet like frying pans, one loose shoe, a Roman nose, long and yellow teeth.

The man seated on the sagging middle of the horse's back wore wrinkled darkblue riding pants smeared with bacon grease on thigh and hip, high boots with rusty spurs, a dirty baggy once-white shirt of weird design (no collar, double row of buttons up the front), the dusty black scarf (of anarchism?) tied about the neck, dirty white gloves with high gauntlets, and a dirty white ten-gallon comical hat with four-inch brim.

He also packed a brace of silver-plated, ivory-handled, .44 magnum Ruger revolvers, each in its leather holster, strapped to his waist by a broad ammo belt studded with cartridges, some of them empty brass. For reloading.

Dark dense Ray-Ban sunglasses shaded his eyes, looped to his neck by a strap like hotdog skiers wear.

He was a thin gristly man, narrow-shouldered, concave in the chest, not tall, not short. He looked old, older than his horse, three times older than his horse. He needed a shave. He needed a bath. His nose came to a point. His ears drooped. His hair was a greasy brown with streaks of gray. And his eyes, dimly visible behind the sunglasses, did not match. There was something false and alarming about one of his eyes.

In any case he merely sat there on his withered hams, in his worn saddle, on his worn-out horse, doing nothing practical or useful. Only watching, waiting, listening, making a fool of himself, because he was the scout.

Meanwhile, below, the little pink ribbons fluttered on the survey stakes. Old man turtle lay stiff as a stone in his grave. The muddied stream rippled in its channel, gurgling over the fresh mud, and flowed down canyon between the parallel bulldozer tracks, around the bend, through a rocky gorge with springs where pink penstemon and scarlet bugler flowered, around another bend into a broad vale thick with wild Indian ricegrass (no cattle in here yet), where the bulldozer roads diverged at the far end and disappeared up opposite side canyons.

But the stream went on mile after mile, down ledges and terraces of stone, forming clear pools and waterfalls, and descended a deeper more narrow gorge into a daring canyon, a canyon of drama and fantasy, deeper than wide, a thousand feet deep and two hundred feet wide, where the water leaped from chutes in bluegray limestone, passing more springs, acquiring more volume, plunging still deeper, deeper, toward the master canyon of them all.

*　　*　　*

A cove at the canyon mouth. Two wooden dories, flat white with gunwale stripes of red and green, lay tied to willows on a sandy beach. The name of one dory was *Lost Eden*, of the other *Paradise Regained*. Golden oars at rest, the bright high-riding pretty boats bobbed in the sandy shallows, sterns in the water of the river, their cockpits stacked with Gott coolers, ammo cans, lifejackets, waterjugs, rocket boxes, cases of beer. On the cans and boxes were round stickers, each with its upthrust green fist in a red circle on a field of white. A trail of discarded clothing led from the two boats up a path winding among boulders on the side of the busy, flashing stream. Here lay a long-billed boating cap in desert camouflage brown, and there a white T-shirt, on its back a picture of planet Earth and the legend in green *We Stand For What We Stand On*. A girl's halter top. Ragged bluejean cutoffs, shockingly brief. A black bandanna. Another sloganeering T-shirt: *Down With Empire!, Up With Spring!* A pair of man's shorts. One flip-flop sandal. Lime-green panties. A black string bikini. A sweat-stained salt-encrusted felt hat decorated with hand-tied trout flies. Somebody's boxer-style swim trunks. . . .

The path wound among pastel boulders the color of hardrock candy, under willow trees and fat-trunked cottonwoods, into the creek, across a fine sandbar, and disappeared in the depths of an emerald pool fifty feet wide. The water was agitated, turbulent: the creek poured into the upstream side from an overhanging spout of travertine fifty feet above, creating a bold but strangely pleasing sound, the white noise of waterfalls.

Water nixies played in the pool, three of them brown as Indians, brown all over, with long loose flowing hair, sparkling eyes, buoyant and rose-tipped breasts. One was short and chubby, one slim and tall, one bobbed up between: all were beautiful.

The three boys squatted on the bankside watching. One of them — wearing only a T-shirt — played a tune on a recorder. He grew a reddish beard on his chin; his curly brown hair flared up in pointed tufts above each ear. His mates, naked, darkskinned and hairy riverboatman types, passed a little Zig-Zag placebo back and forth, sucking noisily on the illegal fumes, grinning at the girls and feeling their erections grow to unbidden, unprecedented, unwieldy, unconcealable enormity. Where to hide them, that was the question. No doubt an answer would, at any moment, present itself. They waited, watched, shy as unicorns in a field of maidens, half stunned by the wild primeval clamor of their own blood.

The swimmers leaped in the water, supple bodies gleaming like trout. . . .

The musician lowered his instrument, feeling the tug of that more powerful instrument below. He looked at his eager comrades. They nodded. He pulled off *his* T-shirt (*"Hayduke Lives!"*) and dropped it to the sand. Rising together, primed like torpedoes, the three young men plunged into the water. The girls shrieked in mock alarm, scattered out, backed off, then regrouped and dove like dolphins for the deep center of the pool, flashing glossy bottoms at the hot pulsing leer of the sun.

Everything is better in the out-of-doors.

Everything?

A strand of red mud, iridescent with a trace of oil, appeared in the clear green of the waterfall.

5

The Cleaning Lady

The Suits gathered about the boardroom table, an architectural structure three times wider, near half as long and twice as polished as a bowling alley. Overhead an extravagant chandelier, glowing. . . . The older men puffed on obligatory cigars (the CEO was a smoker), the younger men chewed their lower lips, the one representative woman — handsome, hollow-cheeked as a fashion model, smartly and soundly costumed in a business suit of checked wool, skirt to her calves, silk blouse with frilled collar, discreet and genuine necklace of cultured pearls — she drew languidly on a slender cigarette of black and gold, thin as a pencil. Her fingernails, painted primrose red, were long, dangerously long, indicating to all who might notice or care that she did no useful work. Labor, that is. Manual, as with the hands, labor. Her male colleagues, some of them younger than she, some of whom might be presumed to be at least capable of pushing a lawnmower from time to time across the lawns of their Longmont estate homes, they too wore their fingernails long. Unpainted but scrubbed, buffed, trimmed, immaculate.

(Pushing a lawnmower? Pushing? A lawnmower? Nobody, nowhere, nobody in all of America, Japan or western Europe *pushes* a lawnmower. They *ride* them, pushing levers, buttons, horns. Or their gardeners do. Their children, maybe, sometimes.)

Waiting for the chief, the eleven men and one woman idled about the giant table, stared out the great wall windows at the thick brown air of the city, the streets far below, the dim snow-dappled distant mountains of the Front Range, the eastern plains extending through an infinity of haze toward the darkening East.

The Big Blue Behind was late, they noted, checking chronometers. Unusual for him. Like most great men in the upper echelons of Nuclear Fuels Inc. (U.S. subsidiary of Syn-Fuels Ltd.) he prided himself on his punctuality and demanded it of others. When one's virtues are singular one makes the most of one.

The twelve vice-presidents glanced at watches, gazed at the familiar scenery through the tinted Thermopane, mentioned certain items on the agenda.

" . . . Mountain States Legal Foundation?"

"Hell yes. They'll never get rid of old Wort. He's the founder."

"What about the appeal?"

"No problem. The judge understands."

"I hear he has this weakness for Indians."

"He'll go along. He understands the situation. They're not one of his tribes anyhow. Only two hundred on the whole reservation and half of them are drunks and the other half are children, he'll go along."

"They get that thing assembled?"

"Finally. Two months behind schedule. Some asshole trucker kept losing the welding equipment. You have any idea how many welds in one of those machines?"

"You mean the walking dragline?"

"I mean the 4250-W. About ten thousand. Damned welders pulling down thirty-five an hour, too. But we're working on that. Got the whole southern Utah school system training more welders now. More welders, pipe fitters, plumbers, electricians, diesel mechanics, operating engineers — "

"What the — ?"

"Yeah I know what you mean. Operating engineers. That's what they like to call themselves. Operating — "

"Drives a tractor, calls himself an operating engineer?"

"Herself too. We're getting girls into the program too. That'll whip the union into line, get them out there putzing around on Cat D-9s. Good workers, those girls. Take the work seriously. Don't drink, smoke dope. Really want the job. Put the screws on those rednecks once and for all, teach them a little humility, show them there's nothing special about running big equipment, nothing special at all, anybody can pull a gearshift, turn a crank, breathe through a respirator can drive a bulldozer, backhoe, fuel tanker, ore hauler, dirt scooper, dump truck, earth mover, core driller. That's what the boys don't believe yet. They're in for a shock."

"Might be too much."

"Keep 'em scared. Bit of affirmative action, that's all it takes. Hire more girls, blacks, Mexicans, we'll soon have the union crawling around on all fours begging for a swift kick in the — hello, Mary."

"Hello, boys."

"Talking about the strip project."

"I'm sure you were. Did we get the permit already?"

"No problem with the Feds. No problem with the county. They're eager to cooperate."

"Then we've already got the permits?"

"They're in the pipeline, in the pipeline. All routine procedures under way, a few more hearings here and there, usual crap, regulation bullshit, everything's set."

"But I heard the machine was already moving."

"Sure is, Mary, it sure is. We can't wait forever. Summer monsoons coming, muddy weather maybe, flash floods in the canyons, that sort of problem, had to get started while the time is right."

"Really? But suppose — "

"You'll find out, Mary, it pays to jump the gun. Every time. Any hitch in the permit process, any more goddamned appeals, we show the court we already spent seventeen million, seventy million, whatever the hell it is, got four hundred men at work — "

"Men?"

"Men, girls, women, blacks, Hispanics, Native Americans, whole community depending on us, Judge, don't dare cut off the project now."

"Show some pity on those poor folks, Judge."

"Don't be cruel, Judge."

"Have a heart."

"New day-care center, Judge."

"New school building. New Dairy Queen. New McDonald's."

"Seventeen million dollars, Judge."

"Seventy million."

"Lecture fees, Judge. Ten thousand a night. All yours."

"No, no, we don't mention that. Sensitive point. Never mention the lecture fees."

"Or Antigua? Cancun? Palm Springs? Honolulu?"

"Don't mention it."

"Et cetera?"

"Especially not that."

"You boys have it all figured out, don't you?"

"Mary, you must be as smart as you look."

"Me? Little me?"

"Nobody could be that smart."

"Except Mary."

"Why thank you, gentlemen. Really. And where *is* the big blue behind today?"

"Mary, we always speak that sacred name in capital letters. Italicized. The *Big Blue Behind.*"

"Reverential, like. With muted awestruck voice."

"I see. Of course."

"And — "

"And here — he — comes. . . ."

They heard the gold key slip into the gold-plated lock. They saw the gold-plated latch handle turn on the massive, planked, hand-tooled, mahogany door. In the sudden silence, all conversation stilled, the eleven big men and one tall woman watched the heavy door swing slowly inward, without the faintest creak or squeak. A well-hung door.

The cleaning lady entered.

She trundled behind her a huge and filthy steel mop bucket on wheels, a bucket brimming with a sulfurous-yellow, slick, foaming sludge. With her free hand she dragged an industrial-size mop, trailing a greasy smear through the open door and into the boardroom. Her own special mop, nobody else's, with her own initials engraved in the hard ashwood of the handle: H.I.S.

The cleaning lady was a big woman, hips an ax-handle wide, bosoms large as vine-ripened muskmelons. (Those splendid female gourds!) Her belly bulged — pregnant again, obviously, planning to get back on the old public welfare titty, undoubtedly. (Beulah, how come you keep has'n all dese chillun, Beulah? Well suh, Mistah Social Warfare Investigation suh, dat simple as dog-poo on de front walk: de mo chilluns we has de mo money we gits.) Half-concealing the black face, shining with sweat and/or grease, the woman wore granny glasses with blue lenses and on her head a mop, another mop, of thick blond polyester curls, evidently a wig, resembling that of Harpo Marx. Her gown, loose and full in the Mother Hubbard style, a grimy cotton print with dirty roses, long-sleeved, buttoned to the throat, came down to the toes of her large wide flat sneaker-shod feet.

She was a powerful a magnificent an awe-inspiring cleaning lady.

But a bit early on the job? The handsome board members stared. One of the bigger, older, more important of the Suits nudged the younger man at his side. A firm elbow jab to the ribs. The hint.

"Ah, yes," the younger man began, lowering his cigar and taking a step forward, "pardon me, ah, madam, but we're, I mean, this is, that is, you're a couple of hours early, aren't you? Furthermore — " He looked at the bucket, the mop, the floor with its rich carpeting, wall to wall.

"Where'd you get that key?" the older man asked.

Ignoring him, the cleaning lady dipped her mop into the foul liquids of her bucket, let it soak for a moment, then pulled it out — dripping on the rug — and stood it against the wall, close to the frame of the open door.

"Wait a min . . . I mean," continued the younger man, "just what do you think you're doing, woman?"

The cleaning lady looked at him. Hidden by the blue glasses it was hard to read the expression of her eyes, but judging from the firm bite of her jaw, the prim grim set of her grotesquely overpainted carmine lips, she would appear to be glaring at her interlocutor.

"I mean," he said, "ah, well, madam, if you prefer, or even, *ma'am*, if you wish . . ." Glancing aside at his fellow board members (Aryans all), the man allowed himself a slight snigger, a small smirk, and shrugged, helplessly. Receiving no verbal assistance from any of them, plainly stuck with the odious chore of clearing the master boardroom of this curious intruder, he faced her once more. "My dear woman," he began, again displaying his company manners (M.B.A., Harvard '75), "we know you have your work to do, but, as you can see, we are having a meeting here, and besides . . ."

The cleaning woman glared at him.

Casually, but with shaky hand, he raised his burning cigar to his lips, nearly inserted the wrong end, reversed it hastily, tried again, got it right, took a puff, coughed. "Besides . . . this room, as you see, this carpet . . ."

The cleaning lady spoke at last, her voice a high-pitched fake falsetto. "What, boy," she said, "you jivin' me?"

"What?"

"Cain't you talk plain talk? You human or what, boy?"

"Well, sorry but, all I mean is, Jesus, woman, you don't *mop* a *carpet*. Nobody mops — "

"Not here to mop no carpet."

"What?"

Taking her bucket of yellow slops in her big gloved paws, the cleaning lady lifted it waist-high and stepped toward the gleaming splendor of the boardroom table. "Got a message for you folks," she said, "straight from the slime pit of you-all's Moab Utah uranium mill." She swung the bucket backward — " 'Bout five gallons pee-ure liquid radiation" — then forward, dumping the entire contents over the surface of the table. The members leaped away, dabbing frantically, with dainty breast-pocket hankies, at the steaming glop splashed upon their Savile Row suiting.

"What's more," the cleaning lady yelled, falsetto falling, failing, "you can keep your bucket too." And she hurled it upward, with mighty arms — strong woman — at the immense blazing gold-leafed intricate chandelier that hung, like a canopy of radiance, above the table. The bucket smashed through the middle tiers of glass and glitter and jingling incandescence, fell end over end in a shower of shards to the center of the table, bottomside up, steel wringer down. Scoring the table's mirrorlike perfection with a long scrawl, it skidded to the farther end and plopped like a field goal into the chairman's discreetly but substantially superior chair.

"Radiation," howled the cleaning lady, backing toward the doorway, "is good for you!"

"Grab that nigger!" commanded the older man, pointing, the senior vice-president. "Kill her!" Looking down, aghast, at the stinking smoldering splotches on his thousand-dollar suit, he fumbled for the bank of telephones on the shelf at his rear.

Three of the bigger, bolder, huskier vice-presidents made threatening advances toward the cleaning lady. She grabbed her mop and brandished its sloppy hank of radioactive yarn in their faces. The men hesitated. The woman backed through the open door, into the subdued lighting of the wood-paneled hallway, turned suddenly and dashed for the executive elevator, its door wedged open with another mop bucket. Forgetting to lift her lengthy skirts, she nearly stumbled, but recovered and plunged into the elevator two paces in front of her pursuers. There she turned again, thrusting out her loathsome mop, held them at bay as the elevator doors slid shut. A gagged and trussed-up body wriggled on the floor behind her.

The men gaped at one another, then at the blinking lights above the sealed door, Otis Descending.

"There was a body in there. . . ."

"Him?"

"Yeah — looked like him. Same old blue suit."

"My God, he's being kidnapped."

"Terrorists!"

Security was alerted — basement parking, utility floor, lobby, main floor, first floor, all ground floor exits. The entire body of vice-presidents rushed for the hallway exit, ran clattering and falling down the bleak emergency stairs in a mad race against the sinking elevator. All but the senior vice-president, still barking into the telephone inside the boardroom, and the woman called Mary, junior vice-president for Marketing Research, who was leaning on the button that would summon up the alternate elevator. As she waited she noticed that the cleaning lady's elevator had paused for some reason on the second floor. When Mary stepped into her own elevator the cleaning lady was still at the second floor. Shrugging, smiling, lighting a fresh new gold-tipped slimline cigarette, she touched her little button and sank sedately, like an executive goddess in an air-conditioned space module, down down and down to the grandeur and hysteria of the main floor. But she'd had enough blustering male foolishness for the day. Without inquiring into the fate of *Big Blue Behind,* she slipped out through revolving doors to the crowded five o'clock sidewalk, strode through the mob on elegant heels in swishing nylon to that dark sleek little bar round the corner where her lover waited, her darling, her sweetheart, her little mate, her ingénue, her petite treat, her trim trig tasty little trollop for the night, for the week, for the year, Trixie by name and Trixie by nature. Toward love and life. True love, real life. So long for another sixteen hours, you foul-breathed oversized blue-suited forever-yammering arseholes.

The V.P.s and the uniformed guards arrived together at the stalled elevator on floor 2. Again they found it with door jammed open by a bucket. On the floor was the wet mop, the blond wig, the blue granny glasses, and a heap of rags — the cleaning lady's Mother Hubbard. And the body, the fat Suit, writhing in its bonds, furious, bellowing at them before they even fully removed the gag:

"He went down the hall, you idiots, down the hall! Some kind of ape-man in blackface. Has a gun. Has a big coil of purple rope over his shoulder. That way, yes, after him, run, you blundering fools, run!"

But all they found, at the terminus of an adjoining corridor, was a neatly tapped-out window panel and a heavy-duty zinc-alloy carabiner, like mountain climbers use, snapped securely to the window washer's spring-bar safety hook. No sign of the purple rope. In the dark alleyway thirty feet below, running behind the building, they saw nothing but a wino sprawled on the greasy pavement, grinning, blinking, shouting up at them:

"Jump. Jump. You can do it. He could do it, you can do it. Jump, you bastards, jump."

6
Working on #12

Night:

Zap! Zip!

In the blue glow of the electronic bug killer mounted to the wall outside the window, two bodies on the inside, on the bed under covers, struggled for a fruitful union. Both were "obese," as we say these days, to an extent inconvenient (though not impossible) for a functioning carnal connection. Especially the woman, a victim of that condition physicians term "grand multi-parity" — too many pregnancies. So great was her excess of fat that her husband, probing in the dark, always had difficulty in finding the proper opening, or sometimes any orifice at all. Or found too many pseudo-vaginae, chose one, only to discover upon the climax of his sweating labors that he'd been making love to some incidental, temporary crease between his wife's lower belly and her upper thighs. From modesty, indifference and aversion to another pregnancy, she never helped him, never guided. Let him do the work; it was his manly role.

Snap! Crackle! Pop!

"Did you take your digitalis, today, Dudley?"

Panting a bit, he replied, "Yes, dear, I took . . . my digitalis . . . huh!

huh! . . . today. Phew! . . . Hah . . . Huh . . . Can you . . . can't you give me some . . . a little help here . . . Mother? Huh?"

"Oh, Dudley. Please, Dudley. Do we have to do this again? Every month? Dudley?"

"It's the right time, ain't it? Right time of month? Right? Ain't you . . . like you say . . . oval . . . hating? Huh! Ain't it, Mother . . . ? Got to preserve . . . that nucular family . . . that nuke . . ."

The blankets heaved on the groaning bed, tangled and tumbled by the struggling couple, seen as by strobe in the bluish lightning of electric sparks. Each jet of light — zap! — announcing, as it performed, the execution and death of another flying beetle, another June bug, another kissing bug, another mosquito, another moth, another miller, another praying mantis, another innocent little mayfly with its lacy, gossamer wings. They came from miles around, converging multitudes of small nocturnal creatures, drawn by the blue seductive glimmer, to die — zip! zit! zing! fried alive! — under the bedroom window of the house of Love.

"I know, Dudley, but it's such an awful . . . please . . . such a messy . . . oh . . ."

"Well doggone, Mother, how we gonna make . . . heh? huh? . . . that lil ole Number Twelve if . . . if we don't . . . don't keep . . . keep on a . . . huh! huh! . . . keep on a tryin', hah? This it?"

"But, Dud — can't we settle for eleven? Ain't eleven kids enough? Dudley?"

On the dressertop near the jangling bed, propped in a long curving row, were the framed and matted photographs of eleven smiling children ranging in age from two years to thirteen. Genetically tidy, each and every child had the same thin lips, the identical snub pugnacious nose, the imitative little blue eyes, the selfsame fine and flaxen hair, as the father. All were girls.

"God He said be fruitful, honey . . . He said be fruitful and multiply and we . . . we shall make . . . shall make the desert blossom . . . blossom as . . . the . . . ho! . . . the rose? Replenish the . . ."

"But why us? Why do we have to do it all?"

" 'Cause if we don't . . . who will? The Gentile? Them . . . those . . . hmmm . . . oh jeez . . . they won't do it, Mother, cause they're steeped . . ."

"What?"

"Steeped. Steeped in sin. Abortion. Contra . . . contracep . . . ceptives when the Lord says . . . He said . . . replenish the earth."

Zip! Zap! Crackle! Die!

"Well I wish we could get it over with and be done with it. Seems to me like there's too many replenishers already. You should see the lines I got to stand in at the supermarket." She stared at the ceiling as he worked. "Utes. Paiutes. Navajos. Meskins. Even some Nigras showin' up now, God knows where they come from. Didn't think we had none of them in Landfill County. And ever' single one of them colored women, I mean Indians and all, ever' single one of them buys their food with food stamps. You should see it, Dudley, carts full of nothin' but Pepsi-Cola and Wonder Bread and Hostess Twinkies and white tortillas and potato chips and cases of refried pinto beans, that's what they eat, no wonder they are all so fat. And lots and lots of Pampers. Just as bad at the bank, lines of 'em, all waitin' to cash their welfare checks. And then layin' around the bars all afternoon, right smack dab in the middle of the sidewalk, men and women both. And the schools, Dudley, the schools, all that fightin' in the halls now, kids gettin' stabbed in the restrooms, things stole all the time, and thirty-five forty kids in ever' class, it's bad, Dudley, bad. Somethin's wrong somewhere. . . ."

Snip! Snap! Dead bugs falling from the light, falling, failing, electrocuted by automated cybernetic process, death on the industrial mass-production plan. Little bugs, big bugs, piling in a heap on the ground beneath the spastic sparking blue electrodes.

"Yeah, I know, Mother, I seen . . . seen it too, what . . . what'd you think we ever talk about . . . talk about, the school board . . . school board . . . school? . . . heh? huh? hmmm? . . . but right now I got to . . . got to . . . concen . . . concen . . ."

"Gettin' sleepy, Dud. . . ."

"I know, Mother, I know. One more. One more time, Mother. Just one . . . more and then . . . then by God . . . then by God we . . . by God we . . . Am I . . .? Is that . . . ? Hold on, one more min . . . minute and I . . . This won't hurt."

Zoot!

"Did it?"

The mercury vapor yardlights glared beyond the house. The Lombardy poplar and the Chinese elm shook their little leaves in a sudden sighing release of air. Relief of wind. Then heard the braying blat, as from a Wagnerian tuba, of one clam barking through a window. ("Sorry, honey. . . .") One desert clam, alone in the night. Files of parked automobiles, pickup trucks, cattle trucks, enameled steel gleaming by streetlight, waited under the dancing shadows of swaying tree limbs. Down the asphalt street, past more suburban ranch-style tract houses, the last of the winter leaves skittered before the breeze, past the offices of Love Realty: "Get Your Piece of the Future Today!," past the franchised Ford agency: "Love Ford — Dudley Deals in Honest Wheels!," past the headquarters of the Love Trucking & Construction Co.: "Building a Bigger Utah for a Better Tomorrow!," past the stately red brick structure of the Church of Jesus Christ of Latter-Day Saints, past the whitewashed plasterboard warehouse of the Jehovah's Witnesses and the little white box, with token aluminum steeple, where the local Baptists met to meet their Maker, its illuminated marquee announcing the title for the coming Sunday's sermon: "No Job Is Too Big Or Too Hard For God," Dr. Harry Palms, Pastor. . . .

And out of town and down the narrow highway into the dark of the desert night, past the goodbye billboard at the last cattleguard on the other side of rancher Love's bob-wire fence: "Leaving Hardrock, Utah, Pop. 3,500 Today 35,000 Tomorrow! Have A Happy And — Come Again When You Can!"

"Well, honey . . ."

"It's all right, Dudley, don't fret."

"I tried, honey. . . ."

"Sure you did."

"Maybe in the morning . . . ?"

"Sure, Dudley."

7

Bonnie Abbzug-Sarvis Reviews Her Life

She bent over the crib, contemplating her sleeping child, and thought.

He is so beautiful. So perfectly beautiful. Those rosebud lips, that eatable little bit of a bite of a nose, those black eyelashes so long and fine they look fake, those rosy cheeks, that curly dark-brown Yiddisher hair, I could eat him, eat him, gobble him down like an apple turnover, my little boy, my Reuben sandwich, that sweet bellybutton in the center of the cute round belly, his little dingdong all *complete* (no 20 percent rabbi's discount there, no sir!), his tight soft little scrotum, oh my but the girls will love him!, and his chubby legs, his chubby knees, his fat little feet with the ten pink toes you want to nibble on like corn niblets, I could eat him, I could I could, my darling my pet my sweet my doll my baby my bundle of joy my little bungle from Heaven. . . .

Suppose. Suppose they ever tried to take him away from me. Who? Never mind who, just suppose. Don't even think of such a thing. It couldn't ever happen. But suppose. No, no, no, think of something else, anything else, such things could never happen. But they do. Kidnappers. But we're not rich anymore, old Doc works more hours and makes less money than any doctor in the whole city, should've stayed in heart surgery, everybody knows that. Hardly anybody knows that. Sick people everywhere. Child molesters. Every week a child disappears, turns up later in a . . . No. *No!* But they do. Those scum, we ought to dump them on an empty island in the middle of the ocean, for life, those murderers and rapists and child molesters, dump them on a desert island in the far Pacific, let them eat breadfruit, let them rot, let them kill and rape and molest each other. Never let them off. Put them all there. But we watch him, watch him, never let him out of our sight, never for a single second, but those other women out there, old hags that never had a baby, those weirdos from the rubyfruit jungle with their dry hard tits and withered wombs that get the idea all of a sudden when they're forty years old that they . . . Not mine. They try even touching mine, those hagfish, and I'll bust them in the mouth, a knuckle sandwich for lunch, a mouthful of bloody chiclets if they so much as lay a hand on even look at my little Rube.

Bonnie. Such talk. You sound like a crazy girl. A certifiable loony from the bottom bin. Hate. I could feel the blood boiling in my head, anyone, anyone at all try anything, anything at all, with my baby, my boy, my Reuben. Men, women, bears, lions, alligators, scorpions, any animal comes near my baby with malice aforethought and I'll fight to kill. Simple. Absolutely fundamental. Axiom Number One, as Doc would say. Fuckin' A-right, as George would say. The bottom line.

Look at him. He smells so sweet. I love to watch him sleep, his little chest goes up and down, that's the heart beating, of course, the little round belly goes up and down, his diaphragm breathing, like a little bellows, pumping air into those pure pink untarnished lungs.

Untarnished? We hope so. That air's not so good around here anymore. Damned garbage from the freeways, the smelter, all those projects, half a million too many cars and trucks, we're breathing dirt. Pure filth. Maybe we should go back to Green River, live on the houseboat full time again. But Doc couldn't do it, keep that job at the U. And then he'd fall off the boat when I wasn't looking and drown. Takes only three minutes, Doc said. Three minutes, no more, no more life. Gone. Absolutely *gone,* man. Forever.

Child molesters. There's danger everywhere. Look at him, not a care in the world. But he does have bad dreams sometimes. How could a little boy only three years old have bad dreams? I don't know but he does. Danger. Danger. Rattlesnakes in the grass, alas, and zero at the bone.

There's somebody out there in the dark, watching me, watching us, close that blind, draw those curtains, can't be, nobody there, stop scaring yourself, wish we had a dog, a big fierce killer watchdog. I hate that kind of dog. A pooch, that's what I want, a little yellow-haired mongrel mutt with big brown eyes and a stubby tail he keeps wagging all the time. Would bark though when strangers came sneaking around. We're getting paranoid as pigeons, Abbzug, what the hell's the matter with you, woman? Wasn't like this before. Didn't have a baby before. And now the second on the way, poor Doc he didn't really want a second, I know, he would never admit it but I know I can tell I can read his mind like an open book, he's about as subtle as a monkey in a cage, poor old guy.

Men.

They all think they're so smart and they're all so dumb. Crude. Crude people, men. Dense as rocks. They think like rocks, in a straight line, nothing but gravity, straight down the hill, that's how they think. No feelings. They think they feel but they only feel with their skin, that's how they feel. Skin deep. Nothing makes sense to them unless you can explain it. Have to draw them pictures, diagrams, charts, formulas, equations, simple propositions with a subject and a verb and an object, that's it, that's all they, only way they, no sensitivity, no inner understanding, no empathy. Sympathy, sure, that's on the surface, only skin, they understand sympathy and can do a pretty good act with sympathy but empathy — ? Wouldn't know what you were talking about.

I feel sorry for men.

All horn and push, they don't even understand sex, the one thing they think they're really good at, the idiots. I'm a man, he said, and I insist on my right to act like a child all my fucking life. Hayduke? Seldom? Jack Kerouac? Who said that?

Wish Doc would come home. He's late. So quiet here. Should play some music. Get back to that piano, Abbzug, you used to be pretty good on the old 88s. Long time gone, honeybee. Look at my fingers. The diaper expert. Shopping carts. Laundry. Good for cooking. You're a good cooker, Mummy, Reuben says, bless his sweet little heart. Hell of a lot nicer than what that bastard George Hayduke used to say. Called me a good fuck like he was handing me a bunch of fresh long-stemmed roses, the pig. The swine. Most men are swine. You can take that for granted.

Feel sorry for men.

Too quiet here. Wish Doc would come.

So crude. Sawing down that awful billboard, he kept snarling at me, growling don't bend the saw don't bend the saw just ease it in, your job is just to guide it, keep it in the old groove, he said he'd do the push and pull. Gross. Vulgar. No real sense of humor, just that kind of crude sexual innuendo, that's all they understand. The old double entendre. And they think it's so funny. So fucking funny. Just sick if you ask me.

And weak. Frail. Always getting sick. Always feeling sorry for themselves. Come on strong, fade fast, that's *them* for you. Big talk, small cock. Big truck, puny fuck. The bigger the buckle the teensier the weeny. Those little shriveled tubes they're so proud of, you'd think they'd paint them red, let them hang out all day. But wouldn't dare, some little bird might come along, snip it off. Snip snip snip, said little bird, now I've got your little worm, take it home and feed it to my nippers. Luncheon tidbit. Hors d'ouevres and horsecock, it's all the same old baloney.

Men.

Thank God I'm a woman.

Whatever became of my life? Twenty-nine years old* and where have all my days gone? I could have been a doctor too, I had the brains, I knew the tricks, was always good at biology, Latin, hydrovascular epidermiology, not so hot at math. But that's okay, nobody with any sense likes math. A litmus test: if he likes math drop him. Like a cold potato. Because that's what you've got, a cold potato in your hands. Never knew a decent man who liked mathematics.

Such simple creatures. No subtlety, no suave, no savoir faire, most of them no savoir vivre either, only one thing on their minds, all the time. When you're fifteen they start looking at you. When you're seventeen they're staring at you, drooling, tongue out, pressing up against you in crowds, trying to see down the top of your blouse or up under your skirt, following you up stairways, escalators, steep hills, that awful dumb sad pleading look in their eyes, like starving beggars, always watching, be careful how you cross your legs, they're watching, keep your knees together when you sit because that's where they're always looking, right up between your knees, be careful how you bend over at drinking fountains if you're wearing something short, bend your knees instead, they're always staring at that one place, you'd think they thought you had some kind of very valuable precious jewel there, rubies maybe — hah! — a kind of gold mine, and never look them in the eyes they think that means a come-on, don't smile don't talk don't show you even know they're there, they'll take it for an invitation, all they want is do is grab you, fold you over

_____
* Thirty-two in point of fact.

the back of a couch or the tailgate of a pickup truck and plant their slimy little seeds in you, that's all most of them really care about. Plant a baby in you and then run. On to the next one. And the next and the next, just like a rooster in a chickenyard or a bull in a cow pasture, they're all that way, all the same, those horny pimple-faced adolescents, those young men in their new suits and BMWs that think they're such hotdogs, those smug fat middleaged men with wives and children and too much money that should know better, even those old wrinkled gray-haired codgers like my Doc, looking at the girls all the time, pretending not to, they're all basically the same. Animals.

And then you're twenty-two and they're still interested. Only maybe not quite so much. And then you're twenty-five and over the hill and you notice they're looking past your shoulder a lot. And then you're thirty and you're invisible, you're not there, they don't see you, and a woman's supposed to spend her next twenty years trying to look nineteen again. They want you to stay nineteen forever. To *be* nineteen. To be a *girl*. Or get out of the way. An actual grown-up woman they can't handle. A woman with some experience who really likes sex and by the time she's thirty or thirty-five probably can't get enough of it, at least if it's with the right man, I mean *her* man, a real man, a woman like that who knows what she's doing and what a man likes and still has her looks it's not good enough for them, it scares them. Scares them off. Panting after you all those years and then when you want it they don't.

And then what're you supposed to do? Raise children, I guess, if you're lucky enough to have a man who'll stick with you and support you. More likely he's gone and you have to go to work in some godforsaken huge office with fluorescent lights buzzing on the ceiling and a little green video screen glaring in your eyes all day giving you headaches and cramps and your poor kid dumped at a day-care for eight nine hours with a mob of sick brats with infectious diseases and two or three lesbian deviants and faggoty child molesters running the place and you don't see your kid again until evening. Quality time. Some quality. The quality of bullshit if you ask me. Women's liberation, the women's movement, feminism, they didn't change a thing except make things worse. You can't stop progress.

So what do you do? Avoid trouble, marry an old man with some property and a good steady income who'll be grateful just to be allowed to get into the same bed with you every night even if he can't get his tool up anymore or keep it up or keep it in or get it off, he'll be grateful to you anyway and even if he's silly enough to play around a little on the sly he's not so likely to run off with some scheming little baby-faced sexpot named Cheri or Teri or Kristi or Misti. Or Bonnie? Like he did before. And if he does you've got his money and his house and his ski chalet and cabin cruiser and even his lawyer's on your side. So he probably won't.

So he dies instead. Of a horrible smelly expensive disease.

And you're a widow at thirty-nine. Then what?

And then you're a grandmother and hell really begins. And then suddenly you're dead. Then what?

Poor little Reuben, look at him there, sleeping away as if the world was a good safe kindly place where everybody loves you like Mummy and Daddy and everything you need you get and nothing can ever hurt you. It's enough to make you weep.

If I were a man I'd cry. Right now.

There's got to be something more. Doc says we should be happy with what we have and stop whining for life after death or before death but he's not, he's not happy, not always, not very often, not really, look at him tired all the time, that mournful look in his eyes, and why *not* believe in another realm of existence? Maybe even right now, that other realm, waiting for you, like changing planes or buses or trains or men, you step off one step on another, now and then, for the adventure of it if nothing else and anyway there's got to be something better or at least different after death. Why? Because. And before birth too, reincarnation means preincarnation and if we tried hard enough we'd all remember that former existence. Sometimes I think I do. I was a lioness on the African savannah. I was a Commanche princess racing my pony across the Plains of San Augustine. Once I was an Egyptian queen named Cleopatra, this simple jerk Mark Antony hanging around all the time (but handsome, strong, knew his job) and that potbellied asshole Julius Caesar. The hairy one. Water skiing with Mark behind my golden barge, boy did we make those big black Nubian bastards row! Good for them. Good exercise. But things ended badly. Like they usually do. Bit on the ass by an asp. But croaking like a queen, by God, beautiful slaves bawling around me, the ones I hadn't already poisoned I mean, and my little darling Charmian weeping her heart out. Those were the days. Those were the days, my friend, when would they ever end, those were the days, thank God that's over.

But really. Easy to make fun of it but there really is something more to life than just merely living and dying. I can feel it. I know it. There's a world of spirit beyond this crude materialistic world, a realm of beautiful spirits floating like little golden Fourth of July sparklers through a kind of heavenly rose-colored circle of clouds spiraling around a great sacred pure blue eye or like little innocent fireflies on a summer evening glowing off and on in the dark as they circle closer and closer to the beautiful blue light of God.

Jews don't believe in that crap, Abbzug. Some Jews do, look at Saul Bellow. You look at him, God if I had a face like that I'd believe in life after death too. I'd prefer it.

Reuben, my little darling, sleep my darling, sleep and sleep, scrunch up your pretty little eyes and close your sticky little fingers and wiggle your toes and sleep my lamb, my baby, my sexy little sexless little androgyne, really neither boy or girl, you lucky kid, just a sweet lovable perfect little firefly of a bug. Thank God you don't know what's coming. If anything. You won't be jealous, will you? We'll love you just as much as ever and you'll be so happy to have a little sister, a nice little sister named Debbie with diapers full of yellow babyshit and her little mouth latched like a leech to Mummy's breast, you won't mind, will you? Of course he'll mind, he'll hate it. Well . . . tough. Tough titty, any kid of mine he's got to grow up, I refuse to be another Jewish mother even if I am a Jewish mother.

Where is that Doc?

Why do they keep watching our house? Day and night they're out there right this minute watching and waiting, Doc thinks I'm imagining it but I know, I mean like man I *know*, I feel them out there, somebody out there in the dark watching this house, watching this very window, waiting. Waiting for who? You know who. Him, that's who. Doc says he's gone, dead, dead as a doorknob, but what does Doc know, Doc reads the papers, watches the TV news, anybody does that will believe anything. Him dead? — not bloody likely. I can feel him, I know he's around somewhere, and I know he's coming right here. Coming again. Yes, he coming, I can feel it, I can feel it deep inside, I can't believe it but I feel it, yes he's coming again, that ugly squat hairy evil grinning son of a bitch — yes! oh God! — he's coming, he's coming, he's coming again — !

Doc . . .

Dear sweet Doc of mine. Please hurry home. Baby needs you. Bonnie needs you.

8

J. Oral Hatch, R.M.

Four men sat in a darkened, gloomy motel room — Little America — smoking cigarettes. Drapes drawn close, night-time anyway, only one light on, the blue smoke hung waist high above the floor, flat planes of smoke hovering at various levels on the overheated air. The television set was turned on but silent, its screen depicting what appeared to be a perpetual snowstorm. An electronic snowstorm, a blithering whirligig of mesons, photons, neutrons and neutrinos, a lacy fleecy blizzard of queerish quanta, the dance of the woolly masters.

The four men were formed in two groups, one group of three and a somewhat smaller group of one. The one, whose name was J. Oral Hatch, sat in a hard chair confronted by the one light, a floor lamp with the beam of its three high-wattage bulbs aimed directly into his face. Hatch was a young man, no more than twenty-five years, which is very young indeed for a man, an American Mormon man in the city of Salt Lake in the state of Deseret. He was dressed, quite uncomfortably, sweating, in the black shoes, black suit, white shirt and red tie of an R.M., i.e., Returned Missionary. (Appointed to the slender pendant barely tumescent damned Gentile nation of Norway, he awoke one night, near the end of his mission, to find himself nude, strapped to his boardinghouse bed, body under physical assault. Two girls, nearly naked, giggling like children, were coaxing his virgin penis into a state of manly rigor. Birgit and Erika, chambermaid and sea-captain's daughter, he thought he knew them well, he'd converted them both to Mormonism only a month before. Now Birgit straddled his loins, waiting to advance, while the other, very busy, head toward Birgit, seemed to be clasping Oral's ears with the inner side of her calves. It was painful on the lobes. "Oral," explained Erika later, a twinkle in her big startling sea-green eyes, "ven effer I see your darlink face I tink, Erika, always you haff place to sit."

He did not report the rape but departed the country soon after, Erika's farewell in his ringing ears: "I alvays haff chob for you, Oral, if effer you come again in Norge." They waved as he boarded the train for Oslo. "Gott bless Council of Twelve," they shouted, "also E. Power Bricks and Z. Norman Tabernacle." Their cheery rosy faces and the depot glided backward, out of vision; against a dark glassy background of fir and spruce his own face stared at him, frightened, pale, with haggard eyes, his mission impossible, a failure, and his intromission involuntary, all too brief. Perhaps he should grow a mustache.

The other three men sat or lounged behind the lamp, obscured by shadow, nearly invisible to young Hatch. Although a free man, a fellow agent, in official status an equal to two of the three, he felt like a subject under criminal investigation.

"Then what'd he say?" inquired a faceless voice, harsh from too many cigarettes, too much whisky.

"He said come here, Oral, I got a job for you."

"What did he mean by that?" asked a second, equally harsh.

"Would you fellas mind not smoking? The smell makes me sick." Hatch removed his eyeglasses, looked at them, put them back on his nose.

A moment of silence. A third voice, a senior type of voice, smoother, well modulated, suggesting higher rank, a better education and superior intelligence, spoke softly from the shadows on the king-size bed. "Be good to Lieutenant Hatch. Put out your rotten Marlboros. This is his town."

Grunts of assent. The smoke cloud rose, after a moment, to slightly higher elevation, lesser density. "For Lieutenant Hatch," said the first voice, "and Mr. Moroni." A smothered laugh.

"And please don't make fun of my religion."

"Don't make fun of his religion."

"Yes sir." Another pause. "Now Oral, to get back to the question. What do you suppose he meant by that?"

"I don't know."

"Think maybe it was an offer of employment?"

"I didn't like the tone of it."

"So what'd you do?"

This was better. Young Hatch relaxed a bit, permitting himself a tiny close-lipped smile. "Gave him a chop on the neck. Then — "

"A job?"

"A chop. Karate chop. Searched him."

"And found?"

"He was queer all right. Had chicken entrails in both front pockets."

"What else?"

"What?" Young Hatch sat up straight. "I tell you he had chicken entrails in his front pockets and you ask me *what else?*"

"How do you know they were chicken entrails?"

The young man sighed. "I know my entrails."

"You must get pretty personal with chickens."

Hatch frowned. "I was born and raised on a farm. I used to kill and clean a chicken every week. Gee whiz, fellas."

Lieutenant Hatch was a large young fellow but looked small. A two-hundred-pound six-footer with wide shoulders, deep chest, flat stomach, narrow hips, pale-haired, Nordic and jut-jawed as a store window mannikin, he nonetheless looked somehow oddly under-sized. Perhaps it was his head; his shoulders too broad, his frame too big for the head. Not that his head was small either; his head was of average size; but the hairline came down within an inch of the eyebrows, giving his brow a flattened, compressed dimension, as if, when a boy, he might — in normal boyish curiosity — have put his head in a trash compactor and flipped the switch. Whatever the cause, no damage was done; young Hatch was equipped with perfectly normal intelligence. His intelligence quotient, in fact, as tested by the agency, proved out to be precisely 100.00, a numerical value that matches, interestingly, is indeed identical to and with, the American national average. Few Americans have an average I.Q., an alarming piece of data when fully considered, because it implies that half the brain power in our nation must fall below the average, half rise above, excepting of course the statistical sliver, like the brain of young J. Oral Hatch, which corresponds exactly *to* the average. Only the average, he himself liked to point out, are truly exceptional. Furthermore —

"Forget the chicken entrails," the senior voice said, interrupting a resumption of that discussion. "Who did in the BLM bulldozer, Oral? Federal property. Who dumped the sludge in Syn-Fuels' boardroom? Interstate commerce. Who reset the survey stakes at Radium Canyon? Forming a spiral that crossed state lines. Who's behind that Earth First! crowd? Terrorism."

"Yes sir." Lieutenant Hatch tried to see beyond the bright light flaring in his eyes, looking for the face of the Colonel. "Well sir, those were all misdemeanors."

"But who was involved? How many? Conspiracy to commit a misdemeanor, Lieutenant Hatch, is a felony. Did you know that?"

"No sir. I mean I knew it, of course, but so far as I can find out there's only one person involved."

"Who?"

"I don't know his name."

A pause.

The first interrogatory voice, coughing, broke the awkward silence. "You know his sex? Man or woman? Old or young or in between?" Pause. Hatch shrugged: no answer. "So who was this guy in the BLM comfort station?"

"Just a bum. No I.D. on him, no car keys, no money, nothing. Just another old pervert, I mean gay, just another old gay pervert using our public facilities for a private shelter. Maybe a child molester. Anybody with chicken entrails in his pocket, God knows what he was looking for." Again Hatch removed his glasses, wiped off the steam, put them back. "But that detail doesn't interest you, does it."

"Maybe he was waiting in there for a chicken. What'd it say on the door? Hens? Roosters? Maybe he was a chicken molester. I hear they're the worst of all. Catch a live chicken, jam its head under a toilet seat, whip out the old whangdoodle, they say there's nothing like it."

Silence. Smothered sniggers. "Chicken toilet . . ."

"Christ, Oral, didn't you even talk to the man?"

"He wasn't conscious."

"Chopped him pretty good, eh? You kill him?"

"No, no, he was all right, he was breathing normally, I checked his pulse. There was this glass eyeball on the tiles."

"You checked his pulse to see if he was breathing. Good technique. What color eyeball?"

"What color? What kind of a question is that? Sometimes I wonder if you guys are serious. Don't you even want to know where this god — this darn glass eyeball came from?"

"It popped out of his eyesocket when you chopped him. So you left him there?"

Hatch sighed, patiently. "I had work to do. There was this danged old gray horse outside in the parking lot, making a mess on my right front fender."

"Horses, chickens, glass eyeballs," the coughing voice continued, "we're getting nowhere, Oral. You're paid to watch people, not this funny farm. You must have some idea who reset those stakes."

"Not for sure."

"Who pulled the linkage pins out of that bulldozer so it runs right off its own tracks."

"Not for certain."

"Your job's to watch certain people, Hatch. Where were you?"

"I was there, like I told you. Had my eye on Doc and Bonnie and Smith and Susan and Kathy all the time. All we did was play poker."

"Seems like that's all you ever do, Hatch. No wonder you run up such a big expense account. Don't you — "

"Pardon me," the senior voice, that of the Colonel, interjected. "Tell me a bit about these people, Lieutenant. You have tapes on all of them, I understand."

"Yes sir." Hatch slipped a video cassette into the player mounted on the television set, pushed the PLAY bar. Patiently they waited. After what seemed like rather an undue interval, a series of numbers flashed across the TV screen, then the name "SMITH, Joseph Fielding III, a.k.a. 'Seldom Seen' " appeared, followed at once by the still photo, in color, of a man in his forties, the honest homely incorrigibly bucolic face of Smith himself, complete with dangling forelock, upstanding cowlick, big ears and customary broad and bucktoothed grin. He seemed to be scratching the back of his red neck with his dirty sombrero.

"What's the record on this cowboy type?"

"He was a member of the so-called Monkey Wrench Gang," Hatch said. "Served six months in jail, along with the so-called Doc Sarvis and his gun moll Bonnie."

"What was the crime?"

"Rolling rocks."

"I see."

"Destroying property, actually. A lot of it. Rolled boulders down on people's cars. Also suspected of arson and felonious use of high explosives. He might have been mixed up in the destruction of a coal train but they plea-bargained their way out of that charge. That's him there on his watermelon ranch. . . ."

Smith appeared on the TV screen in motion now, grinning at the camera, holding up a gigantic watermelon, then tucking it behind his shoulder with one hand, other arm extended forward, as if preparing to throw a great bomb of a pass deep into the end zone. Jerkily, the hand-held camera swung about to show a bulky bear of a man in suit and tie stumbling through the melon patch, pretending to run, to catch the pass, to score a touchdown.

"That's Sarvis," Hatch commented. "The one they call Doc."

"The one they call Doc. The so-called Doc Sarvis. Tell me, Lieutenant, is he or is he not an actual doctor? I mean an actual M.D. — *Medicinae Doctor.*"

"Yes sir, actually he is. Rather distinguished in his field, as a matter of fact, before his disgrace. He was chief of surgery at the University Medical School. Wrote a book called *The Human Heart: A Romantic Disease.* Used to pull down a fee of two thousand dollars an hour — if he liked you." Hatch consulted his little black pocket notebook. "Once treated the President. After he got out of jail he switched to pediatrics. A baby doctor. Not much money in that."

The TV screen showed Smith shoeing a horse, grinning over his shoulder at the camera as he gripped the beast's forefoot between his knees, tacking on a new shoe. Hatch pushed the FAST FORWARD button, then the STOP, then the PLAY. The videotape proceeded at normal viewing speed, presenting Doctor Sarvis and his moll lounging about on the deck of an old-fashioned, wooden-hulled houseboat, large and comfortable but in need of paint, repair, plaster. The main cabin had been stuccoed to resemble adobe but the stucco was flaking off, exposing the rusty chickenwire beneath. The doctor himself sat on a folding canvas chair, book in hand, huge floppy straw hat shading his face, while Bonnie Abbzug, a fine figure of a woman in a high-cut black swimsuit, led a naked child up a ladder to the roof of the cabin. From there, hand in hand, laughing, they jumped off. Into the river. A sheet of muddy water leaped toward the eye of the camera, blacking out the light.

"Not sure I get the point of this home movie, Lieutenant," said the Colonel. He sounded cross. "Why are you showing us this home movie?"

"Well, sir . . ." Hatch shifted nervously in the hot seat. "For the record, sir. Doing my job. Keeping these people under observation."

"This won't serve as evidence. We need incriminating shots, pictures of them actually tampering with mine equipment."

"Yes sir."

The abrasive voice cut in, speaking from the shadows. "What about the other one, that Hayduke? Got any action film on him?"

"No. Nothing. Only some old snapshots. Anyway — "

"Let's see them."

"Sure." Hatch played the machine, fast forward, stop, partial rewind, stop again. The face of George Washington Hayduke, father of his country, filled the screen. Heavily blackbearded, wearing a bandit's greasy wide-brimmed leather hat, he scowled at the photographer, squinting against the light. Unlike the others, Hayduke had a suitably villainous face, a visage savage, hot-tempered, ruthless, uncompromising.

"There's our boy." The second voice, long silent, had finally spoken. "Now *he* looks like a terrorist should look. A real psychopath. Where is he, Hatch?"

"In that picture? Well, that picture is five years old."

"Where is he right now? Where does he live? Hang out? Hole up? Bed down?"

"How should I know? I mean, I can't keep track of all these characters all the time. Doc, Bonnie, Smith and his wives — they're off probation now, they come and go when they feel like it, they are four, five, maybe six separate people. I'm just one guy, I only have two eyes." He adjusted the glasses on his nose. "Anyhow — "

"You have four eyes."

"Anyhow we think the one called Hayduke is dead. Nobody's seen him for several years. Got shot, body disappeared in a flood. Or maybe accidentally blew himself up, that's what Love thinks."

"Who's Love?"

"He's that small-time bigshot down in Landfill County. Bishop Love. Mine operator, trucker, rancher, County Commissioner. Wants to be a U.S. Senator. Can't even get elected to the state legislature. Works as front man for Syn-Fuels. Does what the mining execs tell him to do, like any smart Utah politician."

Pause. The Colonel spoke: "Don't let yourself become cynical, Lieutenant. Cynicism is a cheap emotion, a craven substitute for thought and action. Cynicism corrodes the will, dulls the conscience, blunts your sense of right and wrong." The Colonel paused before rounding off his mini-lecture. "Stay alert to fine distinctions: become a pessimist like me." Chuckling in the dark.

Young Oral stiffened in his chair, the helpless flush of youth red-dening his cheeks, his simple clean-cut square-jawed Eagle Scout R.M. countenance. "I'm not a cynic, sir." That jab hurt. "Absolutely not. I'm an optimist. All my people are optimists."

"I know," the older man said. "That's why I'm a pessimist."

"Wasn't this Hayduke in pretty thick with that doctor's girl friend?" the harsh voice broke in. "Didn't he get his operating funds from the doc himself?"

"They're married now," Hatch said. "The doctor and the woman, I mean. And yeah, I've had their house staked out ever since the Denver thing and that business with the bulldozer. Just in case Hay-duke is still around. No sign of him."

"And so this is all you got? No other suspects?"

A moment of hesitation before Hatch said, "Well, there is talk of some crackpot wandering around the canyonlands on a horse. The one they call the 'Lone Ranger.' Just talk. I can't find anyone who's actually seen him or knows anything about him. Or her. Those people down there, they're cranks. Too much isolation from the rest of the world. Lots of inbreeding. They don't trust outsiders. That little town of Hardrock, for instance, didn't even get regular mail service until 1935 and then only once a week by mule train. Didn't get a paved road until 1965. They think Herbert Hoover is still President. They like him. Half of them are polygamists like Smith."

"Lieutenant," the Colonel said, "do you know who the Lone Ranger was?"

"Who he *was*? Yes, sir. The guy with the mask and the silver bullets."

"You've heard of Tonto, too, then?"

"Yes, sir."

"You know what Tonto means? Tonto means 'fool' in Spanish. Tonto's name for the Lone Ranger was Kemo-sabe. That means 'Shithead' in Paiute. Eventually they split up. You can see why. What was that fellow wearing?"

"Wearing? Who? What fella?"

"The old bum in the restroom."

Hatch stoked his memory. "Well, let's see, dark in there, his clothes were so dirty I hated to even look at them, smelled terrible. Like chicken entrails." He paused. Went on: "Sort of a riding outfit, I guess. Black boots, tight pants, funny kind of shirt with two rows of buttons on the front. . . . Big white ten-gallon hat . . ."

Silence. They waited for Hatch to continue, staring at him. He squirmed in the hard chair, averting his eyes from the fierce light. Changing the subject, he said, "I'll need more expense money."

"What for?" the smoker asked. "You're not doing much with what we already give you."

"I need more money for those poker games."

"Why?"

"They like to play poker. I always lose."

"Why?"

"If I don't lose they won't let me play."

"Nobody loves a loser."

"They do."

"We don't."

"You want me to stay in close with that gang or not? They still think I'm their probation officer."

"What about that other one, what's his name?"

"Greenspan? They think he was transferred."

"So they trust you?"

"Trust me, who knows." Young Hatch was getting impatient. "Maybe. As long as I keep losing they trust me. You think — ? Do I get the money or not?"

"Sure, Oral," said the first voice, "you'll get the money. But concentrate on the game, Oral. Remember the Federal deficit."

"Watch out for that old bottom-card mechanic," said the second voice. "That Doc. Listen for a swishy noise. How'd you ever get into playing poker with a man named Doc? Not very smart, Oral."

"But he is a doctor," cried young Hatch, running a hand through his fine pale hair, then wiping the sweat from his upper lip. "He cured my toe fungus."

"But does he always cut the deck?" said the first.

"And do you keep your mind on the game?" said the second.

"Or on Bonnie Abbzug?"

"Don't let them bluff you."

"What?" Exasperated, Hatch burst out again. "Bluff? They're always bluffing. All of them. All the time. I can't trust any of them. She's the worst. My God, you should . . . And that Smith, that so-called Seldom Seen Smith, always talking, always telling stories, how'm I supposed to concentrate in a situation like that, I ask you? Holy . . . cow."

Another pause in the proceedings. Quiet laughter in the dark. The TV screen flickered quietly, the silent video film unreeling yard after yard: Bonnie in her housedress suckling a baby, flashing one big tit at the camera and pointing, all smiles; Doc pedaling his three-speed Schwinn bicycle up a long grade in Salt Lake City, waving, behind him a mile-long column of steaming garbage trucks and laboring cement mixers; the laughing Smith sitting in a submerged dory, water up to his neck and a good-looking woman in each arm, all three of them making funny faces at the jiggling movie camera. . . . This home movie like all home movies went on and on and on. . . .

"Please," asked Hatch, "can we go now? I'm tired, fellas."

"Yes," said the Colonel. "We've had an entertaining evening and it's time for you to go home. But do try to remember that we're not playing a humorous game with a handful of jolly pranksters. I'm talking now to the three of you. We're here on a matter of national security. The nuclear industry is of vital importance to the Department of Energy and the Department of Defense. The White House is concerned. Bear that fact in mind. Attempts to sabotage uranium mining is an attack on the national interest. We are not here to deal with your ordinary well-meaning harmless environmentalists. We're here to root out a gang of determined, skilled, well-financed international terrorists. Is that understood by all and sundry?"

The Colonel paused, waiting for the usual grunts of agreement. Hearing them, he concluded:

"In other words we're talking about business. I mean business of critical national value: money. And now — no sniggers, please, I'm serious — just one more question for you, Lieutenant, and I'm letting you go."

"Yes sir."

The Colonel allowed a moment of silence to emphasize the importance of his questions: "Was he wearing a black mask?"

"Sir?"

"Was he wearing a black mask?"

"You mean — ?"

"Yes. Him. The bum in the toilet. Was he wearing a black mask over his eyes?"

"He only had one eye. The other was glass."

"That makes two. Answer my question."

Young Hatch pondered the question. He was in shit and he knew it. Deep shit. Deep bad liquid mucilaginous shit. I cannot tell a lie, he thought. Why not? his devil said; your career may be at stake. But Daddy said and Mummy said, Never never tell a lie.

Tell it anyway.

I can't.

Sure you can.

I'll go to Hell.

No you won't, I promise.

You promise?

Promise.

Well . . . but I shouldn't.

Only this once, you'll never have to lie again.

You mean that?

Yes, Oral.

That's a true fact?

Oral, have I ever lied to you? Ever?

Shading his four eyes with one hand, young Hatch endeavored to see around the glaring light, to look the Colonel in the eye. Either eye. Any eye. He swallowed, swallowed hard. He opened his mouth to speak. His lips were dry, his tongue felt like a lead toad. He tried but could not speak. He tried and tried. Could not do it.

Close to pity, the three hard men behind the light stared at young J. Oral Hatch. The silence became cruel.

"All right, Lieutenant," the Colonel said. "You can go now. You did your best, your best is none too good, but maybe it'll improve. We'll give you one more month to close this case. You too are on probation, as you know, from the point of view of this agency. Goodnight, Lieutenant."

The young man rose shakily from his chair, shook hands with his three employers, mumbled the formalities of departure and left the room, closing the door gently.

The others waited, listening. One man rose, looked out the door and came back. The second man restored the floor lamp to its original place at the side of a motel desk, where the Book of Mormon rested on a tourist's guide to the flamboyant fleshpots of Salt Lake, principal city of Deseret, Shithead Capital of the Inter-Mountain West. He switched on the zero volume television. MTV: some humanoid with an orange crest bristling on the centerline of an otherwise shaven head, wearing a cut-off black leather tank top and skin-tight black leather pants, knelt at the front of a stage with a microphone at his mouth, howling in mute anguish from the violent convulsions of his pelvic girdle.

The first man poured drinks, three tumblers of straight bourbon, no ice, passed two to his fellows, sat down. They stared at the soundless agony on the TV screen.

"He forgot his cassette."

"Belongs to the company now."

"You suppose he really thinks he's a lieutenant?"

"You wrote out the commission. You typed it, you signed it."

"But does he believe it? That kid might be brighter than he acts. Got to be. He might be investigating us. Is he under surveillance? Who knows what he's up to behind our backs."

"Who cares. Kid's so uptight his asshole squeaks when he walks."

"If he believes he's a lieutenant he'll believe anything."

They fell silent, watching the silent commercial. The commercial seemed to be promoting the latest hit number of the latest hit band. *You Too? Mötley Crüe? Screw You? Mee-2?*

"That's not a commercial."

"Sure it's a commercial."

"No, that's the program. The commercial was the thing before, the thing in black leather. What channel we got here?"

"You turned it on."

"All I did was turn the thing on, I didn't select the channel. Where are we?"

"It looks like MTV."

"I mean what city?"

"What's the difference?"

"There might be a Playboy Channel, we could see some T and A. Some basic Western values. There might be a plain-talk straight-talk talk show. Hear the white man's side for a change." But nobody got up; they watched a fuliginous hominid in purple jumpsuit, androgynous face, mincing upstage with a single lacy white glove.

"Why'd you hire somebody like that Oral? *Oral,* for godsake. What a name. How could anybody do that to their own kid?"

"He seemed all right when I interviewed him. Kind of simple but honest. Has a college degree."

"What school?"

"Brigham Young University."

Nobody said anything. The men finished their drinks. The first man stood up to pour a second round. The man called Colonel finally spoke: "Excuse me, gentlemen. If you don't mind — I really should get to bed. Have to fly back to D.C. in the morning."

Of course, of course, the others muttered. Yes sir. As they left, the Colonel said, "And don't worry about your boy Hatch. He's young, he's healthy, he's Mormon, he's American, he's of perfectly average intelligence. He'll believe anything. And he's dedicated. He'll make a good agent."

9

Seldom's Nightmare

Seldom was having the nightmare again. Twitching and mumbling like an old hound dog on the parlor rug, he lay in his big domestic bed with Sheila, his Bountiful wife, and dreamed again his dream of doom. Damnation. Death and transmogrification.

A blue glow hovered above his haybarn. The UFO again — some kind of Unidentified Fucking Object. The light revolved upon an eccentric axis, a wobbly disk of blue flopping in the night, making the tinny humming sound, semi-musical but sinister, of a child's toy, a spinning metal top. Attracted by the light, tiny winged creatures, like angels, flew toward it, vanishing one by one in brief bright flashes of self-immolation, their only sound the buzz and crackle of electrocution. Far above the blue glow, high as a hotel, higher than a grain elevator, two small beady red lights, like a pair of spider eyes, blinked slowly on then off, on then off, from the midst of an A-frame rigging black against the stars.

He heard the horses galloping round and round in the pasture, panicky with fear. Seldom drew his revolver, aimed with facile grace at the blue disk and fired. The light stopped revolving; he heard the clatter of falling crockery. Got the insulators, he thought, by God got the goldang insulators that time. Can't always miss. Even a blind hog's a-gonna root up a acorn some of the time. Pleased with himself, he blew the smoke from the muzzle of his old-time black powder penile repeater and aimed again, this time at six o'clock — the lower edge of the disk — figuring that his first shot must have gone high.

Far above the red eyes squinted, looking both cross and cross-eyed, toeing in and downward at the insect life before its shoes. The blue glow was suddenly transformed into a thin precision beam of laser-like intensity directed into the open bore of Smith's revolver. Psssst! said the beam. The revolver's barrel drooped like a wilted flower, an impotent daisy, and poured in a puddle of gray molten steel to the ground between his bare feet. Holy Moroni! Smith turned to run, as any sensible hero would.

The machine stepped forward, lifting its 130-foot shoes (both together) and bringing them down on Smith's barn. The barn disappeared in a cloud of dust, smashed flat as a seaskate — tractor, wagons, manure spreader, hay baler and all. Completing the cycle, the machine rose from its butt, swung forward on its pelvic arch, like a duck doing the bump and grind, and sat down again. With a crash. The ground trembled. The shoes rose —

Smith ran for his life, for the safety of his bed, the comforts of his wife, straight toward the little gray vine-covered board-and-batten ranchhouse. Kathy's place, the old dude ranch near Hardrock in Utah's Dixie. He seemed to be running in glue, a mucous mud that clung to his feet like quicksand. The blue beam, now a spotlight with revolving mount, blazed on his back, projecting his antic shadow fifty feet before him. He saw the shadow of something else swoop down, heard the rush of wind and the iron clank of pulleys, cables and boom in action, looked back to see the monster's great excavator bucket, fanged jaws spread wide, big enough to hold four Greyhound buses or twelve Eldorado Cadillacs, striking at his rear.

Smith leaped.

The bucket plowed deep into the ground scant inches short, flinging a wave of dirt and debris over Seldom's back. Missed, he rejoiced, it missed. The bucket's lower jaw slid forward beneath his feet, making the ground ripple like a carpet, while the upper jaw passed over his head, cutting off the light. Whoa! thought Smith, it got me. The iron mandibles clanged shut before him, square teeth interlocking like the links of a zipper. He was trapped inside the iron bucket like a rat in a box. A small rat in a very big black box.

They got me. He waited; nothing happened. Fear overcame his soul.

Kathy! he bawled. Mama! Jesus!

No succor came. He heard the rattle of machinery and felt himself being suddenly raised, as in an elevator, high into the air. He could see very little through the chinks in the wall of the bucket — a spray of stars, clouds of rising dust, the wild bluish glare of the spotlight, a pair of red eyes high above, blinking.

The bucket rose up, back, and partly down, slamming with brutal metallic force into a square dock high in the complex superstructure of the machine. The jar knocked Smith off his feet. Stunned, he waited, groped his way to his hands and knees, felt his head. No blood. No leaking brains. Didn't hurt me a-tall, he thought. Only the head. He waited.

Silence. Then the iron clamor resumed, the jaws of his trap opened wide, the blue beam glared into Smith's eyes. A pause, the buzzing noise, and a recorded voice began to speak, a gentle mellifluous feminine, almost human, well-trained in elocution but scratchy, badly transcribed:

> Welcome, K mart shoppers. Today's Special is our new patio dinette set, regular price one hundred thirty-five dollars, reduced for one week only to ninety-nine fifty. Please visit our Home Improvement Department for a free no-charge no-obligation look at this truly unique value. Brief pause. [*Sic.*] Bienvenidos señoras y señores aficionados de K mart. La especialidad de hoy —

The tape stopped abruptly. The blue light wobbled on its crazy pivot, watching Smith. Far above, the two red eyes gazed forward, blinking into deep space, deep time, searching for the significance of existence in the spiral galaxies beyond Andromeda while the machine lurched onward, smashing Kathy's house, Kathy, and Kathy's garden.

So far so good, thought Smith, blinded by the light — but now what?

After further hesitation and a few moments of electronic hemming and hawing, a different recording got under way, this time in the voice of a more masculine android, deeper, richer, with standard American accent and a quality of barely repressed enthusiasm, as if announcing the Second Coming. However, the surface noise was conspicuous; tapes getting dusty.

> Welcome, project visitors. Welcome aboard "GOLIATH." No doubt you are wondering what's behind the world's largest drag-line bucket? Answer . . . the world's largest dragline! The 4250-W

Walking Dragline, a twenty-seven-million-pound giant that walks to work, is the biggest mobile land machine on earth!

This is a new age, folks, an age requiring better ways to lower costs to meet ever greater demands. And that's why a machine this size has come into being. The 4250-W's record size and design enable it to uncover vast areas of coal, uranium, potash, molybdenum, or other minerals that before now could not have been economically mined. Operated by one man scratch that [*sic*] by one person in an air-conditioned cab the 4250-W walking dragline "GOLIATH" is the latest example of how Bucyrus-Erie keeps pace with our world's most urgent requirements.

Look at these 4250-W fantastic facts!

One: Overall length four hundred and ten feet! Three times longer than the Wright brothers' first aerial flight! Longer than a row of nine average size railroad coal hoppers! Almost one and a half times the length of a football field!

Two: Twenty-seven million pounds weight! Thirteen and a half thousand tons! As heavy as one hundred fifty fully loaded average-size railroad ore hoppers! Equal to the weight of nearly fourteen thousand automobiles!

Three: Height sixty-seven feet one inch from base to top of powerhouse enclosure! One hundred nineteen feet eleven one-quarter inches from base to top of A-frame! Two hundred twenty-two feet six inches from base to top of boom at highest operating angle!

Four: Two hundred ninety thousand square foot working area! Equivalent to a six-acre park! Lifts loads three hundred twenty-five feet, dumps six hundred ten feet away. . . .

Smith began to find the jubilant lecture wearisome, even tedious. He was having trouble keeping his eyelids open. He felt about for the steel wall of the dragline bucket, found it and propped himself erect. The proud and happy voice brayed on, sprinkling Smith with a tepid vapid insipid drizzle of amazing facts and fantastic figures. When he heard the words

. . . prior to mining the land was used to a limited extent for cattle grazing. However the mine area is classified by the U.S. Department of the Interior as marginal to submarginal at best and is nearly uninhabited. . . .

he reached for his revolver, found it intact and holstered, drew and looked beyond the rotating spotlight for a suitable target. Public address speakers, for instance. He heard them rasping and rattling somewhere above his head but could not see them. He aimed instead at a point between the pair of blinking red eyes far up in the topmost rigging. Blast the goldamn critter's brains out, he thought, that'll stop the sumbitch. Knock him down, stomp on his paws, cut off the rattles and skin the beast. When he heard the words

> ... serving the needs of our changing ever-growing world economy ...

he fired five times in quick succession, aiming casually from about the middle of his belly, natural shooter style like his father always did. He blew the puff of smoke from the pizzle, opened and reloaded the cylinder, reholstered his weapon and waited for results.

The spotlight wobbled hysterically, screaming like a toy tin top in full career, turned its beam skyward and inspected the damage. Smith had missed the brainpan — there was no head up there, only the eyes, like those of a crab set high on stalks — but hit and severed an electrical conduit. One eye blacked out, the machine swayed and stumbled on, a drunken mechanical bum winking at eternity, blinking from a nervous tic. As it moved, the dangling cables, fuming with blue sparks and the stink of overheated insulation, bounced against a steel box-truss, creating an intermittent short circuit in an electrical system of 13,800 volts (" . . . enough energy to pull ten average-length freight trains! enough to power 75,000 TV sets!").

Slightly injured but neither stopped nor slowed, the G.E.M. of Arizona tramped forward, step by step, flattening a sheet-metal warehouse on the outskirts of Kanab, Utah, stamping down the LDS church across the street, crushing a troop of Boy Scouts sleeping in their pup tents in City Park, liquidating the maternity ward of the county hospital (the biggest ward), and squeezing, like toothpaste from a tub, the dozing occupants of a speeding Greyhound bus caught and suddenly compacted in a curve of the highway south of town. The bus split open at the rear, the passengers squirted out. Any odor? Oh no. They came out like a ribbon, lay flat on the sagebrush.

Smith meanwhile . . . was having difficulties. His brief whingding of a party was over. Paralyzed in the spastic blue glare of the spotlight, he was seized by jointed, whip-like tentacles, disarmed, stripped to his shorts, pulled from the dragline bucket and transported instantly to a point in space ten feet above and to one side of the operator's control cab.

> ... separately air conditioned and provided with large picture windows for a full two hundred seventy degree view ...

The guide tape stopped.

Smith waited, dangling in mid-air, helpless as an infant, musing upon his sense of déjà vu.

Somewhere in the bowels or brains of GOLIATH a new cassette was inserted in the cassette player. Unreeling automatically, the tape played one full minute of computerized digital static — one of high technology's more characteristic refinements — before a third voice began to gibber, in extreme high frequency (like R. Buckminster Fuller at 78 rpm), from the P.A. loudspeakers. Mounted on the masts above the A-frame, loosened by the machine's constant vibration, the speakers functioned badly; Smith could hardly make out a word. But he felt, he sensed, he *knew* that this message was addressed directly to him and to no one else:

> Welcome to our new control cab operator . . .

The tape stopped. Why? Smith waited, wondering. The tape replayed itself, this time at a speed too slow. The androidal voice assumed a deep Dopplerian adenoidal tone, not inhuman as before but subhuman. The speech of Frankenstein's dying monster recorded on a sick compact disc, *hecho en Mejico* by carefree fun-and-family-loving *maquiladores*. The sense, however, was clear:

> Welcome to our new control cab operator. Having completed the ten-minute factory training course, we know that you are eager to begin your employment as a 4250-W Walking Dragline control cab operator. You will be pleased to learn that this position is permanent, full-time and guaranteed for the life of either the 4250-W Walking Dragline or the 4250-W Walking Dragline control cab operator, depending upon which event precedes the other. . . .

For life? Smith became aware, for the first time, of a semi-human figure strapped to a contoured plastic seat inside the control cab. Hands attached by rivets to the self-adapting control levers, the operator was being yanked back and forth in the jerky movements of a windup toy.

> . . . such tenured employment contingent upon satisfactory performance of control cab operations . . .
> . . . You will note that the present control cab operator is not functioning properly but has succumbed to metal fatigue and molecular stress. Having expired in accordance with terms of original agreement . . .

The creature in the control cab looked up at Seldom Seen, forcing a weak and terrified grin, and shook its head. It wore an airtight Plexiglas helmet sealed to the neck of a pressurized, separately air-conditioned, aluminum foil bodysuit by Ralph Lauren. (Halston?) Whether man or woman Smith could not say, but he/she was pale as a fish, sweating, and desperately frightened. Looked almost like a much older Bonnie Abbzug.

Wait, thought Smith, do I really want to be a Super-G.E.M. control cab operator? What about fringe benefits? Ain't heard no mention of them. And then, shamed by the operator's pleading eyes, he forgot personal concerns and reached once more for his revolver. Gone. The belt was gone. His pants were gone. GOLIATH lumbered on.

. . . we will now terminate employment of present 4250-W Walking Dragline control cab operator and install the replacement component. . . .

The voice on the tape halted, waiting, as a large hatch opened itself in the roof of the control cab. The dragline bucket, until now suspended far ahead on the point of the forward boom, came sailing back through the air on creaking cables and halted above the hatchway. The huge jaws gaped wide, far too big themselves to enter the control cab, and extruded something that resembled the forked tongue of a serpent. This was, however, merely the specialized replacement adapter, a forceps-like instrument with teeth that dropped into the cab and snatched the struggling operator, straps, rivets and all, from the control chair. Arms and legs writhing in reflex terror, the operator was swung to maximum boom extension two hundred and twenty-two feet above the ground, and freed, i.e., released, that is, dumped, directly into the path of the machine's advance.

(*Smunch!*)

Smith heard, above the fuel-thirsty roar of engines and the clanking, clanging, banging uproar of chains and cables and pulley-wheels, he heard — or thought he heard — that tiny, mouse-like squeak, remote but human, of the plunging body's final scream.

Have a nice day [the tape said]. Install next operator, please.

The blue light, until now occupied elsewhere, turned its cranky woozy wobbling spot upon the face and naked limbs of Seldom Seen Smith.

"No," he groaned. "Not me. I quit."

Moaning in his nightmare, he fumbled about, felt the warm abundant flesh of his wife, clutched her to him in a drowning man's embrace.

"Seldom," she said, coming slowly into wakefulness. Then louder, sharply: "Seldom! Wake up." She squeezed his encircling arm, the heavy leg thrown across her thighs. "Seldom, wake up!"

"Ohhhhhhhh. . . ." He opened his eyes, saw in the gloom the sweet anxious face of his wife peering at him. "Kathy . . ."

"Guess again."

"Huh?" He blinked, trying to emerge from his bog of horror. "Susan . . . ?"

Sheila frowned, not amused. "You get one more guess, buddy, and it better be right."

He stared at her, smiled, drew that pretty face close and kissed her on the mouth — a long wet slobbering desperate kiss of relief. "Bonnie," he murmured, "Bonnie. . . ."

10
Man Running

A man was running running for his life, across and up a naked dome
of golden sandstone. Far off in silhouette against an evening sky, dark
figure running across a field of gold, a flush of gashed vermillion, the
flaring fanned-out rays of setting sun peering for one final moment,
under a reef of purple clouds, into the slickrock desert, over the rippled
sea of golden lifeless petrified dunes of sand . . .

He ran, ran, ran to live, up the rising skyline curve of rock, across
the huge plasmic crimson bulge of sun, black running human animal
caught forever, in perpetual motion, eternal in his fear, upon the red
sun and background of the yellow sky of Utah.

A stocky man in boots, jeans, no shirt, big hat, puffing like an
engine, hoarse and gasping in despair, laboring at ever-slower pace up
the barren and unsheltering incline of monolithic stone.

He ran because he was pursued. Fifty yards to his rear and
gaining rapidly came a snorting ramping bellowing machine, the
diesel-powered forty-ton dirt scooper, product of Caterpillar Inc.,
bouncing after its prey on rubber-tired wheels each taller than a tall
man. The operator's cab projected forward above the front wheels;

the windows of the cab, covered with dust, splattered with mud, obscured the nature of whatever it was, if anything, that guided and propelled and animated the machine. Reaching the upward slope, the machine redoubled its efforts, bounding ahead. Puffs of black smoke jetted from the upright exhaust stack, floating like little balls of dirty cotton up and backward on the pure golden backdrop of the sky.

Hopeless flight, implacable pursuit. The running man stopped running, stopped climbing, stopped and turned to face the iron black joggling goblin that approached him, closer, closer, with spinning wheels and howling motor, towering above him, about to run him down, crush him like an insect, leave him smeared in a paste of hair, calcium, protoplasm and blood across the gritty surface of the rock.

The man drew a small object from his belt, something not much bigger than his fist, dark against the sunset light, impossible to immediately identify. The man raised this object and pointed it toward the blunt flat advancing snout of the machine. His finger twitched.

A red flame leaped from the tip of the object in the man's hand. Leaped and disappeared, followed presently by the report of a small compact explosion. The man froze, waiting. The machine slowed, stopped as if surprised, and jiggled for a moment, up and down, on heavy springs, twelve feet short of its victim. An arc of cooling liquid spurted like blood from the creature's nose, spouting under pressure into the air then looping down to spatter on the stone. Hurt, baffled, astonished, the machine remained at a standstill, one dark and solid silhouette of steel, rubber, glass and iron upon the forlorn red flare of dying sun, a complicated outline of angles, joints, hoses, couplings, wheels and linkage rods flat back against the horizon. As the light faded the engine died, the coolant drooped in a smaller arc and petered out, the surrounding sea of desert silence closed in complete upon machine and man.

Silence. Stasis. Creeping darkness.

The man replaced the object in his belt. He turned away from the stricken machine — dead tech — and walked upward on the ridge-line, descended the farther slope and vanished into a dense violet twilight.

We heard him singing. Singing, that is, as a wolf sings, a proud prolonged profound Promethean howl of triumph and of joy, a hymn that dwindled after a time to the faintest vulpine vibration on the air but never died, never died completely.

New moon. New moon and evening star.

The new moon, signal of hope, glowed in the western sky. Quite near, almost within the moon's embrace, hung Venus planet of love, rare as radium pure as platinum more precious than gold.

11

The Night Watchman

At midnight, right on time, the new night watchman drove up to the entrance gate in a rusted slab of Detroit iron, stopped at the security station and presented his credentials.

The guard looked them over. He wore a uniform, a visored cap, a gun, a Motorola. So did the new night watchman. "Casper W. Goodwood," the guard said, reading the name and I.D. number on the embossed plastic card, checking the photo on the card against the face in the driver's window of the pickup truck. The faces matched: both were blue-eyed, beetle-browed, ruddy-skinned, crude-featured, red-necked, basic native-American white male working-class chump, the only social stratum in America subject to legal and socially approved school, job and advancement discrimination, accompanied by slurs and sneers. Both faces were clean shaven except for a bushy, drooping, skunk-black Vietnam veteran's mustache.

"Casper W. Goodwood," the guard repeated, squinting first at the card and then at its holder. "Unusual name, Casper. What's the W stand for?"

"Wilbur." Goodwood's voice came out as a throaty growl, less than sociable, but the guard seemed not to notice.

"Where you come from, Casper?"

A moment of silence. "Same place you do, Jasper."

True fact: the guard's first name was Jasper. The plastic card pinned to the breast pocket of his short jacket gave away that painful true fact. Blushing, the guard said, "What do you mean?"

Goodwood smiled. His smile was broad, deep, sincere, but somehow . . . somehow not heartwarming. "I mean shit, Jasper. Fuck-all shit, you know. I mean we come from nowhere. You know what I mean, nowhere." The smile contracted slightly, becoming an unwholesome and unfriendly grin. "That's why we work in a dump like this, Jasper. You follow me? Let me know if I'm going too fast."

The guard stared. He was a big man, six-four, overweight but strong, pressed iron, pumped barbells, never dodged a fight. He carried the .357 magnum on his hip. And a two-foot Mag-light, heavy as a club. He shoved his wife around with one hand. One finger even. He lacked a sense of physical insecurity. And yet, staring at the face of this smaller man, Goodwood, who was smiling at him, the guard hesitated, feeling a rush of novel sensations. Though all he could see of Goodwood through the pickup window was the visored cap, the face, the mustache, the grin. And of the course the shoulders. They looked padded.

The guard said, "Well what the hell, Casper, we're working here together." He returned the I.D. badge, the employment papers and watched as Goodwood, wearing gloves, pinned the badge to his green twill night watchman's jacket. The big shoulder patch read Ace Security SLC. Same as the station guard's. "Might as well be friends," the guard went on, "what the hell."

"Sure, Jasper. We'll work it out." Goodwood gunned the idling engine of his truck. He looked around. "Where do I park?"

The guard pointed inside the gate. "Right over there. Lots of room at the end. Got your punch clock?"

Goodwood lifted the solid round metal gadget, thick as a canteen, with its winding key and shoulder strap, from the seat beside him and showed it to the guard. The guard nodded, started to speak again. Engine racing, Goodwood popped the clutch and lunged forward with a screech of rubber, yanked the truck ninety degrees to the right — twice — and slammed into a tight slot between two immaculate new company sedans. His front bumper, dipping then rising, just *barely touched* the woven steel of the security fence. Ten feet above, in sympathetic resonance, the coils of razor wire shimmered and tinkled and flashed.

The station guard watched as Goodwood got out of his pickup and rewired the door shut. Short fella, the guard noted, kind of heavyset type. Knuckles drag on the pavement. "You know the rounds?" the guard shouted. Goodwood was at least fifty yards away.

The new night watchman nodded. "Got the training course this afternoon." He started off into the lights and shadows of the motor pool, following the fence. Already on duty. Eager beaver.

"Drop in when you feel like it," the guard shouted after the broad, retreating back, "got lots of coffee here." No answer. "That grave-yard's a long shift," he shouted again. No reply.

What a shit, the guard thought. Where do they get these new guys? A real shit. He was glad to see Henderson, the swing shift watchman, emerge form the shadows, Doberman on leash, coming off duty. And Hankerson, his own relief, driving toward the gate. Happily Jasper poured three cups of coffee. None for the dog. The dog had his water dish, full of stale water and drowned and swimming insects, near the station door. While the dog refreshed himself Jasper and friends would drink their greasy coffee, fiddle with their peckers and talk about the quality of these new young security men. City boys, most of them, dope smokers on the sly, poor attitude toward the company. Thanks be to Jesus they weren't stuck with any female gun slappers yet. A man could still talk. Probably won't last long.

Henderson leashed his dog to the doorknob. Hankerson parked his car and joined them. Jasper mentioned the new night watchman, asking about his background. Henderson said the man was all right, had a solid employment record, good references, picked up on the job easily. Hankerson complained about his teenage kid: damned boy had left the key in his uncle's pickup, somebody stole it only hours before. And no insurance on the old heap — hardly worth reporting. Jasper said there were a lot of strangers in town these days, looking for jobs, passing themselves off as miners or construction workers. Some of them not too honest. That's the trouble, Henderson complained, we get this new mill under way here, those new mines, then two thousand dink-heads from Idaho and Colorado and Timbuktu come rushing in, grab the jobs that should go to our kids. That's the price you pay for progress, Jasper argued; can't have everything perfect.

They drank the coffee. They watched the nervous and irritable dog. They listened to the new watchman checking in, by Motorola radio, every ten minutes, as required.

"Goodwood here, 505, Post Six, everything ten-four."

"Ten-four," Hankerson responded on the entrance station radio, "501 clear."

"505."

At about 0030 hours (12:30 A.M.), Jasper said his so longs, picked up his lunch bucket and his Thermos jug and his *True West* magazine and went home. Grudgingly. He didn't really want to go home but in Hardrock, pop. 3500, there was nothing else to do. Even the Atomic Bar, outside of town across the Arizona line, would be closing soon. Anyway Jasper drank only Pepsi-Cola, the officially sanctioned LDS beverage. The Church owned stock in Pepsi-Cola. The Church owned Jasper, full name Jasper Benson Bundy; he often wondered why he didn't go by J. Benson Bundy, like anybody else in Utah would do. Sounded better, looked more . . . businesslike. Maybe he would.

When Jasper left Henderson left, dragging his whining dog. Hankerson sat alone at the gate, listening to the low static of the squelch on the intercom. There were now only eight men within the entire Syn-Fuels compound: himself, the new guy Goodwood patrolling the perimeter fence, an engineer, a foreman and the four welders working overtime somewhere deep in the complex guts of the ore reduction and processing plant. Patching boo-boos, playing catch-up; the mill, still under construction but nearly complete, was only five months behind schedule. Not bad for any project in Landfill County.

At 0200 hours (2 A.M.), the voice of Casper Goodwood crackled from the speaker of the base radio. He sounded different this time, somehow, and Hankerson, a calm and stolid fellow, felt his skin prickle.

"Hankerson . . . ?"

Hankerson responded, sticking to the code: "501."

"Full alert, Hankerson. . . ."

"What? What's up?"

"Bomb."

"What?"

"Found a bomb, Hankerson. Clear the plant."

"A bomb? You sure?"

"I know demolitions, Hankerson. This fucker's ticking away and it's big. I mean fucking big. Clear the mill. The whole fucking place. Quick."

Hankerson smashed the glass over the red alarm ignition switch, yanked down the handle. At once the system began to function, activating ten heavy-duty factory klaxons installed at strategic points within the compound. Bellowing in counterpoint, they sounded like a chorus of lunatic mules risen from Hell, tortured by Lucifer and amplified one hundredfold by God.

Hankerson waited for the sound of running feet. Sticking by his radio, he said, "Where are you, Goodwood?"

"Post Seventeen. Down here in the cyanide leeching plant, I think. Lots of ducts and pipes and motherfucking valves and things. It's a fucked-up mess."

"What do you see?" Christ, thought Hankerson, that's the most delicate expensive tricky section of the whole damned complex. "You sure it's a bomb?"

"I'll soon find out. I'm gonna disarm it."

"Wait a minute. Don't you touch that thing. We'll fly in the Salt Lake bomb squad. You get out of there."

A bunch of men in hardhats came pounding out of the reduction mill. Hankerson counted: . . . three, four, five. Where's that other guy?

"Everybody out yet?" Goodwood asked.

"No," yelled Hankerson. "Wait." He saw the men running toward the rank of parked automobiles and pickup trucks. Stepping outside the station, he motioned them on to the open gate. "Bomb," he yelled, "time bomb. Keep running."

Amazed, they stopped, gaped at him, then ran past and through the gate and into the unlit gloom beyond. There they stopped again. The sixth man, the chemical engineer, middleaged and fat, emerged from a maze of pressure tanks and panted toward the gate house at a strenuous waddle. His yellow helmet fell off, bounced from a circle of light into the shadows. He stopped, clutching his roll of blueprints and a clipboard.

"Come on, sir," shouted Hankerson, "there's a bomb behind you. Better clear out."

"Oh to hell with the bomb," the engineer replied, looking back. "To hell with Syn-Fuels and Hardrock and to hell with the Pipe Fitters Union and the state of Utah."

Hankerson heard the voice of Goodwood on the radio. "Everybody out? I'm gonna see if I can disarm this fucker."

Hankerson rushed inside, grabbed the transmitter. "No, hold it, hold it, one man still in there."

"It's ticking. Might blow any minute."

"Hold on a second."

The engineer arrived, slumping into the doorway of the station, red-faced and panting, sick with disgust. He wiped his sweating face with a pocket handkerchief. "What a place," he mumbled, sagging against the doorframe.

"Okay?" asked Goodwood. "Everybody at the main gate?"

"Everybody but you."

"You can see them? Everybody?"

"Yes, sure."

"Okay, here goes. Stand clear. Keep your hardhats on."

The transmission went dead. Hankerson snatched a pair of hardhats from a shelf, gave one to the engineer. They put them on, sat down on the floor, waited. Hankerson kept an eye on the big wall clock. The sweeping red second hand completed one full revolution. Hankerson reached for the radio mike.

"Goodwood — how are doing?" No answer. Hankerson waited a few more seconds and called again. "505 this is 501. 501 calling 505. Come in, please." No response. Hankerson looked at the engineer, who was leafing through a copy of *Nuclear Times* magazine. "He must be busy. Needs both hands, I guess."

"Bomb scares are bullshit," the engineer replied, not looking up. "Two pounds of bullshit in a one-pound bag."

"This was reported by our night watchman, sir." Again Hankerson radioed Goodwood. "Goodwood," he said, "Goodwood — are you okay?"

This time the radio answered, but poorly, the voice of Goodwood coming through broken and scratchy. "Okay, okay . . . I've got it . . . open . . . Keep everybody . . . out. . . ." Goodwood seemed to be breathing hard, like a man engaged in strenuous labor.

Stress, thought Hankerson. My God, the stress must be terrible. "He's trying to disarm it," he said to the engineer. "The stress must be terrible."

"Heroes are bullshit. Five pounds of bullshit in a cellophane baggie. Pour me a cup of coffee."

"Yes sir. Just a minute." Squeezing the transmitter button, he said to Goodwood, "What do you think? You need some help?" He looked at the clock. Three minutes had passed since Goodwood began the disarming operation. "Want me to call in the experts?"

The voice replied, still puffing a bit, "I'm the expert, shithead. Stop bugging me. This is extremely fucking delicate fucking work. You should see the wires in this motherfucker. Looks like the inside of a switchboard. With batteries and digital clocks and bubblegum. All wrapped around about a hundred fucking pounds of trinitrotoluene." The engineer looked up, interested. "That's TNT," Goodwood continued, "to you simple laymen shits out there. Is everybody clear?"

"Yes sir," Hankerson replied, deferring automatically to the sound of authority. "Seven of us. All but you."

"Okay, I think I see the key to this little fucking electronic cundrum here. I think I see the nipple on the cocksucker. What the hell, let's try cutting this wire, see what happens."

They heard Goodwood laughing. They heard the clink of metal. They heard what sounded like a horse's fart. "Wait up, Jack," they heard him say, "I'm — "

The radio fell silent.

Hankerson and the engineer stared at the speaker. The foreman and the four welders, clustered at the gate, stared at the two men inside.

They waited. Hankerson squeezed his button.

The cyanide leeching plant blew up.

In the morning, searching for Goodwood's remains among the twisted, smoking, sputtering, blackened ruins, they found no trace of him. He was obliterated. Vaporized. Transported far beyond all mortal ken. What they did find was a hole in the back fence big enough to lead a horse through and a pile of horse dung under a juniper tree and a set of horse tracks — two sets, eight shod feet — leading south of town and into the slickrock wastelands of the Strip. A half-breed Paiute tracker and his dogs were able to follow the trail for only three miles into Arizona before the dogs, distracted, confused and maddened by chicken entrails laced with capsicum pepper, gave up the spoor.

Casper W. Goodwood's name was not given in the news accounts, pending notification of next of kin. But the next of kin proved hard to find. Rechecking the man's employment application, the company clerk found only one actual person identified by Goodwood as a blood relation, namely his uncle, Mr. Henry James Jr. of London, England, typist by trade, defunct in 1916 (AIDS). No parents, brothers, sisters or wife revealed. As such, the police report was then released to the press, which ignored the matter, having already passed on, a week later, to more current events.

Syn-Fuels Inc., Denver, subsidiary of Nuclear Fuels Ltd., Brussels, made light of the incident, preferring a minimum of publicity, blaming the affair on "routine labor troubles." The union president, Antonio "Scarface" La Scala, interviewed in his suite at a New York state correctional facility, refused comment. "Gedda fug ouda heah," he said, "fuggin' paparazzi. . . ." The explosion — whether sabotage or accidental valvular malfunction — cost Syn-Fuels about two million, a trifling charge passed on through a daisy chain of Federal subsidies to the U.S. taxpayers, and it set back the production schedule by only eleven weeks.

The machine marched on.

12

Earth First! Rallies

When the two Mitsubishi bulldozers from BLM reached the head of Lost Eden Canyon, a little-known but magical branch of Radium Canyon, which leads in turn to Shivwits Canyon and the Grand Canyon of the Colorado, they found — the operating engineers found — the route blocked by a chain of chanting dancing flag-waving placard-hoisting T-shirted human bodies.

The Mitskinners halted their iron beasts, letting the mighty Mitsu diesels throb and champ. A thin bearded man of thirty, a pink-cheeked chunky teenage girl, they sat on their vinyl seats under canopies of two-inch steel and gazed in wonder, then in irritation, at the spectacle confronting them. What in the hell . . . is the meaning . . . of shit like this?

Unprecedented.

In the center of the chain, perhaps a leader, stood a tall young woman with blue-black hair reaching to her rump, a red headband with hawk's feather around her brow, and a pair of startling fjord-green eyes that blazed within her charcoal lashes like radioactive emeralds of the finest purest deepest water. She wore — but who cares except the author? — faded Levi britches shrunken to a perfect fit (and what they fit was perfect), track shoes, and a snug sweat-soaked white T-shirt which proclaimed, with green fist and words of red across her proud upstanding jugs,

EARTH FIRST!

At her side posed a nearly naked lad, clean-shaven, golden-haired, with the sculptured muscles of a professional body builder, bronzed hide glistening under a becoming film of perspiration. Like everyone else in the group he was unarmed, prepared only for passive resistance and peaceful demonstration. The tool he carried at his side, on which at the moment he was gracefully leaning half his weight, was not as it might appear a primitive Neanderthal warclub but only a simple old-fashioned antique monkey wrench, of the type employed by early railroad mechanics when tightening nuts and bolts on the drive wheels of a steam-powered mogul locomotive. It was four feet long, with oaken handle and adjustable head of cast iron, and weighed only forty pounds.

The remainder of this gang, thirty in all, about half of them girls and the rest only boys, spread out from the center pair on either side, flaunting their youth and health, their black scarves, blue jeans, red rags and green flags —

No Compromise In Defense of Mother Earth!
We Stand *For* What We Stand *On!*
AMERICAN WILDERNESS:
    Love It or Leave It Alone!
GOLIATH Go Home!
Syn-Fuels Is Sinful! Sunshine Is Good!
See One Grand Canyon You've Seen Them All!
BLM Means Bad Luck, Mother!
CAUTION: Land Rapers At Work!
Save Our Canyons: SOC It To The BLM!
Nuke Pukes Eat Carnotite!
Radiation Is Good For *Who?*
Down With Empire, Up With Spring!

Etc., with exclamation mark the clearly favored weapon of punctuation. (There was a time men loved ideas; now they get by with slogans.) The placards and flags lent a jolly, festive, subversive air to the occasion but the press, the media, the TV cameras and videotape recorders, though notified, had failed to show. They'd covered an Earth First!® demo only the month before, in the same region and for the same hopeless cause — why repeat themselves? Time to move on. On this day, for example, most of the Utah-Arizona media corps —

and who else could care less? — had assigned itself to the twentieth anniversary celebration of the erection of the Four Corners Boundary Monument, an obelisk of cement and brass four feet high (economy model) planted upon that theoretical ideal Euclidean point where the four states of Colorado, New Mexico, Arizona and Utah meet, each to the others, in an arbitrary spatio-temporal surveyor's event of total perfect, absolute and neo-Platonic non-significance. With speeches by Governors Lamm and Anaya, Babbitt and Bangerter, emceed by the Bureau of Land Management's own beloved boss bureaucrat Bob "Beefburger" Burford, also known as Burford the Hereford, himself another public-lands welfare rancher appointed to his job in order to defend the public lands against people like himself. Dracula in charge of the blood bank. Reynard to caretake the chicken coop.

The whole world, therefore, was not watching the meeting this day of Mitsubishi with the rearguard of Earth First! (Exclamation mandatory.) No television, no radio, no video, not even the morning or evening or local papers, nothing, nobody, no one reportorial but that seedy old buzzard from nowhere who called himself a "literary journalist" and sometimes appeared at events like this, listening carefully, nodding, smiling, deaf as a stump, taking notes, getting his facts wrong but interviewing the prettier women at exhaustive length, exploiting public bravery for private profit and calling it . . . calling it what? He called it Art. Nobody knew his name, but his *T-shirt* read "Readin' Rots the Mind." Disregarded by all, he faded quickly and naturally into the background whenever violence loomed, as it always did when Earth First! appeared.

The crowd refused to budge, although the operators revved their engines, raised and lowered their gleaming dozer blades in threatening gestures, backed off and re-advanced and pawed the ground a couple of times, like timid grizzly bears not quite certain exactly who was king of the ridge. Finally they simply stopped, motors idling — always cheaper to keep a diesel running than to shut it down and start it up — and waited for their support team, the BLM police-trained ranger in the pickup truck to arrive and disperse the mob.

But looking back the dozer operators could see no sign of the BLM pickup, or of the four-person survey crew redoing a survey job they had completed four times so far, or of any wandering deputy sheriff looking for trouble. Earth First! had alerted the media but forgot or failed to do the same for the Law, obeying the sound principle that there is no situation so bad that the cops can't make it worse.

No help coming, the road-builders perceived, except that towering mushroom cloud of smoke and dust, always back there far in the rear, and the vague rocking yellow form, within and below, of GOLIATH, Super-G.E.M., advancing slow and sure but still ten miles behind.

Meanwhile the rioters besieged the two operators with cold beer, organic apples, bean sprout sandwiches and wry advice.

"Chentlemen," said the tall woman, leveling her rare sensational green eyes upon the patient bearded one, "in Norge vee luff your Grand Canyon off Arida zona. Vee neffer *dream* you tink to dig it up for making thermonuclear bombshells."

"Lady," he said, and groped for answers — "Lady, I need the job. Got a wife, seven kids, a pony and a half-ton four-by-four with camper, $229 a month."

"You call me Erika," she said, "I call you Joe."

"My name is Orval."

"Oral?"

"Orval. Orval Jensen. You're a nice girl, Erika, but please get your hand off that fuel tank cap, please. Takes two hands to unscrew it anyhow. Unless — " He held up one huge oil-grimed sinewy paw and grinned at her.

"Oh yes, Joe, I see you ferry ferry strong man. So vye you bulldoze zis beautiful canyon off Grand Canyon?"

"This ain't Grand Canyon. We ain't nowhere near the goddamned Grand Canyon. This one's called Lost Eden Canyon or some dumb name like that."

"But iss part of Grand Canyon. Vill pollute zee drainage, destroy desert turtle habitat, destroy beautiful cottonwood trees and waterfalls and swimming pools." Squatting long-legged on the mud-caked steel tread at his side, one slender bare arm resting on the fuel tank behind his back (hand on the cap), she gazed sadly, deeply, *greenly* into the impassive and opaque black orbs of Orval Jensen's tractor goggles. Her breasts heaved slightly, nipples aroused from the bounty of her emotion, heart and feelings ill-concealed by the sweat-dampened T-shirt. The old buzzard hovering near, making his mental notes, groaning with lust, observed this dialogue with his usual ambivalent interests. "Vye Joe?" she asked, "vye?"

He tried not to notice. Hands spread in helpless confusion, mouth agape, Orval raised his goggles to the sky — blocked by the steel roof — and said, "Christ, lady, what do you want from me?" Then he looked at her, or seemed to look at her, from behind the goggles, and said, "What's more important to you, people or a goddamn desert turtle?"

She considered the question. She thought about it while the man waited. At last she said, gently and softly, "Vye not haff both, Joe?" And she explained, simply, briefly.

Hah! thought the buzzard, reading her lips, she's hit it, square on the head. While those young punks on the other side of the engine block, funneling emery powder into the crankcase via the dipstick pipe, missed the whole thing.

Orval was silent, thinking hard. The odor of burning particle board floated on the air. People and nature, he thought. Too many people, no more nature. Just enough people, plenty of nature for all. Nature *or* people? Or nature *and* people? Think, Orval, think. It was hard. Especially when you're urgently desperately suddenly full-bore in love.

At the same time, while Orval thought, two young women with beers and the goat-bearded young man with the curly horns and fipple-fingered wood recorder assaulted the pink-cheeked sunglassed teenaged driver of the other Mitsubishi. She refused to look at them, refused to speak, ignored the offer of a beer, even a cold Pepsi or a warm orange.

"My name's Pete," said the piper. "You ever been down in this canyon, miss?" No answer. "I tell you, it's the prettiest place in the Arizona Strip. This side of Pariah Canyon, anyhow. You been there I suppose." No reply. "No? You live around here? Fredonia? Kanab? Hardrock?" No response. "I live at Vermilion Cliffs," he went on. "Got a nice tepee there. Row boats down the Grand for a living. Dories, mainly. Ever been down the river in a dory? No? There's nothing like it. It's fun and it's real." He paused; silence. She would not carry the conversational ball. "Though sometimes it's not real fun," he admitted.

"Come on, let her alone," said one of the two with Pete. "She wants to mind her own business, let her."

"There's somebody coming anyhow," the other said. (The one with the canteen full of blowsand.) "We'd better get back in the line."

The Earth First! platoon reformed its body chain across the survey route, elbows linked in elbows, banners streaming in the breeze, as the BLM patrol truck finally reached the scene. The truck stopped, whiptail quivering, the dust cloud billowed on, enveloping all present in a floating veil of finely pulverized Great Basin Desert soil. The driver surveyed the situation, reported by radio to district headquarters, shut off engine and climbed out.

A rangerette. Another female, naturally — and why not? why the hell not? — stoutly built and looking stern. She wore the uniform, the badge, the massive belt, the ammo clips, the can of Mace, the hand-cuffs, the solid two-foot six-celled Mag-light that doubled as a club, and of course, on her right haunch, the huge holstered high-caliber piece, loaded with hollow points, that weighed as much as all the rest of her hardware together. The name tag above her bulging right-hand breast pocket identified her as "Virginia H. Dick." Ironically, she may or may not have been a virgin. Uncomfortably, her nurturing, mus-cular, heavy flesh swelled at hip and thigh, straining the seams of the trousers she wore like a man.

Actually she was only a shy sweet well-meaning terrified rookie rangerette.

" 'Kay," she barked, glaring at the protestors through bulbous bug-eyed purple shades. Let pass one beat of time. Then said, "Seems to be the trouble here?"

Fists on hips she glared at Erika and the near-naked young man with four-foot tool anchoring the center of the line. She glared at Pete the piper and the sweet young things propping him up from either side. She surveyed the entire row of silent Earth First!ers, from left to right and back again. No one said a thing. Her lip curled with disdain. (Upper lip only.)

"Who's charge this clown show?" Erika raised one hand. "Yes?" the ranger said. "Speak up."

"Pardon, sir," said Erika. "Vee iss no one in charge."

"Looks it. You the leader?"

"No sir. Vee all leaders."

Smiles broke out upon the line of earnest faces. "Yeah," somebody yelled, "we got no leader. We're all leaders." This fellow looked right and left for approval.

"That's right," yelled another, "we're all leaders." Cheers.

" 'Kay!" barked the ranger, lifting one hand for silence. She glared at them all. "So who's the spokesman?" No one spoke. "Gimme a spokesman, spokeswoman, spokesperson. Anybody." A faint smile crossed her face. "Gimme a spoke." Again she glared at Erika. "You there, Miss Cutie Pie. You the spoke?"

Murmurs of objection from the crowd.

Erika stared right back, green eyes blazing. "Excuse, sir, I am not zee spoke. Vee haff no spoke."

"Then shut up." More growls of shock and anger on the line.

"But I speak." Shouts of approval. "I speak," said Erika, "because I luff America and because I luff your beautiful free speak and your beautiful canyon land." Cheers, whistles and the bold flourish of a recorder. "I speak because my heart it cannot be silent." She placed one hand upon that fragrant sweat-filled cleft between her breasts. "I speak because I luff zee desert wilderness. I speak because I cannot sit aside, like bush, like stone, like stupid chump, when zee big machine comes every day closer to ziss place vee luff like home."

Standing tall, back arched, head high, black hair flying, Erika extended her fighting Viking arm full length, and pointed with unshaking hand and straight imperious forefinger at the distant pall of smog, the alien shape, the particle of harsh light that jerked along upon an oblique course, with low but constant grinding irritation, toward them from the east northeast.

"Zat!" she cried, "zat ting zey call what how you say, zat iron brute, zat steel Tyrannosaurus RAX, zat great ugly beast of Armageddon Gog Magag GOLIATH!" She paused for final effect. "Vee here to stop him!" Hurrahs and applause. "Vee here to crush him like a bloody mouse! Zank you."

A moment of doubt, then a shower of cheers, applause, and shouts of defiance from her twenty-nine co-leaders. Smiling happily, proudly, Erika bowed to right and left, clasped hands together above her head and stood like a champion. The piper raised his recorder to his mouth, lips to fipple, fingers to fingerholes, and burst forth in Beethoven's Ode to Joy, the most tragic piece of music ever written.

The ranger waited, giving the crowd its big moment, then raised her hand again. The joy waned, tapered off, died into stillness from lack of good organization.

The ranger smiled. "Pretty speech, honey." Poking a finger beneath her shades, the ranger rubbed at something in her eye. "But now you got to get zee hell out off zee way. Zeese mens — " Too easy; she checked herself. She gestured toward the man and girl on the bulldozers. "Those two have work to do. You're trespassing. You have no permit to demonstrate. You're holding up construction on a Federal project. You're threatening life and safety of men and equipment engaged in lawful bona fide pursuance. I'm giving you two minutes to disperse. If you do not disperse I am calling the county sheriff and the department of public safety and the BLM Helicopter S.W.A.T. Team and placing each and every one of you under arrest on multiple charges good each for six months in the county slammer and fines of not more than and not less than five thousand dollars per individual."

Nobody moved.

The operating engineers revved up their sixteen-cylinder Mitsubishi

engines, brandished their dozer blades, twitched steering levers caus-
ing the machines to pivot left and right, treads grinding down on earth,
on sand, on cliffrose and sego lily, on gopher hole and badger den and
kit fox burrow. A dung beetle died in the first bloom of youth. A
horned toad, lapping up ants at an ants-nest hole, was crushed flat as
a spatula. Ten thousand ants were never seen again. . . .

Arms linked, the mob stood firm.

The ranger glanced at her watch. The time was up. Jeez, she
thought, what the hell do I do now? I wish I was back at Michigan
State. I wish I was back at the drive-in with Marty and Bobbie, holding
hands and popping popcorn and watching *Return of the Jedi*. Oh Jeez,
Momma, where are you now?

She faced the crowd, resumed barking. The lady pit bull. " 'Kay,"
she barked, "you are all under arrest. Don't move." She waited for
them to start running, like bunny rabbits. They must have a truck or
a bus or something up there on that funny hill. She looked where her
thoughts led, to the low mesa on the north where the jeep trail came
to a deadend, but saw nothing except a man loafing on a horse,
watching the human comedy below. A second horse lounged nearby,
tethered to a juniper. Ah for the carefree life of the cowboy, she
thought, taking his crap in the bushes, riding the range in search of
stray heifers, holding his joint in one hand while scratching his balls
with the other.

One of the boys at the barricade flipped the tab on a can of beer.
Sounded like the spring release of a hand grenade. Wind blew, the
flags rippled: green & white and the black & red and the red & white
& blue.

"Don't move, I said," the ranger said. Keeping them under arrest
with her purple glare, she backed to her truck and the radio. And me
with a riot on my hands, some idiot shooting up dirt scoopers, and
Bishop Love on my neck about his stolen Caterpillar and all those
reports to make out tonight. "I'm going to radio for assistance now,"
she yelled. Adding, "If you don't clear out." She waited. Run, you
idiots.

The line held. Nobody broke.

My God, thought the ranger, maybe they did walk all the way from
the river. Thirty miles? Forty? She looked with misgiving at the heap
of backpacks on the rim of a ledge above the next drop-off. But the
beer? Those flags? Surely not. Anyhow — call for help. You're enti-
tled. Resisting arrest. Threatening violence. Look at Miss Glamor
Puss. . . . Look at that one in the middle all hide and muscle, thinks

he's Arnold Schwarzenegger, look at that thing he's got. In his hand. Four feet long if it's an inch. Call for help. (*Help!*)

Ranger Dick opened the door of her ranger truck, then saw the roostertail of dust approaching, at excessive speed over the churned-up earth and smashed vegetation of the road-in-progress. Another pickup? Boys from the crew, she thought, bringing reinforcements. A half ton of rednecks in hardhats, that's what I need all right, got to admit it.

And then the vehicle came close, bouncing over the bumps, and she saw that it was a Ford Bronco four-by-four containing one hat, one head, one man. Stockman hat. Shaven head. Oh shit, she thought, it's the Bishop. Still mad, I'll bet. But at least we got the mob outnumbered now: me, Orval, the Bishop, maybe that kid. Four of us and only thirty of them.

The Bronco skidded to a halt. Landfill Co. Search & Rescue Team, said the decal on the door panel. Always searching for something to rescue. Bishop Love got out, politely smiling at Ranger Dick and more sincerely at Orval Jensen on his machine. The smile weakened a bit for the girl on the other; the Bishop did not approve of hiring women to do construction work. But this was a government job, he had to follow certain guidelines, make at least a gesture toward filling the official minority quotas for the official government minorities.

And then Love turned his eyes upon the ragged line of protesters obstructing progress and he abandoned all pretense of civility. He frowned, he scowled, he spat in the dirt. "Them again," he growled to the ranger and Orval, "the green bigots."

"I'll radio for help," the ranger said. "I warned 'em . . ."

Love eyed the demonstrators, their defiant anxious faces, bare limbs, brazen flags. Eyes full of bale, smoldering with contempt, he muttered, "Help hell, it'll take two hours for the sheriff to get here. I'll clear them out myself."

He nodded to Jensen. "Let's go, Orval." He jerked his thumb at the teenager on the second machine. "Get down, sweetie, I'll take it."

Reluctantly, the girl descended from her high seat. "I ain't afeared of them hippies, Bishop Love."

The Bishop patted her helmet as he climbed past her to the controls. "You're a good girl, honey, but this is man's work." Seating himself in the cramped cockpit of this new Nipponese machine, he thought of something else too: "By the way, Ginny," he shouted at the ranger, above the rumble of motors, "you find my crawler yet?"

Afraid of that question. "No sir," she replied, "but we're on the track." That's a lie, she thought. Though it's only been missing for twelve hours.

The Bishop grinned his tiny creepy grin. "Kind of hard to hide a Cat D-7 out here in the desert, wouldn't you say?" He pulled out the throttle on the Mitsubishi, letting the roar of sixteen cylinders pronounce his opinion of the ranger's explanation. If she had one. Lady rangers, *he* was thinking. Female dozer operators. Next thing you know they'll want to be bishops. In *our* church. Just like the niggers. Yes, it's a fact, true fact, we live in the latter days and the time of judgment is nigh. Sodomy in the streets and fornication in high places, like them naked sky jumpers do. Waxing wroth, he pulled the power takeoff lever and lifted the mighty dozer blade clear of the dirt. He engaged the clutch lever; the tractor lurched forward. Love aimed the machine at the center of the Earth First! line, directly at the slender form of that shameless long-legged harlot in the tight jeans and damp T-shirt.

By God, I'll make her jump. Make her run like a scared bunny rabbit. She's built for speed, let's see her use it.

At full throttle he rumbled toward her, wind at his rear, dust cloud passing. The tall girl did not move. Instead she seized a small American flag from somebody nearby and held it before her, like a crucifix, warding off the devil.

But that only made the Bishop madder. Dirty tricks, he snarled, dirty tricks. At full speed forward he lowered the blade and plowed into the ground, shoving a half ton of stones, weeds, brush and rainsoaked dirt toward his target.

"Out of the way!" he screamed, "out of the way!"

She did not move, except to spread her feet apart for a firmer stance.

Cursing, Love halted the machine three feet short, raising the blade and letting his dune of debris flow over her feet, calves, knees, thighs, planting her crotch-deep in mud. Standing up from his seat, shaking a fist, the Bishop roared, "I'll bury you!"

She turned white with fear but did not struggle to escape. "Vee stay here," she yelled, great green eyes shining, waving her borrowed flag. "You go home. You bury not *me* on zee lone prairie."

Love backed off a bit for better visibility and a second run, his dozer blade high in the air. Something hard clanged against steel. Amazed, he saw another woman, heavy and powerful, heaving rocks at the front of his machine. Like most of the others she wore a proclamatory T-shirt. "EF! Feminist Garden Club," said hers, "Georgia Hayduchess, Pres."

Holy Moroni! thought the Bishop, they're everywhere. But Bishop Love had never run from a woman yet. Nor from any number of women. But he could use some support. He looked around for Orval Jensen. Where was Orval?

There was Orval's machine, still in place, motor idling, but Orval himself was walking away, headed for his pickup truck a mile back down the road. The Bishop stared for a moment — that man is fired — then climbed down from cab to tread to ground. Again he jerked his thumb at the teenager. "Okay," he said, "get back on your Mitsu. I'll take the big one."

Happily the girl obeyed. Love took over on Jensen's machine, flipped the steering clutch levers, yanked out the throttle and roared once again toward the line of protesters. This time he aimed at what he judged to be a weaker sector of the line, a group of smaller, younger girls hanging together, elbow to elbow, on the left. Advancing at full speed, iron treads clattering, engine bellowing like a bull from Hell, he saw them tremble, saw one take a step backward, then another. Hah! he thought, they're gonna break. He raised the dozer blade to make his machine look bigger, meaner, uglier. He glanced aside; his teenage operator was advancing against the right flank, on her pale face a look of rigid hate. Good kid! he thought; nothing like a female driver to scare the pants off anybody.

Whang!

A mighty blow resounded from his blade. Love paid attention. That woman throwin' rocks again? No, it was the huge young punk with no clothes on, hardly any, all meat and muscle, rearing back with some kind of godawful battle club — a mace? — getting set for another swing. Before Love could lower the blade, amputate the kid's feet, he heard

Whunk! the second blow, duller this time, something dead and deadly about it, that tone without resonance which the practiced ear of Love recognized as the sound of weakened metal, distempered steel, of oriental molecules relinquishing their grip on reality. Quickly, the Bishop flipped the dozer lever, letting the blade drop to the ground, but he was too late, the sweating thug had already stepped aside and swung his weapon for the third time

Whack! and cracked the dozer blade from stem to rim. Impossible, the Bishop thought, even as his blade, plowing into the ground, parted itself in twain along the jagged split of fracture.

But he didn't stop. Lifting the blade, broken but still firmly bolted to its iron supporting arms, uglier, meaner, more dangerous than before, the Bishop drove his tractor onward. For the enemy was bolting. They were running, scattering before him like a bunch of panicked calves, grunting with fear. The girl had done it, the kid on his right, couldn't even remember her name, she and her little Mitsubishi, something in her style of operating, her fixed frozen inflexible non-reactive grip on the controls, almost a paralysis of will, had communicated itself to the line of young people confronting her, forced them to realize, unanimously, suddenly, that they were being charged, not by a human driving a machine, but by a machine driving a human.

And so, naturally, sensibly, they unlinked arms and fled, throwing a few useless rocks, each on his and her own, in various directions. Only the tall young woman stood her ground in the center of the field, staying there because she could not move, could not pull her legs from the mound of mud in which they were embedded. Erika the Svenska, and at her side Hayduchess, scrabbling frantically at the dirt with bare hands, trying desperately, hopelessly, to free her.

The loafing horseman on the mesa raised one arm.

Ranger Dick sat in her pickup calling headquarters.

The two yellow bulldozers, circling right and left among the dodging yelling rioters, kept them scattered far and wide. Spotting the mound of backpacks on the ledge, Bishop Love advanced to crush them under his treads, saw the drop-off, lowered his broken blade instead and pushed them one and all over the edge, stopped his machine, reversed, rotated. His assistant was chasing an old graybearded buzzard through the sagebrush. "Press!" the man yelled, "press!," holding up his little shirt-pocket notebook as he ran. It did him no good whatsoever; the teenage operating engineer maintained steady pursuit, engine roaring, blade elevated high to clobber him. (Her engine block smoking a bit, overheated.)

The Bishop grinned. Press, he thought, press — they're the worst of all. I hope she jams him down a gopher hole. He looked about for fresh victims, saw Hayduchess and the young bastard with the giant monkey wrench trying to dig out that half-buried slut with the legs and the eyes and the big sweaty tits. We'll see about that, by golly — that black-haired Barbie doll is mine; that gal is going to the pokey. For six months.

He gunned his engine. Didn't respond quite right at first, he felt a couple of pistons seemed to miss a stroke. Then it took off, raging full bore, and the Bishop clattered happily back toward the struggling bodies in the mud in the middle of the right-of-way.

From the corner of one eye — good peripheral vision here — Love became aware of a patch of dust and yellow steel veering toward him from the right, on a bearing that would cut across his path not far from the objective. The kid? No, not her, she was far off on another tangent, still rattling after that reporter. This was a big machine, much bigger than hers, almost as big as Love's, a Cat in fact, a D-7 in fact, third biggest hunk of crawling iron that Caterpillar makes. Well, good, the Bishop thought, we got them now, we'll round up the whole crazy long-haired bare-legged flag-waving herd. He waved to the dark figure crouched at the controls, a man obscured by thick billows of dust rolling up from the treads. The operator waved back, lowered his filthy red bandanna for a moment to flash a gleaming grin, then drew it up again to screen his mouth and nose from the fine rich dust. Face half masked by the rag, no goggles, big black floppy hat pulled low on his head, the man resembled one of those half-breed Mexican desperados from an old-time Western movie.

Don't think I know that guy, the Bishop thought. He one of my men? Why ain't he wearing his respirator? His safety goggles? His hardhat? Goddamn OSHA's giving us enough trouble already with their goddamn candyass rules and regulations, man can't take a piss anymore without consulting their goddamn rulebook, can't squat to take a shit without a backup beeper. And holy Moroni not so fast there buddy where'd you learn to drive and for the love of petesake why the hell don't you watch where you're —

Ca-rump!

The Cat D-7 slammed hard into the right front side of Love's big Mitsu, jarring it off course.

Now what the hell — ?

Treads grinding into bedrock, the Cat pushed at low speed full power against the forequarter of Love's machine, its massive dozer blade jammed against the Bishop's right tread, tilting him off center, robbing him of full traction, swinging his whole front end around a good ninety degrees. He was now headed toward the rim of the ledge that curved on a bias up the wash, a clear fifty-foot overhanging drop-off, with the man on the Cat continuing to push him toward the closest part of the edge.

Wants a fight, does he? By God we'll give it to him. Love pushed the forward-and-reverse lever into reverse position, attempting to back clear from his opponent, get room for a racing head-on charge, shove that wise guy ass over tincups. Big as the Cat was, his Mitsubishi was bigger, outweighing the other by five tons.

But the other gave him no space for maneuver. No sooner did Love go into reverse, disengaging his right tread from the Cat's dozer blade, than the bandanna bandito rammed full tilt against the inside of the Mitsu's blade, shearing off the broken right half, exposing the vulnerable radiator to frontal assault.

Dirty tricks, the Bishop thought, dirty tricks again! Bastard won't fight fair. Still in reverse, backup signal screeching, he lifted his remaining half a blade as high as it would go, shifted into forward, full speed, yanked back the right clutch steering lever and made a sudden lunging attack directly at the open unshielded cab of the Caterpillar.

Better jump, pal, better jump, or you're one mashed-up Catskinner.

The man on the Cat did not jump. Instead he rotated his tractor face-to-face with the Bishop and caught the Mitsu's dropping blade behind the edge and between the arms of his own. With the clang of iron and a shower of sparks they locked.

Horns locked, like a pair of rutting bull elk, like two stag beetles, they struggled for a moment blade to blade, motors bellowing, both driving forward on slipping treads, each striving to shove the other back, neither gaining an inch.

At first. And then the Mitsubishi's superior weight and power began to pay. To pay off. Despite his slightly uphill advantage, the man on the Cat was forced to yield, foot by foot, before the Mitsu's greater mass. Grinning under his sunglasses, the Bishop turned a hair to the left and then another, forcing the Cat this time toward a corner of the overhang.

The bandanna bandit tried to free his blade from beneath the weight of the other's; he had power enough to cant up both but could not detach his own without the other man's cooperation. (The Bishop grinned.) The Cat driver attempted a sharp turn in reverse, as the Bishop had done, but this time the ploy left the Cat with its rear close to the rim of the ledge and the Mitsu on the uphill side. (The Bishop grinned again.) The man glanced over his shoulder; the edge lay ten feet away. Nine. Eight. Seven. . . .

Jump, you moron, the Bishop thought, his satisfaction smug and complete, jump or die.

But the moron did not jump. Not yet. Looking back, then forward, then back again, standing up but not leaving his place, he remained at the levers of his Cat D-7b.

So okay, thought Love, be that way. It's your funeral. He pulled his throttle out to the last notch. Full power forward. His sixteen pistons danced in their oily vaginae, the black smoke jetted from his stack.

And then, as the bandit tractor teetered on the edge, apparently about to fall, Bishop Love remembered that his shattered dozer blade was caught behind the other man's dozer blade. Well . . . He jammed down the steering clutch brakes, pushed the speed selector into neutral, pulled back on the blade lift lever. We'll let him go over nice and easy, he thought, give him time for a prayer. A short one.

The Bishop's dozer blade rose as instructed.

But the other man's blade rose with it and stayed there, keeping the two bulldozers coupled together, nose to nose.

Out of habit the Bishop stood up to get a clear view of the problem, releasing the brakes. "Let your blade down!" he shouted, making the customary down-pushing hand signal. The man on the Cat seemed not to understand. "Let it go down!" the Bishop shouted again, trying to be heard above the clamor of the excited engines. The man stared at Love, nothing visible of his face but the wild red crackpot eyes between the greasy brim of his hat and the upper edge of his greasy bandanna. The Bishop pointed at the locked dozer blades. "Down!" he shouted, getting angry, "down, you moron!"

This time the man nodded, placed a gloved hand on a control lever, the other on the outer edge of the fuel tank, looked over his shoulder one last time, shifted his tractor into reverse, and vaulted over the fuel tank. Into space.

Both bulldozers clanked over the edge.

The Bishop scrambled down from his, over the rippers in the rear, barely in time to save his ass. He lay on the cool stone for a long time, face flushed, hand on his heart.

Ranger Dick came trotting near, lugging a big first aid kit. She dropped to her knees beside Love, put one ear to his chest and grabbed his wrist, listening, feeling, counting heartbeats.

"I'm dead," he said. Feeling for her hip, his hand came to rest on her gun butt. "Ginny, I'm dead."

"Should be. Bishop Love, when you going to stop doing things like this? Got to take care of yourself. Get your hand off my leg."

"That's your leg?"

"My hogleg. Take your digitalis today?"

"Yes I took my digitalis today. Yes I took my digitalis yesterday. Yes I'll take my doggone digitalis tomorrow."

"Don't get upset. Was only asking." The ranger pulled a handkerchief from her pocket and wiped his damp brow. "Drink of water?"

"Got any Pepsi?"

"No."

"I'll take a drink of water." Laboriously he sat up, leaning a bit on Ranger Dick's strong warm shoulder as she unslung her felt-covered canteen. Unscrewing the cap he said, "How do you feel about polygamy, Ginny?"

"How's your wife feel about it?"

"Yeah . . ." He drank, wiped his mouth. "Yeah, that's the problem. But say . . ." He grinned at her. "Was that a great fight or was that a great fight?"

"Great. Pushed your own bulldozer over the cliff."

"You mean that Cat D-7? That was mine?"

"Hell yes, Dudley; you didn't know?"

He lay back on the ground and closed his eyes. "Hold my hand, Ginny, I feel weak." She took his hand, held it on her warm and abundant lap. "Any man can't recognize his own brand," the Bishop went on, "better get out of the livestock business."

"You're insured."

"The deductible gets higher every year. Last time this happened they said they'd cancel my policy."

"Don't tell 'em."

"Yeah, don't tell 'em." The Bishop smiled. "Anyhow by God I won the fight. Didn't I win the fight, Ginny?"

"Ever think of getting a bypass operation?"

"No. You see that evil bandit bugger jump? God but he was scared, you should of seen the look in his eyes."

"Might do you lot of good."

"There's only one heart doctor in this whole country I'd trust to do that operation and he don't like me anymore. Not since I had my change of heart. And besides he don't do hearts anymore anyhow. What they call a pediatrician." Love's big thick fingers twitched on the ranger's thigh. "Think maybe we oughta take a look?"

"A look at what?"

"At the remains."

"If you want. Make you sick."

He sat up again. Taking his hands she helped him to his feet. They walked to the edge and looked over, smelling the stink of burning diesel fuel. Approximately ninety feet below the two bulldozers lay, belly to belly, like copulating lovers. Treads untracked, blades twisted, internal organs dangling, both were burning, quietly burning in the shade of the drop-off within the generalized desert stillness. Scattered about the wreckage, spattered with fuel and also burning, were the charred melted remains of a dozen or more heavy-duty backpacks, a few of them once pretty fancy.

Bishop Love gazed down at his smoldering machines, the bigger one sprawled upon the slightly smaller one. He turned a sly shy smirking grin upon Virginia. "Wish I was doing that."

She caught his meaning. "Well go ahead, Dudley, they're your bulldozers."

"I mean, you and me."

"Oh come on. Haven't you had enough action for one afternoon?"

"Ginny, you're a caution. Heavens to betsy." A helicopter thumped past overhead, awkward and violent in approach, subdued and sneaky in departing. Like a country lover. The Bishop looked up. "BLM? What're they lookin' for?"

"Your boy."

"My what?" Love stared at her, then up at the dwindling helicopter, then down at the smoking ruins. He noticed for the first time the great slopes of fine sand banked against the canyon wall on the near side, reaching from the floor of the canyon to within ten feet of the base of the overhang. Slanting down the loose dune, from top to bottom, was a series of sitzmarks, like the footprints of a giant hound, spaced well apart. The question that was uppermost on Love's mind he finally brought down to his lips. "He jumped down there?"

"Guess so, Dudley. Time I got here I saw only his rear end going around that next bend down there. He must be four miles down the canyon by now. You all right?"

They walked slowly back toward the original scene of confrontation, holding hands. After the battle of the bulldozers the world seemed strangely quiet in Love's ears. "So they all got away? Every doggone last one?"

"Got two, that long one you planted in the mud and that big one threw rocks at you."

"Who are they?"

"We'll find out."

They shuffled through sand and over bedrock up the wash, emerged from between the sheltering mudbanks into the open terrain of sagebrush and survey stakes, pickup trucks and four-wheel-drive Ford Broncos.

The Bishop stopped. "Where are they?"

The ranger stopped too. "Had 'em handcuffed together. Locked 'em in your Bronco."

"The Bronco's gone."

The ranger nodded. "So it is. Well . . ." She indicated her BLM pickup. "Least they had sense enough not to steal Federal property. Come on."

They reached the pickup. All four tires were slashed. The teenage operating engineer sat on the sunken hood looking discouraged. Also anxious. She held a long shining dipstick in her hand; her Mitsubishi XLT was nowhere in sight. Her story too was fairly simple. Tears in her eyes, she told it:

"Oh Bishop Love, I'm sorry. I'm awful sorry, Bishop Love, and I sure hope it ain't my fault. I almost got that old beaknosed media man, Bishop Love, he sure could run fast but I almost got him and then my engine started to smoke and then it froze up, Bishop Love, seized up tighter'n a Spandex saddle on a corn-bloat cow and wouldn't run no more *a-tall*, Bishop Love, there was blowsand in the crankcase, and I had to walk all the way back here nigh on to half a mile and my feet are sore as snakebit pups."

"Where is it?"

She pointed. They looked, looked hard, and sure enough there it was, a tiny blur of dusty yellow half buried in a gully deep in the sage and gama grass. The ranger checked with her 7x50 binoculars. Far past the defunct bulldozer she saw golden dunes of sand, aeolian sand, the singing sands of the leanest part of the loveliest region in the whole long wide high-lonesome land of horny toads and soaring buzzards and melancholy coyotes. Coyote, she thought — the prairie wolf. Staring at the sands and the blue mesas beyond, she thought she could hear the wolf, its cry, its call, its wild defiant song. She stared, stared, and saw a horseman ride slowly up the dunes, pausing on the summit to peer about, then passing on. He led a second horse, saddled but riderless. They disappeared.

13

Bonnie and the Bag Lady

Doc was gone, off to the trauma factory for an early morning bone marrow transplant. Another poor kid, a little girl only ten years old, from the St. George area. Acute leukemia again. Plus cancer of the lymph glands. Rather common down there in the southern part of the state, considering the relatively small human population. Not enough numbers, of course, to serve as hard proof of anything, though the region lay downwind from the military proving grounds. The Federal government denied responsibility and the Federal judges, appointed to their lifetime $89,500 a year jobs by the Federal government, decided — always — for the Federal government. Nobody knew why.

"Of course," explained Doc, "could be like they say only a statistical anomaly."

"How come children keep dying of these statistical anomalies?"

"Don't take care of themselves. Don't understand probability theory. Mathematical illiteracy all too common in our society. Can be fatal."

"I think mathematics is a fatal disease."

"See what I mean?"

She was glad he was gone. And Reuben still asleep. In nightgown and robe she descended the staircase, opened the front door and rescued the morning newspaper from what looked like an ongoing drizzle. Doc hated to pedal home for lunch and find his *Salt Lake Tribune* in dampish condition. Bad enough, he would say, when it's dry; worst morning paper in the whole state of Utah. It's the only morning paper, she'd say. That's no excuse, he'd say, adjusting his eyeglasses and opening first to the Letters column on the editorial pages. When looking for wit, wisdom, knowledge or intelligence in a newspaper, any newspaper, your only hope is the Letters column.

She carried the paper through the quiet old frame house to the kitchen, made herself a pot of tea, turned on the radio to her favorite soft rock station — Doc could not bear the sound of any music more recent than that of that ancient creep Gregorian and his dreary "chants" — and sat down to enjoy her only hour of solitude before the boy awoke.

She unfolded the newspaper and spread it open on the table to dry. Not even glancing at the front page — for what could be older than the "news"? — she opened Section C, "Accent on Living," which followed "State & Local" and preceded "Sports," to Ann Landers, Joyce Brothers, and the astrology chart. Under Aquarius, her favorite sign, she found this wise counsel:

> Danger. Avoid your regular haunts today. Contact old friends. Reconsider your financial affairs. Beware of strange men wearing big hats, dark glasses and raincoats.

Why? she thought. What regular haunts? This house? The baby's room? The supermarket? The new car dealer's service shop? And what financial affairs? And strangers in raincoats? Sounds like my husband. She conjured up the mental vision of Doc, at that very moment, emerging from the recovery room in his greenish surgical scrubs, loosening the drawstring on his pants to show the young nurses in Pediatrics what an uncircumcised penis looked like when half erect. Absurd.

Well, she had to go to the goddamned store sometime this morning, danger or no danger. And Reuben would raise unholy hell if she didn't take him for his regular after-shopping marshmallow fudge ice-cream sundae. Children believe in ritual, ceremony, custom, tradition, and children are right. Children keep in touch with the ancient underlying rhythms of organic existence. Yeah — like sitting in a pool of their own piss on the elegant white wicker chairs of Snelgrove's Ice Cream Parlor.

They entered the place at eleven, beating the lunchtime rush. Nobody there but a few Mormon matrons with their squalling litters, those large hippo-shaped women with their snot-nosed blue-eyed towheaded brats. Why are Mormon mothers always so fat? They make such cute teenagers, such rosy sexy leggy golden pom-pom girls, and then, a mere ten years later they're all a bunch of buffalo butts, why? Grand multi-parity. Too many babies. Don't believe in birth control and don't understand the mechanical principle of mandibular sex, the auxiliary function, that is, of what you might call the oral hatch. When a fella needs a fellatio, said Doc, he won't get it from a Latter-Day Saint. Female, that is. From the other half, on the other hand, especially if a Congressman, you might get anything. Like genital warts.

Was there no end no bottom to a medical man's crude gross vulgarity? There was not.

Folding her umbrella, Bonnie led Reuben to a table near the window, away from the matriarchs and their bawling vermin. Nobody sat nearby except a couple of tidy fair-haired young men in dark suits, red ties, umbrellas neatly furled at their feet. They looked like returned missionaries — or Soviet functionaries. They wore black rubbers over their black shoes. Nobody wore rubbers anymore, black or any other color. On shoes. Nobody but returned missionaries.

In the corner reading the morning paper through purple sunglasses, floppy wet hat on her curly head, sat a broad-shouldered blonde in a filthy greasy military-surplus rainjacket. Her cheap cotton dress was hiked almost to her knees, revealing thick hairy ugly legs in "flesh-colored" support hose. Her shopping bag, stuffed with God only knows what garbage, rested on the floor at her side. Her overloaded shopping cart, stolen from Safeway, waited outside the entrance. Snelgrove's did not encourage the patronage of bag ladies but this one evidently carried the price of a cup of coffee somewhere on her person. As long as she nursed her coffee they could not legally throw her out.

Bonnie looked at the window, holding Reuben's hand, and watched the spring rain streaming down the glass. Cynical on the outside, soft as mush at heart, Bonnie wept inwardly for the harsh life of a bag lady, whether here in Snelgrove's, Salt Lake City, or under the sewer gratings of midtown Manhattan. (And what's the difference?) She wept for all of the poor, everywhere; she was, as Doc liked to say, the only non-professional anywhere who actually lay awake at night thinking about starving Ethiopians. Who actually worried, at least once a month, about the fate of the Third World's colored people.

"Not 'colored people,' " she corrected him, many times; "people of color."

"Oh? What's the difference?"

" 'Colored people' is racist."

"Sorry. People of color, I mean. Of course. Our swarthier, duskier brothers and sisters, as it were. Okay?"

"Doc, you're asking for trouble."

"Sorry. Was only asking."

The waitress came, she ordered the hotdog & beans and the sundae for little Reuben, a cup of coffee for herself. Surrounded by ice cream in two dozen flavors, Bonnie refrained from the indulgence. She was secretly proud of her trim neat female figure and she meant to keep it. At least for another ten years. Although, as she sometimes worried aloud to Doc, she thought her breasts too large, her buttocks too fleshy.

"You're a woman not a whippet," Doc reassured her. "You stick out in front and you stick out behind like a woman should, for the love of Christ. There's a purpose to it. What more do you want? Anorexia? If you were built like a boy I'd never have noticed you. Probably."

"I want a body like Jane Fonda."

"That old wombat? Listen, you're a hell of a lot better looking than she'll ever be. Or rather, than she ever was."

"My hips are too wide."

"You're Jewish."

"Half Jewish."

"That's the half. You've got a Jewish ass and a colleen's brain. Too bad it didn't come out the other way around but, well, we all have our private tragedies."

"Doc, you're asking for trouble. Someday you're going to go too far. Nobody loves a weisenheimer."

"You do."

"That's not love it's only pity. If I didn't feel sorry for you I'd leave."

"You can't leave me, I'd die."

"That's right. It's an unhealthy unilateral relationship and it's called co-dependency and there's a new therapy treatment group for people with your problem and if you weren't so old and stubborn you could go there and get the help you need, his name is Doctor Maharishi Zit, he's from Nepal."

"Santa Monica more likely. Isn't that the mystical podiatrist who was trying to get us all to walk barefoot on hot coals? If we paid him a hundred bucks.''

"That was last year. You're thinking of Swami Prabhavananda."

"Also, this Dr. Zit fellow, why does he call it *co*-dependency if it refers to a one-sided relationship?''

"What kind of a question is that?''

She had him there. He couldn't answer.

Reuben nibbled at his hotdog and beans, under his mother's pressure, then gobbled up the ice cream when she looked out the window again.

Shark-nosed automobiles streamed in endless caravan through the gentle acid rain, spraying one another with a film of insoluble filth, a vicious servility oozing by in grease. Bonnie's heart sank when she considered the horror of the lives that most men led, trapped for nine ten hours a day in the slave gangs of traffic, the uniformed peonage — suit and tie and digital wristwatch — of the office galleys, the nerve-wracking drudgery of the on-going never-ceasing destruction and reconstruction, backhoes, front-end loaders, jackhammers, wrecking balls, freight trucks, nailguns, concrete culverts, asbestos insulation, I-beams, hardware, software, application forms, medical claim forms, auto insurance forms, income tax forms, garbage, mud, dust, sludge, whole monoclines of paper and anticlines of carbon (press hard) and synclines of silent despair. The world of ''jobs.''

Koyaanisqatsi!

And not only the men. Progress proceeds. Now the women too, driven by need or madness or by simple greed, were plunging into the same nightmare world, unsexed by unisex, becoming office-persons, waitpersons, chairpersons, cowpersons, truck driverpersons, coal minerpersons, machine-gunnerpersons. With their children abandoned all day five days a week in pink and blue Day-Glo Tee-Vee Jailhouse Kiddie Kare storage centers. That is, if the women were lucky enough to be able to afford it. Those mothers, that is, who had their ''jobs.'' The cruelty of it sickened her. Reaching out, she placed one hand on Reuben's curly hair.

Powaqqatsi!

It occurred to Bonnie, and not for the first time, that she was a fortunate woman. She patted her belly. A lucky woman, though stuck with an aging curmudgeon like Doc Sarvis. Her ball and chain, at least, was chocolate-coated. Velvet-lined. Made of hollow aluminum. If I didn't want to be a mother, she thought, I would never have had a baby. I absolutely would not be having a second.

"Momma," said Reuben, "that old woman forgot her bag."

Sure enough. The bag lady, lumbering out the door, had left behind her giant plastic shopping bag. Staggering into the rain, pushing the cart, she seemed preoccupied with her thoughts. Bonnie covered the waitress's check with a five-dollar bill (over-tipping again, spoiling the natives) and rushed out after the bag lady, pulling Reuben with one hand and toting the woman's bag in the other.

The bag lady had drifted two doors down the street, in the direction of Bonnie's parked car, and was now leaning against a wet wall mumbling to herself.

Bonnie approached, holding forth the bag. For so bulky an object it seemed strangely light, as if filled with nothing but the crumpled wads of paper visible on top.

Apparently unaware of Bonnie and her child, the woman glowered at the rain, the traffic in the street, or perhaps at nothing at all, and gibbered to herself, lips moving. "Fuckin' rain," she seemed to be saying, "fuckin' traffic, fuckin' nothin' at all . . ."

How does one address a bag lady?

"Ma'am," said Bonnie politely, clearing her throat for attention, "madame, you forgot your bag."

The creature glared at Bonnie, little red eyes squinting behind the dark shades. Rain dripped from the wide brim of her big sagging Goodwill fedora. Six inches taller than Bonnie, she was indeed a massively constructed female, with the thick neck and heavy shoulders of a steamroller fullback. She must have weighed at least 180 pounds. "You talkin' to me, sister?" Her voice was deep, rough, familiar.

Bonnie stared, dropping the bag on the wet sidewalk.

The bag lady grinned, a wide and savage rictus revealing powerful teeth well-honed for gnawing on the spareribs of a buffalo or cracking the thighbone of a bull elk. The bag lady said nothing; the grin was sufficient.

Bonnie said, "What are *you* doing here?" Instinctively she tightened her grip on Reuben's little hand; instinctively she looked over one shoulder to see if they were being observed. No pedestrians in sight except the two young R.M.s emerging slowly, casually, from the ice-cream parlor, stopping under the awning to open their umbrellas.

"Need some help," he mumbled, still grinning like a wolf. He held out his big right paw. "Spare ten, lady?"

"Ten? Ten what? You're supposed to be dead."

"Fuckin' papers. Exaggerate everything. I mean ten thousand." He looked over Bonnie's shoulder at the missionaries, malingering at Snelgrove's entrance. Couldn't tear themselves away from the smell of ice cream. The Mormon vice: reject alcohol, you plunge into sugar.

"You mean ten thousand dollars? *Dollars?* Now? Today? In one lump?"

He looked down at the little boy, who was gazing up at him. "So how you doin', Reuben? Gettin' bigger all the time, ain't you? Don't even look like a fuckin' sandwich anymore."

"Momma, he said — "

"We're all sick of that joke, George. And watch your language. You want to be a garbage-mouth all your life? Obscenity is a crutch for — "

"For crippled minds, yeah, I know, Jesus, how many times I got to hear that? And yeah, I mean ten thousand dollars. If you can spare it, what the f—— fork. Also — " He grinned again, peering at her through the sliding droplets of rain on his dark sunglasses. "Also, Bonnie, I need your body. Bad."

"Those days are gone. Gone forever, Hayduke. I loved you once, when I was young and crazy, you had your chance and you blew it and now I guess you'll just have to make love to your fist or your horse or whatever you do for recreation out there in the rocks, because things change, you know, things change, George, and maybe it's time for you to grow up anyhow."

He seemed pleased. Still grinning (not smiling), he said, "Good old Abbzug, sweeter than ever. Good lookin' too. But I don't mean exactly what you think I mean. I mean I need your body but not for me."

She glanced down at her boy, whose attention was drifting toward a sycamore leaf floating, like an elfin boat, down the flooded gutter. She glanced back at the men under the awning: still there.

"Don't look at those fuckers."

"What do you mean?"

"I mean I got this special project. You know where. You know what about. And you know why. And I need some special expert help. Something you can offer that I can't and you know what I mean."

She paused, staring at his dark wind-burned face under the hat, his thin grin, his little red porcine eyes behind the misted glasses. "George . . . George, there's something you'd better understand, once and for all. We're married now and we have Reuben and I'm pregnant again and, George, we just don't do that kind of thing anymore, we have responsibilities now, though I don't suppose you could understand that, and we just don't intend to take chances anymore."

"We. We. Who the fuck's all this we?"

"You know what I mean. I mean Doc and myself. We still care but we can't afford to take chances and so we just don't want to get involved in your kind of . . . activity. Ever again."

"You care, huh? What do you do about it?"

"Well . . ." She released Reuben's hand, let him free to pluck a second drifting leaf from the gutter. "Well, we write letters. Doc speaks at hearings. We support the Sierra Club and the Wilderness Society and Audubon and the neighborhood coalitions and Amnesty International and the ACLU and the NAACP and God only knows what else but we give ten percent, every year. Ten percent."

"Ten percent of what?"

"About half what Doc used to make. What difference does that make anyhow? We do all we can, George, and that's all we can do and that's all anyone can do. Lots of things have changed, George, I'm sorry."

"Not me."

"No, not you."

"Let them fuckers change, not me." Looking over her shoulder at the loitering missionaries. "Okay. Just thought I'd ask. You know where to find me if you change your mind."

"If you really need money . . ." She looked in her handbag. "I think I've got a C-note in here somewhere."

"I'll take it. Make this fuckin' encounter look right."

She groped through the jumbled mess of her handbag, among the old letters, old bills, old receipts, lipsticks, combs, a hairbrush, coins, crumpled dollar bills, a purse with I.D. cards and credit cards and more coins and more paper money, medical prescriptions, checkbook, bankbook, address book, pencils, ballpoint pens, a pair of dirty kid's socks, a compact foldup raincape, Doc's spare set of reading glasses (which he'd been seeking for a month), bent photographs, a badly misfolded city map ("Never did know a woman," Hayduke once said, "who could fold a map"), nail clippers, makeup kit, magic crystals, sacred feathers, a Tarot pack with half the cards missing, three of Reuben's lost marbles, mystical postcards from Benares and Kyoto and Naropa Colorado, a crushed flower, nail files and emery boards, rubber bands, and barettes . . .

"Just a minute, it's in here, I know it's in here somewhere."

       . . . sunglasses without a case, a case without sunglasses, old shopping lists, old lists of important things to do carefully enumerated in descending order of importance, important telephone numbers without names and names without numbers, a pack of chewing gum, dental floss, a toothbrush, a water pistol loaded with ink (leaking) for repelling muggers and murderers and dope-crazed sex fiends, and green beret? a *green beret?*, a number of other — many many other — essential items.

"Well I thought I had it, sorry, George, must've spent it, will a twenty do?"

"I'll take it." He took it. He piled his shopping bag of crumpled newspapers on top of his shopping cart of stuffed garbage bags, wiped the rainwater from his dark glasses and flashed his big hearty evil grin. "So long, Bonnie, you sexy slut. Goddamn but you make me horny. You always were a fuckin' good — "

"Don't be gross." She held up her hand. "Don't say it. Don't even think it anymore, it won't do either of us any good at all. Are you still living in that cave?"

"Me?" Grinning. "What cave? So long, kid."

"Who rubs your back these days? I suppose you're on your seventeenth teenybopper by now."

"Seventeenth?" Grinning again. "Just me and my memories, kid, what else do I need? Better go." Glancing over her umbrella at the dawdling pair obstructing the entrance to Snelgrove's sugar den. "Yeah. Say hello to Doc for me, that lucky old fart. And goodbye. Bye, Bonnie; bye, Rube. . . ."

He was gone. Suddenly. Vanished. Like a dream.

She stared at the broad doors of ZCMI, the great vast crowded horrible Mormon department store, into which the bag lady and her shopping cart had somehow, suddenly, magically, disappeared. The rain slackened, stopped. One of the young men, brushing hurriedly past Bonnie, attempting to follow the bag lady, was delayed at the doors by a spontaneous, unpredictable eruption of shoppers. Hastily collapsing his umbrella, he tried to force his way into the store but was stymied by a barrage of exiting umbrellas exploding in his face.

The other watched Mrs. Sarvis.

Bonnie raised a forefinger and cleared the welling moisture from her eyes. Re-slinging her handbag and retrieving her little boy, she walked slowly around the puddles, over the cracks, down the sidewalk to her car.

14
Code of the Eco-Warrior

Doctor Sarvis, laboring on his bicycle up the long grade of Ninth South toward his home on 23rd East, was not unaware of the pressure of the traffic accumulating in his rear, the clamor of horns pounded by impatient fists, the motorized hatred fermenting at his back.

But he thought, Fuck 'em.

Let 'em wait. Let 'em fester. Let 'em walk. Let 'em ride a bike like me, would do me and them and everybody a world of good. Cleanse our city's air, reinvigorate the blood, tone up the muscles, strengthen the heart, burn up that surplus fat, stave off arteriosclerosis, cut down on bypass operations, eliminate transplants, lower the cholesterol count, prolong lives. Yes and reduce oil consumption, slow down the waste of steel and rubber and copper and glass, free human labor and engineering skills for important work — anything bad for the auto industry and bad for the oil industry is bound to be good for America, good for human beings, good for the land.

Terra primum, god fucking damnitall, as somebody used to say. And don't forget the exclamation mark: *Terra primum!* This above all: to the earth be true and it must follow, as the night the day, thou canst not then be false —

Some fellow in an ancient boat of rusted-red Michigan sheetiron was trying to force him off the street. Him, Doc Sarvis. Yes, a swarthy halfbreed in an antique GM convertible, top down — Buick, Caddie, Olds? — was actually jamming Doc against the right-hand curb. Gently. But firmly.

What the — ? Canst not then be false to any, any what? Any man, god, planet, organic system? I say there, sir, do watch your bloody manners or I'll have you horsewhipped through the streets like a dog!

Doc saw his opening and took it, humping his rubber over the curb and up the sidewalk between a row of Chinese elms and a ragged, unbarbered hedge. The Hindus lived here, the Samoans, the newly arrived Koreans and Vietnamese: not the sort to fret over trimming shrubbery.

Thinking he'd escaped his tormentor, Doc was horrified to discover, suddenly, that the oversized motorcar was right behind him, following him up the sidewalk, clipping twigs from the hedge. One glance to his rear and there it was, the wallowing low-slung ragtop, the huge chrome grin of the grille mimicked by the flashy grin of the dark-faced driver. Doc flipped the man a finger; the man replied likewise. Up yours, monsieur.

Well — ! We'll show this character something he's not going to find so funny.

Dropping off the curb ahead, Doc veered sharply down an alleyway, threading a narrow lane between battered and overflowing garbage cans. Smell of rotten fruit, plastic diapers full of oriental babyshit, broken wine bottles, the boiled bones of cat, dog, rat, fishheads, burnt olive oil, curry, buffalo milk, rancid butter . . .

He heard a great clangor of banging metal behind. Yes, the car still followed, knocking garbage cans to right and left. The man was mad, malevolent, clearly bent on homicide. Unable to escape, Doc resolved to make a stand, face and face down this lunatic.

He halted abruptly behind the corner of a broken-down garage. The car pulled up and stopped, angled in, blocking him off from further flight. Doc reached inside his suitcoat breast pocket and pulled out his only weapon, a leaky fountain pen. He unscrewed the cap, put a thumbnail under the vacuumatic lever, loosened his necktie and waited.

The driver of the car (a 1963 Eldorado in shabby condition, needing body work, new rubber, shock absorbers, a paint job, headlights, a new windshield, hubcaps, chrome trim, etc.) shut off his throbbing, rumbling, guttural engine (500 cubes in there) and grinned at Doctor Sarvis.

The good doctor waited, ready for trouble.

"Doc," the man said, his grin growing broader, "good old Doc . . ."

Sarvis stared, trying to remember the identity of that dark-skinned, smooth-shaven face, the eyes concealed by dense sunglasses, head covered by a sporting cap of dirty tweed of the kind that hobos and burglars traditionally wore, the heavy shoulders and beer-barrel chest clad in a field jacket of desert camouflage, faded, greasy, frayed at the seams. Not the Banana Republic type of camoufleur. Nor yet your ordinary freeway-interchange transient derelict either. This bum belonged to and had created a class with only one member. One was enough. One was all it needed. One was an excess. In a nation of pansies one nettle formed a majority, one prickly pear a quorum.

Nevertheless it seemed he wanted help.

Still unrecognized, he pulled off the sunglasses. "It's me, Doc. Holy shit, you blind?"

"Is that you?"

"Fuck yes, who else."

"You're dead."

"Not yet I ain't."

"What happened to your beard?" Doc felt his own for reassurance, his formerly salt and pepper bush now largely salt, but respectably trimmed, professorial, smelling faintly of shampoo, cigar smoke, merthiolate. "Never saw you baldface before, George."

"Camouflage, Doc, camouflage. I'm the man with a dozen faces now and a dozen different sets of I.D. Last month I was Casper Goodwood. Month before — "

"Where'd you get that name? Casper Goodwood?"

"Out of a phonebook. Where I get them all. Before that I was Eugene Gant. For a while I was Julien Fuckin' Sorel. One day in Denver I was Daisy Miller. Liz Bennett. Zuleika Dobson. And so on. It's easy, you pick out a fuckin' name, go to the right place, put down your bucks, pick up your new I.D. Anybody can be anybody in this fuckin' country if he's got the dough. What're you lookin' at?"

What am I looking at? I wish I was looking at the road map of Crete. Of Provence. Of central Africa. "What do you mean?"

"I mean you don't look happy to see me, Doc. All I want is some help, Doc, just a little fuckin' help for one fuckin' little project and then I'll go away and you'll never see me again."

"I don't have my checkbook, George."

"Checkbook?" The man laughed. "How do you like this piece of iron, Doc? A Caddie classic. What could I do with a check? Me — in a bank? I need cash, Doc, cold hard U.S. of A. paper currency. Also I need your body. Just — "

"My what?"

" — just a warm body, stand watch for me, just one fuckin' night, Doc, that's all, then I'll handle everything on my own."

"Code of the eco-warrior."

"The what? Right. Yeah, code of the eco-warrior. That's me, that's it, Rule Number One: Don't get caught."

"No, you've got it wrong already. Rule Number One is, Nobody gets hurt. Nobody. Not even yourself."

"Sure, Doc." Hayduke crumpled his beercan, tossed it out the car. Into the alley. He reached to the floor and drew two more, yanking them from the plastic collar, opened one and offered the other to his mentor. Doc shook his head. "What? You won't drink my fuckin' beer? What does that mean, Doc?" Hayduke looked hurt, then sad, then wise. "Leaves more for me." He slurped a throatful from the open can. "You tryin' to lose weight? The old belly sloppin' over the belt again, eh, Doc? You do look kind of soft."

"Rule Number Two is, Don't get caught."

"That's right, Number Two, that's the important rule."

"And Rule Number Three is, If you do get caught you're on your own. Nobody goes your bail. Nobody hires you a lawyer. Nobody pays your fines."

"Shit yes, Doc, that's the way I operate. Code of the eco-warrior, that's me. But just this once — "

"But there's more, much more. The eco-warrior works alone, or with one or two old and trusted comrades that he's known for years."

"Right. Sure you don't want a beer?"

"The eco-warrior forms no network, creates no club or party or organization of any kind. He relies on himself (or sometimes herself) and on his little cell of two or three, never more."

Hayduke grins, white fangs glinting. "That's right. Like in the old days, just you and me and Bonnie and old Seldom Seen Smith."

Enchanted by his thoughts, his new program, Doc rambled on, ignoring the proffered cannister of Coors beer. (A low-grade brew anyhow.) "To summarize so far: The ecology warrior hurts no living thing, absolutely never, and he avoids capture, passing all costs on to them, the Enemy. The point of his work is to increase *their* costs, nudge them toward net loss, bankruptcy, forcing them to withdraw and retreat from their invasion of our public lands, our wilderness, our native and primordial home . . ."

"Right on, Doc." Hayduke belched, farted, scratched one armpit and slapped dead the fat horsefly that was reconnoitering his — Hayduke's — unwashed neck. "Let's hear it for Mother Teresa."

". . . relies on himself and a small circle of trusted friends, a tiny felonious conspiracy to commit non-felonious misdemeanors against the perimeters of the techno-industrial *ordnung*. But this is merely the beginning, a mere preliminary, and Mother Teresa, bless her sweet misguided soul, has nothing to do with it. Avoiding organization and all forms of networking, operating strictly on anarchic principles of democratic *de*centralism, the eco-warrior must also be a man or woman of heroic dedication to the work. Not fanatic dedication — no place for fanatics here — but heroic dedication. Because the eco-warrior must do his or her work without hope of fame or glory or even public recognition, at least for the present. The eco-warrior is anonymous, mysterious, unknown to any but his few if any chosen comrades. He wears no uniform, is awarded no medals, is granted no privileges of rank. Not only does he win no taste of personal fame, he must expect the opposite, namely and to wit, public obloquy and vilification, verbal abuse and — "

"Pardon, Doc, what's the word?"

"What word? Try not to interrupt, young man."

"That word, oblo-key? Oblo-kie?"

"Obloquy. Oblo-kwie. From the Latin *obloquium*, to speak against, i.e., to censure or to subject to concerted and widespread disapproval. Get it?"

"Got it."

"Good. E.g., you cut down a powerline somewhere, sabotage a trucking terminal, monkey-wrench a delicate and expensive computer bank assembly, you must then expect that certain elements of the power structure will murmur against you."

"Yeah? Okay, I get it. Obloquy. Like oh be quiet."

"Yes. Jam a wooden shoe in the gearbox, drop a monkey wrench in the transmission, throw a Spaniard or a spanner into the works — you will not be loved. Editorial writers will denounce you, anonymously, from the safe security of their editorial offices. Commerce chambers will burn you in effigy — or in person if they catch you. Congressmen will fulminate, senators abominate, bureaucrats denunciate and all the vipers of the media vituperate."

"Music, Doc, music, it's music in my ears." Sprawled across the front seat of his enormous and worthless motorcar (birdshit on the hood and stains of catpiss on the boot and a live pet gopher snake coiled among the wiring behind the termite-riddled walnut-paneled dashboard), young Hayduke tossed his empty over the side and popped the top from another can of Coors Curse — the sweet green death from the Eastern Slope. He propped a waffle-stomper booted foot on top of the dash, draped his other leg over the back of the sagging passenger's seat, and listened carefully.

"True," said Doc, "regard it as music. But you won't find it so musical when those who should be your admirers also denounce you. When the official conservation societies and wilderness clubs and wildlife federations and defenders of fur-bearers and national resource defense councils scramble and scurry to place maximum distance between themselves and you, insisting that they deplore your work and even going so far as to offer monetary reward for information leading to your capture and conviction. Yes, hard to believe but a fact."

"True fact?"

"That's a fact, true fact. Furthermore — " Warming to his subject, Doc put his pen away and felt inside his coat pockets for a cigar. All gone. He held a hand toward Hayduke. "Guess I'll take that beer now."

Hayduke looked at the beer in his hand, half consumed, and then at the floor of his spacious Cadillac (body by Fisher), carpeted with crushed beercans, beercan collars, beercan tabs, crumpled six-pack cartons and a moldy puke-green plush of old vomit and stinking beer-stain spills. All the paraphernalia but no actual drinkable beer. He pulled the keys and tossed them to Doctor Sarvis, M.D. "Try the trunk, Doc."

"Furthermore," continued Doc, leaning his bicycle with care against the wall of the garage, "not only does the eco-warrior work without hope of fame and praise, not only does he work in the dark of night amidst a storm of official public calumny, but he works without hope of pecuniary recompense." He stepped to the back of the car. His bicycle folded its front wheel and collapsed. He unlocked the trunk and raised the lid. A pack rat scampered out, followed by a pair of cone-nosed kissing bugs.

"Triatoma," mused the good doctor. "Triatome protracta." He reached, somewhat gingerly, for the twelve-pack of Budweiser resting on a heap of log chains, tow chains, tire chains. A tarantula glowered at him with its eight near-sighted but fearsome eyes. Doc brushed it gently aside, lifted out the twelve-pack.

"What do you mean ·no pecuniary recompense?" said George. "Hell's fuck, Doc, us terrorists got to live too."

"True, but only on a subsistence level. We want no mercenaries in the ranks of our eco-warriors. As I said, you do your needed work out of love, the love that dare not speak its name, the love of spareness, beauty, open space, clear skies and flowing streams, grizzly bear, mountain lion, wolf pack and twelve-pack, of wilderness and wanderlust and primal human freedom and so forth."

He started to put the carton back in the trunk; Hayduke signaled otherwise. Doc heaved it forward. Before closing the trunk lid, Doc made a quick scan of the trunk's contents: the mass of chains, a spare tire, the big bird-spider, a dozen one-gallon milk jugs full of water (or something similar), a five-gallon fuel can, assorted gloves both new and old, a prise bar, a tool case, bolt cutters, a small plastic funnel, a pair of old sneakers, a pair of smooth-soled cowboy boots, greasy coveralls, a blue hardhat, a coffeecan full of lapidary grit, a can of spray lubricant (WD-40), and an incomplete set of rusty golf clubs, in a bag, to camouflage everything else. And of course a case of canned pork and beans in a dynamite box.

Frowning, he returned to his previous place at the garage wall. Our boy is getting careless. Even reckless. His old urge to self-destruct? Or the carefree exuberance of winning trivial battles in a losing war?

"Don't forget Rule Number Two," Doc said, opening his beer.

"Don't hurt anybody." Hayduke had already opened another himself. "Murder only in self-defense."

"No no no, that's Rule Number One. Rule Number Two is, Don't get caught, remember?"

"I know, I know, got to clean out that trunk one of these days." He guzzled his beer. "Doc . . . ."

"And George, you've got to stop drinking so much alcohol. You'll get kidney stones, liver trouble, pancreatitis, varices. Remember the code of the eco-warrior: keep fit. The eco-warrior is strong, lean, tough, hardy. The eco-warrior can hike twenty miles overnight, over any terrain, in any kind of weather, with a fifty-pound pack on his back. Maybe sixty pounds. And do it night after night, through brush and swamp, cactus and rattlesnakes, mountain and forest. The eco-warrior does not chain-drink beer or chain-smoke cigars. The eco-warrior takes care of himself, herself, bounces back from injury and exhaustion, never gets sick or if sick carries on despite sickness. The eco-warrior is tough, the eco-warrior is brave, taking on the risks of a soldier in frontline combat, the dangers of a commando behind the lines. The eco-warrior is a guerrilla soldier fighting a war against an enemy equipped with high technology, tax-extracted public funds, legal privilege, media protection, superior numbers, police and secret police, communication police and thought police. Fighting them all, the eco-warrior cannot even carry a weapon; his own Code of Honorable Conduct forbids it."

"What? Not even a sidearm? Not even some knife? How about toenail clippers? How about a live duck, Doc, to beat on his head? How about a snow shovel to whup his ass down the street? No? Nothing?"

"The eco-warrior does not fight people, he fights an institution, the planetary Empire of Growth and Greed. He fights not human beings but a monstrous megamachine never seen since the days of the Late Jurassic and the carnivorous dinosaur. He does not fight humans, he fights a runaway technology, an all-devouring entity that feeds on humans, on all animals, on all living things, and even finally on minerals, metals, rock, soil, on the earth itself, on the bedrock basis of universal being!"

Silence, silent applause, a sitting ovation.

"Great speech, Doc, great speech. You took the words right out of my mouth. Now about my personal problem . . ."

Doctor Sarvis felt in his pockets, pulled out a small wad. "I can lend you a twenty."

"I need about ten thousand. But I'll take the twenty on account. On account of I can use it. Tired of eating beans and slow-elk jerky. But, Doc, what I really wanted to ask you . . ." Hayduke paused, stopped, waited.

Doc waited, staring at Hayduke. "George . . . maybe Seldom can help you. I can't. I'm a married man now, George, have a wife, a little boy, another child in the oven. Which reminds me of Rule Number Four: No domestic responsibilities. That lets me out. The eco-warrior does not marry, or if he marries he does not breed. Better not to marry. She does not marry or breed. The eco-warrior, like a priest or priestess, like a samurai, like a dedicated revolutionary, forgoes the personal pleasures of ordinary life, forgoes ordinary life, for the sake of the great cause. For a time only, naturally. When he reaches the age of forty, or she of thirty, if they're still alive and not in jail, then they retire from the war against Goliath and rejoin the natural, evolutionary mainstream of organic life. The eco-war is only for the young. That also lets me out. Maybe I could lend you two twenties, George, I'm in a generous mood today."

"I'll take it." He took it. Smiling now, not a grin but a sad almost winsome smile, Hayduke said, "What the hell, Doc, sorry to bother you. Maybe I can do it by myself. Wouldn't want to get you guys in trouble again, would I? Fuck no. But you know where to find me if you change your mind."

Doc felt a surge of sympathy for his young friend but fought it down. One beer and reason threatened to yield to the heart, to those reasons that reason knows only so much about. "Where's your sidekick the Lone Ranger?"

Hayduke opened another beer, gazed at the wisp of CO_2 wafting from the hole. He smiled. "That old fucker? Doc, he's older than you are. And crazier. Senile, maybe, talks to himself a lot about some fuckin' horse named Whisky, falls in love with somebody named Oral or Opal, carries chicken guts in his pants pocket, damn near shot himself in the foot practicing his quick draw, not really much help. Good with horses. But I don't need a horse for my special project, I need an ultra-light fucking flying machine. Where can I get one, Doc?"

"So it really is the dam this time?"

"Dam? What dam? That dam? We're savin' that damn dam for maybe next year. Wrote a letter to Omar Kaddafi, he never answered yet. No, the Special Project is something new, wanta hear about it?"

"No."

"I'll tell you all about it."

"I don't want to hear anything about it."

They hesitated, paused, each waiting for the other to say something intelligent, useful, sentimental, nostalgic. Doc too thought often of the good old days and when he did he shuddered. Never again. What he wanted now, at this moment, was to extricate himself in graceful fashion from George Hayduke's compromising and always dangerous company. To say goodbye to his old young friend and hopefully — hopefully? in a hopeful way? what is my diction coming to? — to say goodbye, *hoping* never to see him again. Forty dollars would be a tiny price to pay for such great good fortune.

"And now, George . . ."

"You're excused, Doc."

". . . If you'll excuse me, I really must pedal away, pedal home. Can't be late for supper, you know, Bonnie would be hurt." You insolent devil, he thought.

"Flap her big eyelashes at you and break your heart, eh, Doc?"

"Goodbye, George." He offered his hand. They shook, fraternal eco-warrior style, each clasping the other's wrist, like alpinists ascending a rotten crag of rotting dolomite. Doc glanced at the sky. "It's going to rain again; better put that top up."

"It's automatic. Don't work."

"What do you do when it rains?"

"Drive fast."

"When it rains hard?"

"Drive faster."

Hayduke grinned his great hearty sardonic grin, started and gunned his V-8 engine, flipped into Drive and blasted off. Down the alleyway they roared, man and motor, centaur of flesh and steel. Garbage cans danced in their wake, rolled in the aisle, spun like tops. As he turned the corner at the street, Hayduke tipped his cap to the doctor, grinning his farewell grin, then disappeared downhill into the evening twilight of Greater Salt Lake City, the Wasatch Front, the Kingdom of Zion, the Land of Deseret.

Doc waved back, picked up his bicycle, straightened the front wheel, mounted heavily to the saddle and labored off in the opposite direction, uphill toward wife, child, home, safety, comfort and virtue.

15

Seldom Seen in the Field

Seldom Seen Smith stirred the coals of the fire with a stick of green willow, added another cup of water to the grounds in the coffeepot and placed the pot on the fiery coals. One more bourbon and coffee: then he too would retire for the night. He looked at the dim forms of the little Springbar tents, five of them, scattered out among the junipers on the slickrock. His customers, his clients, were all asleep, he reckoned, all but that one, that gorgeous what's-her-name the stewardess — beg your pardon, ma'am, flight attendant! — who was waiting for him. A candle flickered in her tent, its soft glow illuminating the translucent canvas walls, revealing the woman's graceful silhouette as she brushed her hair.

Seeing that classic female form outlined against the light, he thought, How come I can't never git enough that there kind of living? How come I'm stuck on good-lookin' wimmen in lacy underwear? How come I get a harder-on ever time I see a pretty girl a wagglin' her be-hind inside a hula hoop? straddin' a horse bareback? a-high-divin' off a springboard? a-touchin' her toes in a black string bikini? a-climbin' onto a hay wagon in a minidress? turnin' cartwheels in a cheerleader skirt? What the hell's wrong with me anyhow?

What's wrong with you, Smith?

Guess I'm just a doggone ol' pervert, always was and always will be and ain't nothin' I kin do about it except put a stout rubber band around my balls 'till the ol' family jewels turn black and dry up and fall off like a dead kumquat off a kumquat tree and if that don't do the job stick my pecker in a sausage grinder and whittle it down about nine ten inches maybe that'd work but goldang even then I'd still keep on a-recollecting and a-recollecting the good ol' times we used to have, me and Slim Jim here. Hot dang . . . ! That long-haired gal in the short Levi britches in that there Earth Fist bunch or whatever they call it, goddamn I mean the way she walked, the way them hindquarters of hers kind of scrunched up and rubbed together when she moved, why I bet she could pull a cork or chew peanuts with that thing. What's wrong with me, Smith? You queer?

Guess I'm queer. I like women. Women and horses and little wooden, lap-straked dories. Full of girls.

He thought of an old frontier ballad, an anonymous song from the days of Joseph Smith and Brigham Young:

> I love to go swimmin'
> With bare-naked wimmen
> And dive between their legs . . .

Yep. Queer. You're queer, Smith. But I'll grow out of it someday. When I'm dead I'll grow out of it. That's the best time to grow out of it anyhow.

He looked again toward the lady in the tent, brushing her hair, turning, yearning, candle burning, waiting for him, Seldom Seen Smith. Her name was Julie, no, Cindy, or was it Candy? — brain damage, Smith — and she'd been on several trips with Smith before. Down the Colorado River, down the Escalante River, into Grand Gulch, into Pucker Pass, into the Black Box of the San Rafael, through Muley Twist in the Waterpocket Fold — all them there tight hot juicy all-natural scenic wonders places (no preservatives added) that he loved so much.

Queer, Smith, queer, you're queer as a double-ended horny toad. To hell with another cup of coffee I'm gone to bed. *Right now!*

The pot was steaming. He jerked it off the red coals, kissed his scorched fingers and stood up. Somewhat creakily. The squatting position didn't come as easily for Smith as in former days. Knee joints getting a mite stiff. Hip bones wired together. Middle joint maybe not quite as stiff as it should be. But she'd take care of that. Them stewardesses know their job.

He limped toward her tent, dick-swole, bow-legged and sore-footed. Old Seldom needed the exercise. Never walked when he could ride. Even kept a horse tied to his front porch for trips to the barn, ninety yards away. Even invented an extra-long long-handled hoe so he could hoe his cantaloupes from the saddle, only man in Dipstick, Sawdust, Snakeweed, Greasepit, or Landfill Counties (Utah) to think of a labor-saving device like that.

Smith heard a faint disturbance among the horses. They were tied in a bunch in the tamarisk thicket by the stream. If he could break them animals to eat tamarisk he'd be the richest man in the whole Four Corners region. He paused, looking, listening.

The horses stamped their feet, shifting about. Sounded nervous. Mountain lion? Rattlesnake? Smith's handgun was in his saddlebags, heaped with the saddles and saddle blankets under a staked-down tarp. Only weapon on his belt was the Buck jackknife in its little holster. He glanced once more at his sweetheart in her tent — give me just two more minutes, honey — pulled the flashlight from his hip pocket and lurched into the dark beyond camp.

The great rolling eyes of the horses glared in the beam. Knothead, Ginger, Nelson Eddy, Miss Peach, Hook the big sorrel, Fred the giant Appaloosa, Billy Buckskin, Dirty Gertie the fence jumper, Shithead Dudley the Shirt-Eater — saddle horses, pack horses, all present and accounted for. No sign of snake nor lion.

"Take it easy, fellas, whoa there, Billy, you boys and girls settle down now, what do you say. Daddy's here, nothin' to fear. You smell a cat, Fred?"

The big gelding stood with noble Roman head up high, peering into the dark, velvet nostrils flexing like over-anxious pudenda. Smith put a hand on his shoulder and stroked him; the horse was trembling. "Relax, boy, relax, goldamnit anyhow. . . ." Anxious himself, he glanced back toward camp, looked for the glow in Cindy's, yes, Cindy! — Cindy's little canvas boudoir. Still burning — but how much longer? Can't expect a gal to wait all night long, not even for him, S. S. "Superslick" Smith the easy-riding slow Wham! delayed Bam! jack-Mormon man. Well, *he* would if he was her but he wasn't her he was him. Try to keep that straight.

The horses quieted. Smith gave each a final pat on the nose, a rub between the eyes or a caress on the neck, and turned away.

A hand fell on his shoulder, gripping hard. "Whoa there, pard-ner," said a basso profundo, sotto voce.

"Awwwwffff!" Smith twisted away, stung by terror. Backed against a tree, he switched his light beam to and fro, seeking the nameless horror in the night. He saw a pair of little red eyes squinting at him, below the eyes a shining toothy excessive and disembodied grin. Only that, the eyes, the teeth, floating on the darkness, before supporting features became apparent: broad brown face, immense shoulders, a deep and hairy chest.

"George . . .?"

"Shit, Seldom."

"That you, George?"

"Oh for chrissake, Seldom, you blind or stupid or drunk or some-thing? Or what?"

"They said you was dead again."

"Who said that? He's a fuckin' goddamn liar and I'll peel his fuckin' skull. Who?"

"They all said it. Everybody. Not me."

"Who? I'll remove his jawbone. I'll tear off his arm. Who said it?"

"Not me, George, hell I knew it all the time you'd be around somewhere, come back to see me sometime, you sure you ain't dead? George?"

Hayduke looked aside. "Get that light out of my eyes." Smith lowered the beam, turned off the light. Hayduke looked toward the camp, the illuminated tent, the lissome silhouette within. "Got com-pany again, huh? God, Smith, but you're a horny sumbitch. Don't you ever get enough? You got three wives, you got these all-purpose horses, yeah don't lie to me, Smith, I know you're a fuckin' horse lover, never knew a cowboy yet didn't like to bugger the livestock."

Still shaky, Smith essayed a joke. "Cowboys, they make better lovers, George."

Hayduke forced a sour grin. "Sure, ask any cow. Look, Seldom, I won't take much of your time, I know she's waitin' for you, so I'll make this short."

"No," said Smith.

"No what?"

"Can't do it."

"Can't do what?"

"Can't do whatever it is you're a-plannin' on, George."

"Well you got to. I need some help. Just one night, then I'll turn you loose." Eyes adjusting to the darkness, Hayduke surveyed the other tents, unlit and silent. "They all asleep? Who you got here this time? Any nosy young returned missionary, maybe?"

Smith looked where Hayduke looked, at the five little tents spread out under starlight over the sandstone bench. "Yeah, they're asleep. All but one." He smiled. "No R.M.s, though, except Oral, he's my personal private probation officer, always hangin' around to watch over me, keep me out of trouble and it's a good thing too. He likes to play poker and can't win for losing. Took six dollars from him this evening."

"Yeah, I'll bet. He's an informer for the FBI or CIA or something and you know it."

"I know it but he don't know I know it."

"Don't be too sure of that." Hayduke peered about in various directions, eyes penetrating the darkness. "You sure he's in his tent?"

"I seen him go in never seen him come out."

Hayduke paused, listening hard. Lowering his voice to a rasping whisper, he said, "Seldom, I need you to give me a hand with that you know what. It's creeping closer to Lost Eden every day. If you and me don't stop it — "

Smith put a hand on the other's massive arm. "George, you think I don't feel bad about it too? I lay awake nights thinkin' about that goldang monster. I get nightmares about it. I get the feelin' that thing is a-comin' after me personally. After everybody. But George, dog-gone it, George, we're whipped, there ain't nothin' we can do any-more, we fought it ever' way you can and they beat us. They own the guvmint, George, you know that. They own the politicians, the judges, the Tee Vee, the army, the *po*-lice. They own ever' damn thing they need to own."

"They don't own me. They don't own you."

"They don't need to own us."

Pause. Hayduke spat on the ground. He raised his head and stared into Seldom's face as if unable to understand or believe or even quite hear his old buddy's words. All that Seldom could see of Hayduke's eyes were two tiny red dots, like the "Power On" bulbs of a large and mysterious night machine. Like two glowing sparks in a fire nearly dead. Like . . . like the dim distant receding taillights of a departing — never to return — runaway express. One cool breath of reality would extinguish those twin pinpoints of hope forever.

Why me? mourned Smith, why do I have to give poor ol' George the word? Where's Bonnie? She could make it a little easier and one hell of a lot sweeter for him. Where's Doc? He could explain it for him.

Doc can explain anything to anybody, he's our doggone goldamn State of Utah philosopher, ain't he? Why, ol' Doc could explain to Gawd Hisself exactly where He went wrong — and make Gawd feel good about it too.

Why me? "Besides," he mumbled, "I got responsibilities, George. You know what I mean. I mean it ain't merely the fact I got three women to keep happy and them little childern to boot and all these damn worthless horses and them watermelons and cantaloupes and this here non-profit guide business but, well, to tell the truth, George . . ." Smith gulped, feeling his eyes moisten, watching that film of pity and self-pity descend between himself and George Washington Hayduke. "To tell the truth . . ."

"You don't have to do it."

"I don't?"

"I mean you don't have to tell me the fuckin' goddamn truth. I know what you mean for chrissake, you don't have to spell it out."

"Maybe you don't. The truth is, George, I wanta stay out of trouble. But the real truth is I'm afeerd of them nucular power people. They're something different. They ain't like ol' Bishop Love and his comical Search and Rescue Team. They ain't like him or us. They ain't even human. They ain't even people. They ain't even alive. They — I mean *It* — It comes from some other world, George. Saturn, maybe. Maybe Pluto. You understand what I'm a-tryin' to explain, George? They scare me. *It* scares me."

Hayduke was silent, gazing in something like astonishment upon the solemn, sober, serious, incorrigibly bucolic and irredeemably honest face — homely as a hound dog — of Seldom, his old comrade Seldom Seen Smith. The name acquired, at that very moment, a whole new world of significance.

As Hayduke failed to respond, Smith made further attempt at explanation. "The way I see it, George, if we don't fight It anymore why then maybe when It takes over It won't hurt us. Maybe It won't even notice us if we lay low, you see what I mean? Stay out of sight? Keep real quiet? You know what I'm talkin' about, George?"

Hayduke cracked a wan and crooked smile. "Can't believe this," he muttered. "Can't believe my own fuckin' ears."

"The way I got it figured, George, It'll leave us alone if we leave It alone. Won't even see us, most likely. Well, anyhow, I can loan you a twenty? That help some?"

Hayduke turned his eyes again, looking left and right, over and about. Maybe the government did have its sensors out here now, even in the wilderness, and Smith knew it. Looking around, he held out his right paw.

Smith fished through his pockets, pulled out matches, a rawhide string, a greenish penny, three .44 shells, a crumpled pack of M&Ms. Even good jack Mormons have the sweet tooth. "Well, sheet, guess I don't have it on me, George. Left my billfold in the truck. Back at trailhead. Meet me there about four days from now, we'll be a-comin' up outa here then."

"Maybe. Not fuckin' likely."

"Sorry I can't help anymore, George. But you know how it is." Seldom held out his hand for the parting handshake. Hayduke took and clasped his hand but without the usual rough vigor, without warmth, and without sliding on down to his wrist and the mountain soul-brothers' grip of mutual aid and a shared fate, whether for good or ill, for life or death. "Sorry, George . . ."

Hayduke kept averting his eyes now, apparently unable or unwilling to look his old friend in the face. Staring instead into the darkness, beyond the tamarisk and stream and the horses and the canyon walls, he spat on the trampled ricegrass at their feet, and merely said, merely out of habit, "Well, you know where to find me. Guess I better go, what the fuck."

"You still a-hidin' out there, George?"

"Sometimes. Why not? It's a good fuckin' camp, nobody's spotted it yet, so long, Smith."

He was gone. Silently, abruptly, like a phantom, Hayduke vanished. Smith, listening with care, could hear no sound of booted feet in motion, no swish of grass, no scrape on stone, no slip and slide of gravel on a talus slope. He knew that Hayduke might have a horse out there in the dark, half a mile off, tied to a juniper and waiting, or again he might not; old George, he was like as not to figure on a-walkin' all the distance to wherever he was headed next. Ten miles in the night, twenty, even thirty, that was nothing but routine transportation for old George. Sighing with relief, faintly guilt-struck but happy to be rid of Hayduke so easily, Seldom switched on his flashlight and turned toward the tents. He sighed a second time, again with relief, to note that the candle still burned in Cindy's tent.

But halfway there he saw her silhouetted shape half rise within the tent, a slender arm reach forth — and the candle was snuffed. Out.

He halted in dismay, a sudden pang of unrequited love coursing from his heart to groin and back again, several times, the effect much like that of an electronic impulse flashing between two points on the screen of a video game. Pac-Man, perhaps.

After a moment Smith recovered his courage, his resolve; he proceeded on to her tent, shut off his light, knelt at the zippered entrance. Dark inside. The entry was half closed.

"Honey," he whispered, "it's me." On hands and knees, he waited for her sweet invitation. He could hear her steady breathing but there was no word. "Me, honey, your ol' Seldom come to check for buzz-worms and horny-headed ticklebugs. . . ."

Another pause. "You're late, Smith. Too late with too little."

Cold words, striking at the core of his manhood. He cudgeled his feeble brain for an apt reply, but the best he could come up with was, "Reckon small is beautiful too, honey baby."

"Don't call me baby."

"Sorry, honey-pie."

"I'm not a pie."

Holy cow, thought Smith, cain't say nothin' right right now. This little gal is mad. "Well doggone, ah, darling, I sure am sorry I kept you a-waitin'. Somethin' was botherin' the horses. Had to go look."

"You kept me waiting half an hour, Seldom." At last, she was softening a bit, a touch of sympathy in her tone. "What was it? Snakes?"

She feared, as she was fascinated by, snakes. Any snake, all snakes — long, short, thin, fat, pink or brown or black, with or without ribbons or rattles, whether rugose as a dry salami, knobby as a cucumber, slick as a mud puppy.

Inspiration: a bulb clicked on in Seldom's head — forty full watts. "Honey, there was just snakes a-crawlin ever' which way all over the ground, it was the most disgustin' sight you ever seen, couldn't hardly find a place to put my feet there was so many of them."

That did the trick. "Oh, Seldom . . ." She reached out through the opening, feeling for his hand. "Maybe you'd better get in here and zip up this door."

He caught her hand. "Cindy," he said happily, "I think you got a good idea." He removed his big hat and lowered his head, preparing to crawl into the tent.

The hand was jerked away. The canvas panel of the entrance door flapped in his face, accompanied by the snarl of a closing zipper.

"Cindy . . . ?"

"Cindy," she mocked.

"Cindy . . . !"

"My name is Debbie." Her voice was short and sharp. "As you should — "

"Debbie . . . !"

"As you should very well know. Go find your Cindy now, Mr. Smith. I'd rather sleep with an armful of big fat black wiggly pit vipers than one slimy old sneak of a snake like you. Goodnight."

He waited for another minute, hoping for mercy. Not for justice, for mercy. But she would not relent this time.

Whipped like a dog, Smith crept away on hands and knees toward the mound of saddles and pack saddles under the rotten plastic sheet. He'd brought no tent for himself. Didn't figure he'd need it. Seldom seldom ever did.

He glanced up at the sky. Not a star in sight. A mass of black clouds, drifting in from the southwest, flickered with inner lightning. As expected, as he'd predicted, she was a-gonna rain for sure. Sure as God made little blue turdbirds he was in for a long cold wet sonofagun night. Him, not God.

And what about George?

Too bad about George.

16

Erika in the Woods

> **TIMBER SALE**
> NW¼ Sect 12
> T 39 S R 15 E
> 160 acres
> Bids Invited
> Kaibab NF
> Flagstaff AZ

"Clearcut?"

"Oh yeah, they always clearcut these days. Whole point of the deal. Timber here's not worth much — old growth yellowpine full of beetles, too much aspen, spruce, scrub oak. Will cost the Forest Service more to build a road in here than the timber's worth. But that's normal too, that's the way they operate now."

"Will cost us, you mean."

"You a taxpayer?"

"Not always. I earned twenty-four hundred dollars last year. Got a refund coming, I think. I hope."

"Vat you mean iss ziss vat zey call zee 'deficit logging,' no? eh?"

"Yes. That's the story. But like I was saying, that's only part of the story. The Forest Freddies don't mind losing money on these timber sales, it don't come out of their agency funds or personal pockets. The real point of the deal is to get all these mixed, old-growth and weed trees, as they call them, cleared out of here, every tree, every bush, every blade of grass, then level the ground, harrow it with industrial-type farm equipment and plant a single, uniform crop of Ponderosa pine or white fir, whatever the market seems to want most, plant it in straight rows, all the same species, like a tree plantation, that's the real objective behind these timber sales, I mean scientific tree farming, what the Forest Service calls stewardship. Managing the land for the best interests of industrial society and fuck anything else like deer or elk or black bear or red squirrels or people who like to get out in the woods and hunt or make love or hunt something to love or get lost or maybe hide from the government, that's the real purpose. To make the forests neat and orderly and easy to cut. Like a cornfield, that's what they want. They want the whole West to look like an Illinois cornfield. Like a farm. We are stewards of the earth, they say, appointed by God to manage the earth (every bit of it) in whatever way seems best (to us stewards). That's our holy mission, to be good little stewards and keep that old raw cranky smelly unpredictable Mother Nature where she belongs, namely in a zoo. Or a museum. Under glass and behind nice neat paved nature trails."

"I looked up that word 'steward' one day in a big dictionary. You know what a steward really is?"

"Rod Steward? Iss rock, yah? Rock star?"

"Not him, beautiful, not that one. No, a steward is a sty-warden. Look it up. It's from the Anglo-Saxon *stigeweard,* meaning guardian of the pigpen. That's what our noble stewards are — people who guard pigs."

"That makes sense."

Laughing, they cruised under the trees on a thin frozen crust of snow, short narrow touring skis strapped to their boots. The rare early summer snow, glittering like glass in the sunlight, blue as pale phlox in the shadows, lay a foot deep beneath them. But they were skiing on the north rim of the Grand Canyon, across the meadows and through the glades of the Kaibab National Forest, eight thousand feet above the level of the sea. The air was clear as crystal, the sky unclouded, the sun fierce and pure, the stillness unflawed by any sound but that of their small human voices, the swish of skis, the crunch and squeak of their metal-tipped poles pivoting in the dry snow. And oh yes, of course, the sound — now and then, from time to time — of steel striking steel.

Three young men, one young woman. Four healthy happy vigorous young animals with souls, with minds, alive and jolly in their work, exuberant with purpose, exhaling cloudy syllables of vapor and laughter as they advanced, now one then another, from tree to tree.

They were not dressed as skiers should be, in fashionable nylon stretch suits of gaudy orange, blazing blue, flashy yellow and hotdog red but in baggy wool pants and loose forest-camouflage coats from Goodwill, Bob's Bargain Barn, Woolco, K mart and Yellow Front. Each of the four carried a big olive-drab pack on his or her back; two of them — the muscular Apollonian body-sculptor and the long-haired girl — carried green canvas ammo bags slung across one shoulder. The athlete also carried a three-pound singlejack hammer, attached by a lanyard to his wrist; the young woman an ordinary carpenter's hammer of medium weight.

At every third tree of saw-timber quality the man with the sledge stopped, pulled an eight-inch helix spike from his ammo sack and drove it into the trunk as high as he could reach, leaving the head protruding slightly. As soon as he moved on the girl followed, driving two 60-penny nails into the same tree, at a lower height, also letting the heads jut forth a bit. Behind them came the young man with another hammer and the bolt cutters. He clipped the heads from the spikes, hammered the spikes deep into and beneath the bark, and disguised the shiny dots of hot metal — where necessary — with a dab of brown ink from a Permo-Marker.

The fourth member of the party, meanwhile, stood watch fifty yards in advance of the other three, his eyes and ears alert for any sign, any sound of other humans at large in the woods. He saw nothing of the sort: the snow ahead was immaculate, virginal and frozen, untracked by snow machine, snow tractor, snowshoe or any trace of skis. He saw the prints of bird and rodent, hare and rabbit, fox and coyote, but nothing man- or woman-made.

He did hear, however, from time to time, the faintest hint of the whining wail of a caravan of snowmobiles five miles to the east, disturbing the peace on the old road that led from Hart Meadow to Point Sublime. No danger from that quarter: those goggled helmeted space-suited androids, encased within the screaming uproar of their infantile machines, drove themselves onward sealed off from everything but the red light, exhaust fumes and thrashing treads of the idiot in front of them. And their leader, for all each follower knew, might himself be following the stinking tailpipe of the blinking jerk at the rear of the column. The purpose of snowmobile recreation is not to get anywhere, see anybody or understand anything but to generate noise, poison the air, crush vegetation, destroy wildlife, waste energy, promote entropy and accelerate the unfoldings of the second law of thermodynamics. For this purpose, then, an endless circling round and round from morn to night could be perfectly satisfactory to all participants, requiring only that road signs be shifted here and there, now and then, so as to provide the illusion of linear progress on a European-style space-time axis.

Everyone knows that.

The spiking party, meanwhile, proceeded happily through the woods, working steadily but not too hard, not sweating, enjoying themselves, vaccinating the trees for protection against a possible chainsaw massacre in the future. When the Forest Service was informed and interested logging companies tipped off, as they would be, by anonymous communication, about the preventive measures taken here, it was then most probable that the timber sale would have to be canceled and this particular patch of forest saved. There is nothing that the clearcutting timber corporations hate more than a tract of forest defended by direct citizen action: one spike in a log can strip the teeth from a ten-thousand-dollar circular saw, put a crimp in profits, deter further logging, and thus preserve those living breathing respiring trees whose right to continued existence is at least as legitimate as that of any other creature including, but not limited to, the human.

When the sun became a burning ball of orange music low in the west, peeking at them from among the black trunks of silent pine and ragged spruce and shaggy Douglas fir, they left the woods and skated on their skinny skis down a frozen watercourse, leaving no trail. They hid their tools and made camp for the night deep in a grove of quaking aspen, their four-man dome tent concealed from view, and cooked their supper on a pair of tiny Primus stoves that made no smoke and cast almost no light.

Yielding however to the ancient human need, they built a very modest wood fire, in a pit in the hard snow within a circling rampart of down trees. Sitting on logs close to the cheery, symbolic, ceremonial flames, removing gloves and warming their hands, they ate their stewed venison jerky (one of the party was a veteran deerslayer and cow poacher) on a bed of wild rice spiced with garlic salt, drank hot cocoa spiked with rum or magic tea (Earl Grey laced with Wild Turkey) and consumed the last of Erika's Norwegian fruitcake in the flickering blue light of flaming brandy.

They discussed the day's work.

"But if zey no belief zee vorning?"

"They believe. They know better than to take chances. The Freddies will send a crew out here with metal detectors, spend days and weeks trying to find our nails, find some of them, and try to pull them out with crowbars. But they can't — no heads on the nails. Or maybe they decide it's a bluff, let the loggers cut down a stand, haul the logs to the mill. The first log that hits the buzzsaw will clarify their thinking and maybe cancel the timber sale."

"Suppose if saw breaks in pieces? If maybe, how you say — ?"

"Will anybody get hurt? Get his head sliced off? Well, he shouldn't, not if OSHA's on the job, not if the sawmill obeys the law, not if the protective shields are in place, not if the operators are where they should be, not if the metal detectors are functioning, not if the company pays attention to our notice, not if the U.S. Forest Circus stops its deficit timber sales and takes the forests away from the clearcutters and the stripminers and the four-leg maggot ranchers. If *they* do any one of those things they should do and are supposed to do then no millhand is going to get hurt."

Pause. "But if zee company cuts down zee trees anyway? I mean zen so we break zee big saw but zee trees are gone all same, logs viss nails but here nossing only stumps. Explain, please."

A moment of thought. The three young men looked at one another, hesitating — Who zee Spoke? — while the young woman with the amazing eyes, the braided black hair, cheeks like wild roses and lips like cherry wine, smiled at each in turn and all collectively. All were sick with love for her; she was sick as well but the shining object of her love, for whom she had crossed the raging Atlantic in dead of winter and Greyhound-bussed the width of an alarming continent from New York City to Salt Lake City, was not present. The Hatch named Oral.

The golden boy shrugged his splendid shoulders, shrouded now within a goosedown parka. Pete the Piper, twiddling his little recorder in his fingers, red beard sprinkled with snow, gaped at the chunks of burning aspen and said nothing. The third man present, the youngish fellow who'd done most of the talking earlier in the day, took on the task. He was a hollow-cheeked big-boned raw-hided youth, with the keen gray eyes of a hunter. He looked, not as Indians actually look, but as Indians are supposed to look, lean and long and liver-eating. He smiled rarely but when he did it humanized his face remarkably. His name was Nielsen. Carl Nielsen. Like most Nielsens around the world he was a Mormon but not a very nice Mormon. He shot things and ate them. (Cows, lambs, sheepdogs, whatever caught his fancy.) He wore a buckskin shirt with fringes. He never attended the Wednesday evening meetings of the Sixth Ward Mutual Improvement Society in his hometown of Short Crick. He was known (by his few friends) to pour liquid concrete into the smokestacks of hauler trucks, road graders, and crawler tractors. Like the goat-bearded flutist and the muscle-bound weight-lifter he earned a minimal living by rowing boatloads of tourists through the depths and heights of the Grand Canyon of the Colorado. Like so many of those macho types, he despised Growth & Progress.

"Erika," he said, "it's the theory of deterrence. You know — worry the bastards so they keep their damn tree clippers out of our public woods. In order to work, the deterrence has to be credible. God, I sound like Henry Kissinger. In order to be credible, we have to actually pound in the nails and maybe shatter some buzzsaws — sacrifice a few trees in order to save many trees. That make sense to you?"

She looked at him then at the fire, her delicious lips moving, rephrasing his words into her native Svenska. "*Ja,*" she said, "*ja ja,* but . . . iss sad. Iss so sad."

"Money," said Nielsen, "that's what it's all about. If we can cut down their profits in the national forests the timber corporations will go back to growing trees on private property. Money is the name of the game, the one thing they care about. Those M.B.A.s from Harvard and Yale and Princeton and the University of Tokyo get very emotional about money. So that's where we hit them — in their hearts."

A tear leaked from her eye.

"Come on, don't cry for those swine. You think they'd cry for you? You think they'd cry for the murder of a living tree? or for the massacre of a whole damn forest of living trees?"

"I vas sinking . . . off somezing else. . . ."

The boys glanced again at one another, eyebrows lifting. The golden-haired Apollo groaned. "Erika — not him again. Not that goddamn missionary."

She nodded. "I vant to find him." Blinking, sniffing, she wiped her fine noble red nose with a half-frozen finger.

"Jeez, Erika, you know how many Hatches there are in Utah and Arizona? About half a million. And half of them are named Oral or Orrin or Orval or Oval or Offal."

"Opal, Ovary, Overalls, Ovine, Overshoe, Onus, Oviduct . . ."

"I luff him," she said simply, gazing at the dying flames.

That silenced them.

A striped skunk padded by on the far side of the fire, half in half out of the light.

"Don't anybody move."

The skunk halted, lifting its lovely bushy tail at the sound of the hunter's voice. The four humans froze, watching the skunk. The skunk waited, then lowered its tail with an elegant rippling movement of fur and sinew, went on, disappeared into the shadows. The humans resumed breathing, mouths opening for speech. The skunk came back.

"Don't move. . . ."

Again the skunk halted, tail up, hindquarters elevated in firing posture, eyeing them from fore and aft — two bright obsidian eyes in front, one red puckered eye at rear, or what some folks would later call the Ev Mecham campaign button.

Again the skunk relaxed, assumed a horizontal attitude, padded delicately away over the snowcrust like a housecat with important business elsewhere. Uncontrollably, three of the humans began to giggle.

"Careful," Nielsen said, "he's still around."

The skunk returned, this time hopping onto the log between Pete the Piper and Pretty Boy. It perched there as if invited, like a legitimate member of the company, gazed calmly at the little fire and began to rub its long pointed nose with both forepaws. Itchy.

Nobody dared speak. Each human struggled to suppress the giggles, while pondering at the same time the furtive and traitorous impulse to leap away, to make a solo break for safety and let the other three absorb the punishment.

Somebody began to choke on her stifled laughter, straining not to burst out. The skunk sprang to full alert, handstand position, belly to audience, head turned around and taking aim.

"Don't . . . move. . . ."

A coyote chose that moment to howl, answered at once by other coyotes in other quarters, everyone sounding close to camp. The skunk dropped to all fours, hopped from the log and fled. Rescued, the four young humans stood, hugged one another in tears and laughter, kicked snow on the fire and prepared for bed, crawling one by one, when ready, into the tent and once inside, into their snug and womb-shaped mummy bags, stripping down to long-handled thermal underwear. The dome-shaped tent could accommodate four, but without a square inch to spare. They ranged themselves, therefore, in alternating positions, head to toe, doing it one at a time — no room for a juggling of full-grown bodies.

"Who sleeps with Erika tonight?"

"Everybody sleeps with Erika tonight!"

"Ja, ja," she cried, the jolly tease, "but nobody zey slip on *top* of Erika tonight." Day by day and night by night her English was improving, acquiring elegance and grace. Elegance from need, grace beneath pressure.

And day by day the machine advanced.

17
Love and Ranger Dick in Love

The big blue Ford Bronco churned through the white sand in four-wheel drive, following the course of an intermittent streambed that led, by serpentine and unhurried route, toward a maze a garden a petrified city of pale buff and rose red domes, turrets, pillars, skyscraping obelisks, cloud-touching towers.

"Dudley . . . it's beautiful in here."

Bishop Love, clutching the wheel with left hand, his right on the knob of the gearshift lever, gazed with pride at the splendid scene on either side and before them, and nodded in agreement.

"Sure is, honey. See that yellowish-green stratum under the Moenkopi? Carnotite, sweetheart, carnotite, highest-grade ore in the whole United States. See them black beds down there under the Chinle? Coal, honey, that's genuine bituminous low-sulfur coal."

Rangerette Dick, out of uniform on her day off, wore a loose partly unbuttoned blouse of pink chiffon (sweetly feminine) revealing the curvature of her generous mammaries, and tight stone-washed acid-bleached designer jeans (from Sears) that shaped her powerful thighs in graceful, swelling symmetry. Her clean petite bare feet, with the scarlet toenails of a designing woman, were perched high on the dashboard of Bishop Love's bouncing machine. She clung with one hand to the roll bars above her head. "So beautiful," she repeated, "so beautiful, Dudley. It's like a fairyland in here."

"You bet your boots, Virginny. Why, someday we're gonna have fifty thousand people living here, mining that uranium, digging that coal, building golf courses and swimming pools and condominiums and selling hotdogs and postcards to a million tourists a year. Also there's tar sands here, and oil shale, maybe potash, and for sure we know there's a big pocket of CO_2 under here somewheres." The Bishop smiled at the view ahead, gratified by the pleasing prospects. "Yessirree bob, this here's mighty pretty country."

"This should be a national park," the woman blurted. And regretted the remark instantly.

"Park?" Love frowned. He scowled. He growled, "Ginny, you know we been parked to death in Utah, Arizona. One thing we don't need is no more goldang national parks or even state parks or god-damn wilderness *pre*-serves. Pardon my French but doggone, Ginny, you know and I know a park attracts them environ-meddlers and Sahara Clubbers like a dead horse draws blowflies. Nosir, we don't need no more parks, we need industry. Jobs. People. I'll take people over rocks and cactus any day and I don't care who hears me say it."

She thought it best to switch the subject, quickly.

"What's the CO_2 good for, Dudley? To carbonate Pepsi-Cola?"

He smiled, smug in his superior knowledge. "Pepsi? Lot more than that, honey. We tap the deposit here, ship it by high-pressure pipeline to the oilfields in California and Texas, they use it to pump more oil out of them old dried-up wells. The geologists estimate we got enough carbon dioxide here to force maybe another sixty million barrels out of them old oilfields. Sixty million!"

Sixty million barrels, she thought. Wonderful. Why, that's enough oil to keep America going for — what'd I read? — nearly eight more weeks. Great. Great thinking, fellas. (What a pack of inbred idiots.) Smiling herself, amused rather than annoyed by the Bishop's techno-industrial fantasies, which she tended to regard as merely one more example of the comic male lust to always improve on nature, to organize, exploit, design and dominate (even the jeans designers were men too, of a sort), Rangerette Dick held to the roll bars, let her right hand dangle out the open window at her side, and tickled the heads of the golden sunflowers, the creamy cliffrose, the purple asters, the cadmium-red Indian paintbrush, the coral-red globemallow, the giant long-stemmed primrose, as they passed, brushing the side of the vehicle. Flowers, flowers everywhere, for as far as she could see, glowing on the sand dunes, shimmering under the junipers, flaring from cracks in the monolithic slickrock. Not only these big ones in this sandy ravine but all those little ones out yonder: sand verbena, blue phlox, purple beeplant, princess plume, alyssum, larkspur, Sego lilies, blue penstemon and scarlet penstemon. . . . A treasure trove of flowers in a fairyland of sandstone across a wonderland of open space and clean air and untrammeled earth.

More or less, she added to herself; the range would be infested with domestic cattle in a few more weeks, once the local ranchers had bestirred themselves enough to stop drinking Pepsi-Cola with their legislators up in Salt Lake City, got out of bed with the state BLM administrators, and came back home and heaved their big potbellies into their airplanes, $15,000 four-by-four pickups, and radio communication centers. She knew the type; in only six months on the job she'd already met every rancher in her district, heard all their complaints about the government not doing enough to poison wildlife, kill off the ravens, clear off the sagebrush, improve the old roads and build more new roads, install more cattleguards and string more barbed wire, increase grazing allotments and decrease grazing fees — why these poor struggling ranchers were even now paying a head tax of $2.25 per month for each cow and calf (and bull) they turned loose on the public lands, one-fourth what they would have to pay to lease similar lands in the private sector. Outrageous? You bet. And they were outraged, those cow-loving, horse-forking, rope-twirling, cud-chewing, crotch-scratching, fly-slapping, old-timey rugged individualists. Goddamned government wasn't doing enough for them. Goddamned ungrateful taxpayers letting them down again. Goddamned bureaucrats not paying as much attention to the Cattlemen's Association as it does to them welfare rights Nigra ladies in their pink Cadillacs.

She knew, Ranger Dick did; she had to listen to it nearly every day. Part of the job. Sometimes she hated her job. But she was coming around, more and more and day by day, to love this queer barren God-forsaken land. There was something here, something in the space and silence, something in the landforms and the cloud formations, that she'd never seen back in Michigan. Or even heard of. Or ever imagined.

The canyon country was not Michigan.

Too bad ol' Dudley here didn't understand that. But then ol' Dudley he'd never been east of Denver, except for important politico-business flights to Washington, D.C. And what do you see from 29,000 feet? Mostly nothing. And in Washington, D.C.? Even less.

She let go of the roll bar. Dudley had stopped the machine. Virginia let her left hand fall from the roll bar and drop casually — and fondly — upon the Bishop's thick right thigh. Close to the pocket. You got a gun in there, Dud? Or you just happy to be with me again?

It had occurred to Ranger Dick, more than once, contemplating the hefty figure in the floor-length mirror of her BLM trailerhouse in Hardrock, that she bore a flattering resemblance to the late Mae West. To the young Mae West, that is, the charming chickadee of stage and film. A century ago, thought Virginia, with some justice and with mild bitterness, the men would have admired my body. Now I'm the type that men call "stout" and dress designers call "full figured." Sheet. Where's the justice in this world? There is no justice in this world. (Even worse in the next.) Life ain't fair. And that ain't fair.

But ol' Dud here, he likes me. He likes his "wimmin," as he says, "well built," quote.

"Honey," he said, coming around to open her door for her (imagine that!), "you step out here. I want to show you something."

Gracefully, taking his rough mitt, which felt like the forepaw of a crocodile, she stepped out of the Ford (recovered, by the way, in a parking lot in Kanab, Utah, with "Thank You" notes signed in lavender lipstick, but no fingerprints nowhere). Hand in hand, like bashful lovers, they walked through the sand, around the flowerbeds and toward what looked to Virginia like the edge of the world. Beyond the high rim of pale sandstone, sparsely but elegantly decorated with isolated junipers, blooming yucca, and the fragrant shrubs of cliffrose — that scent like orange blossoms — she saw and could see nothing but an infinite expanse of Western sky, winedark blue, upon which, with insouciant nonchalance, a few clouds drifted, in unison like sheep, fat, woolly, unshorn, ephemeral, without significance.

"Got your parachute?" he joked.

"Parachute?"

Fifty yards farther, high on the outermost ridge of rock, she understood what he meant. They stood on the verge of a mighty mesa, hand in hand, and looked down for nearly a thousand feet upon a talus of boulders big as buses, boxcars, bungalows that led in turn to a second dropoff and a second precipitous descent and a second disarray of scattered, shattered rocks, pedestal rocks, balanced rocks, hanging rocks, cantilevered rocks, rocks like mushrooms and rocks like hamburgers and goblin rocks and gargoyle rocks and rocks perched like glans penes upon erect and swollen shafts of Moenkopi mudstone — two thousand feet below.

Beyond lay the red desert and further canyons, the Grand Canyon, the snow-covered Kaibab Plateau, the snowy San Francisco Peaks near Flagstaff, one hundred sixty miles off by line of sight, two hundred sixty by road, and beyond all this, all that, obscured within the hazy vistas of central and southern Arizona — Phoenix, Mesa, Tempe, Scottsdale, Tucson, Nogales, where the huddled masses endured their muddled lives amidst a welter of smog, crime, noise, drugs, police, traffic, disease, heart transplants, sphincter transplants, two-headed babies, hydrocephalic preemies, endless conflict, smouldering hatred, an ever-rising Irritability Level, enjoying the pleasures of Growth, Prosperity and Progress.

"Oh, Dudley . . .! It's wonderful! Simply — "

"Ain't it, though. I was thinking right here'd be the spot for a big deluxe motel, like maybe a Holiday Inn. Once we get the Super-G.E.M. in here we can level off this mesa, put a jet strip over there, a by-God million-dollar eighteen-holer along the rim, how's that mess down below for a rough, huh? Ol' Sam Snead hisself might shy away from that, hey?"

"Simply wonderful, Dud . . ."

"Helispot on the roof, nice circular driveway coming up from the gulch, live bands on Saturday night, Sons of the Pioneers or Herb Alpert maybe or Lawrence Welk or that Mantovani fella, they still around?, salad bar, probly a resident physician for the old folks, by God, I tell you, Ginny, it'll be something. Something else. And you know something? This here ain't BLM we're standin' on right here, this here's the corner of a section of state land. *State land,* you get me? Two-thirds of it flops over the cliff there but what the hell that still leaves more'n two hundred acres for development which is more'n twice what they needed for Disneyland, you follow me?"

"Well, sure, Dud, but state land is public land too."

"It is and it ain't. State law requires that state land be used for maximum financial return." The Bishop glanced furtively about for a moment, as if fearing eavesdroppers, though the nearest known or permanent human habitation was the town of Hardrock, twenty miles by helicopter, thirty by mule trail, fifty by dirt road and jeep track — the route that the Bishop himself was pioneering this very day. "That means the state land commission has to listen to any offers it gets, lease to the highest bidder. And if a fella had a forty-nine-year lease, and then we get a good road in here, as we got to get for the uranium pit over yonder in Eden Canyon, well listen, honey . . ."

"And you're on the land commission?"

"No but I got friends who are."

His voice warm and choking with sentiment, rich with the poetry of his passion, the Bishop had to pause for a moment to swallow, clear his throat, regain full and manly control of his emotions. In synchronized but unconscious association, his broad hand gently disengaged itself from the ranger's hand and crept around her full waist, coming to rest upon the comfortable jutting shelf of her abundant hip.

Virginia thought it best to change the subject again, divert his mind from what his hand was up to. Why? Well, she wanted their picnic lunch first. She wanted to hear him talk of something other than money. At least for a few minutes. Perhaps pick a flower for her. Perhaps suggest a dip in a pool; he had mentioned earlier the existence of some magnificent natural waterpockets and potholes among that silent rosepink city of capitol domes, Park Avenue palaces, natural bridges, grottoes and buttes and gorges and pillars that lay now, on the horizon to the east, only a few miles ahead. Where also, they both suspected, the outlaw saboteurs hid out between their dastardly, cowardly, bastardly eco-raids.

"What about the Lone Ranger?" she said. "Rudolf the Red and the Earth First! mob? And that Monkey Business Gang?"

The Bishop's eyes suddenly lost their romantic lustre. Rousing from his daydream, wiping a tear from his cheek, he drew himself erect, stiffened with grim resolution. "Yeah . . . that's right. Come on, Ginny, let's check that place out."

Barely allowing her a final look at the purple panorama below, he drew her down and back to the Ford. Thirsty, he opened the icebox in the back, popped a pair of fizzing Pepsi-Colas, and gallantly offered one to his lady love. She opened a tin of smoked almonds. Drinking, eating, they drove on through the soft sand and up the meandering gully, which was now becoming a small canyon where the "wheels of man," as caption writers for *Arizona Highways* magazine were fond of pointing out, "had never trod." Or alternately, as they also said, "Where the hand of man has never set foot."

Deep among the hoodoo towers and voodoo monuments of stone, they reached an absolute deadend. Drifted dunes, unmarked sand, a young cottonwood tree in leafy April green, a plunge pool of clear water and spongy quicksand, a sheer wall of stone fifty vertical feet high blocked their advance. They got out of the machine, strapped guns to their hips, hung binoculars to their necks, slung the straps of full canteens to their shoulders. Ranger Dick pulled on and laced her hiking boots; she also slipped a slim packet of condoms (you can't depend on men) into the leather case which held two spare clips of ammunition for her U.S. Army Colt .45 automatic. (A handgun that would blow away a bull moose if you could manage to hit anything at more than fifty feet. Every girl should have one.)

The Bishop too snuck a pack of condoms (don't give her no excuses) into a pocket, picked up the plastic icebox containing their picnic supplies, and led the way up an ancient path chipped by hand in the cross-bedded sandstone. The path provided the only access for cattle to a series of natural water tanks in the domes above. The Bishop knew this trail because his own Grandaddy, nearly a century before, had made it, using no tools but a hammer, an iron bullprick and here and there a shot of blasting powder. Pausing often on the way up to blow, to wipe the sweat from his eyes and to regain his wind, the Bishop told the story to his companion.

Virginia found this bit of local history faintly interesting, in its trifling fashion, but had other things on her mind. As they neared the summit of the first great dome, a monolithic mass of stone shaped like the back of an elephant or the belly of a whale, she looked down at their vehicle two hundred feet below.

"Maybe we should've brought the Motorola, Dudley."

He stopped again and set down the icebox, welcoming any excuse to rest. Surveying the strange horizon of naked rock, he said, "Naw, we don't need it. Ain't going far. Just get up here, look around, see the ol' waterholes again. Oughta be full now, with all that rain in March." Get her in for a skinnydip, he was thinking, peel her underwear off, show her what a real man's whanger really looks like. Bet my shirt she ain't never seen one. Leastways not like mine she ain't.

"Suppose we see some sign of that Lone Ranger man or that Rudolf?"

Bishop Love smiled, caressing his weapon. "We take 'em. We take 'em."

"Without any help?"

"Why hell, honey, you're a bona fide BLM ranger with bona fide police training, I'm a deputized Search and Rescue patrolman with thirty-five years field experience, how much help you think we need?"

"They got away from us last time."

"Because I was playing games. Playing Caterpillar tag. This time we don't play no games. This time it's all business."

"I hope you're right, Dudley."

"Doggone right I'm right, Ginny honey."

They labored on under the naked sun over the nude rock, the man in his huge comical Stetson cattleman's hat, polyester non-breathing cattleman's suit, and slick-soled two-tone high-heeled lizardskin cattleman's business-display shoes. Awkward.

"Where's this pool?"

"Not far, honey, honest, just around that red knob yonder." Red knob, he was thinking, wait'll she sees my red knob, the poor gal will shit a brick. But that's love, can't be helped, she has gotta learn to take it like a man. I mean, like a man would if he was a woman which thank the Lord she ain't. Or is she? Could all that meat be fake? Perish the thought, Dudley, and remember to act like a gentleman. Talk like a gentleman. *Think* like a gentleman. Get them evil lustful thoughts of lust out of your mind. I will, I will, soon as I can, Lord, but oh my God, Lord, look at them tits on her. If she was a cow I'd go into the dairy business.

Poor old Dudley, she was thinking, such a sentimentalist. Actually got tears in his eyes talking about that hotel he wants to build. And he's so shy — hand on my hip, arm around my waist, jabbering away about hotels and golf courses and jet strips when what he's thinking about is love. I mean love with a little *l* — romance, real love, the passions of the heart. Who you trying to fool, girl? He wants to get into your pants and you know it and that's why you're here, haven't been laid for six months two weeks and four days now and I'm tired of it. Absolutely sick and tired of it. What about his wife? That old cow? Fatter'n I am; must weigh two hundred pounds. Fuck his wife. Poor old Dudley; no wonder he looks so sad all the time. Wonder when's the last time he had any real good honest-to-God loving? Hope he knows what he's in for. When I wrap my legs around him I'll break his back, I will, I'll bite off his tongue and swallow it, I'll rip the hide from his shoulder blades, I'll suck and fuck and fuck and suck him so dry his old turkeyballs'll turn inside out, I will I will. . . .

The first tank was not exactly where Love remembered it to be. They had to walk a quarter mile farther, around the towering phallic knob, along a purple slope strewn with dangerous little geodes the size of ball bearings, down a narrow crevasse between two vast, plump, smooth, symmetrical globes of stone (one with pimple), into a natural window eroded through a sphinx-like fin, and across a canted bench that led — *voilà!* — to a basin full of rainwater, an elegant oval pool ten feet wide, twenty long, clear and clean with a sandy bottom at least twelve inches deep.

"Oh Dudley . . . it's beautiful. Beautiful, Dudley."

He smiled bashfully but with pride, kicked some old dried last year's cow dung out of the way, and put the cooler down in the shade of a spreading juniper tree at poolside. "Kind of purty, ain't it. Ain't as deep as I remember but what the hell, Ginny, water is water. I do remember for sure there's bigger ones a little further but . . ." He looked at her, his little red, white and blue eyeballs moist with feeling, his voice thick, his fingers twitching. ". . . but I'm kinda hungry, ain't you? Ginny?"

She smiled. "Bishop Love, I could eat a Brangus bull right now, the way I feel."

They sat down in the sweet shade of the tree, removed their boots and dangled their feet in the water. Gazing into each other's eyes they opened the cooler, fetched out her tuna fish salad sandwiches thick with drooling mayonnaise, drew forth a bunch of fat and succulent grapes, unwrapped from tinfoil the breasts and thighs of roasted chicken . . .

"Sure love them breasts and thighs."

"I like necks. Sounds peculiar but you know I really . . . really do. . . ."

"Yeah, hell, honey, my cousin Homer he likes the pope's nose, talk about peculiar. . . ."

"You think they really might be out here?"

"Who?"

"Them. Those terrorists."

He patted his holstered cattleman's revolver, a pearl-handled (not ivory) double-action Ruger .44. "If they are we'll take 'em on. And you know somethin' else, you doggone beautiful lady?"

"What?" Now — the flower?

"Right now I don't give a damn."

"Oh, Dudley."

"That's right. Just don't give a hoot in hell." He grinned at her, a mangled chicken's leg forgotten in his hand. "Wanta go for a swim?"

She lowered her eyes. "I didn't bring my swimsuit."

"Me neither."

Significant pause. They gazed at each other, mouths open, half full, shreds of food dangling in their greasy fingers. . . .

*   *   *

My love, she whispered softly. Then she was in his arms, his hungry mouth claiming hers in a hot and passionate kiss that forged them together as if they had been melded into one.

His arm about her waist held her so tightly against him that she could hardly breathe, but she didn't care. She didn't want to breathe; she wanted to devour him; and her open, seeking mouth inflamed his desire to white-hot pitch.

His other hand caught her head and held it so that they were fused in mutual conquest. A soft, muffled groan escaped him as his senses soared. His hand slipped down to capture a soft breast. Their mouths hungered to prolong this sweet, heady assault. They tasted, sapping the strength from each other's limbs, and they clung to each other as a wild, tempestuous river of passion swept them away.

He bent to capture one hardened nipple, sending a storm of tortuous longing through her body. She closed her eyes as the sheer pleasure of his touch filled her with trembling joy. His hands gently cupped her jutting breasts and stroked her smooth skin, savoring the warmth of her flesh. He gathered her body close in his arms. She was a dream, a release of longing that swept every nerve with intense excitement.

She felt the bold urgency of him searing her flesh and heard his heart beating wildly against her naked breast. Beneath her hands his hard muscles felt tense with broiling vigor. Clinging together, caught in surging rapture, they sank to the tender slickrock. (Ignoring the ants now convening from the neighborhood.)

Her thighs were like satin against his heated skin as they parted to accept him. His kiss touched her, fierce with love and passion, and missed no inch of her quivering flesh. Then he was a hard flame within her. She moaned with the almost unbearable pleasure and they were both caught up in a swelling, surging tide of ecstasy. . . .

"Goldang dadgum ants." He smeared a couple of them across the stone with his heel. "Never let a fella alone."

"Dud — I hear a motor."

"Naw."

"I do."

"Ain't nobody here but us chickens, boss."

"Listen."

He listened. He sat upright, listened again. "Ford," he muttered, "V-eight . . ." He jerked on his boots, slapped on his hat, buckled on his revolver, grabbed binoculars and jogged heavily, like a gutshot bear and naked as a jaybird, up the swell of bare stone to the summit. Except for face, neck and hands he was pale as a fish, like any countryman. She stayed where she was, in the shade, legs in the cool water, and watched him standing up there with binocs to his eyes, entire body — excepting one spare part — rigid with attention. Bad news, she thought. She saw him pull the revolver, cock the hammer, aim, hesitate, think better of it. Reholstering his weapon, he lumbered down the slope toward her. She read his face and saw there a mixture of confusion, embarrassment, exasperated rage.

"No," she said.

"Yes," he said.

They dressed, hurried back to the little box canyon. Indeed, the Bronco was gone. In its place was a pile of their gear — sleeping bags, waterjug, the Motorola two-way radio — and a note, scrawled with the Bishop's pencil on a page torn from the Bishop's S&R logbook:

> Howdy podners motorized veehickles not allowed in this genril area within ten miles yer veehickle wuz impoundered as per rooles & recklations this here genril area and you kin recover remanes of same if yew wish two miles east and 1000 feet belowe here direckt dissent not advized heliklopiters shot on sight cows likewise have a nice day yer friend
> THE LONE RANGER.

Snarling, the Bishop prepared to rip the paper in two.

"No," said Virginia, "save that. Evidence. Might even be finger-prints on it."

"Not goldamn likely."

"I know. Save it anyhow."

They stared down the sandy canyon floor, noting the turnaround arcs near the first bend, the doubled tracks winding around the rock. They looked up at the silent, massive, impassive walls, the humps and spires and arches and hard-ons and gargoyle horns of stone surrounding them. Quintessence of stillness; not even a bird, no canyon wren nor brown towhee nor raucous raven nor haughty soaring turkey vulture disturbed by merest sibilance of feather the glassy stasis of the silence.

"Scary," she said. "You think he's watching us?"

The Bishop touched his gun butt. "Him? I wish he was. I wish just once he'd show his ugly face, whoever the bastard sumbitch is."

"Dudley — I never heard you talk like that."

"I'm a-gettin' mad. He went too far this time. Him, them, whatever it is out here."

"Listen — !"

"What?"

"Listen!"

He listened. They listened. They listened, listened, ears straining, and heard the distant echoes, softened and mellowed by space and time, of a solid body impacting upon rock, the explosion of metallic parts, the clatter of many smaller solid bodies likewise impacting upon more distant rock, succeeded by — *diminuendo à ritardando* — overlapping echoes of fainter sounds diminishing forever, ever smaller ever fainter but as Zeno (the Eleatic) said never attaining the final ultimate absolute neo-platonic perfection of nothingness.

He looked at her. She looked at him.

"What was that?"

"Well . . ." She knew she shouldn't say it but she couldn't help it. "I think they just impounded your Bronco."

"That's not funny, Virginia."

"Sorry, Dudley." Pause. She kissed him. "Let's get out of here."

He checked the radio. It seemed to be in working order. "Wanta call the BLM? Get their whirlybird out here?"

"Let's walk a few miles first." She kissed him again. "Then rest awhile." Significant pause. "*Then* call for help."

He stared at her, confused for a moment; he broke into a slow, begrudging but improving smile. "Yeah," he said at last. "Right. What the hell, we still got half the day. Let's go admire the view — want to show you where we'll build the condos. Then long about sundown . . ."

"That's the idea."

They shouldered as much of their belongings as they could carry, linking straps and belts and hooks and buckles, and trudged together, side by side, holding hands, through the sand toward the westering sun, toward the promise of sunset and evening star, love and beauty, rescue and Pepsi-Cola.

Their walk followed in reverse the prospective route of the G.E.M. of Arizona, the 4250-W Walking Dragline, world's biggest moving land machine, GOLIATH on his march.

18

Hoyle and Boyle

"Well, Mr. Hatch?"

"Yes sir?"

"Mr. Hatch?"

"Sir?"

"You don't mind if we ask a few questions?"

"No sir."

"Why are you so incompetent, Mr. Hatch?"

Pause. Silence. Introspective searching of the motel-room carpet, the blank video screen, the heavy black-out drapes shutting off the outside light at the single window, the glare of the floorlamp blazing on his flushed, youthful, handsome face. "Well, sir, I don't think I'm incompetent." Clenching fingers, rubbing knuckles, a chewing of the lower lip. "I think I had some bad luck but I'm not incompetent."

The harsh and whisky-scored voice broke in. "He ain't incompetent, Colonel. Just stupid."

"Now now, I won't have that kind of talk. We must treat young Hatch with respect, whether deserved or not. Don't you agree, Mr. Hatch?"

"I didn't come here to be insulted, sir."

With mincing affectation the rough voice mimicked his words: "I didn't come here to be insulted, sir."

"Now now." Pause. "I admire your spunk, Mr. Hatch. Stand up for yourself, I like that. It gives me hope for you. But — " The ominous "but" was allowed to hover on the air, in solitude, for a prolonged moment. " — we are finding difficulties with your performance. May I call you Oral, by the way?"

"Ah . . . yes. Yes sir."

"Since our last conference, Oral, only a month or two ago, we've had the shooting of the dirt scooper, the mysterious explosion at the ore reduction mill — "

"Sir," said Oral, "last time you called me Lieutenant."

"Yes I did, Oral, and this time I'm calling you Oral."

Awkward silence. The Colonel continued. "The mysterious and still unsolved explosion — a high felony by the way, that use of explosives — and then the theft of Love's D-7 crawler tractor followed by, what's this?" Rustle of papers.

"Aggravated assault by masked man in bulldozer upon Bishop J. Dudley Love's bulldozer followed by malicious destruction of both bulldozers. What do you have to say about it, Oral?"

"Sir, I was in Green River that day, keeping Dr. and Mrs. Sarvis and that fellow Smith under close surveillance." Oral gulped. "As instructed, sir."

"Close surveillance?" grumbled Hoyle. "How close?"

"We were playing poker."

"For you that's too close. How much you lose this time?"

"I did good at the No Peekie."

"How much you lose?"

"It's itemized on the expense account."

"How much?"

"Thirty-eight dollars and fifty cents."

"Holy Mary. In a penny ante game?"

"Nickel ante. It was a regular nickel ante game."

"That ain't mathematically possible." Pause. "Jim, is that mathematically possible?"

"It's possible but it's not human."

"Quiet!" the Colonel snapped. He continued: "Rumors of further tree-spiking in the Kaibab National Forest."

"Sir, that's not in my jurisdiction."

"It's not a matter of jurisdiction, Oral. You're not merely a cop on a beat, responsible for a certain district, you're an investigative agent assigned to monitor the illegal activities of person or persons engaging in sabotage against an industry of vital concern to the interests of the Department of Energy and the Department of Defense, is that not clear?"

"Including pine trees?"

"Don't be impertinent, Oral. We have reason to believe, as you know, that this Earth First or Earth Birth group may be involved in a diversity of illegal activities including, but not limited to, what they call 'direct action' or — what's this? — '*Eine kleine Nachtwerke.*' "

"Are they terrorists?"

"No, Oral. They're worse than terrorists. These people attack property. *Property*, Oral."

"Yes sir."

"Terrorists we can handle. Terrorism is right down our alley. Leave the TV off, Boyle. Terrorism we understand. But this other thing, this so-called 'ecotage,' we haven't had to deal with anything like that since the A.G. wiped out the I.W.W. back in the twenties."

"A.G., sir? I.W.W.?"

"Attorney General, Oral. His name was Palmer. And the I.W.W., well, that's history, Oral, history. Happened over sixty years ago. Ancient history, of course, to you modern college graduates. Ever hear of Joe Hill, Oral? Joseph Hillstrom? Or Joel Hagglung?"

"Ah . . . no sir. None of them."

"Curious. All the same man, Oral, folk hero to the American Labor movement, died here in Utah, shot through the heart by firing squad, Oral, by court order, happened only ten miles south of here at a place called Point of the Mountain."

"You mean the state penitentiary?"

"That's right, Oral, where the penitent are sent to pay penance for their sins and let that be a lesson to you, Oral, think you'll remember a word of it?"

"Yes sir."

"Doubt it. Hands off the TV, Hoyle, for the love of Jesus, Joseph and Mary can't you take our work seriously?"

Growls of discontent. ". . . Signed on to fight a war, Colonel. We got real live Communists to kill in Panama, Nicaragua, Salvador, Honduras, Guatemala, didn't join this fuckin' company to check out Halloween pranks in Za-Boobieland."

"You know why you're here, Hoyle. You too, Boyle. Who helped plan the Bay of Pigs? Who predicted the Tet Offensive would hit on Mother's Day? Who told us Somoza was in for keeps? Eh?"

Silence.

"Now if you'd both lay off the sauce for a while and get this Boy Scout job cleaned up we can all go back to where the real thing is." Pause: silence. "Right?"

Grumbled assent.

"Now. As for you, Oral, I will say only that I'm disappointed in your work so far. Who was that bag woman you caught talking with this Doc Sarvis's shack-up job?"

"They're married, sir."

"Answer the question."

"She got away. Woman ran like a wide receiver, up the down escalator, down the up escalator, couldn't get near her, sir. Darn near killed me with her shopping cart — heaved the whole thing at me on the escalator."

"What was in it?"

"Garbage."

"Fingerprints?"

"Was all wet garbage, sir. Stuff from some supermarket dumpster — rotten fruit, rotten vegetables, bloody newspapers, soggy bags, plastic diapers full of baby doodoo."

Vulgar laughter.

"Doodoo, Oral?" inquired Boyle. "Or poopoo?"

Both men broke down into wheezing hysteria, Boyle rolling on one of the double beds. Hoyle convulsing deep in a sagging armchair.

Young Hatch waited in quiet dignity. The Colonel checked his wristwatch against the digital clock on the sound recording equipment. Outside in the Salt Lake twilight, two stories below, the evening traffic flowed through the slush and grime of Sixth South and State Street. Horns honked in forlorn desperation, anxious for stable, dry straw and feed stall; sirens wailed like banshees from Hell; giant jets screamed through the smog above, their landing lights aglare, the pilots popping pills.

"I'm going to give you one more chance, one more chance, Lieutenant Hatch, to redeem yourself and prove you have the makings of a true undercover agent. I want you to infiltrate this Earth Fist or Birth First or whatever it's called, find out precisely what they're up to. We'll let your friend Orlen shadow the Sarvis family."

"Yes sir. It's called Earth First! . . . Earth First exclamation point. From what I hear you can't join it because they don't have members, or officers, or dues or any kind of organization at all. But I'll hang around if I can find where they . . . hang out. There is supposed to be what they call a Rendezvous pretty soon, on the North Rim. I'll be there."

"Good boy." The Colonel stood up, terminating, without undue prejudice, this second interview. "*I'm* going now, boys." The Colonel had a date, a heavy date, coming up in thirty minutes. A certain United States Congressman from Utah and he had discovered, one evening in the Sam Rayburn House Gymnasium, that they had more in common than merely their imperial politics; from urinals to teak-paneled sauna, romance blossomed.

He checked his tie in the mirror, ran a brush over his silvergray hair. "You boys clean up this mess before you leave; I'll be back in a couple of hours."

Outside, on the street, in the gloom, striding toward the appointed meeting place, the Colonel passed one hand over his fine, interesting, intelligent eyes, as if to clear away an invisible irritant; he felt the aura of another migraine coming on and had forgotten to bring his Sansert. Never mind, there was no pain he could not surmount by scorn alone. Walking rapidly, feeling the first twitch in his right cheek, the first tear forming in his right eye, he raised both hands to the gray, leaking, sulfur-smelling sky, and cried aloud, "Man is a useless passion!"

There were few pedestrians on the sidewalk. Very few. But those that heard him stopped, turning their heads to watch the march of the tall bareheaded man in the black topcoat, his face uplifted to the hidden stars.

19

Dr. Wiener

Dr. Wiener (as his I.D. badge asserted) entered the Syn-Fuels computer center at lunchtime, wearing the customary white smock over his white shirt and black tie. A thick blond mustache drooped from his upper lip, dark purple sunglasses concealed his eyes, and a mop-like helmet of blond curls, encasing sides, top and back of his head, gave him the adorable cuddly appearance of another Harpo Marx. He held a fat briefcase in one hand, a stout cane in the other, on which he leaned as he walked. His gait was awkward, a painful spastic stagger that carried him one foot to the side for each three feet forward.

A young woman held a door open for him. The fleeing crowd of clerks and tapers, surging out for lunch, parted respectfully before him. Some looked back at his lurching figure as it disappeared into the central computer rooms; they'd never seen him before, but he had obviously been cleared by Security in the lobby upstairs. Anxious to escape their labors, pushed on by the mob, they promptly forgot the man, and raced up stairways, escalators to street level, daylight, open air (such as it was) and their sixty minutes of allotted freedom.

Dr. Wiener meanwhile, reaching the double steel doors (RE-STRICTED! Authorized Personnel Only) that guarded the computer banks, drew a passkey and entered, closed and relocked the doors. The room was large, high-ceilinged and well-cooled by heavy-duty industrial air-conditioning equipment. Ranks of computers enclosed in steel cabinets of gray and blue occupied most of the floor space; the steady murmur of their busy little brains filled the air with an oppressive vibration. At least Dr. Wiener found it oppressive.

Against two walls stood metal desks supporting the computer terminals, their keyboards abandoned for the lunch hour, their video screens blinking in holding patterns of green, red and gray. Dr. Wiener placed his briefcase on one of these desks, opened it, pulled out a pair of cheap cowhide gloves and pulled them on. Taking a two-foot screwdriver with plastic handle from his case, he walked the perimeter of the room (with neither cane nor limp) until he came to the grille that covered the recirculating air vent for the cooling system. He pried off the vent cover and set it aside, then advanced directly to the largest computers and jimmied off the access panels, revealing row on row of glittering, immaculate, intricate circuit boards. When all of the computers had been opened he replaced his giant screwdriver in his fat briefcase and removed two empty one-gallon milk jugs, their caps on tight but their entire bottoms cut off. He entered the men's room and filled the jugs — holding them upside down by their handles — with clear cool chlorinated ethylene glycol–enriched Phoenix City tap water.

He hurried on rubber-soled sneakers back to the rank of great computers, their innards now on display like the intestines of a row of surgically flayed mammals. Pitcher of water in each hand, Dr. Wiener was about to continue his work when he heard a key in the lock, the entrance doors opened and a supervisory type walked in. Female, thin, middleaged, she had the haggard face and jerky movements of a woman trapped in a permanent state of agitated irritation.

"What the devil are you doing?"

Dr. Wiener grinned in friendly fashion but gave no answer except to toss the contents of his water containers over the exposed circuit boards. Clouds of steam arose at once from technetronic bowels, scintillating with sparks and glints and zigzag jigjags of bewildered little electrical currents, fizzing like dry ice in a punch bowl.

"You damned fool," the supervisor screeched, "you're frying the circuits."

Dr. Wiener smiled again, nodded, and hastened — with spastic limps — to the men's room for refills. The woman tried to follow; he pointed to the gender label on the door, grabbed his crotch and lunged clumsily inside. The woman hesitated, stared at the horror of the steaming computers, then raced for the doors.

Dr. Wiener emerged from the men's room, doused two more open computers with water, moved quickly to the entrance doors and locked them by jamming his heavy ironwood cane through the interior pair of handles.

Not a moment too soon. The banging on the doors began as he completed his treatment of the computer banks, becoming urgent as he ranged with open briefcase before the ranks of keyboards and terminal screens, popping a golf ball through each and every cathode ray tube. Haste was vital but he was determined to do a good job. The room filled with fetid vapors, the buzz of electronic fusion and confusion, the caustic smell of burning circuitry; the floor sparkled with shards of glass from the imploded CRTs.

When the doors seemed about to yield beneath the pressure from without, Dr. Wiener stripped off smock, mustache and wig and stuffed them deep inside a burning computer. He poured cooking oil over the floor, turned off the overhead fluorescent lights, sealed the switches with duct tape, crouched under a desk beside the entrance doors and waited.

The cane cracked apart, the doors burst open, the security guards swept in. Into the dark.

"Lights, lights, turn on the lights."

"Can't find the switches, where's the switches?"

Feet slipped and slid, bodies tumbled to the floor. One man found his Mag-light: a piercing beam stroked through the smoke and fog. He saw the detached vent cover of the A/C duct. "Hey, this way, he's in the cooling duct, dumb cogsucker tried to get out through the duct, we got him, this way, boys. . . ."

Four men scrambled on the greased floor, slipping and sliding, struggling for traction. One guard managed to get to his feet, peel the tape from the light switches and turn on the lights. Groping through the dense smog, the others pounded on the cooling vent with clubs and flashlights. "Okay, fella, it's all over now, come on outa there. . . ."

Dr. Wiener meantime was strolling down the hallway through the empty offices, decently dressed in tweed cap and his blue serge suit from Goodwill, lugging his big but mostly empty briefcase. Smiling, he passed the lady supervisor standing in the doorway to the corridor, nodded politely and stepped onto a rising escalator. She said nothing but stared after him, watched him floating motionless, in miraculous assumption, toward the lobby. Suddenly she screamed, pointed: "That's him, that's him!" She started up the moving stairs in hot pursuit. Dr. Wiener emptied a bag of marbles in her path, tipped his cap, disappeared.

20

Bonnie's Return

Deep in the outback back of beyond, far into the hoodoo land of naked
stone she walked, she walked, she walked and walked. The noon sun
blazed down from a semi-clouded sky and there was no wind, no trace
of breeze. She stopped often to drink from the canteens she carried in
her small backpack and when she came, from time to time, upon a
pool of rainwater evaporating silently in a slickrock basin, she dropped
to her knees, as if in prayer, cupped her hands and drank from the
pool. The water was lukewarm but clean, sweet, pure, inhabited by
nothing but mosquito larvae, a few of the strange little crustaceans
called fairy shrimp, and the occasional spadefoot toad. Their presence
in the pools, far from repelling her, attested to the water's purity. She
carried two liters of city water in her pack but preferred to save that
when she could. She remembered this trek as requiring five to six
hours of dogged hiking but — but that had been years ago, in cooler
weather, and without a fetus in her womb.

The route — not a trail — was difficult to follow. His old cairns were
in place, three small flat stones piled vertically, placed on strategic high
points along the way so that, from any one, at least two others could
be seen. But there were no other markers of any kind and the route

led mostly over solid slickrock, following the contours of the ledges, avoiding shortcuts across sandy basins and cryptogrammic flats that would leave a footpath discernible to the eye. Of course, even on stone and especially on sandstone, enough foot traffic would create a trail. But this was a secret route, rarely used, known only to its discoverer and his few friends.

She plodded steadily on, wearing her big straw hat to shade her face, a loose long-sleeved cotton shirt soaked in water to keep her cool, baggy knee-length shorts, good stout lightweight old walking shoes on her feet. She carried a long staff in one hand, for snakes and for descending steep pitches of stone, and a rolled topographic map in the other, large-scale, which she consulted now and then when the way forward seemed doubtful.

She remembered most of the landmarks, for she had named them herself (he refused to apply human labels to natural objects older than humankind and destined to outlast humankind): the Goblet of Venus, a twenty-foot vase-shaped boulder perched on a tall and slender pedestal of Moenkopi mudstone; Candlestick Spire, a thin tapering pillar of sandstone one hundred feet high; Cleopatra's Throne, a monolith of golden Navajo sandstone about the size of Ayer's Rock in central Australia; the Playhouse, a winding maze of tunnels, windows and intersecting corridors corroded and eroded through a mass of fractured stone; Manhattan Skyline, a file of blocks and pinnacles high on a ridge; the Spectacles, a pair of natural arches, each big enough to fly an airplane through, set side by side in a free-standing tailfin of Entrada sandstone; Deception Arch, not apparent until you entered deep within it and suddenly discovered the huge skylight beyond, up through which the route led; Seldom Seen's Often Seen Prick, a massive shaft of purplish mudstone topped by a bulging red knob of sandstone (Entrada member); the Joint Trail, a sinuous crevasse in the rock six hundred feet long, fifty to one hundred feet deep, and two to three feet wide. At the narrowest point, which she had named Fat Girl's Misery, she had to remove her backpack and turn sideways in order to squeeze through; once beyond that the going was easier. Not far beyond the mouth of the Joint Trail she came to the first of a series of natural watertanks — Salvation Pools — sat down beneath a big juniper, took off her shoes and socks, and lit up a joint. Relaxing, soothed by the stillness surrounding her and the pleasant shade, she was about to lean back against the trunk of the tree, close her eyes and dream, when she noticed, with shock and disgust, the used condom on the ledge nearby, ill-concealed beneath an inadequate stone. Not very old either; a file of little black ants was coming and going at the mouth of the thing, gorging on what remained of its rich contents and lugging them, by the sacful, back to headquarters.

The woman broke a dead twig from the juniper, picked up the condom — "Yuck" — and carried it away from the pool to a clump of brown bunch grass on the edge of a sand flat. Pulling a book of matches from her shirt pocket, she lit the dry grass and watched the condom curl, shrivel, smoke, burn and vanish in the flames.

That bastard, she was thinking, that son of a bitch, he brought some girl out here, to *our* place, *our* secret sacred pools, and screwed her right there under *our* personal special tree. The dirty slut — I wonder what she looks like? probably not even legal age, some stupid little teenybopper barely out of junior high, the rotten bastard, how *dare* he do such a thing? Here? In *our* magic fairyland right out of Rudolfo Tamayo and Salvador Dali and New Age Art and the Hearts of Space, how could he do it? that ugly dirty hairy ignorant foul-mouthed two-timing treacherous toad of a no-goodnik.

Her first reaction was to sling on her pack and tramp straight back to the end of the jeep trail and her little Suzuki four-by-four. But when she felt the weight of the pack — like an ingot of pigiron between her shoulder blades — and recalled the six seven eight miles of rock and then sand under the afternoon sun . . . why then she hesitated, thought again, returned to the shade of the juniper and thought some more.

Why not go on? she asked herself. We'll give him a piece of our mind, the rough edge of our tongue, drop a rock on his head. Let him know what a bastard he really is, in case he's forgotten, which is all too likely for a rotten son of a bitch like him.

Besides . . . it's closer. He'll maybe have something good to eat, e.g., poached beef on cornpone maybe. Fresh spring water. I can sleep on his cot tonight (alone of course) and not have to curl up on the ground with the tarantulas and kissing bugs and scorpions and those tiny whatever-they-are that crawl in your ears at night and go roller-skating on your eardrums. And what a delight to tell him what I think of him face-to-face and if he tries to grab me I'll, I'll . . . I'll what? Run like hell? Climb a pinyon pine? Try to knee him in the balls? Pull out my little .32 and shoot him in his hairy old beerbelly? He'd pick me up by the ankles and whirl me around his head like a, like a . . . ? apache dancer! Guess not.

Smiling unconsciously, she marched on and over, between, beneath and around further marvels of patient erosion and ancient geo-logic until she arrived at the last of the big potholes before his hideout camp. This was no mere ornamental pool like the first, where she'd found the condom, but a genuine slickrock waterpocket ten feet deep, ten wide and twenty long, enclosed by steeply sloping walls of nude sandstone. Two small junipers grew nearby. The water was dark green but inviting, certain to be cool and offering her a final chance to freshen up a bit before descending on the bandit's lair. She undressed quickly and eased herself toward the water, hunkered on her heels, began to slide, and jumped the last three feet into the pothole. As she jumped she remembered something she was not supposed to forget: the rope.

Too late. The waters, colder than expected, closed above her head. Her feet did not touch bottom. When she came up she gulped for air and reached the edge of the water in two swift strokes. Fighting off a wave of panic, she clutched at the sloping stone and tried to pull herself up. No go; she could find no purchase for hands or feet, fingers or toes, on the smooth, if slightly gritty, sandstone.

Relax, relax, she told herself; take it easy, try to think. Forcing calm, she floated on her back and gazed up at the oval of blue above her head, the hard-edged crest of a snowy cloud beginning to show itself at one side of her piece of sky. It was like looking up from the bottom of a well. Again she felt the surge of cold fear in her bowels and heart. Again she fought it off. Think, woman, think.

Howl for help? Possibly, just possibly, if she screamed loudly enough, often enough, he might hear her from his camp below the rim, not more than a mile away. Possibly — not likely. Too much massive monolithic Navajo sandstone between here and there, too many walls and towers and hills, humps, holes, and hollows for the human voice to thread, too much for even the wailing cry of extreme distress to penetrate.

She'd attempt it anyway, of course. At the moment she could think of nothing else to do. She backstroked to the nearest bulge of stone, got her head and shoulders out of the water's pressure, and essayed a couple of tentative yelps.

They sounded strange, pathetic, utterly useless. Even if he heard me, she realized, how could he locate the source of my voice? — down there among a spreading ripple of echoes and the echoes of echoes.

Oh my God, this is ridiculous. Absurd. Reuben, she thought, Reuben, I can't die now, dear sweet precious little Reuben, I can't die now, here, so soon, much too soon, he needs me, needs me, oh my one and only darling little solitary angel of a boy . . .

Told Doc I'd be back tomorrow night. Didn't tell him where I was going, naturally. I lied about that, naturally. He'll know where to look for Reuben when I fail to show up but he'll never dream of where to look for me. And even if he did and even if they found me — I'd be — I will be — ah, hmmm, how they say, dead. All pale and bloated-up and dead, nothing showing but my big white ass, floating in this deathtrap.

She remembered a strange line from a strange book: "The mute, implacable buttocks of the drowned." That's me. That's old Abbzug all right, mute, implacable, mouth under water and shut up finally, forever. She giggled; she trembled; she felt the tears of self-pity flowing down her cheeks.

Poor Doc, he'll miss me. Poor bumbling helpless old man, how will he ever manage without me? And with a three-year-old child on his hands?

Seldom'll miss me. Good old Seldom, that sweet and wonderful man, he'll miss me. He always loved me. I could have been Wife #4, anytime. Should've done it too, maybe, except — no Reuben. Yes. No Reuben without Doc.

Forgive me, Doc.

And what about him? *Him?* The oaf. The toad. The gorilla. The lying sneaking unwashed bastard. Him and his crazy projects. Him and his urge to self-destruct. His pissing in the kitchen sink. Blowing his nose in his hand and wiping it on a rock. Wiping his ass with juniper twigs. Drinking beer, always drinking beer, and throwing the cans along the road. Old garbage-mouth, always swearing, can't talk unless I swear, he said, can't even *think* if I can't swear.

I think, therefore I swear.

I think I think, she giggled. I guess I think, therefore I guess I am.

And such a violent brutal aggressive reckless lover, the bastard, always in a hurry, always looking over his shoulder like he thought someone was watching, somebody with a gun, an enemy. *The* Enemy, he said. The Enemy is everywhere. Good thing I'm an easy comer, quick on the trigger. . . .

"George!" she screamed, loud and clear. "George!" she screamed again.

She waited, gasping for air. She listened. No response but silence. Not even the croaking of a raven, not even the cry of a redtail hawk. No canyon wren, no desert solitaire. Nothing. The only answer anyone ever got, appealing to the sky. Not even the bluegray feather of a dove, spiraling down and down from the false beatitude above.

She trembled. The cold was seeping through her flesh, crawling into her bones. Think, my dear, think, there must be a way to, well, weasel out of here. Ouzel out. Ooooze . . . like a snail, like a banana slug, like a slimy thing with pseudopods.

She looked about the pool again, taking some care to gauge the angle of the various curving slopes of stone. The closer to the water the steeper, but a few feet higher, only two or three or four feet higher, the slopes began to curve outward, gently, toward the horizontal.

She swam toward what appeared to be the easiest gradient, swam hard, swam fast, and coming close, hurled herself up out of the water like a hungry trout, arms outspread, clutching at the rock. Her fingers found nothing, but something else, something vacuumatic, glued her to the slope of stone, and held her there, out of the water from the waist up.

My tits, she thought. Thank God for big tits. Big wet tits, the suctorial power of a pair of plumber's helpers, by God they're going to get me out of here. I always knew they'd be good for something.

Maybe. She was half out of the water. But how to proceed? If she tried to move now she'd break the seal, lose suction and slide in her bare and tender skin down into the tank again. The sacrificial well. But by God I'm no virgin, I'm a veteran, and if they think they can drown old Bonnie Abbzug like a rat in a barrel they got another think to think, the swine. I'll show 'em.

Keeping hands, arms, chest and belly flat to the rock, vacuum-sealed, she spread her legs frogwise, wriggled her hips, and succeeded in oozing, like an amoeba, several inches upward. Now her bottom was half out of the water; she felt the cooling evaporation in the cleft between the cheeks. She rested for a minute, then performed the movement again and gained another six inches.

Again she rested.

"Give up yet?"

She recognized that mocking voice but dared not look up. One careless move and she'd be floundering in the middle of the tank.

A rope of braided blue and gold Perlon slid down beside her, touching her right arm and hip. "Grab the fuckin' rope," he said, "I'll pull you up."

Go to hell, she muttered to herself. I can get out of this without any help from you.

He waited. "No? Okay, wiggle out like a tadpole, see if I care. Always did like a free show."

You bastard, she thought. She took hold of the rope with both hands, a firm grip, pulled her knees beneath her and walked up the curving sandstone, using the line only for support, disdaining his outstretched hand.

He stood there by her pile of clothing, the rope belayed around his waist, grinning at her in the customary way. The way she hated. "Thanks," she said politely, picking up her underwear.

"What's the big fuckin' idea, swimmin' in my fuckin' drinkin' water? Ain't you got no manners, woman? No desert etiquette?"

She ignored the remark, twitching the hem of the panties over the swell of her buttocks; she slipped into her bra and reached between her shoulder blades to fasten the clips.

He stared, fascinated. "Why do they hook those things in back?"

"Don't gape. It's not polite." She bent for her shirt and shorts. "Reel in your tongue."

"You're beautiful as ever, Bonnie, I can't help it." Coiling his rope. "You know the last time I saw a naked woman?"

"Why do you always say something nice and then spoil it with something stupid?" Buttoning the shirt, shaking the long wet hair from her eyes, she pinned him with her coolest stare. Those violet eyes. "Anyhow this is strictly a business trip, George. Don't get yourself all hot and bothered. Strictly business." She pulled on her hiking shorts. "Anyhow I'm not beautiful anymore anyhow. I'm getting fat. Look at this — " She showed him her plump abdomen. " — stretch marks."

"Stretch marks, what the fuck. I like stretch marks. Stretch marks are beautiful. *You* are beautiful, I don't care what everybody says. You got a beautiful belly. Let me kiss it." He dropped the coiled line.

"Back off, George. Relax. Go for a swim." She zipped up the shorts, tucked in her shirt, sat on the rock to put on socks and shoes.

Hayduke looked below at the dark pool. "As a matter of fact that is what I came up here for." He nudged off his sandals.

"You didn't come to rescue me?"

"Oh I heard the hollerin'. If I'd knowed it was you I'd have gone back to sleep." He unlatched his gunbelt, unbuttoned and peeled off his ragged Levi cutoffs. Since he wore no shirt or underwear, that left him naked. He looked around for his rope, planning to tie one end of it around the closest juniper. Bonnie, her back braced against a ledge, planted one foot on Hayduke's hairy butt and shoved him over the lip, into the pool. Arms and legs flailing with involuntary reflex motions — "Falling!" — he crashed on the surface in a mighty bellywhopper, went under and came up, floating dead-still on his front. Head and arms and legs hanging under the water, Hayduke presented to sky and Bonnie's eyes the *mute, implacable buttocks of the drowned.* He made no move, merely rocking gently on the waves.

Bonnie stared. "George?" No response. "George!" she yelled. No answer. "Oh my God . . ." She took a step forward, about to leap into the pothole, then remembered the rope. Quickly she snatched it up, whipped one end around the trunk of the juniper, tried a bowline knot, couldn't remember the pattern, compromised on a granny and ended up with two accidental but satisfactory half-hitches. Tossing the coiled free end toward the water, she kicked off her unlaced shoes and prepared to jump.

But George had held his breath as long as he could. Roaring with laughter and snorting for air, he flung up his head, tossed the hair and water from his eyes, took a deep breath and jackknifed under the surface, mooning Bonnie with his small pale rear, his puckered asshole, his wrinkled balls. Not a pretty sight.

She stepped back from the edge. She watched Hayduke emerge from the water again, grinning up at her like a dolphin as he swam toward the rope that lay draped upon the stone, its running end underwater.

Bonnie jerked the rope upward. Hayduke heaved himself into the air, flinging one hand at the rising line. He missed, grunted and slipped back into the water, coming to rest at the pool's edge. As Bonnie had done he scrabbled about, searching for a handhold, a foothold. As he well knew, there was none. Relaxing, he floated on his back and looked up at her. Coiling his rope, she dropped it at her feet.

"Very funny." He grinned, but not so heartily as before. "Well, shit . . . so come on in, the water's fine."

"Guess not." Pulling on her shoes again. "Had enough myself."

"Yeah, well, okay, throw me the rope. You got it anchored?"

Bonnie's turn to grin. "Use your tits, bit shot." Lacing her shoes. "If I could do it you can do it."

He smiled, running a hand over his cold little nipples, his bulging hair-covered barrel of a chest, his flat and muscle-corded stomach. In fact Hayduke was in good shape, despite the beer; no soft tissue or loose suctorial flesh on him anywhere, except perhaps inside the braincase.

Bonnie stood up and slung on her pack, ready to go. "You coming?"

"Throw me the fuckin' rope, Bonnie."

"What? Big he-man like you needs a rope to climb out of that little dinky pothole?"

He sighed, feigning boredom, and examined his fingernails. She picked up his belt, massively heavy with its holstered revolver, sheathed combat knife, loops full of extra cartridges. "Want your gun? I'll throw you your gun . . ." Using both hands, she prepared as if to toss the whole rig to him.

"No, no, don't do that, you drop that in the fuckin' water I'll spank your . . . I'll . . ."

"You'll what?"

"I'll kiss it. Okay? Now throw down the rope, Bonnie."

"What's the magic word?"

He grinned his broadest fakest homeliest grin. "Please? Pretty please? Pretty please with icky poo?"

"That's better. But there's something else you better explain, Hayduke. Who'd you bring here yesterday?"

He looked puzzled. "Here? With me? What do you mean?"

"You left your condom up here, Hayduke. Full of ants and you-know-what, you lousy fornicating litterbugging slob."

Bewildered, he stared at her. Then light came. "Oh — yeah. Love. That was Love, Bonnie. Day before yesterday. Love and that — "

"Love you call it? I call it whoring around, you bastard. God, you men make me sick, you're all the same. Worse than little dogs."

"*Bishop* Love, *Bishop* Love." Sighing with exasperation, he explained.

"You sat over there," she said, "spying on two people making love? That's disgusting. I mean that's really sick." She started to walk off. "I think I'll let you drown."

"Bonnie!" She paused. "For chrissake, Bonnie, that old fart was only a mile from camp. My camp I mean. And that fuckin' fat pistol-packin' rangerette with him. They were lookin' for us. *They* were the spies."

"I still think it's sick. Degenerate. Don't you have any sympathy, George, any respect for one of the most sacred, holy beautiful things a man and woman can do together?"

"You mean fuck? Well, sure, only . . . sure. Only I'd rather do it than watch. Any day. Any time. Like right now."

"You're out of luck, Hayduke. I'm a married woman." She flashed her gold ring at him. "And I'm staying that way."

"Okay okay." He shivered, gazing up at her. His lips were turning a little blue. "Can I have the rope now? Anyhow? Please? Please, Bonnie? Pretty please with sugar on it? Brown sugar? White? Powdered? Fucking *granulated*?"

She kicked the coiled line in his direction and disappeared. When he reached the top of the rope five seconds later she was gone, together with his shorts and sandals. Bareassed, barefoot, lugging his military equipment, massaging his chilled, shriveled and retracted organic equipment, he danced over the hot sandstone and caught up with her at the great dome of naked rock that overhung his secret camp. Hayduke's place, the raider's roost, the outlaw hideout. Fort Heiduk, as Doctor Sarvis once had named it.

Bonnie waited by the iron eyebolt driven into the rimrock of the overhang. Smiling at her memories, she squatted on her heels, chin resting on her thumbs, and stared across the labyrinth of canyons below, of pinnacles and needles and arches and fins and balanced rocks and canyon walls beyond, toward Grand Canyon and the maze of buttes, volcanic necks, mesas, plateaus and blue-hazed snow-crested mountains in the distant south.

Hayduke approached, also squatted — the naked ape — and without a word passed his rope through the slick smooth eye of the bolt to the halfway point and tossed the doubled line over the brow of the cliff.

Aroused from her reverie, Bonnie looked at bolt and rope and shuddered. "Oh God, George . . . do we have to go that way? *Abseilen?*"

"No, you don't. Take the fuckin' trail if you want to. That way's two hours, this way's two minutes. Your choice." He pulled a diaper sling of new white nylon webbing and three locking carabiners, two with brakebars, from the pockets of his shorts.

She stared at the rim, the abyss of insubstantial air below. "I hate going over that edge."

"Your choice." He held the ready-made sling toward her; it resembled, sort of, a man's jockstrap.

"Oh Lord." Sighing with dread, she stepped into it and drew it up, snug in the crotch and firm around her hips. Hayduke watched, his interest showing. "Put your pants on," she said.

Ignoring her suggestion, he clipped the doubled rope to the sling with the carabiners, running it over both brakebars, screw-locked the gates, and checked and double-checked, tugging hard, for safety.

"Okay," he said, "you're ready. Over you go."

Her back to the edge, she looked over her shoulder toward the awful drop-off. Fifty feet straight down, a free rappel, and then a sixty-yard traverse across a pitch of steeply sloping slickrock (with aids) to Hayduke's cave.

"Oh I hate this." She faced him, her lovely eyes wide, her full red lips trembling. "Will you belay me?"

He grinned. "Say that again?"

"*Be*-lay, schmucko, *be*-lay."

"Only got the one rope here, Bonnie."

"There's one in my pack." She turned her back to him. "Bottom pocket."

He unzipped the bottom pocket and pulled out her ninety-foot climbing rope. Heavier than needed, much shorter than it should be, but it would do for a belay here. Standing behind her, he looped one end around her slender chest, under the arms, and secured it with a bowline. And then, unable to resist such proximate temptation — and what man could? — he embraced her, cupping her breasts in his hands, and nibbled on her neck and ears, nosing aside her fall of wavy, fragrant, chestnut hair.

She stiffened but did not resist. "George . . . George . . . Strictly business, remember?"

"I remember."

"Anyhow I'm pregnant."

"Me too."

"Yeah, well, get that leaky thing out of my back." She turned in his arms; now it was nosing at the buttons of her shirt, impinging on her bellybutton. "Gross. Will you put your shorts on please!" She started to back away but the abyss lay behind her. "Business," she repeated, "I'm here on business. Business only."

He grinned, all teeth and whiskers and crazy eyes and hairy hide. "What kind of business you have in mind?"

"You know what I mean. You said to come. Now belay me, god-damnit, or I'm going home. Stupid to come here anyhow. . . ." She leaned back on the ropes, looking down. "God, this is sickening." She closed her eyes and started to descend, very slowly, easing the doubled rope through the carabiners and over the brakebars, clutching at the belaying line with her guide hand. Not from necessity but from instinctive fear.

Hayduke belayed her, one leg braced against the eyebolt, Bonnie's rope around his waist, across his chest and over one shoulder. Both hands on the line, he paid it out as she went down.

"Okay," she shouted from below and out of sight, "gimme slack. Off belay."

He slackened the rope and looked over the edge. She at the moment was inside the alcove below, as the course of the ropes revealed, still out of his sight. "Belay off," he shouted. He pulled up the belaying rope, coiled, tied and hung it over one shoulder, buckled on his weapons, took up the doubled-over rappel rope and prepared to descend. He meant to go down boot-camp style, hand over hand, rather than wait for Bonnie to get out of the seat sling. Absolutely against all safety rules, of course, but with arms like his, his hands, Hayduke didn't worry about a fall. Also, he avoided the friction and rope burn of a bareass body rappel.

Whoa there, pardner — almost forgot the short britches. He pulled the garment on, not for modesty's sake but out of vanity, thinking of the spectacle he would otherwise offer to his waiting friend below. Vain as he was of his well-muscled body, he did not want Mrs. Sarvis studying his perineum as he came down. Not really a thing of beauty, in itself. Furthermore and anyhow he needed the five pockets. A man without pockets is like a . . . like a what? Like a kangaroo without a pouch? Like a man without a kangaroo? without a woman? That's it: a man needs a place to put things. Grinning and desperate, sweating and happy, absurd and hungry, just his own old normal self, George W. Hayduke stepped off the brink and glided from sight.

Fifteen seconds later that taut rope twitched, began to slide one-way through the eye of the bolt, swift and easy but not too swift. The free end came up, slipped through the eye and vanished, like a long Perlon snake in a considerable hurry but refusing to panic.

Silence. Soft voices.

Then the sound of a faint feminine squeal — then the sequel, feminine laughter — then the warm and happy sound, the reassuring sound, the universal and irresistible and conclusive sound of two laughing voices, male and female, commingled in universal play.

Only the hawks and eagles listened, from the rim above, only the doves and quail and bluejays from the canyon below. Nobody here but us chickens, Doc.

21
Doc's Return

Doc's turn.

Pleading physical, mental, moral and nervous exhaustion (quite justified) and the need, in consequence, for a brief interlude of open space, clean air, stillness, solitude and spiritual renewal, he borrowed her little Suzuki Sepuku jeepette and headed for the desert. As any wise man must, in springtime, in the autumn of his soul, when the need is great. Where all the Hebrew prophets went to regenerate their visions, where the Indian shamans and Hindu mystics found their oracle, where the great Lao-Tzu was headed (Sinkiang) when the border guard detained him for long enough to write his tiny little open-ended giant of a book (the *Tao Te Ching*).

Told her he'd be back within four five days. But had to have that metaphysical break. She understood, his bonnie wife, and sped him on his way with kisses, homebaked cookies, flowers, a roasted turkey and a final farewell frenzied abbzuggian fuck that shook his teeth, wrung out his loins, fibrillated his heart and left a sweet golden glow of peace upon his mind.

Yes, he had observed a renewed zest for the sexual act (and amplified tenderness) in that woman of his, ever since her return, not

long before, from her own vacation solitaire. Wherever that had really
been. Doc never inquired into such matters, respecting her private
need for whatever it was she needed on such occasions. Possibly an
offstage lover? supplemental sex? Very well, he could accept it pro-
viding that she didn't bore him with details, flaunt names in his face,
do anything malicious or cruel. He knew that he was no great lover,
never had been, and nearly twice her age could not hope to satisfy the
legitimate animal desires of a healthy, wholesome, full-blooded
woman. Doc despised the notion of what was sometimes called "open
marriage"; to him such a practice seemed more dismal and lonely than
no marriage at all. But he could understand and live with the idea (or
so he thought) of Bonnie enjoying a secret paramour, male or female,
so long as she kept it *secret*. I.e., in good taste.

So he thought. We civilized men — such bloody *decent* chaps, you
know. Passion sublimated to the love and pursuit of intellectual
titillation. Honest anger perverted into benign tolerance, joy degraded
to mere pleasure, rebellion channeled into . . . legal procedures, gen-
teel letters to the editor, the political process.

Somewhere south of Panguitch, not far from the Big Rock Candy
Mountain, Doctor Sarvis pulled off the lonely highway for a few
minutes of rest and recreation. Concealing himself behind a bush of
purple sage, like a gentleman, he unzipped and peed upon a small
anthill. The ants scurried forth howling with rage, feelers dripping,
jaws spread for a bite of flesh.

Doc backed off in time, rezipped, removed a plastic milk jug, a
plastic funnel, a can of WD-40 and a pair of gloves from the car, and
walked to the yellow front-end loader parked nearby, first in a row of
silent, giant, murderous machines, all of them spattered with what
looked, at first glance, like dried blood. Red mud, perhaps. He pulled
on the gloves.

How many months, perhaps years have I wasted? he thought,
besieging politicians, bureaucrats, and the *New York Times* with letters? . . . saving the world? . . .

He withdrew the dipstick from the loader's engine block, checked
the oil. Half quart low. He inserted his funnel, uncapped the milk jug,
poured sixty grams of lapidary grit into the crankcase, flushed the
dipstick pipe clean with a squirt of WD-40, and replaced the dipstick.
He proceeded to the next machine.

. . . sitting through tedious public hearings? questioning smug af-
fable evasive Senators at cocktail parties? contributing funds to
doomed campaigns? . . .

A car zoomed past on the highway. The driver waved. Doc waved back. Red sun sinking on the west, purple twilight creeping from the east. He pulled the dipstick from the block of a Komatsu sheep's-foot roller and repeated preceding procedures.

. . . in quixotic opposition to campaigns funded by Union Carbide, United Technologies, Exxon, Texaco, Getty Oil, Nuclear Syn-Fuels, Bechtel Construction, General Motors, Nissan Motors, Mitsubishi, Komatsu not to mention Dow Chemical, Du Pont, Monsanto, Georgia-Pacific, Weyerhauser, Westinghouse . . .

He treated a Case road-grader, a Mitsubishi crawler-tractor and a Caterpillar backhoe as he had the others, playing fair, and then — jug empty — returned to Bonnie's Jap jeep and drove on, southward into the dusk, bound for what he had not mentioned to his wife: Fort Heiduk.

. . . Hayduke. Heiduk: heiduk (hī′ dūk), n. [Hung. *hzei,* beyond, outside of < *djuzk,* wall, enclosure, sty], 1. bandit, brigand, outlaw. 2. rebel soldier, insurgent, guerrilla warrior. Saving the world. But how, why? Saving the world was only a hobby.

At midnight he drove through the town of Hotrocks — nothing open but a Circle K store, where he refueled the Suzuki — crossed the state line, passed the Buckskin Tavern where two cowboys were puking on their cowboy shoes in the parking lot, left the paved highway and followed a graded dirt road deep into the Arizona Strip. Public land; no man's land, no, nor woman's either; a region free of human habitation but not "uninhabited." *Tout au contraire!* Inhabited most fully and complete by pronghorn antelope, bighorn sheep, mule deer, wild horses, desert tortoise, mountain lion, black bear, coyote, fox and badger and a host of smaller mammals, reptiles, birds, bugs, butterflies and obnoxious quite unnecessary arachnids. And the usual seasonal infestation of subsidized beef cattle. Shifting into four-wheel drive, he left the main dirt road for a secondary dirt road, for a tertiary dirt road, for a primitive trail road, for a jeep track, opening a number of barbed-wire gates en route, and leaving them open. The unwritten rule of the range was "Always leave gates as you find them." Doc found them more attractive in the open position. Someday, he thought, we'll drive all these stinking public-lands cattle onto the highways, where they belong, herd them back to Texas, where they come from, feed them to the alligators, where they'll serve a purpose. Force the ranchers off the welfare rolls.

Weary but excited under the blazing shoals of stars, exhilarated by his sense of an ancient freedom now recovered, however briefly, Doc set up his folding cot among the sand dunes and flowers, unrolled his sleeping bag on the cot and went to bed. Now I lay me down to sleep. His last vision, before the dreamtime overwhelmed him, was of two meteors with intersecting paths, falling across the southern sky. Combatants crossing swords? An omen of cosmic conflict? George Heiduk's signature?

Old men wake early, no matter when they turn in. Doc's eyes opened in the gray twilight of dawn. He saw a morning primrose, petals folded, nodding at him in the breeze. Saw beetle tracks like sutures stitching a bank of damp sand. Heard the whisper of wild ricegrass sweeping its arc of dune. Saw the legs of a horse. Many legs.

Horse?

He looked higher, saw the Roman head of an aging gray, the shaggy mane, the dark red-veined bulging eyes big as cueballs mounted in the sockets of a thin-skinned skull. The horse stared at Doc, strands of ricegrass dangling from its flabby muzzle, green drool dripping from a nickel-plated bit.

Bit? Bridle? Reins? A rider? Yes. The Masked Man sat upon his saddle on the middle of his sagging horse. His gloved hands rested on the pommel, holding reins and a lead rope. His huge hilarious Hollywood-cowboy hat, once pure white and stiff as cardboard, now gray with filth and sweat and salt, floppy and frayed around the brim, rested on his small head. He wore the tight pullover shirt, no buttons, with lace-up collar, and the pants and the boots and the two big ivory-handled shooting irons in the tooled and silver-mounted holsters.

A second horse bridled, saddled but riderless, stood behind the first.

Doc raised himself on one elbow, alarmed by these apparitions. The man was obviously mad; was he also dangerous? Doc carried no weapon, never did, nothing in his pockets but a tiny penknife, his lucky crystal, a few coins. He looked around in all directions: no sign of Hayduke, although he knew he had entered Hayduke space. The trouble with the concept of Hayduke space, of course, was that the boundaries of Hayduke space were vague, indefinite, fluctuating, highly variable, resembling in some respects the singular universe postulated by the mathematician Albert Einstein, viz., finite but boundless.

"Morning," Doc mumbled.

The Lone Ranger stared at him, mounted motionless on a motionless mount. Except for the movement of hairs in the horse's mane, stirred by the winds of dawn, the rider and both the horses might have been carved from wood.

"Well . . ." Doc unzipped his bag, swung out his legs, fumbled on his loose khaki trousers, stepped into his loafers. Something wriggled against his bare foot. In sudden horror, thinking of scorpions, he kicked off the shoe. A black beetle fell out and froze rigid on the sand, posterior elevated in defensive posture. Doc slipped the shoe on again. He looked at the man on the horse. "Get down," he said, "I'll make some coffee." He shuffled about, pulled a Coleman stove from the cargo area of the Suzuki Sepuku, set it up on the hood. "Where's Tonto?" He pointed his nose at the second horse.

The Lone Ranger made no reply to this query. It was indeed a senseless question: if accompanied by Tonto, how could he be, actually, a lone ranger?

"Split the blanket, eh?" But Doc did not pursue the matter. Everyone knew anyhow the end of the saga. Doc poured water into the pot and set it on the gas fire. "So where's George? He around?"

A faint smile flitted across the Masked Man's lips. The mask, in this case, had become merely another pair of dark sunglasses. His glance shifted, for a moment, from the tall bulky figure of Doctor Sarvis to the even taller bulkier sand dune at Doc's side.

Doc opened a small paper sack of his favorite, specially ground Colombian coffee. He'd been boycotting bananas, and table grapes, and Coors beer, and rainforest beef, and then all beef, for years now, but he could not and would not give up coffee, no matter how noble the cause. "I said," the doctor repeated, hearing no reply, "is George around? You two hang out together, don't you?"

Sand began to spill from the slipface of the dune. Two big hands appeared, a head with leather sombrero, a grin with whiskers. "What's up, Doc?"

Sarvis was startled but concealed it well. "Thought I smelled you, George. You still have that jungle rot under your big toenails?"

"Yeah . . . and I ain't takin' no fuckin' Nizoral neither. What do you got for breakfast, Doc? I'm hungry. My buddy here's hungry. We're both hungry."

"Anticipated, my young friend. Open that cooler. You'll find everything your redneck heart desires: James Dean sausage, Sowbelly bacon, Canadian bacon, Israeli bacon (kosher), Francis Bacon, Triple-A eggs, cow butter, half-and-half, and of course a case of Dos Equis — breakfast beer. Should not have brought it, I know, don't want to encourage your kidney stones, but, well, frankly . . ." Driveling on, talking talking saying nothing, Doc did his best to steady the tremor in his hands, the cold dread in his heart. Why? Why did I come here? Why did I do this? What madness overcame me? Never meant to see this satanic lad again for so long as I lived. . . .

Hayduke emerged fully from the dune, dripping sand, like Michelangelo's David from Carrara marble, sort of, when he heard the word "case". No, won't do, try again, Doc. Doc thought. He thought, like some rough beast slouching from the sands of Sinai, hitchhiking toward Bethlehem? No, not right. Think again. What creature, mythological or biological, ever came forth from sand? The Sphinx from its ruins? sidewinder? Lawrence of Arabia? whiptail lizard? sand Papago? sand witch? wizard? wog? frog? turtle? tortoise? No go. He measured enough coffee for nine big cups into the simmering water and added one for good measure.

Hayduke tossed a bottle of beer to his companion sitting on the gray gelding — the horse shied, the bottle flew beyond the Lone Ranger's grasp — and opened one for Doc and one for himself. They touched bottles. "God old Doc. I knew you'd show up."

"Cheers. Didn't really mean to, George. Got lost on the road last night."

Hayduke grinned. "Sure. You betcha. Bring any H.E.? *Plastique?* gelatin?"

"We don't touch that stuff anymore."

"All right, I'll raid Love's powder magazine again. Get it free there. How about money? Need about ten thousand."

"What for?"

"You don't need to know. Not yet. Got it?"

"Maybe and maybe not, George. You won't believe this, but Bonnie and I don't really have that kind of ready cash these days."

"Never heard of a poor doctor. About as rare as poor fuckin' beef ranchers, poor Senators, poor land developers, poor corporation lawyers, poor fuckin' CEOs."

Doctor Sarvis filled three coffee mugs and passed them around, handing one up to the silent man in the Ray Ban mask. He didn't seem to want to get off his horse. Maybe, like Seldom Smith, he was at home nowhere but on a horse, rowing a boat or wedged partway inside a woman. He came back to Hayduke. "What's the plan, George? I suppose I could cash in a few C.D.s, although they don't mature till August. You have a plan? The Super-G.E.M., I suppose?"

"Don't even suppose. Yet." Hayduke dropped his beer bottle, empty already, and sipped at the hot coffee. "What's a C.D.? What do you mean they 'mature'? Sounds like some kind of fuckin' — premature baby maybe?"

"No need to know, George, no need to know. You'll never need to know that. But if you want me to finance one of your schemes again you'll have to tell me at least a little about it." Sarvis glanced at the Lone Ranger; the man had drifted off — coffee mug in hand — toward the summit of the highest nearby dune. Keeping watch.

"Don't worry about Jack," Hayduke said. "He was cutting fence before I was even born. Before you got out of fuckin' prep school. Old Jack there, he's got only one thing on his mind: revenge."

"Revenge for what?"

Hayduke looked surprised. "What country you live in, Doc? You forget what it was like out here, only forty years ago? Only twenty? ten?"

The good doctor looked about. Sand dunes, flowers, beetle tracks and scrubby little junipers flourishing their limbs from sandstone slickrock. Wolf Hole Mountain to the northwest. Pariah Plateau to the east. Kaibab Plateau on the south. Grand Canyon on the southwest. Hayduke's never-never land of pinnacles and caves, box canyons, minarets and mighty phallic hard-ons in between. Lost Eden and Radium Canyons with their waterfalls and pools, hanging gardens and cliff dwellings, arches, alcoves and natural bridges. Mountains with real timber and real bear and real snow in the distance.

"You mean here?"

"You know what I mean. The fuckin' West, that's all. He wants revenge. And so do I."

"Still looks good from here."

Hayduke finished his second beer. "Tell you what we're gonna do," he said.

22
Seldom's Return

Smith hobbled his horse near the stream in the ample shade of a cottonwood. A deposit of dried cowdung attested to the popularity of this particular tree. He looked up and down the canyon floor, listened, heard nothing, then looked aloft at the secret eyrie four hundred feet above on the south-facing canyon wall.

There was a great cave there, under the rim, its roof a royal arch formed by ancient conchoidal fractures. Inside that cave (or grotto or recess) was space enough to enclose the capitol dome of the state assembly building. Shady in summer, mostly sunny in winter, it seemed an ideal site of an Anasazi village, but had never been so utilized. Why not? Because access, up steep pitches of bare rock, was too difficult, and because the vertical distance from the canyon bottom, where the bean patches and cornfields would have been, to the cave made it undesirable. An idyllic place for a desperate last stand; very nice for fighting and killing and dying; but for raising a family, keeping your wives happy, getting along with the neighbors, re-enacting tribal traditions through ritual and dance, a place for the kids to play — not practical.

Such, at least, was Seldom S. Smith's theory.

He unsaddled his mount, brushed its sweaty back with juniper twigs, crushed a blood-fat horsefly sucking on the horse's neck and started up the slope toward the base of the cliff. He carried a pair of saddlebags filled with such delicacies as bourbon whisky and tinned baby clams over one shoulder, his coiled calf rope over the other. The big one-gallon canteen he left behind in the shade of the saddle tipped on its horn. No need to carry water on this hike; there was a small but permanent spring, as Seldom knew, deep within the cave.

At the crest of the talus he came to a wall of bare, smooth sandstone ten feet high, sheer and overhanging, unscalable. Smith removed two pitons with snap links and loops attached, from their hiding place beneath a juniper log, advanced to a certain point on the wall, felt about, and placed the pitons, one above and to the left of the first, deep in a pair of holes drilled into the stone. The holes were invisible from below. Aided by these devices, he ascended easily to the narrow bench above, pulled out the pitons from above, and went on, following an unmarked route. Traversing back and forth, climbing from ledge to ledge with the aid of the pitons, taking his good old time, he reached the big cave in about half an hour.

Robber's roost:

Standing in the sunshine, on the level dusty rock-strewn floor of the cave, Smith could make out nothing of the interior: the glaring contrast between light and shade was too profound for the human eye to span. He looked down, saw his horse far below, standing in the shade of the cottonwood, nosing at the ricegrass. With his eyes he followed the shining little watercourse, its pools and pale sand, on a meandering journey under the canyon walls, around the next bend and out of sight, toward the junction with Radium Canyon miles beyond. Nobody down there. Nobody human.

He looked into the cave, shading his eyes, listening. He could see very little, heard nothing. A board leaned on a stone, the words "BEWARE SARPINT" burned in its surface. Smith smiled and limped on high-heeled boots into the darkness, out of the glare, shut his eyes for a minute, opened them.

The outlaw's den:

A narrow tattered mattress on the ground, folded tarp, tightly rolled sleeping bag. Wooden crates containing a few fire-blackened pots and pans, tin plate, skillet, G.I. canteen cup, knife, fork, wooden spoon. Canned goods. Canteens and waterjugs. A half-dozen greasy paperback books. A stack of topographic maps. A few crushed beercans lying in the dirt. A pint bottle of Wild Turkey, empty. Nearby was a fireplace with iron grill, black as soot, and a stack of dead juniper and scrub oak. Two Desert brand alkali-stained waterbags of Scottish flax hung from pegs in the wall of the cave; both were dry, contents evaporated.

Smith noted the dry waterbags. He felt the ashes of the fireplace: cold. Thirsty from the strenuous climb in the noon sun, he stepped farther into the interior, under the smoke-blackened stone, deep into the cool dark recesses of the cave where the ceiling curved down to meet the floor. A small side of beef hung on baling wire from a piton driven into the rock: slow elk, range maggot, some cow's calf that had failed to clear out of the territory in time. Served the little bastard right, trespassing on our public land — but he felt, nevertheless, the twinge of culture shock, the horror of lese majesty, the violation of a deep taboo, that came to anyone born and raised in the American West. A hanging offense, worse than murder.

Holy cow, thought Seldom, that boy he done poached another of Love's little beeves — just hain't got no proper fear of nothin'. Instinctively, with a shudder of dread, Smith glanced back over his shoulder, half expecting to see, huge against the light and sky at the cave's mouth, the black silhouette of an irate, outraged and all-powerful cattleman. With rope. Or *cattleperson*, as he understood they were called these days, in deference to the growing feminist element among ranch owners.

Smith thought of Ol' Waylon:

> Let's all help cowpersons
> Sing the blues

And of Willie & Waylon:

> Mamas don't let your babies
> Grow up to be stockpersons

Or if a waitress is now a waitron then a cowboy should be a cowtron? Or if a chairman is only a chair then a cowboy is only a cow?

Smith was troubled by these subtle distinctions.

But not much. And not often.

He knelt at the spring. Water dripped from the ceiling and walls of the cave, which were streaked with alkali and other salts, but the water was sweet enough to be potable. In fact, after that half-mile four-hundred-foot climb over bare rock, at an angle mostly of sixty degrees or steeper, the water here always tasted pretty doggone good, in Seldom's opinion. He was not a connoisseur of arid-land springs, seeps, *tinajas*, potholes, waterpockets, log troughs, bogholes, frog ponds, stocktanks, irrigation ditches, mining flumes, hoofholes in a mudslide and such, like his old buddy the wilderness avenger, but he had tasted some H_2O here and there, form time to time, when the absence of same would have meant uncomfortable death by leisurely degrees, and thought he knew the essential difference between drinking water and that peculiar solution of chlorine, nitrates, industrial solvents, herbicides and reprocessed sewage effluent that came when summoned from the taps and faucets of Tucson Arizona, Salt Lake City Utah, Denver Colorado, and similar apogees of high techno-civ. He'd been there, several times; once was enough.

The walls were sweating with moisture. The moisture leaked and dripped and oozed from hairline seams in the stone, converged in minute rivulets over beds of pale algae (here where the sun never shone) and pooled a foot deep behind a tiny dam which human hands had fashioned, from mud and rocks, across the bottom ledge. An old tin dipper, its blue enamel flaking off, rested on the dam. Smith dipped the dipper into the little reservoir, lifted up the cool clear water, and drank. Simplest of ceremonies, sweetest of rites, in the land of stone and sun.

Thirst slaked, he got up and wandered about the cave, not meaning to snoop, but lured irresistibly by the fascination of poking around in another man's private quarters, seeing his secret life exposed and vulnerable. Not that there was much to see or anything revealing a hidden side. He found a string of beef jerky drying on a line, a small footlocker in which his friend probably kept a medical kit, spare clothes and an ammo supply, a pair of K mart's Taiwan sandals in the dust, a ragged pair of denim shorts, a packbag heavy with coiled rope and mountaineering hardware, two folding camp chairs, nothing much else. Nothing that could possibly be seen from the canyon below. Or even from an airplane flying low; everything was cached, stashed, set up or laid down back from the cave's opening, deep in the shadows.

He walked across the width of the cave, a hundred fifty feet or so, from the secret camp to an ancient granary of stone mortared with mud, four feet high, in which some Anasazi farmer had stored his corn, his beans, his squash, seven or eight hundred years ago. The only opening was in the roof. He set aside a blocking stone and looked down inside. Darkness, black as sin and dense as pitch, greeted his eyes. What's my boy got in there, I wonder? Don't think I wanta know.

Smith returned to the cave's living quarters, satisfied with his explorations, ready to sit a spell and build a drink, wait for the caveman's return. He reached for one of the folding camp chairs leaning against an apple-box, started to pick it up. At once he felt a thrill of vibration, like an electric current, and heard the warning whir of rattles. He dropped the chair. Staring at it, he saw a fine nylon string, like fishing line, leading from a leg of the chair over the stone floor and into the dust behind the crates. Unable to resist temptation, Smith tugged on the line and a fat diamondback, five feet long, came gliding into view, black tongue out, tail up and twitching.

Smith dropped the line. The snake stopped, watching him, recoiling itself in defensive position. Well, sheet, thought Seldom, who but *him* would keep a goldarn buzzworm around for a watchdog. Smith picked up the chair again and dragged the snake — tied by the neck tethered to the chair, furious with indignation — about fifty feet away, what he judged to be a comfortable distance. He returned to the living quarters and unfolded the second chair, muttering to himself:

Picket that there ol' rattler. Never did much like em' around myself, particular at night when a man needs a little shut-eye. Like my daddy always said, if them other snakes can get along without poison why can't a rattler? Stands to reason.

Hobble them snakes. Or stamp your brand on their hip and turn 'em loose but why keep 'em around camp at night? No sense in it. Man gets up in the dark to take a leak, unlimbers the wrong snake, then what? Dangerous critters. Kind of cute to look at, maybe, but no comfort a-tall when they get chilly and crawl inside your bedroll at two o'clock in the morning. Gets awful crowded awful quick.

The rattlesnake grew quiet. Smith opened his saddlebags, took out the quart of bourbon, unsealed the cap, had a sip. Out of habit he nearly threw the cap away but thought better of that. Never drank alone here before. Should never drink alone anywhere. He recapped the bottle, went to the spring with a waterbag, filled it, returned to the chair and mixed himself a decent highball, half and half, in the Government Issue canteen cup. Hain't my fault he ain't here; maybe I will drink the whole damn quart my loneself.

Out of curiosity he looked at the books in the wooden crate. *The Blaster's Handbook* from Du Pont, the Holy Bible, Dr. Fishbein's *Complete Home Medical Guide, Welcome to Australia!* by the British Ministry of Prisons, *Complete Poems of Robert Service, Welcome to*

Leavenworth! — An Inmate's Guide, The Cadillac Owner's Complete Shop Manual, Oriental Despotism by Wittfogel and *Decline of the West* by Oswald Spengler. And yes, a cheap paperback copy of *The Monkey Wrench Gang*, tattered, greasy, dog-eared, heavily annotated with scornful exclamation points, mocking question marks, sneering and searing commentary. Smith had inspected all of these books before, several times; nothing new had been added for years.

He poured himself a second drink, listening to the profound stillness of the cave, the canyon below, the sky above and beyond. Profound but not absolute: he heard a wren's clear rippling song, the distant drone of a light airplane. Could get the hell outa here before he comes back, Seldom reflected, save myself some grief later. 'Course he'll know I was here, bootprints all over the floor, smell of Wild Turkey in his cup, fresh horseshit below. But if I don't see him, don't talk to him, I don't make any promises, right? And no promises, no misery. I got a good idea what that boy has in mind anyhow and I don't think I need that kind of trouble.

Smith noted the position of sunlight and shadow on the cave's floor near the mouth. Give him one more hour. Then I skedaddle. Nobody can't say that ain't fair. He want to talk to me so bad let him come visit at Green River. Or Cedar City. Or Hotrocks. He knows where I live. (So does Oral and Love and them secret police men from Washington, D.C. Well, that hain't my fault neither.)

Holy Moses but it's lonesome here. Wonder how he can do it. No wonder he ain't here but now and then. Him and that Lone Ranger. Wonder where that old screwball stays? Probly too stiff and creaky to climb up here. Probly has his own cave anyhow, somewhere close by, two three miles away. Them types like their privacy. Would sure kill me but I guess they like it. If you could keep a nice woman here might not be too bad. Maybe two of 'em — one for each end. Of the cave I mean. And one more down in the canyon, build her a cabin, spade up a garden for her, run a ditch in, plant melons, keep her barefoot and pregnant, be just like old times.

Only women don't care for that kinda life anymore. And never did, probly.

Can't say I blame 'em one bit.

The shadow of the overhanging wall had advanced to the granary at the far corner. Smith downed his third drink, unloaded the presents he had brought — the tinned clams, a sack of pistachio nuts, a loaf of Susan's homemade bread, two pounds of real longhorn cheese, pipe tobacco and a new corncob pipe, most of the bottle of bourbon —

slung his rope and empty saddlebags over his shoulder and left the cave.

Through sunlight and shadow he descended the scary spooky dizzy canyon wall, following no trail, for there was no trail, no marks blazes cairns, no clue to the one only possible route except his memory, climbing down from ledge to ledge by rope (cowboy style), traversing the narrow benches in between, sometimes making a mistake and being forced to seek again, feeling the tremors of fatigue in his knee joints, thighs, hams, until finally he reached the safety and ease of the talus slope at the foot of the wall. He rehid the pitons in their place — surreptitiously in case he was, despite appearances, under hostile observation — and angled down to the canyon floor, taking care to leave no tracks. (Hard to hide anything on the open tabula rasa of the desert.)

He found his horse, undid the hobbles, led her back to the saddle, saddled up. Still no sight sound nor smell of the man in the leather sombrero. By Gawd, he thought, smiling inwardly with relief. By Gawd . . . He put his foot in the stirrup and mounted up. Never really wanted to come here anyhow. Whole trip some kind of funny mistake. Ducking his head, he rode from beneath the big cottonwood and headed up-canyon at a smooth-gaited trot, following the dim path beside the stream that led to Pucker Pass, Joint Trail, the secret shortcut over Whale's Back and down through the Whale's Eye to Slickrock Towers, The Silent City, Goblin Valley, Red Knob, Hoodoo Arch and the open sand dune country beyond — from there an easy day's ride to Hotrocks or to Kathy's ranch, if you knew the route and if you knew where to look for water and if your horse was in good condition. No sir, Smith said to himself, nobody can't say I didn't try. Not my fault you can't never find that boy when you're a-lookin' for him. Smiling, heart at ease and riding easy, he watched the evening shadows stretch before him, the rich amber light that glowed on rock and sand, juniper and cottonwood, the purple bloom of sage. Yessir, should be home for breakfast. . . .

A horse and rider stepped from behind a boulder, blocking his path. A big horse, an armed rider, a big grin flashing in the shadow of a wide-brimmed smoke-colored salt-rimed old and ridiculous leather hat.

Smith stopped. He looked up. Another rider watched him from the rocks above; he too was armed. Naturally.

Silence.

"Lookin' for somebody?"

"No sir, not me. Horse got lost. Give this beast her head she always goes the wrong way."

"You're fuckin' late."

"Not me."

"Yeah you. Late."

"Late for what?"

"We'll talk about it. You got some time?"

"Reckon I might or might not. How much time?"

"Oh fuck, I don't know, all night maybe and a bottle of whisky, that should do it. What do you say, pardner?"

What do I say? he thought. Goldang it all anyhow, what can I say? Goodbye Susan, goodbye Kathy, goodbye Sheila, goodbye peace and quiet, goodbye world, here we go again. . . .

23

The Baron's Attack

The Baron taxied the little Cessna to the end of the dirt strip and stopped beside his truck. Working fast and efficiently, he removed the door on the passenger's side of the plane, then the passenger's seat. Quickly he loaded this enlarged cargo space with one-gallon plastic containers, the cheap lightweight kind used for the retailing of cow's milk. Each jug was bulging, filled to capacity with black latex all-weather paint, caps taped on for security. The jugs, taped together through the handles in sets of ten, totaled one hundred gallons or eight hundred pounds. Such a load exceeded the safe carrying capacity of the aircraft, but the pilot had calculated that if he over-ran the south end of the airstrip and dropped into the Grand Canyon beyond he could probably gain enough momentum to become airborne. If not he would simply crash-land on the river, preferably above or below the whitewater rapids at Badger Creek; his chances of survival should be excellent. If he didn't forget to fasten his lifejacket. As for the plane, no problem, it wasn't his.

All was ready. He lowered the goggles on his leather helmet, fastened the chin strap. Revving the single engine to maximum rpm's, the Baron released the brakes and lunged down the runway toward the gaping abyss of the canyon one-half mile away. The brush, slabs of sunburnt rock, scattered horses, flashed by on his left and right. A cow and calf stared stupidly at him from the end of the strip. Gaining speed. Should be in the air by the time he got that far. Faster, faster; he adjusted the wing tabs, as he had seen it done before, pulled the throttle out farther, drew back on the wheel. Nothing happened; heavy as a truck, the Cessna sped forward but did not leave the ground.

So. Committed. He pulled the throttle to full speed and kept going, racing onward at seventy, eighty mph. The cow and her calf, hesitating, gaping at the metal bird roaring toward them, scampered aside within inches of destruction. The plane burst through the warning lights at the runway's end, charged over blackbrush and prickly pear, bounced over some rocks and cleared the canyon rim a hundred yards beyond.

Now, quite suddenly, he had plenty of air.

The river wound like a thread of silver far below; the opposite canyon wall loomed above his nose, approaching rapidly as he dove toward it. Elevation: 3800 feet above sea level, 700 feet above the river. Airspeed: 122 and accelerating. The Baron banked the plane to the right, heading upriver and directly toward the foaming tumult of Badger Creek Rapids. He could see a flotilla of rubber rafts forming a line in the pool above the rapids; a teeming mass of pale faces, staring up at him, came closer and closer at a brisk velocity.

The Baron checked his lifejacket. Christ! he'd forgotten to fasten the damned thing. Too late now. He needed both hands simply to control the mad dive of the aircraft. He stepped on the footbrakes: useless gesture. He pulled back on the wheel; slowly, steadily, the plane began to level off. He roared above the cringing humans in the rafts, clearing their heads by a safe and sane three feet, and continued upriver, fully airborne at last, more or less, though having difficulty gaining altitude.

He whipped around the next bend in the canyon. A bridge popped into view directly before him, an arch of steel spanning the canyon from rim to rim. He flew under it, aware of clusters of tourists on the roadway staring down at him, boatloads of tourists staring up.

Airspeed: 110. He struggled for altitude, eager to get above the narrow winding confinement of the canyon walls. The plane climbed a couple of hundred feet, the walls dropped away, the boat ramp at Lee's Ferry swept past beneath his wings, the deep dark narrow gorge of Glen Canyon — like a hairless vagina, solid Navajo sandstone — beckoned from ahead.

He plunged into it. Not that he really wanted to. But he'd gone too far to attempt to circle and climb. He flew onward, banking right, left, left again, then right, with the snakey meanders of the canyon, wingtips almost grazing the stone ramparts. Gradually the plane climbed. He had nearly reached rimrock again, four thousand feet above sea level, when suddenly, dramatically, completely, unavoidably, the dam appeared.

The dam. *That dam.* Glen Canyon Dam. That goddamned unforgivable dam.

The Baron's lips twisted in a grin of fiendish glee. At full speed he shot beneath another highway bridge and flew straight toward the vast blank concave cement face of the world's most despised and hated dam. He aimed himself to the right and a little above the powerhouse at the dam's base, took his foot off the brakes and jammed it against his cargo of black milkjugs, pulled back on the wheel and soared steeply upward to the left.

He pushed. The milkjugs tumbled out, set after set, sailing in graceful arcs toward the dam's facade. The Cessna climbed, slowing quickly; stall warning lights glared red, a buzzer snarled, the plane oozed over the rim of the dam like a sick butterfly and on to safety while in its rear the black jugs exploded one by one, *a staccato,* against pale gray concrete.

The Baron was not finished. Half his jugs remained. He banked above the bilge-green waters of stagnant Lake Powell, circled west and approached the dam's face for a second bomb run, this time coming in from the left and climbing out to the right.

He shoved and kicked them out, the last five sets, fifty gallons of black latex, cleared the rim of the dam by a few feet, leveled and gained speed, banked and climbed and circled high for a good look at his work. On the way he noticed clots and clutches of sightseers, bouquets of pink dim faces staring up, and even detected a few men in uniform scribbling notes, jabbering into radios. They'd have the Cessna's I.D. number now. So what? The craft was the property of the U.S. Bureau of Reclamation — a taxpayer-financed article.

The Baron circled again for one more viewing, pleased with what he saw, what all the tourists on the highway and in the visitor center saw: a huge black spattered "X" upon the dam's massive face, the "X" of condemnation, of doom implacable, inescapable, complete and certain. The Baron's sign, his mark, his signature.

Grim grin on his thin lips, stern satisfaction in his goggled eyes, the Baron waggled wings in farewell to the onlookers below and set his course south-southwest, bearing for the dirt strip where this flight began, for his waiting motor vehicle which would bear him away in quick escape to the high cool forests of the Kaibab, cocktails and dinner at Jacob Lake, a restful evening in a reserved motel room, an hour of meditation with the Book of Mormon. Then beddy-bye and a well-earned sleep.

First, of course, he had to find that little airfield beyond Badger Creek and set the airplane down in one piece and comfort at the proper attitude. The task would require thought and some concentration but he felt confident; he had seen it done before. Many times.

24
Earth First! Rendezvous

They straggled in from everywhere that's dim, obscure, unsavory, crawling from the woodwork and creeping out from beneath stones, coming by jeep and bus and horse and bicycle and pickup truck and railroad boxcar and Cadillac convertible from Barton, Vermont to San Diego, California, from Key Largo, Florida to Homer, Alaska, a motley crude Coxey's army of the malcontent, the discontent, the madly visionary, the vengeful revolutionist, the pipe-smoking field-trained deep ecologist, the misty-eyed tree-hugging Nature Lover, the sober conservationist, the native American 1/16th Chippewa Mother Earth Goddess, the mountain man in buckskin with fringes, the mountain girl in doeskin gown and flowered headband, the beer-drinking fun-loving gun-happy trailbusters in sweat-rich camouflage T-shirts and worn-out steel-sole jungle boots, the zealot-eyed unisexual fun-hating sectarian Marxists in corduroy and workman shirts, the pot-smoking flower kids sagging into middle age, Vietnam vets hiding in the woods, desert rats baked on the rocks, swamp hogs soaked in muck, misanthropic redneck pseudo-intellectuals steeped in Thoreau and Garrett Hardin, a few wolf-howling goose-honking owl-hooting elk-bugling Neanderthalian macho mystics, three socio-feminist Furies in baggy dungarees and steel-toed ball-crushers, straw-haired Ned Luddites in bare feet and faded Osh-Kosh B'Gosh bib overalls, Pleistocene naturists with firedrills and panpipes and no clothes at all, a shifting number of uniformed observers from the Park Service, Forest Service and Bureau of Land Management and shifty numbers of spies and informers garishly disguised as 1960s hippies representing the same (and other) Federal, state and county law-enforcement agencies.

Plus Erika, Girl-Viking, Nordic goddess of beauty, last name unknown, representing the song of Norway, the mind of Arne Naess, the spirit of Grieg, Nielsen, Sibelius, the beauty of Greta Garbo.

And somewhere in the mob young J. Oral Hatch, R.M., masquerading as a flower child from Dipstick, Utah.

Totally absent from this convention were any bureaucrats above the rank of patrol ranger, any elected official other than county sheriff, any officers of national conservation or environmental organizations, or any correspondents from the national press. Many such had been invited; none appeared.

Maybe they'd tried to come but got lost. The Rendezvous convened this year deep in a national forest, high on the Kaibab Plateau, far out on the north rim (the clean and decent rim) of the The Awful Grand Canyon of the Colorado. State of Arizona. Land of the horned toad, the Gila monster, the cone-nosed kissing bug, the sidewinder rattlesnake, the lung fungus, Barry Goldwater, congressmen Eldon Rudd and Bob Stump, jumping cactus, whiptail scorpion, the Udall brothers, hairy tarantula, brown recluse, black widow, *Arizona Highways* magazine, *American West* magazine, slime mold, eight-inch centipede, No-See-Um, fire ant, killer bee, a newspaper known as the *Arizona Daily Estrellita* ("La Voz de Lata Mejico en Baja Arizona"), cowshit, cowfly, barfly, buttonfly, cowperson ("Yoohoo buckaroo!"), cattleperson ("Who ya runnin' for State Senate this year?"; "Huh? I'm spozed to remember the dingbat's name?"), solpugid, Jerusalem cricket, giant cockroach, coral snake, diamondback buzzworm, Dennis DeConcini, bubonic plague, Peter McDonald, fetal alcoholism, liver fluke, bark scorpion, vinegaroon, Phoenix-Tucson, giardia, Syn-Fuels, Phelps-Dodge, Del Webb, IBM, Hughes Aircraft, commercial astronomy, kidney stones, Roy Drachman, U.S. Air Force, the Bonano brothers, old drug money, old real estate money, old multiple-organ inverted-sphincter transplant money, and — growth. *Growth.* GROWTH. GROWTH. . . .

True sagebrush patriots, the Earth First! Sixth National Round River (from a phrase by Aldo Leopold) Rendezvous began, as always, on the Fourth of July. Independence Day. War & Revolution Day. Death Before Dishonor Live Wild or Die Don't Tread On Me Give Me Liberty or Give Me Damnitall Coors? or Budweiser? Day. Seven days of fun, frolic and anarchy.

The welcoming address to some five or six hundred assorted riffraff was delivered by Dave Foreman, unacknowledged non-leader ("We're all leaders"), founding father (one of several), editor of the *Earth First! Journal,* and principal Earth First! Spoke:

Big and burly, bearded and bellicose, native-born son-of-the-pioneers Southwesterner, one-time shoer of horses, packer of mules, Marine Corps Officer School dropout, bow hunter and fly fisherman, lover and husband, he opened his wide smiling loud mouth and bellowed to the multitudes, to the listening pine trees, to the hovering clouds in the sky, to the rosy walls and purple depths of the Grand Canyon —

"Welcome, you posy sniffers, tree-huggers and toadstool worshippers. Glad you made it."

"Fascist!" screamed a shrill voice from the far fringes of the assembled mob. Alecto the Red-eyed —

"Eco-fascist!" screamed another. Tisiphone the Red-beaked —

"Creeping eco-fascist hyena!" screamed a third. Megaera the Red —

"Terrorist, sexist, racist, rightwing libertarian eco-brutalist!" screamed all three in chorus, snakes writhing in their hair.

" — Welcome also to the social ecology delegation from Berkeley," Foreman continued, barely missing a beat.

"Eat shit, Nazi Foreman!" screamed a slightly deeper, somewhat normal maler voice.

"Tofu to you, Doctor Mushkin," Foreman replied, and waited for the screaming, howling, grumbling and laughter to die away. "I'd also like to welcome our friends the Freddies, both those in uniform and those in the tie-dyed shirts and love beads. Please feel free to penetrate, infiltrate, conjugate or copulate whatever and whoever you can. We appreciate your interest. No secrets here. Like you heard, we're just a bunch of fascists, racists, terrorists, sexists, anarchists, communists, Young Americans for Freedom, Democrats and just plain folksy eco-freaks. If you find anybody acting respectable report them to Igor and the goon squad. If you see any illicit sexual activity report them to Bruce and the vice squad. If — "

"Homophobe!"

"If you see anybody having fun report them to the Rednecks for Social Responsibility Committee."

Foreman raised his big right fist, squeezing a beercan and spraying the front row audience with a fine mist of sweet green watery Coors. "Earth First!" he bellowed.

"No, Earth second!" the crowd responded, eager to follow wherever not led, raising a forest of fists, a thicket of flags, an effervescence of beercans.

"No, grizzly bears second!" the leader corrected.

"Naw, women!" came the response. "Men!" cried others. "Red squirrels! Dolphins! Desert turtles! Old-growth forest! Rainforest! Central Park! Bats! AIDS! Band-aids! International Monetary Fund! Androgynes! . . ."

"Down with Empire, up with Spring!" Foreman went on.

"Up yours!"

"We stand *for* what we stand *on!*"

"Shoes! Feet! Linoleum!"

"Earth First! *Terra primum!*"

"Sieg heil! Beer! Sex! Condors! Park rangers! Cowboys! Erika! George Hayduke! The Common Man! The Unknown Soldier! Jesus H. Christ! John Muir! Aldo Leopold! Henry Thoreau! Walt Whitman! Emily Dickinson! Doctor Norbert Wiener! . . ."

"Who?" said Foreman. He chugalugged his beer and shouted, "No compromise in defense of Mother Earth!"

"Yeah! No! Maybe!"

"And I thank you all for your unanimous support!" Grinning, waving tossing his empty beercan to the platform floor, Foreman started to descend, then remembered his emcee duties: "Now if you'll . . ." He waved both hands above his head, begging for some attention in the midst of the uproar of laughter, screaming, yelling. " . . . If only you'll . . . please . . . please . . . we'll now have . . . the invocation by . . . by the Reverend Mike Roselle and the Virgin Grove . . . the Virgin Grove. . . ."

The bedlam grew in all dimensions, a swelling sea of laughter capped with shouts of mock derision, rolling cheers of approval, polite hand-clapping, and a little constellation of silent "sparkling" (burning matches) by envoys from the Rainbow Gathering, a group that regarded any form of audible demonstration as disruptive to the true higher communal spiritual experience. The Rainbows were set upon at once, however, and rudely, by a pair of uniformed USFS rangers concerned about human-caused forest fires. Sheepishly, the Sparklers blew out their matches, held them till cold and broke them as instructed by the outraged Smokey Bears. "Only *you* can prevent forest fires," sez Smokey — a lie, of course, since 95 percent of the nation's forest fires are caused by God and lightning, but the kind of lie that easily becomes religious dogma in the bureaucratic mentality.

Still trying to get the crowd's attention and complete his introduction of the next act, Foreman threw back his head, raised both hairy paws to his muzzle and began to howl like a wolf. He started low and deep in the chest, rising in slow crescendo toward an apogee of animal liberation, the blood-cry of the eternal untamed, the true and original call of the wild.

That did it. That caught their interest. The mob echoed his howl in antiphonic recapitulation, male and female, adult and child, human and canine, six hundred voices soaring through the cathedral of the trees, into the listening sky, over the yawning abyss of the world's one and one only Grand Canyon, where a waxing young moon, at this very moment, was shining like a platinum shield above the Powell Plateau, the Great Thumb Mesa, the towers and temples of gods far older than any ever imagined by man. (Or by wo-man.)

Even the cops and rangers were impressed by this mass outburst of angelic demonology. Not frightened, not disturbed — hard for them to imagine so anarchic and jolly a multitude becoming dangerous — but impressed. They listened, they stared, their hearts beat faster with the power of the primitive — *be primordial or die!* — and they remembered, under the thin imposed film of cultural consciousness, something older, deeper, richer, warmer, lovelier and finer than anything they'd ever been taught in school, heard from Church and State, or osmotically absorbed from TV, radio, newspapers, billboards, politicians, evangelists, priests, experts, M.D.s or Ph.D.s.

What? What was it? It was that sense of life that cannot be expressed — or depressed — through mere words. It was the message of the wolf's cry, the lion's roar, the whispering of the forest, the thunder of a storm, the silence of the canyon, the wail of wind, the meaning of the moon. The fire of the blood. The drumming of the heart. The beating of the drums.

Drums, drums, drums and tambourines and flutes, all present heard the coming music, the procession of the dancers.

"Mike Roselle," announced Foreman, "and the Virgin Grove Spikettes!" He leaped from the stage, snatched a beer from a careless hand, and melted into the mass.

"Nazi!" squealed a heckler, recovering his hatred. "Animals!"

Useless protest: the crowd ignored him, shoving him aside as they cleared a path for another hulking brute of a man in antlers, whiskers, T-shirt, bluejeans, boots, tools, who sprang onto the stage followed by six girls in gowns of white and green and gold, impersonating an aspen grove. Chanting, they danced in a circle around the horny satyr with his grin, his can of Michelob, his singlejack sledgehammer, the canvas bag of spikes slung from his shoulder.

The meaning of the pantomime seemed obscure, at first, until Freddie climbed on stage, a man dressed in the brown-shirted uniform of a U.S. forest ranger and lugging a gigantic cardboard make-believe chainsaw. At sight of him the six aspen girls stopped their dance, quaking with fear. Freddie yanked the starter cord on his chainsaw; snarling like a two-cycle engine he approached the trembling trees, menacing them with his implement of massacre. They skipped in a circle, round and round, chased by the ranger until — Oh *terra primum!* — the bold satyr interposed himself with uplifted hammer. A brief clash of weapons and the forest ranger fled, yelping with terror, pursued by Roselle deep into the shadows of the evening woods.

Cheers, whistles, applause.

"Sexist!" screeched the Furies from Berkeley, "male chauvinist piggery!"

Vain outcry: the drumming resumed, the piping of the flutes, the dancing. The Virgin Grove, hand in hand, jumped from the stage and led the crowd in a whirling spiraling joyous dance that wound about the stage and across the meadow and through the forest and every which way but loose. . . .

Sundown. Moonshine. Smoke of burning oak in campfires, juniper incense, guitars and banjos, drums and flutes and panpipes. Smell of barbecued spareribs, corn on the cob, refried beans, Mex-Tex chili, avocado dip. Burning hemp. Sweat. Seminal ideas. Porta-johns. Baby diapers. Gasoline. Dust and pine duff. Tennis shoes and foot powder. Silverleaf lupine in midsummer bloom. Cliffrose. Sacred datura.

"Oral," she gasped, stroking his cheeks. "At last I find you my crazy handsome Mormon-Moroni man!"

"Oh no," he said, backing off, glancing furtively about, "not me, you got me mixed up with somebody else, my name, my name . . . ah . . . is J. Bracken Benson, that's right, I come from, from Moab, Utah. You know, Moab? Land of Moab?"

Oh Moab, thou art my washpot. — Psalm 108
Moab, alas! thou art undone. — Numbers 29

"Oral . . . !" Reaching out, she flung her arms around his neck and clung, clung (clang?) like a twining woodbine, like a kudzu vine, like the running blackberry of clearcut and/or fire-scorched woodland. "Oral, my little Oral Hatch I miss you so much so long your Erika she comes all zee way to America to find you and now at last — "

Whimpering with fear, he managed to break free from her strong sweet arms. "No, no, sorry, miss, you got the wrong, I'm not . . . you better look again, us . . . we . . . we Mormons do kind of look alike but really, honest, I'm not . . . see? look, mustache, brown hair, no glasses, Oral wore glasses, right?, didn't he? . . . did he? . . ."

Young Hatch ran, ran like a man in fear, into the fringes of the swirling crowd, into the darkness of the wood, and vanished. For the time being. Erika stared after him, astonished, eyes wide in wonder and shock. Could she be wrong? True, true, most young male Mormoni tended to resemble one another like pease in a pot, like ants on a hill, like sheep in a flock, but she knew her Oral, how could she ever be mistaken in those adolescent lineaments, those perfect fluoridated teeth, that small peenhead without neck set like a soccer ball midway between the shoulders? The first great love of her life. And he denies her.

She sank to her knees on the pine needles of the forest floor, mindless of gaping bystanders, and wept freely, loudly, with the fariytale abandon of the lovelorn Svenska maid. The dour Norse? That Nordic phlegm? The dull and sluggish Norwegian permafrost? *Tout au contraire:* they are a wild and hearty breed, whose emotions from joy to despair and back again run deep, fierce, true and hotly energetic, untainted by the cynical affectation of Latin posturing, the operatic gestures of the lukewarm worn-out thin-blooded Mediterranean soul. If ever turned loose from their self-constructed cage of inner doubt, guilt neuroses and liberalistic angst, these northern races could subjugate the entire planet in approximately two weeks. (Well, Japan might give them trouble. And the Israelis. And the cheerful little Bushmen of Southwest Africa.)

Erika wept for a while, absorbed in her grief, then rose to her feet, wiped her nose, her reddened but spectacular seagreen eyes, and rejoined the dancers at the central bonfire, where music by Dakota Sid, Wobblie Bab, Lone Wolf Circles, Bill Oliver and the Austin Lounge Lizards, John Seed and the Canyon Pygmies kept the party alive.

The moon went down, the fire faded, the night took over, the last of the revelers staggered, crept, wandered and wobbled to their tents (if any), their pickup truckbeds (where relevant), their swags, kit, bedrolls and sleeping bags scattered through the forest (if they could find them).

Erika slept alone beneath a pinyon pine far out on the tip of a peninsula of limestone along the rim of Parissawampits Point. One thousand feet below a lion crept, with burning yellow eyes, with twitching tail, on padded claws, toward a browsing deer. Erika dreamed of calving icebergs, caving glaciers, Tapiola love.

Hoyle and Boyle rose at dawn, grumbling, from their rented camper-trailer parked on a side road four miles north of the Rendezvous. Hoyle stirred bacon and scrambled eggs in a new skillet on a brand-new Coleman stove. Boyle popped the top from a can of Budweiser Lite, drank deep, his morning preliminary to the customary Bloody Mary and Hoyle's All-American grease fix. He drank and drank again and felt, almost at once, the thin diuretic beer trickle through his kidneys, into his bladder, down the conduits of the urethra. He walked to the edge of camp, scuffed at an anthill until a few sleepy black ants crawled forth. Unzipping, he pissed on them. "This Bud's for you."

Young Hatch appeared in neatly patched bell bottom jeans, strings of beads around his neck, a leather headband around his brow, a pack of Zig-Zag papers showing in one pocket of his loose, baggy, ruffled Bengali shirt. An array of large metal buttons proclaimed his doctrine: Flower Power, Give Peace a Chance, Nuke the Whales, I'm Clean for Gene, Girls Say Yes to Boys Who Say No, Free Angela Davis, Free Huey Newton, Free Eldridge Cleaver, Free Bobby Seale, Zap Clap and Free Love. His hair was drawn to a stubby pigtail in back. He alit gracefully from his ten-speed Stump Jumper and prepared to give his morning report.

"Jeez," said Hoyle, staring at young J. Oral, "what a sickening sight so early in the morning."

"Enough to make a man puke his guts out," Boyle agreed. "That coffee ready?"

"What's wrong?" Oral said. "You don't like my disguise? What's wrong with it? Whose idea was this anyhow? You think I like it any more than you do? I feel like a doggone dope fiend in this outfit. You don't like the way I look let's see one of you guys try it. You wouldn't last five minutes down there. Those people are crazy. I mean they are absolutely the craziest kookiest freakiest mob of . . . of whatever they are I ever saw. Half of them beating on drums while the other half hop around like frogs. There's one bunch not wearing any clothes at all. Another bunch dressed up like Jeremiah Liver-Eating Johnson, walking around with muzzle-loaders and coontail hats and bearclaw necklaces and Bowie knives two feet long. Little children all over the place, most of them bare naked. A bunch that look like Hell's Angels — they even ride Harleys. Some guys in sportshirts and bolo ties smoking pipes, they might be the weirdest of all, talking about biocentric land ethics. And there's a little bunch called Sparklers and Twinklers, they think that cheering or handclapping is 'rude and disruptive,' they tried to get the whole insane mob — there must be a thousand by now — tried to get them to ban yelling, whistling, handclapping, any kind of noise — and the Twinklers believe you should sort of twirl your hands around in the air, kind of like this — " Hatch attempted to illustrate his words with grotesque limp-wristed birdy-like gesticulations in the vicinity of his ears; Hoyle and Boyle watched him with fascinated contempt.

"I feel sick," Boyle said.

"Yeah. It's like one of them old army V.D. movies."

" — and they actually managed to get the idea on the agenda and then the emcee, that's Barbara Dugelby today . . ."

"Who?"

"Barbara Dugelby, sir."

"Who's she? She on the Index, Hoyle?"

"We'll check it."

" — so Barbara called for a vote, all those in favor so indicate by twinkling, she said, and the whole lunatic crowd twinkled away like little butterflies and then she said all those opposed so indicate by clapping, yelling, whistling or wolf-howling and the whole crackpot mob except for the Twinklers and Sparklers started to hoot and holler and whistle and howl like a pack of animals." Young Oral stopped for air.

"We heard it. Four miles away we heard it."

"Yeah," Boyle said. "The sound of Hell at Yankee Stadium when the ump called Winfield out on three pitches in the fourth game of the Series. You burnt the bacon, cocksucker, tastes like something somebody scraped off a brake lining."

"Is that right? Well fry it yourself next time, shithead."

"Well today they're mostly broke up into what they call workshops."

"Work? These eco-freaks work? Love says they're all on welfare."

"There's a workshop on wolves and endangered species. There's one for first-time Earth First!ers. There's one on what they call deep ecology and another on the Rites of Summer and — "

"Rights of summer?"

"That's what they call it. Some woman named Dolores LaChapelle teaching people how to chant and dance and braid flowers in their hair and attain deep spiritual intimacy with the organic rhythms of Mother Nature."

Boyle began to choke. His Bloody Mary fell from nerveless fingers and splattered on his wellingtons. Tears streamed from his eyes. He gasped for breath, wheezing like a concertina. Hoyle slapped his back, harder than necessary. Boyle's bridge fell out, his hat fell off, his toupee slid forward over his eyes.

"Oral," said Hoyle, "you better take it easy. Poor guy's got a heart murmur. Ain't near as tough as he thinks he is."

Oral stared. "I'm sorry, sir."

"Just stick to the illegal stuff, Oral. Terrorism, PLO contacts, homicide, explosives, felonious conspiracy and so on. Skip the organic rhythms, Boyle can't take it."

Boyle recovered. Eyes watery, he readjusted his hairpiece, reinserted the bridge, replaced the hat, rebuilt his Bloody Mary. Humming a tune from *Oklahoma!*, he sat down carefully on a new aluminum camp chair, sipped at his drink, blinked, swallowed, cleared his throat, braced himself. "What else, Oral?"

"Well . . . there's the Redneck Women's Caucus. Somebody called Georgia Hayduchess and the Feminist Eco-Warriors organized that one. Doubt if they'll let me in. There's Art Goodtimes and the Seminar for World Re-enchantment Through Pure Earth Poetry."

Hoyle raised a warning hand. "Careful."

Oral nodded. "Somebody who calls himself Art Goodwrench is giving a course in diesel mechanics. I think I'd better check that one. Sounds significant."

"Does indeed. What about Syn-Fuels, the Super-G.E.M., all that?"

Pause.

Oral said, "They're talking about what they call an 'action.' " He hesitated. "Erika's giving a speech about it this evening at moonrise."

Hoyle and Boyle both glanced at their wristwatches. "Moonrise?" Hoyle said. "What time is that? Don't these bubbleheads own watches?"

"They don't go by the clock. They claim they're on what they call Earth Time. Something to do with natural organic — "

"Erika," Houle interrupted sharply. "This Erika, who's she?"

Oral began to turn red.

"Erika," Boyle said, "she's that juicy lookin' long-legged cunt from Norway, right?"

Oral turned pale.

"Jeez," Boyle went on, musing over his drink, "sure could get into some deep organic rhythm with that little piece of snatch." An idea twinkled in his soggy brain. "Wonder if she's legal? Tell her we're INS, Border Patrol, maybe make a deal. Put out or get out, Furline What's-yernameanyhow?"

Oral stiffened. "Mister Boyle . . . "

Sensing trouble, Hoyle attempted to change the subject, quickly. "That Foreman's the one we got to nail. Him and Mike Roselle, Howie Wolke, Georgia Hayduchess, Karen Pickett, Bill Haywood, Roger . . ." He consulted a list in his hand. "Roger Featherstone? suspected bolt-weevil? Nancy Morton? And what about that Hayduke character himself? There's the one the Colonel really wants, dead if possible, alive if necessary, but we'll discuss that. . . ."

"Me first," Boyle said, grinnng at Hoyle, "sloppy seconds for Oral."

". . . later?"

Young Hatch strode forward charged with adrenaline, grasped Boyle by collar and tie and hoisted him from his chair. And Boyle was a large and heavy man, two hundred pounds if an ounce. Through gritted teeth, eyes glaring, Oral breathed, "Apologize."

Smiling, Boyle set down his drink. Both hands free, he was prepared to kill young Hatch — kill him instantly — with a single chop to the Adam's apple. This was exactly the kind of situation he most enjoyed. Lived for. Dreamed about. Another notch on his coup stick. "Apologize?" Eyes half closed, lazily reclining in Hatch's grip, he repeated, "Apologize? For what?"

Oral hesitated. How explain without revealing that he'd already blown his cover? But honor came first, the code of the gentleman Mormon missionary. "What you said. About her. You apologize." His right fist hovered in striking position.

Hoyle intervened, breaking Hatch's grip with an expert application of pressure points to the boy's hand. Boyle slumped down in his chair, relaxed and smiling. Oral froze like a statue in Hoyle's one-handed clutch.

"All right men, no foolishness. At ease, Oral. Boyle, give the kid a break, apologize."

"What for?"

"Just do it."

"Sure. Yeah. Okay. Okay, I apologize. Didn't know you was in love, Oral."

"I'm not in love. But you can't talk that way about her."

"So she knows you?"

Silence.

"How about it, Oral?" Hoyle said. "She spot you?"

"Yes."

"How much does she know?"

"I don't know. But they all think I'm a spy anyway. She will too, I guess. None of them seem to care. But . . ."

"But what?"

"She says she loves me." At once he regretted the words.

Another silence. Boyle and Hoyle glanced at one another, then stared at the young man. He stared at the coffeepot simmering on the stove. Now what?

"Oral," said Hoyle, "are you still working for us?"

"Yes sir. But not for him." Glaring at Boyle. "Not for you either. I'm working for my country. For America."

"Okay, good, that's good enough. That's the main idea. So here's what I want *you* to do: go back to that Twinkies nuthouse jamboree. Observe. Listen. Talk. Make suggestions. Sit in on the workshops. And stick close to that Norwegian cutie. You say she likes you, we know you like her, make the most of it. Opportunity. Move in close, you lucky dog. If she's suspicious now, tell her you're a double agent. Tell her how much you really secretly love rocks and cactus and chipmunks, that kind'll believe anything. Tell her your connections in Libya, Iran, Nicaragua, see what she makes of that. Find out if she knows Hayduke. You follow me?"

Young Hatch considered. "Yes sir."

"Good. You've got your orders. Don't forget your oath of loyalty to the Company. Don't forget your pledge of allegiance to the flag. Don't forget you're an American first, a boy friend second, a nature lover third, right?"

"Yes sir."

"Am I right?"

"Yes, Mr. Hoyle."

"Right. Now how about shaking hands with this stinking booze-hound here, our good buddy Boyle. He apologized like a gentleman to you, you should show him there's no hard feelings. Okay, Oral?"

Boyle stuck out his big moist right hand, palm mottled like a sausage, assuming on his red fat face an expression of solemn sincerity. Young Oral hesitated. Boyle waited. Oral hesitated. Boyle waited. Again Hoyle intervened.

"Better idea." He placed his hand on his heart. "Let's all recite the pledge."

Boyle snapped to attention, hand on heart. Young Hatch did like-wise. Lacking an actual flag, they faced each other. In unison, more or less, they chanted together, sort of, like Druids at the sacred oak, Lakotas at the sun pole, Christians at an execution, Hebrews at a penis party, Aztecs at a heart transplant, etc., the holy formula:

"I pledge allegiance . . . huh . . . to the flag . . . hah . . . of the United States of America . . . ho . . . one nation indivisible/under God [con-fusion on that point] . . . hey . . . with liberty . . . hoo . . . and justice . . . hi . . . for all . . . yah!

"Great," Hoyle summarized. "Okay, Oral me boy, hop on your trike I mean bike here, pedal your rosy ass back to your . . . to the randy-voo there and see what you can see. Captain Boyle!"

Again Boyle snapped to attention. "Yes *sir*, Major Hoyle!"

"Give Lieutenant Hatch a formal military dispatch with full military honors!"

"Yes sir! With pleasure, sir!" Boyle raised both hands to his mouth — while young Oral, sunk in thought, slowly mounted his bicycle — and bugled forth, in perfect imitation of the real thing, a stirring cavalry charge, *presto fortissimo*.

Oral pedaled off, not very fast, wobbling a bit on the rutted dirt road, and dwindled off, down, away and out of sight among the colonnades of *Pinus ponderosa*.

They watched him go.

"What do you think?"

Boyle shrugged. "Stupid punk. I shoulda broke his throat. Why'd you stop me?"

Hoyle shrugged. "Can't stand the sight of blood. Hate the paper-work. Have the Colonel on our backs again. Besides, might still get some use out of that kid."

"Double agent. You make me laugh, Hoyle. He ain't smart enough to make a double highball — or a single agent. You see those dumb badges?"

"Sure. What the hell, those Earth Firster types probly think it's a joke. And he's not as dumb as you think."

"He's dumber."

"He's simple. But he's not dumb." Hoyle stared down the single-lane dirt road to where it curved out of sight deeper in the forest, joining the main dirt road a mile beyond. "He's not only not stupid, he's not only gonna play double agent, he might even turn out to be a triple agent. We got to watch him; he might be smarter than us."

"That's not smart."

"But he takes the flag stuff seriously. That's why I trust him. He really was an Eagle Scout. He really is a Mormon. He really does like apple pie."

Sagebrush Patriots, unite.

Flags rippled in the evening breeze. The flag of anarchy, red monkey wrench on a field of black. The green fist, red lettering and plain white of Earth First! The red, white and gold, with rattlesnake, of American independence. DON'T TREAD ON ME. And centered as a backdrop to the stage, and fluttering on hand-held staves throughout the assembled mob of misfits and mavericks and crazy kids, Old Glory herself — *our flag* — the red the white the blue the stripes and stars of the Fucking United Fucking States of America by God and by Christ. This was a mucho-macho patriot crowd, fanatic lovers of the land, of liberty, of a glorious tradition, and they were proud to show it.

GUNS, GOD, GUTS & GRASS, THAT'S WHAT MADE AMERICA GREAT! (sang a scarlet pennon waving in the air). MORE ELK! LESS COWS! said another.

And more (of course):

AMERICAN WILDERNESS: LOVE IT OR LEAVE IT ALONE

ANOTHER MORMON ON DRUGS

BACK TO THE PLEISTOCENE

DREAM BACK THE BISON, SING BACK THE SWAN

ESCHEW SURPLUSAGE

HUNT COWS, NOT BEARS

HUNTERS: DID A COW GET YOUR ELK?

MALTHUS WAS RIGHT

MUIR POWER TO YOU

NATURE BATS LAST

REDNECKS FOR WILDERNESS

NEANDERTHAL AND PROUD OF IT!

PAY YOUR RENT: WORK FOR THE EARTH
WALT SAYS: RESIST MUCH, OBEY LITTLE
THINK GLOBALLY — ACT LOCALLY
SUBVERT THE DOMINANT PARIDIGM
HAYDUKE LIVES!

And so forth and so on. Flags, pennants, T-shirts and buttons, clenched fists and flying monkey wrenches, the import might be construed as suggesting a certain vague dissatisfaction with the "oligarchic swine" (as one wag put it) who "own and operate America" (in the phrase of another).

But all in the spirit of good clean fun, no harm meant.

Sun going down in a volcano of gruesome gorgeous clouds, that great big pizza in the West where God Hisself was splattering tomato sauce, melted cheese, purple anchovies and rotten salami clear across the celestial dome from Shithouse Mountain on the north to Dead Cow Butte on the south. Divine abstract expressionism!

So where's our comely young mistress of ceremonies this evening? Why here she comes, Miss Barbara Dugelby from Muleshoe, Texas, picking her way through the milling mass of ragged anarchists, fanatic conservatives, environmental blowflies, unwashed preservationists, neat clean tidy wildlife biologists, sly sneaky courageous eco-saboteurs, wild and beautiful young women with wilting posies in their long and Herbal Essence–scented hair, gnarly unshaven handsome young men with naked chests, bulging biceps and no hips at all, nudist naturists wearing only sandals and magic crystal necklaces, wild and happy children chasing one another yon, hither and back, and all the others heretofore mentioned: the spies in hippie costume, the ecologists deep and shallow, the conservationists both respectable and disreputable, the founding fathers and sustaining mothers, the redneck women, the socio-femmes, Igor and the goon squad at the perimeters watching for a rumored night attack from the Posse Comitatus and Search & Rescue Team, a few free-lance correspondents like the aging geezer with whiskers and buzzard-beak gaping up at Barbara from the front or "Pervert" row, and such. As young Hatch had said, the festering crowd had grown close to a thousand, with hundreds of others still groping about through the woods all over the fifty-mile-wide Kaibab Plateau, snarling to themselves Where the fuck is this Pissy-wampitts Point, this fucking Round River Rendered View?

And the leaders, where were they? What leaders? There weren't none. They were all leaders.

Miss Dugelby adjusted the mike (solar-powered, of course, by a portable array of purple panels mounted on a trailer), sent a few electric crackles through the ambience and spoke:

"Greeting, *compañeros y compañeras*. Hope you all had enough to eat. Don't forget to recycle your garbage at the garbage separation centers. Hope everyone who likes them has found the porta-johns by now and that you appreciate the location; Dave and the boys did their best to set them up in places with a good view. The rest of you, I trust you're digging your catholes deep and at least a mile back in the woods. Burn your toilet paper with care or we'll have the Forest Freddies on our necks with a hundred firefighters and pumper trucks rampaging around all over the place. What else? More bio-regional and deep ecology workshops tomorrow: see the schedule at the EF! propaganda booth. Please contribute as much as you can to the kitty; some people put out a lot of money to rent those stinking porta-johns and the solar power unit. Tonight we're having more music and moonlight dancing: a midsummer night's maypole dance, a square dance with music by the Organic Nutty-Gritty Peanut Butter Jug Band, a sacred ritual holy Druid Dance over in the scrub oak thicket, general free-style dancing in the meadow, music by the Lounge Lizards, and another cowboy stomp dance out on the point, music by Peter Gierlach and the Rusty Spurs. First though, an announcement from Erika about the action she's planning at the Neck pretty soon. Erika, where are you?"

Erika, tall, slender, beautiful, Princess of Moon Power, appeared from the shadow of the pines and began to work her way through the packed crowd toward the platform. Before she reached it there was a small outburst from the Berkeley group up front. A portly fellow stood there waving a document, shouting at the emcee: "Equal time, equal time . . ."

Dugelby hesitated, glancing at Erika still some distance off. "Okay," she said to the man with the paper, beckoning him onstage. "Five minutes." She looked at the moon, rising pale and round and waferwise through the crowns of the trees.

The portly fellow struggled at the edge of the stage; there were no steps, his legs short, his belly large. Barbara leaned down, gave him a hand, hauled him up. Bernie Mushkin took the microphone, red in the face and panting. A man of sixty or so, bald on top, flatfooted at bottom, wide-assed narrow-minded and slope-shouldered, he resembled in shape a child's toy known as Mr. Potato-Head. (Life is not fair.) He suffered furthermore from inadequate chin whiskers: despite forty years of concentrated effort he still had not succeeded in growing a man's beard. Like that aging teenybopper balladeer Bobbie Dylan, the best he'd been able to do was sprout a scraggly furze of pale fuzz along the jawline, while the chin itself remained downy as a boy soprano's. Even his voice had a tendency to break — up an octave — at inconvenient moments of stress, Sturm und Drang, stormy weather and clogged-up drains.

Nevertheless: Bernie Mushkin, old-time Marxist, sectarian revolutionary, tenured professor, academic writer, pedagogue, demagogue, ideologue, was drawn to political controversy as a moth to the flame — or a blowfly to a rotting hog. Inept and passionate, fiery-tempered and humorless, graceless but relentless, he had acquired a reputation, over the decades, among the far-out fringes of the urban-American left wing, as an intellectual blowhard. Which meant, in that element, leadership. (Who's your leader? What leader, we got no leader, we're all followers, baa baa baa. . . .)

Clutching the mike stand with his left fist, Professor Mushkin raised his right in the good old Nazi salute. *"Sieg heil!"* he barked, standing on tippytoe to bring his lips close to the microphone, which he'd neglected to readjust (downward). Barbara approached to do it for him; impatiently he waved her aside. *"Sieg heil!"* he repeated, *"sieg heil!"*

If he hoped to provoke a howl of outrage in response, he must have been disappointed. Most of the crowd, who knew nothing about him, stared in bewilderment; a few tittered and laughed; some twinkled, waggling hands at ears, in mock approval.

Mushkin raised his paper and read his statement. "Earth First! eco-fascists," he announced, "I congratulate you on setting back the cause of justice, decency, ecology and environmentalism by at least fifty years in America."

Cheers. Applause. Scattered twinkling.

"Your well-publicized advocacy of sabotage and monkey-wrenching has made Earth First! a synonym for terrorism."

Scattered applause. Polite cheers. Faint twinkling.

"Your well-known support of famine in Africa, as preached by your official spokesperson Foreman, has revealed you as fascist, neo-colonialist and anti-humanitarian."

Heavy twinkling. Sporadic sparkling, quickly doused.

"Your enthusiastic support of immigration control, as preached by your official ideologists Hardin and Abbey, has revealed you as nationalists and xenophobes, quite the opposite of the fun-loving anarchists you pretend to be."

Cheers, applause, twinkling.

"I might add that your opposition to immigration, especially your opposition to immigration from Third World nations, which means of course immigration by people of color — "

"Colored people?" someone shouted. "That's a racist term, you lousy bigot!"

"I said people of color," Muskin shouted back, his voice abruptly squeaking into boy-soprano range again. "People of color, I said." Trembling with rage, he fought for self control; the microphone shook in his hand. He looked at his paper. He continued: "Your dogmatic opposition to immigration by people of color from oppressed Third World nations — oppressed mainly by capitalist America, I might point out — exposes you, *exposes you* — " he emphasized, "as not only nationalists, xenophobes, neo-colonialists, cultural chauvinists and running dog lackeys for economic imperialism, but also I must say, and it pains me to say it — "

Cheers. Applause.

" — exposes you as a hypocritical mob of *creeping fascist hyenas and elitist Nazi racists*. Emphasis added. *Sieg heil!*" He saluted.

No one returned the salute except for the Three Snake-Haired Furies from Berkeley stationed up front. *"Sieg heil!"* they screeched in perfect unison. *"Sieg heil!"*

"Furthermore," Mushkin went on, glancing at his notes — easily distracted, he was not a good extemporaneous speaker — "Furthermore, and with this point I conclude — "

Loud and prolonged cheering, whistling, yelling; massive twinkling and a brief outburst of sparkling.

"Your basic doctrine, laughably called 'deep ecology,' a ludicrous term better rephrased as 'deep *zoology*' . . ." Mushkin paused to relieve himself with a scornful laugh; his acolytes, catching the cue, barked like seals. "Your so-called deep ecology or 'eco-la-la-la!,' as sketched so far by Naess, Sessions, Devall, Snyder, Leopold, Flowers, Manes and who knows what other intellectual bantamweights — " Mushkin curled his lip; his claque cackled. " — is basically anti-human misanthropic people-hating bigotry. Not philosophy but bigotry. Biocentric, you call it, or eco-centric. I call it *ec*centric, in the most vicious sense of that term. All living things are equal, you proclaim. Does that include the bear and the lion?"

"Yes!"

"The cockroach and the rat?"

"Sure . . ."

"The centipede and the pit viper?"

"Yeah."

"Yes? Well what about the smallpox virus and the AIDS virus?"

Confusion in the ranks.

Mushkin paused, awaiting an answer. Tough talk; he smiled his scornful smile as the silence spread, his rhetorical question sinking deep.

A fat little boy, wearing a T-shirt that argued "No Guts No Glory," broke the silence by piping up. "Mister Munchkin" he squeaked.

"Yes?"

"Wanta get rid of ten pounds of ugly fat?"

"What?"

"Cut your head off!" the boy squealed and broke down howling. Every child in the audience, and there were at least a hundred of them, listening intently when they heard the tip-off line, joined in the chorale of laughter. The contagion spread, the hilarity became general.

Professor Mushkin waited. When the laughter waned at last, he said, "Finally — "

A storm of applause, cheering, whistling.

"Finally, I'd like to point out that your gross display of flags here, with clenched fists, coiled rattlesnakes, red monkey wrenches and the feared hated brazen banner of capitalist militarist imperialist racist Amerika — I spell it, of course, with the appropriate 'k' — reveals the basically macho, redneck, sexist, violence-prone frontiersman mentality of your Earth First! image makers. Your own symbols give you away, reveal and expose you for what you are: a drunken ignorant low-class (but not true working class) lumpen-proletariat led and misled by a power-greedy clique of petit-bourgeois shop clerks, writers manqués, failed academics, corrupt journalists and petty businessmen, *the traditional raw material,* as seen in Italy, in Germany, in Latin America, *of Fascism and Nazism.*" Mushkin paused. "And so I say, once more, '*Sieg heil*' to you Earth First! right-wing pigs and if you want to hang me for it, hang me!"

Defiant, proud, heroic, hands at his side, Professor Bernie Mushkin tilted back his head, baring his pale plump wattles to the screaming mob.

The screaming mob gave him a sitting ovation, with full Twinkler honors, while one of the aspen girls draped a garland of flowers around his neck, and others helped him lower himself from the stage, pressed a frothing can of Schlitz into each Mushkin hand, slapped his shoulder blades in congratulation and hustled him back to his waiting disciples. Those three worthies, sternly facing down the wolf pack, took Bernie's beers from his shaking hands, emptied them — with full socio-feminist contempt — upon the dusty pine needles, and escorted the professor back to his rental car (a Nipper of the Komatsu brand). From there they drove him to his hotel in nearby Las Vegas only three hundred miles away, in their eyes and in his the nearest outpost of proper civilization in the entire northern Arizona-Utah-Nevada region. At least there is a university in Las Vegas. Hospitals. A foreign-film cinema. Fern bars. Lesbian bookstores. And a synagogue or two or three. And Wayne Newton and Liberace and Bette Midler and a four-lane superhighway leading direct to the airport, with connections for L.A., Bakersfield, Fresno and Berkeley-by-the-Bay, Home of Advanced Thought, Third World Liberation, the Livermore Nuclear Radiation Laboratory.

The crowd simmered, waiting. Then a chorus of cheers rose high as everyone stood up.

Liberté mounting the barricades. A hard act to follow but Erika the Svenska Maid was obliged to try. Taking the mike, raising it a foot, she thrust her right fist *ad astra* and shouted at the milling mulling moiling musing merry multitude —

"Zee Eart' She First!"

This time the crowd responded properly, as they had not done for the others. The battle cry, "Zee Eart' She First!" echoed and re-echoed from a thousand hoarse throats. Hoarse from too much laughter, too much bawling of huzzahs, despite the lubrication of a thousand quarts of beer. They wouldn't do it for the others, but who would not do anything for Erika? Looking at her standing there, regal, tall and slender, rosy, bright-eyed, radiant, lovely as a Nordic flower in her snug T-shirt, her skintight cowgirl jeans, her dark and glowing hair falling like a lion's mane from crown of head to swell of crupper. My *Gawd* but she was beautiful, so beautiful that she existed somewhere beyond the envy of other women, safe from the animal lust of even the simplest young men. All loved her, all looked upon her as a work of natural art rather than (as simply) an object of sexual inspiration. Erika herself, Princess of Moon Power, lived within and lived throughout all through her youthful beauty, conscious of it not as a lucky attribute but rather as an expression of her unconscious zest for life. Her beauty was not hers; she was beauty's; and living what she was, and being what she lived, in essence and appearance one and the same vibrant harmonious whole, she melted every heart.

"Down wiss empire up wiss spring!"

Both hands palm upward spread toward the sky, smiling like an

angel, body arched and breasts upsurging, she waited for the anti-
phon.

"Down wiss empire up wiss spring!" they roared in perfect mimicry,
amplified a thousandfold. The trees shivered. The secret police grinned
nervously. Young J. Oral stared in awestruck adoration. The old
graybearded rednosed wrinklenecked correspondent in Perverts'
Row — too perverse and old for purity — gaped up with wonder in
his bleary eyes, a silent groan of archaic desire rising from his groin
through heart to throat and brain. Silent? He meant it to be silent. But
a number of people standing nearby glanced his way for a moment.

In the brief stillness that followed the antiphony, a woman shouted:
"Erika! What do you say to Bernie Fuzzchin?"

Erika hesitated only a moment. "Vat do I say? Vat do *vee* say?"
Pause. "Vee say . . . ven you haff fight zee beeg bulldozer you no haff
time worry about zum housefly buzzing round your head."

They loved it. The ruffian riffraff, *hoi polloi* of American environmentalism, ate it up, howling with delight. She had them eating from
her hand, licking at her palm, drooling in her spoon, slobbering on her
graceful instep.

"Ven you face zee great GOLIATH," she went on, "you no wess
time wiss insex crawling up our leg."

They roared with approval, whistled, yawhooed, twinkled, sparkled, yawped and yelled and pounded palm on palm.

Insex, the old gringo journalist noted in his notebook, I like that. I
love that. And crawling up her leg! Holy Mary, Mother of Gawd, to
be an insex on a moonlit midsummer's night. What foolishness these
morals be. Puck, Puck, you skipping scamp of lust, stop plucking at my
scrotal hairs. Oh the itching and the twitching, the bitching twitching
itching of romantic love.

". . . which brings to zee point of ziss announcement. Ven
GOLIATH he gets to zee Neck I am being there to stop him. I put my
body where he comes. But not all by my alone person must I surely
hope. I ask for sisters, brothers, comrades, put your body where I put
my body. I say — and ziss iss joke, yes? but also more zan joke, I
say — put your body where your mouse is. Vee talk big, vee talk very
tough, now iss time to show vee act like talk, no? Yass? *Ja?*"

"*Ja, ja,* Erika!"

Mouse, the correspondent noted, puts her body where her mouse
is. Good. Very good. The girl's a poet. The blood of Ibsen, Hamsun,
Laxness, Strindberg, Bjornsen, Lagerlof, Undset, and J. V. Jensen
flows through those splendid Viking veins.

". . . ask for one t'ousand bodies meet at zee Neck between Last Eden Canyon and zat how you call? Radium Canyon? when Super-G.E.M. he finally get to zat point which is what? maybe ten days? two weeks? Zere vee stop him, he no can go around, Neck iss only forty meters wide, vee pile up livink human bodies, my bodies, your bodies, everybody's bodies, on zee solid rock, vee stick monkey wrench in works, vee put flowers on zee Big Bucket, vee put flowers on zee driver's neck and hug heem, her? it? and kiss and luff and squeeze and make GOLIATH stop. Make it turn around, go home, nevair come back to God country, your country, my country, our country, are you coming wiss me, folks? vill you join to your body my body?"

"Yes!" they thundered, male and female. "Yeah!" they rumbled, girls and boys alike, as they whistled, sparkled, twinkled, hollered, cheered and clapped. "We are coming, Princess Erika, one thousand bodies strong!"

We are coming, Father Abraham, one hundred thousand strong. Ga-lory hallelujah! The journalist, on his feet, yelling and cheering with the rest, scribbling madly in his notebook, felt tears trickling down his bourbon-rubicund cheeks. He sniffed, furtively rubbed the tears away with back of hand, glanced left then right beneath his shaggy eyebrows and saw on every side young pink firm glossy cheeks likewise glistening with tears of joy. Okay then. He wept, he scribbled, he rejoiced.

"Eart' First!" called Erika, shaking both her little fists at the moony sky, stretching that splendid body toward the stars.

"Eart' First!" the mob howled back.

"No more zat fuckink compromise — !"

"No more fucking compromise . . ."

" — in defense ziss Mutter Eart'!"

" . . . in defense of Mutter Eart'!"

An uproar of cheering. "Let zee revels now begin!"

The young woman leaped from the stage with a Valkyrie's cry of triumph (a perfect high C, 2093 hertz, cycles or vibes per second) above the arms of Perverts' Row into the arms of those beyond, where she was promptly hoisted onto some eco-freakish hulking bearded brute's shoulders and paraded around the platform and across the meadow and through the woods and back to the meadow and around the bonfire, followed by a thousand or so dancing shouting laughing maniacs.

Viz., From San Diego up to Maine, on every field and hill, where eco-folk defend our Earth, it's there you find our gril [sic]. As Joe Hillstrom himself might have sung it, had he lived another fifty years, and seen the evolution of the I.W.W. into the IEF!

"Well?"

"Well what?"

"What do you think?"

"What do *I* think?" He relit his cigar, which had gone out during the height of the joyful hysteria. "Well . . ." puff, puff. "I've never seen so gay a mob of hero-worshipping anarchists. I think they really yearn for a king — or a queen, rather. Like most Americans, really. Or, where all think alike, no one thinks much."

"Gay? You call them *gay?*"

"Why yes, gay. You don't think so? Look at them out there, prancing around and around like red savages, beating drums, laughing like idiots, howling at the moon, wrapping themselves in one fantastic tangle around that maypole. If these are revolutionists, they're the happiest jolliest craziest ones I've ever heard of. Wasn't it Emma Goldman who said, If there's no dancing at the revolution I won't come?"

"Emma Goldman? I don't recall."

"Maybe it was Jesus. Anyway . . ." Puff, puff, puff. "They're happy now. But how many will actually show up at Erika's body-heap demonstration? Bet you ten dollars to a dime there won't be twenty-five."

"You're such a cynic. Such a defeatist. Such a pessimist."

"Pessimist, yes. But a very wise man once said (I believe it was me), a pessimist is simply an optimist in full possession of the facts."

"Oh, bull. Bull-loney. You think she's beautiful?"

"Beautiful? Who? Whom?"

"That chick that doll that — come on, you know who I mean. Don't pretend you weren't leering at her like everybody else. The men, I mean. Is she?"

Puff. He considered. Carefully. "Not bad, not bad, in the conventional, cinematic, show-biz sense of the term. She'd make a nice *Cosmo* cover girl."

"Bet you'd rather see her in the middle of *Playboy.*"

"*Playboy?* Not familiar with that — is it a periodical?"

"Nobody loves a weisenheimer."

"You do, I hope. Where's Reuben?"

She stared across the moonlit meadow toward the bonfire, the lurid fifty-foot pole swirling with paper streamers, the dancing dark mass of human forms, the musicians bobbing on the stage. "Out there somewhere with Seldom and Susan's kids. I hope. You think we better find them?"

"Let them play a little longer. It's a Kiddies' Konvention. Susan's with them." He dropped his soggy cigar in the dust and ground it out. He drew her close. Lifting her chin, he kissed her, fair and square, on the sweet full rosy mouth. Withdrawing an inch or two, he muttered, "Baby, what say let's me and you back off under the trees over there, like to show you my new tattoo."

"Yeah? You sure it's me you want?"

"Cynic." He gazed into her violet eyes, dark and deep, lustrous and loving in reflected moonlight. "Listen, my love, my only one, there's cover girls, there's starlets, there's sexpots and sexbombs and sleek blank blond bimbos everywhere, but not too many real women. Me, I'll take the real woman anytime."

"You mean that?"

"Yes."

"Then shut up and take me."

"Yes."

"Talk talk talk — let's have some action around here."

"Yes."

She squeezed his hand. He was trembling. She stroked his fine hair, his smooth cheeks, his tender ears. She locked her hands behind his neck, tugged him gently down a bit, kissed his thin prim stiff lips. He stood rigid, arms pressed to his sides. She caressed his shoulders, his back, feeling the tension in the muscles. Delicately, she led him farther out upon the point of rock, close to her sleeping bag rolled on its foam rubber pad, the pad resting on a nylon poncho. They looked down, down, down, into the hazy depths, through the mists of moonlight and shadow to the dim forms of trees a thousand feet below — Douglas fir, pinyon pine, Gambel oak, juniper, hackberry. Far beyond and much farther below, the great river glided through its inner gorge toward its mothering fathering androgynous sea.

He stared into the wonder of the ages. She looked up at his youthful wonder.

"Oh for so long I sink off you. . . ."

He made no answer.

She ran her fingers through his hair, felt the absurd pigtail with its rubber band, leaned her fair head against his chest, under his chin, and stroked and squeezed the muscles of his brawny arm.

"You sink off me . . . ?"

He mumbled something unintelligible, words that caught and never quite emerged from his throat. Ziss silly poor boy: if only I could rub his back. He need massage. Good strong healthy Svenska massage. She kissed him at the base of neck. Slipped a hand up inside his shirt, caressed the hot bare skin of his lower back and waist. She thought of something else, pulled a tidbit from her shirt pocket, unwrapped a chocolate-coated truffle with one hand and held it to his lips.

"Oral . . ."

"Huh?"

"I haff surprise for you. Open wide, plizz."

"Whah? What is it?"

"Somesing mos' ex-*quis*-eet, darlink. Open lips, plizz." A joke occurred. "Open little hatch." She unsnapped her cowboy shirt, pulled up her EF! T-shirt. She wore no bra. Naturally. (Support them pectoral muscles.)

He did not open his mouth. She brushed his lips with the bit of chocolate. No good Mormon can resist chocolate. His tongue came out to taste. She lowered the bait, he bent down to follow, she lowered it further. His head was now below *her* chin. She clutched his hair with her strong right hand. Again she touched the delicious trifle to his mouth. His lips parted. Her right breast was bare, the nipple like a rosebud, erect and eager.

"Open wide, my Oral, I pop it in."

He opened wide. She arched her back, elevating her firm young mammaries to his face, to the moon, and popped it in.

"Don't bite, my luff. It melts in mouth."

"Well sheet," he growled, "just a lot of fuckin' goddamn bullshit if you ask me. One thousand kooks is all I saw." The horses shuffled through the pine duff, soft plopping iron shoes scuffing dust that floated like molecules of matter, nothing in particular, Lucretian atoms, on the slanting moonbeams. "Am I right, pardner? What'd you think?"

The other, up ahead, riding his old gray mare (once a silver stallion), mumbled something vague that sounded like "Good kids. Bunch of nice kids havin' fun."

"Yeah? Well, maybe. But they sure the fuck ain't gonna stop GOLIATH by layin' their bodies on the line. You and me know what'll happen. The construction goons will beat up a few girls and skinny little hippies while the cops watch. Then the cops will arrest the girls and hippies."

"For what?" asked the old man leading the way. Slow and cautious. Dark out there in the woods at two in the morning, moon setting low. And Freddies prowling the forest.

"What for? Come on, Jack, you been there. They arrest you for anything. Anything. Disturbing the peace. Obstructing Giant Earth Mover traffic. Hanging flowers and sticking stickers on the dragline bucket. Damaging private property. Any old thing will do, anything to make more trouble, give the cops an excuse to manhandle some good-lookin' women, make the demonstrators pay fines and hire lawyers and serve time in the county slammer, same old fuckin' crap, you know the story. You ever in your life see a situation so bad the cops couldn't make it worse?"

No reply to that question. No reply needed.

They rode on, almost silently, through the pine and the aspen, the fir and the spruce. Hearing nothing, seeing nothing, smelling nothing suggestive of the enemy, the man in the rear continued aloud with his train of thought. "After the cops and the troopers drag 'em all away, and everything is quiet, and the dust settles down, and the fuckin' dragline crew decides to take a break in the shade, pop some beers and celebrate, that's when we make our play."

"At the Neck?"

"The Neck is the place."

"Only me and you?"

"With a little help from my friends."

"Friends? You got friends? You?"

"Hard to believe, maybe. But it's true, pardner. I ain't got many but they're all I got and they're all we need."

"The Gang."

"That's right, Grandpa. That fuckin' old gang of mine."

They rode on, falling again into silence. They listened, watched, sniffed the currents of the air for trace of woodsmoke, gun oil, gasoline fumes, diesel smoke, Freddy's Forest Ranger eau de cologne, Smoky Bear. The old man peered intently ahead with one good eye, remembering the route, alert for any sign of something new. After a while, not slowing, he turned in his saddle, looked back and said,

"How'd you like that filly with the long mane and the high-set tail? Good hindquarters, too." Pause. No answer. "Pretty good points all over, wouldn't you say?"

His gold tooth gleamed in a grin; his bright glass eye glinted with what, in the moonlight, could pass for wit.

The younger man merely shrugged his ursine shoulders. His face, shadowed by the brim of a greasy leather sombrero, revealed no expression of emotion. "A woman's only a woman." He pulled a cigar from his vest pocket, shucked off the wrapper, stuck the cigar in his teeth. "A good cigar is a smoke."

But he did not light the cigar. He chewed it. They rode on, into the dark. The moon was down.

25

Love Proposes to His Wife

Zip! Zap!

"But Dudley . . . what would the neighbors think?"

Pssst! Fssst!

They stared at each other in the blue glow from the bedroom window. A poor vague light but sufficient for him to perceive the anxiety in her eyes, the tremor on her lip.

Zit! Zat! Zick!

"Honey pie, don't you worry none about them. They think what I tell 'em to think. And when. Am I Bishop this here goldang ward or hain't I? Huh?"

Snick! Snack! Snap crackle pop!

"You're Bishop, Dudley, but isn't that, I mean, you sure that won't raise a ruckus up in Salt Lake? Them Elders hear about it they might excommunicate."

Blip!

"Naw. They wouldn't dare. They know doggone well half the men south of Panguitch got plural wives. Like right here in Hotrocks. Look at that dang jack rabbit Smith, for one. And all them people straddlin' the border at Short Crick. Not to mention Glen Canyon City and Old

Pariah and Stocktank and Feedlot and Greasepit and Dipstick and Landfill and Flyspeck, what about them? And Page, Bluff, Mexican Hat, Kanab, Escalante, Boulder? And Herkin, Springdale, La Verkin, Mesquite, Fredonia? They wouldn't dare. They'd lose half the Dixie membership roll. And Moab and Hanksville and Green River and Blanding. *Blanding!* Gawd that Blanding now, there's a cesspool of sin and sex and drugs and AIDS and incest and sodom and gonorrhea if I ever heard. Teenage mothers. Putative fathers. They got actual Indian grave robbers livin' in that town. Talk about ghouls. Their own Bishop a pot collector."

Zap! Clapp!

"We're talkin' about polygamy, Father."

"Yeah I know, Mother, and that's my point, there's plenty things goin' on in the canyon country lots worse than a man takin' a second wife. That Smith with three, two of 'em half his age, look at him. Anyhow you think them Council of Twelve give a hoot in Hell —"

"Dudley!"

"— what anybody does down here? They sure as shootin' don't. Wasatch Front, that's all they care about. Wasatch Front and their doggone foreign missions in Norway and New Zealand and Patagonia and Gawd only knows where else. We don't count for old cowshit in their eyes."

"Mister Love!"

"Pardon my French, Mother, but gosh all golly them square-headed stuff-shirted dingdong dickless old farts up in Provo and Salt Lake make me sick sometime. How come there's a million a half people livin' up there and not four thousand in all of Alkali County? Only county in Utah with world's highest birthrate that's a-losin' population. Some kind of Wasatch Front International Communist Sahara Club Federal Government United Nations environmental-extremist conspiracy if you ask me. Get the U.N. out of the U.S. Get the U.S. out of the U.N., we should of done it years ago."

Fsssst! Fiiist!

"Now now, Dudley, don't get yourself all excited about them United Nations again. You know what it does to your blood pressure. Did you take your digitalis today?"

"Yes, Mother, I took my digitalis today gawddamnit."

"Father!"

"Sorry Mother. But gee whiz . . ."

"Anyhow it's illegal."

"What's illegal?"

"Bigamy."

"Bigamy? Who's talkin' about bigamy? We're talkin' about polyg-amy."

"What's the difference?"

Zip! Zip zip zip!

He smiled with tolerant condescension. "Oh come on, woman. Bigamy means two wives. Polygamy means two or *more*. Anybody knows that. Bigamy is a terrible sin. Polygamy is what them Hebrew old-timers Abraham, Jacob and Isaac and then Joseph Smith and Brigham Young done."

"You got a third in mind too, Dudley?"

"Huh? What? Naw, Mother, just the one." He smiled at the thought. "Two's plenty for your old Dudley. You know that. Don't forget my leaky valve."

"Just a-wonderin' where-all it's been leakin', Dud. What's her name?"

"Not that valve. Heart valve. What's her name? You really want details, Mother?"

She stared out the bedroom window, through the blue glow of Love's bug-zapper toward the dry pale beetle-infested leaves of the Chinese elm, the neighbor's blue-glaring mercury vapor yardlight, the distant but pervasive radiation of the uranium mill south of town. No stars available. No moon. Technology hath vanquished night and sometimes the Bishop's wife regretted that particular conquest in the onward march of progress. Though she'd never dare say so aloud. Not in Hotrocks. Not in Utah. Not in America the Beautiful.

"How come that bug-zapper don't kill them elm beetles?"

"What?"

"Seems like the more bugs that thing electrocutes the more bugs we get. Like maybe we're a-breedin' a tougher smarter breed of bug."

He smiled. "Never did know a woman could understand *ec*-lectricity."

"I'm not talkin' about volts, amperage, wattage or electrodynamics. I'm talkin' about natural selection. Evolution."

"Mother!"

"Well you been takin' up cursin' lately, why can't I say that word?"

"Let's not try to change the subject. Her name is Miss Dick. She's a rangerette in the BLM."

"How old is she?"

"Oh? Oh, about thirty-five, forty, I reckon." Liar; he knew very well she was barely thirty.

"That's too young for you, Father. She'll kill you. And then what about the will? What about your eleven children? What about me? We been married nigh onto twenty years, Dudley, and now you talk about a second wife. You bored with me already? And does she get part of your estate — our estate — when your heart gives out tryin' to keep her . . . satisfied?" He failed to answer. "Father, you're too old to take a young wife."

"She ain't young."

"Too young for you. You're an old man."

His manly pride was stung. Too old? he thought. Me, too old to do it anymore? Guess I done all right out there on the slickrock. Took a while but I done it, by Gawd, I got it up and I put it in the dock and I made her happy. I think. Didn't hear her complain none anyhow. Anyhow, like ol' Seldom says, if I ever get too old to get it up I'll turn the girls upside-down and *drop* it in. Like a plumb bob.

"Nothin' to say, Dudley?"

"Huh? I got plenty to say."

"Like what?"

"Like don't you worry none about that will. Ain't gonna make no changes in the will. She understands that. She ain't marryin' me for money. Why, with that goldang equal rights and affirmative action law (that tain't a law a-tall) she'll be state bureau chief inside five years. You know how it is these days. If you ain't a woman or a Nigra or a homo or a Jew or a Meskin or one-sixteenth Chippewa or better yet an illegal lesbian alien from Haiti in a wheelchair with a disadvantaged I.Q., you ain't got a chance in government work. That girl she's on the fast track to the top. Equal rights? What about equal rights for us native-born free white and twenty-one plain old-stock Gawd-fearing native Americans? It's Communism, Mother, that's what it is, Communism, and we might as well all go back to Siberia now. Makes me so *gawddang* mad . . ."

"Easy Dud, easy." She put her tender hand on his hoary-haired chest. "Heart's beatin' too fast, Father. Try to calm down now. You sure you took your digitalis?"

"Yes I'm sure I took my digitalis. So don't you worry about Rangerette Dick and the estate, she ain't gonna touch it. Not that she wants it. Everything we got goes to you and the kids. Anyways I don't mean to kick the old bucket or cash in my chips or settle the bill or meet my maker or ride an ol' paint with our faces to the West for a while *yet*, Mother, why you so interested in that anyhow? So don't fret."

They lay in bed holding hands, watching the blue glow of the insect killer, listening to the erratic, intermittent buzz and snap and zit of tiny executions. The faces of eleven children, framed in gilt, looked down upon the large comfortable if sagging conjugal bed. Eleven sweet and innocent kids, all girls, each and everyone with the face of Daddy, the brains of Mother. Talk about the handicapped, the disadvantaged! Though Mother had been showing signs of cerebral independence lately. Evolution. Natural selection. Electro . . . electro what? Where'd she see them words, he wondered, drifting toward slumber. Has this woman been hangin' around the library lately? Never did trust that new librarian we got now. She's Mormon, of course, but too young for a dangerous position like that. And she didn't even go to Brigham Young. Went to Utah State. In Logan. Hotbed of beer drinking and anti-Christ and atheism and English majors. . . .

His sweet drifting languor was broken by the one question he dreaded most, that he hoped would never come.

"Dudley . . . you still love me?"

"I sure do, Mother." He squeezed her hand. "More than ever."

"Then why do you need a second wife?"

Silence. Painful silence. Because every bull needs a bunch of cows? every rooster a flock of hens? every stallion a string of mares? The truth was too crude, too brutal, too obvious, too simple to be grasped by the fine subtle intuitive mind of the human female. What's more he loved the ranger and she loved him, sort of. The truth was not good enough. Not adequate. However, Bishop Love had anticipated this heart-breaking question from his loyal and loving and long-time wife and he had prepared an answer. Now was the time to try it out and hope for the best:

"Mother . . . the twelfth child?"

"What do you mean?"

"I mean our Saintly duty to create an earthly body for another one of them little kiddie souls waiting up in Heaven. I'm a-talkin' about Child Number Twelve, Mother."

"Oh Dudley . . . please Dudley . . . Dudley, I can't go through all that again. Dudley, Dudley, ain't eleven kids enough? Sometimes they drive me crazy, Dud. I'm old before my time. Don't make me do that again. I know it's our duty and all but Dud . . . please . . ."

Inwardly he smiled. She'd walked straight into his trap. But he couldn't resist the mean temptation to lock the trap, to clinch his argument. "But Mother, I'm the Bishop. You're the Bishop's wife. We got to set a right example for the Saints in our ward."

"I know, Father. But please . . . look at me. I used to have a nice body, now I'm shaped like Mrs. Potato-Head. Remember when you thought I was a pretty girl? Remember? And if that don't matter to you anymore, and I guess it don't, what about my nerves? What about my mental health, Dudley?"

He squeezed her hand, stroked her shoulder. She was crying again, silently. "Now now, Mother, you're the soundest strongest level-headedest woman I ever knowed. Forty-four kids and sixteen husbands couldn't drive you crazy. And that mental health talk, that's Communist, that's part of the Communist international environmental — you hear? Environ-*mental?* — conspiracy. That's why we made the state shut down that what they called 'Mental Health' Clinic. That's why we run them Jew headshrinkers outa the county."

"Sometimes I wish you hadn't done that, Dudley. That Doctor Robinson was a nice man. Everybody liked him. He done some poor women around here a world of good. I know three might of killed theirselves wasn't for him."

"Is that right?" The Bishop was uncomfortably aware that he was losing control of this dialogue. Somehow she had put him on the defensive again. "Well your nice Doctor Robinson is gone and them three women are still alive, ain't they?"

"Two of 'em. You know what happened to Darnelle."

"That woman always was crazy. She was a drunk. She had no business tryin' to drive a car. Anyhow, I said it then and I'll say it now, we don't need no Communist brain-washin' clinic around these parts. We don't need no Mental Health in Alkali County."

She fell silent, quietly crying. Where was I? he thought. Yeah — the twelfth baby. "Anyhow, Mother, we got to have that Child Number Twelve. It's our Christian duty as Latter-Day Saints to be fruitful and multiply and replenish the earth."

"Do we always have to do it all by ourselves?"

"No and this is what I want to tell you. If —"

"I just can't do it anymore. Why can't them Gentiles help? I'm plumb worn out, Bishop Love."

"I know that, Mother, so listen to me. We'll have Number Twelve by Ranger Dick." We? *We?* Never mind. He waited, staring at the ceiling, grinning in his guts. Now I got her. Let that sink in. Now she'll see the light of reason.

After a pause his wife said, "She'll do it?"

"Yes."

"And that'll count for us?"

"That's right, Mother."

"She'll be the surrogate mother?" In Mrs. Love's mouth the word came out as sorrow-gate. And sometimes as sore-gate.

"Ah — that's right." Love wasn't certain about that point but now was not the time to fuss over fine distinctions.

"It'll really be our child?"

"Ah — yes."

A pause. Another silence. "And who gets to raise the child, Father? Who gets to take care of it every day?"

Another pause. A further silence. Careful now, Dudley. Watch out. Think. He thought. And said, "She'll take care of it. It'll be our child but she'll raise it. Unless —"

"Unless what?"

"Unless you want it."

Zip! Zap! Zat! Zit!

This time Mrs. Love raised her head from the pillow, elevated herself to one elbow and looked at her husband. In the semi-darkness she could see only his square handsome massive head, the big shoulders, his arms. A faint bluish glow, like a halo, like an aura, seemed to emanate from his face and outline his head. For a moment she was startled.

"Dudley — you been eatin' carnotite again?"

He twitched in surprise. "What? Eatin' what? What're you talkin' about, woman?" With difficulty he shifted mental gears.

"You look radioactive."

"You're crazy." He looked at his hands, saw the pale luminosity, touched his face. Felt normal. Touched his hair, ears, neck. Everything felt normal except his heart, which seemed overexcited, under pressure, strictured. Staring at his wife, he saw the blue glow in the bedroom window behind her. He smiled. "For godsake, Mother, it's only the bug-zapper." He took her nearest hand again, stroked her warm palm with his thumb. "Now you relax, sweetheart. Don't worry none about me or her or that Number Twelve child. Everything is gonna be A-OK. We're gonna work this out so everyone is happy. Everyone."

She lay down flat again, on her back. Both of them wide awake, terrified by life and love and death and marriage and sex and reproduction and the future, and by what would the neighbors think, they stared at the opaque obscurity of the ceiling. After a while, before they finally got some sleep, Mrs. Love said,

"But Father . . . what *will* the neighbors think?"

He also had an answer for that. Grinning in the dark, he replied, "Who told 'em they could think?"

26

The Last Poker Game

The canyon winds blew softly.

The old houseboat rocked gently on the wavelets.

The old Green River flowed homeward to the sea.

Toward the sea, pardon. Suffering evaporation in the Lake Foul National Settling Pond, then the Lake Merde National Recreation Slum, then diverted into canals, conduits, channels and ditches to die by slow degree among the surplus-cotton plantations of Arizona, the sorghum fields of the Imperial Valley, the beanfields and alfalfa farms of Mexicali, the cisterns, swamp coolers, car washes, fire hydrants, Laundromats, golf courses, swimming pools, sensory deprivation tanks, kitchen sinks, toilet bowls, septic tanks, leach fields, sewage lagoons and sewage treatment plants of Greater L.A. . . . this ancient and noble river never achieved union anymore with its parent body, the Sea of Cortez and the Pacific Ocean, but expired in poisoned trickles and polluted dribbles on the baked cracked desiccated mud of the barren delta, far above its natural outlet. Centipedes crawled, flies buzzed, cows stumbled, vultures cruised, spiders crept, weeds grew where once upon a time and not so long ago a living river flowed and sparkled, fish danced, herons stalked and falcons gyred and stooped, with a green fragrant forest, on either bank, sheltering the secret lives of deer and ocelot, jaguar and javelina, gray wolf and black bear, red fox and puma, armadillo and snapping turtle, anhinga, elegant trogon, ivory-billed woodpecker, kingfisher, bald eagle, marsh hawk, sea gull, pelican, fucking albatross, magnificent fucking frigate bird. . . .

Gone. A river no more.

"So what?" she snapped. "So who cares?" In mock disgust she whipped her cards to the table while Doc, as usual, with apologetic smile and stinking cigar, raked in the pot. Bonnie the bad loser. But next dealer.

"How'd you do that, Doc?" says Seldom.

"Control, friends, control. Same as always."

"Naw, somehow it ain't the same without Oral here."

"Oral the Provider," Susan says (Mrs. S. S. Smith #3).

"Oral the Moral," Kathy says (Mrs. S. S. Smith #2).

"What happened to that kid anyhow?"

"Well you seen him there at that there Rando-voo. Poor guy's in love with that Miss Universe type from . . . where's she from? Italy? Spain? Greece? Germany?"

"Norway," Doc said. "The Svenska maid. The King of Norway's daughter, fair Sigrid with the Emerald Eyes."

Bonnie looked up from her fingernails. "Emerald? How would you know? We were fifty yards away."

"Deal the cards."

"So what's the game?"

"Dealer's choice. You're the dealer."

"All right," says Bonnie, shuffling the deck, "this time it's Abbzug Wins, also known as Montana Gouge. Everybody ante one buck. How'd you know they're green?"

"Hey, two-bit limit."

"Special game. Ante up or shut up." Bonnie led with a dollar bill.

Reluctantly, each player pushed or dropped or tossed four blue chips onto the center of the table, the middle of the soft beguiling green. The dealer reached out and pulled in the five dollars. The others stared. Bonnie stacked the chips before her, tossed another dollar into the pot and repeated the dealer's command: "Everybody ante another buck." She shuffled, riffled, interleaved the cards, watching her husband. "How'd you know, Doc?"

"Hey, dealer, what kinda game is this?"

"How'd I know what?"

"He said dealer's choice. I'm the dealer. You want to play poker, Smith, or you want to go home and cry?"

"Tough broad, this here Mizz Abbzug."

"Also she forgot to cut the deck."

"It's a tough game, country bumpkin. You in or out?"

The big Aladdin lamp swung gently overhead, casting its mellow radiance upon the chips of red and white and blue, the paper dollars and the silver coins, the redback cards, the rednosed Doc, the strawhaired Seldom, the comely and serene young faces of the three women. Bonnie's Reuben and the Smiths' five kids were sleeping forward on the bunks in the wheelhouse. Outside of the grand master salon, where this sporting game of chance took place, the only sound was the faint moan of the night wind sweeping up the river, the lapping of little brown waves, the slap of beaver tail on water, the occasional tramp and thud of Seldom's horses grazing on alfalfa in Seldom's twenty-acre riverside pasture. You might also have heard, if you listened with extreme acuity, the rustle of vines creeping over sandy, well-tilled, drip-irrigated and well-manured soil in Susan Smith's two-acre melon patch. The constellations of the stars, blazing with holy light through the dark clear desert sky, could not be heard by any array of human ears. Nor the arc of meteor, the shower of shooting stars. Nor the vast approach, from far beyond Andromeda, of the Lord of the Universe, Uranus, seeking out his bride, Gaia, green-bosomed, brown-thighed, rosy-bellied Earth.

Listening, Smith stared blankly at the ceiling.

Grinning, Bonnie returned the false ante to all players, and dealt five cards face down to each. "Straight draw," she announced, "nothing wild, jacks or better to open. Everybody ante up. How, Doc?"

"By me," said Kathy.

"Only a guess. Black-haired Sigrid with the Emerald Eyes — from a poem I read somewhere, long ago, in another country. An odd and interesting genetic type."

"By me."

"Seldom?"

He fanned his hand, looked, clapped it shut. "Pass, podner." Still listening, his gaze went over Bonnie's shoulder, out the little curtained port, into the windy dark.

"What do you hear?"

Doc tossed a blue chip into the pot. "Two bits."

"Nothing."

Bonnie looked at Smith intently for a moment, accepted his statement, announced Doc's bet. She called. The others called, no one folding. No one had folded yet in this night's game; without young J. Oral Hatch taking part, their secret tapline to the U. S. Treasury, poker was merely a playful *divertissement* among family members, Sarvis, Smith & Co. Inc., lacking seriousness. Not much fun. If most of the chips ended up before Doc Sarvis, as usually happened, it mattered little to anyone. He bought the whisky, soda, Pepsi, beer and chips, Bonnie made the dip and salsa, cake and coffee, no one really lost. The game was merely background noise, like Mozart or Muzak, as in the Archduke's court, for the sustenance of conversation. Manual persiflage, as Doc would say, to keep the KGB confused, the FBI off the streets, the CIA amused, the Interpol entertained.

"Her name is Erika, right?" Bonnie checked the pot. "Somebody's light again."

"It's you, my darling. As always."

"Izzat right, Hawkeye?" She added her blue chip — "Pot's right!" — picked up the remaining deck, thumb, forefinger, middle finger poised for action. "Cards!"

Three for Kathy, three for Susan, one for Seldom, two for Doc. "Doc takes two," the dealer announced. "He's trying to bluff again. On your guard." She peeled off one card for herself, quickly, and dropped the deck. "Dealer tay . . . mmm . . ." she mumbled, furtively. Loudly: "Your bet, Sarvis."

"Five beans."

Bonnie studied her hand, lips moving. Eyes bright, tail bushy, nostrils dilated like a vixen smelling blood, she chirped, "Raise *you* five beans, old bean." She flipped two blue chips on top of Doc's one. Called, called, called, and "Raise you back," said the good gray balding doctor, tossing his fifty cents into the pot.

Bonnie stared at him, locking eyeballs. He stared back through foggy glasses. She stared, watching for the hint of fraud or irresolution. No such hint forthcoming: Doc's poker face was implacable, unshakable, redoubtable.

"You're called, you quack." She matched his raise. "And raised again." She flipped her second chip upon the pile. All blue. Heavy stakes. She looked at Kathy on her left. "That's fifty cents to you, my dear."

"I'll stay."

"Susan?"

"Stay."

"Seldom?" He was gazing up at nothing, frozen, mouth agape. "Seldom Seen Smith? This is Mission Control calling Smith."

"Yeah?" He returned to earth. "What's it to me?"

"Two true blue."

He checked his cards again, cupped deep in his large grimy left hand. "No game for shoe clerks." He collapsed his hand and spun it face down upon the discards. "I'm out. Go get 'im, ladies. And that's right, her name is Erika. Now what you spoze a classy gal like that sees in a simple Utah kid like J. Oral Hatch?"

Doc raised again: fifty cents. He stared at his wife, his face immobile, blank, dumb, devoid even of any trace of curiosity in her response.

Mrs. Sarvis — Mrs. Bonnie Abbzug-hyphen-Sarvis, to be precise — stared right back, her face heartbreaking in its rosy loveliness, exasperating in its stubborn will to triumph even at the risk of severe financial loss ($1.50? $1.75?). "What do you have in your hand, you old bluffer you?"

Doc fanned out his cards — close to the chest — and looked. "Bullets," he said. "Three bullets and a pair."

"You liar." Bonnie looked again at her own hand. Ten high straight. She'd drawn the eight, smack dab in the middle. Pretty damn flashy maneuver. But he had her beat if he was telling the truth. And sometimes Doc did tell the truth, especially when bluffing. Sometimes he lied. Sometimes he did both. Bonnie hesitated, hesitated. She glared at her husband. She glared at her perfect straight. (Is there any other kind?) She was dying to show it, aching to tell about it.

"Full house beats a straight," he reminded her. "Beats a flush too."

"Keep him honest," Susan said.

Bonnie picked up her last greenback. "Raise it again, big shot." She slapped the bill down on the pile of chips. "And no more raises, that's it. Right, Seldom?"

"House rule," he agreed.

Kathy dropped out. Susan dropped out. Seldom was out. Only Doc stayed in, facing the determined dealer. He squinted at her with his small evil red eyes, the dingy smoke from his cheap cigar encircling his head like a wreath of pure smog. He grinned. He dropped two blue chips in the pot. "You're called, dealer. Let's see what you got. Put up or shut up."

Bonnie displayed her pretty little straight. "Beat that, wiseass. I did it the hard way too."

Doc grinned again, cigar jutting from the corner of his loose, sensual, slack-fibered mouth. Crumbs in his beard. He smacked down his cards, one by one, with heavy, melodramatic flourish. One: Ace of spades. Two: Ace of clubs. Three: Ace of diamonds. "Three bullets," he pointed out, a sneer of mean and petty malice on his lip.

"So?"

"And the pair." He looked at the two in his hand, just to make sure, then slapped them, one at a time, onto the table. Four of hearts. Three of hearts. "Pair of hearts," he explained. "Big two-hearted bluffer."

Seldom clapped, the women cheered, Doc smiled, as Bonnie raked in the biggest pot of the evening.

Kathy shuffled the deck.

Seldom Smith listened for the sound of strange horses.

The old houseboat creaked at its moorings. The little riverine waves gurgled and played, flipped and flopped at waterline, splashing against the hull. The boat rocked, the lanterns swayed from their hooks in the ceiling beam. Shadows wavered on the walls. From far away along the river's shore they heard the cry of an owl. The hoot of the great horned owl, calling for his friends.

Come out and play. . . .

"You think he's around?" Bonnie said.

"Who?"

"Him."

"You mean —?"

"Yeah. Him."

"Doubt it," Seldom said. "Last I heard . . ." He paused.

"Yeah?"

"Last I heard he was headed for Australia. That's what I heard."

Bonnie cut the deck, Kathy named the next game — seven-card Hi-Lo — and began to deal.

"The last good country," Doc mused, talking to himself. "We should all go there to live."

"Any of you see him lately?" Bonnie asked.

"Not me," Seldom said.

Doc looked up. "Not me. You?"

"Me? How would I see him? I don't even know where he lives anymore. Do you? Or even if he's still alive."

"Is he still alive?" Doc asked.

"Goldarned if I know," Smith said. "Last I heard he was down in Mexico, as I recollect, a-tryin' to figure a way to sink the boat."

"What boat?"

"That big boat they used to haul the nucular reactors through the Panama Canal and up the Sea of Cortez to Rocky Point."

"You mean Rocky Point, Mexico? Punta Reñasco?"

"That's right, honey."

"The Mexicans are building a nuclear power plant? The *Mexicans*? Good God, we are in trouble."

"King," sang Kathy, dealing the third cards face up. "Three. Ten. Jack. Another cowboy. First king bets."

Susan bet the nickel — one white chip. Doc raised. The rest stayed.

"They was for that nuke plant at Phoenix, Arizona, honey. Palo Verde. America's biggest. Was the only way Bechtel could get them from New Orleans to Phoenix was what I heard. Anyhow that's the last time I seen him. About two three years ago, maybe."

"The Mexicans brew fine beer," Doc said. "Paint great murals. Started a good revolution once, which will soon be resumed, I expect. I won't hear a word said against them."

"Did he sink the boat?"

"Pair of jacks bets."

"He got on board somehow, ten miles out of Rocky Point and tried to scuttle it: opened the seacocks, monkey-wrenched the pumps. But they was too close to port, crew managed to limp in and get the nukes unloaded before the ship went down. In thirty feet of water."

"What happened to him?"

"He got away. He always gets away. Ain't no jail on earth can keep that boy shut up. They'll have to kill him. The government's probly figured that out by now."

"So now we have the world's biggest nuke plant setting thirty miles upwind from Phoenix." Disgust in her voice, Bonnie peeked again at her hole cards. "Sickening."

"That's right, Bonnie. But it's only Phoenix."

"One million human beings live in Phoenix."

"What kind of human beings would live in a town like Phoenix?"

"Jacks still high," sang Kathy. Your bet, Doc."

"Raise it two beans." The dime — a red chip. "Some of those million are children," he said. "That's the point."

"You don't like grownups?" Susan asked.

"Not much. Only my friends. As the years go by, one by one, I find it harder and harder to feel any respect, or even much sympathy, for the human race."

"You some kind of misanthrope?"

"Some kind. More and more I prefer women to men, children to adults, the other animals to the naked ape."

"People are no damn good," agreed Seldom. "Take 'em one at a time, they're all right. Even families. But bunch 'em up, herd 'em together, get 'em organized and well fed and branded and ear-notched and moving out, then they're the meanest ugliest greediest stupidest dangerest breed of beast in the whole goldang solar system far as I know."

Doc nodded. The women glanced at one another, raising eyebrows, calling bets, rolling eyes.

"You two belong in the Badlands," Susan said. "Out there with those clay hills and petrified logs and nothing alive but a few horned toads and sidewinders. You'd be happy there."

"I been a-thinkin' the same thing," Smith said. "How about it, Doc?"

"Me too."

"Come to town about once a month, hold up the bank, clean out the liquor store, rob the supermarket, rape all the good-lookin' wimmin if any and then gallop back to them calico hills, what do you think, Doc?"

"Sounds about right."

"The good life," Bonnie snorted. "The life of reason. What about the toy store, boys? And whose bet for chrissake?"

"Yours."

"Then I raise. Two bits." She tossed in another blue chip. "So he actually sank a ship. Was it in the papers?"

"Papers said it was an accident. Nothing about who done it nor why. Government don't want people to get hold of no funny ideas."

"Mexican? American? Which government?"

"Any government."

"Three jacks win," announced Kathy.

Doc pulled in the pot. Susan shuffled the deck. Seldom cut and stared out the window. If we're going to do it we better do it soon, Bonnie thought. And felt at once the cold, deep, clammy, paralyzing fear. No, no, not again. But I promised.

"How'd that Round River Rendezvous turn out?" Susan asked, dealing the cards with slick finesse. "After we left?"

"What's the game for chrissake?"

"Anaconda. Pass the Trash. Anybody hear?"

"We only stayed one more day ourselves."

"One of my nurses stayed for the whole week," Doc said. "Ac-

cording to her things got lively after we geriatrics left. According to her
we missed the good part."

"Like what?"

"There was a raid one night by the Aryan Nation," Bonnie said. "Or
Alien Nation, something like that. They rode through on those big
motorized kiddie-cars from Japan — those — what are they called?"

"ORVs," Kathy said. "Off Road Vermin."

"Yeah. Right. Anyhow this Alien Nation bunch drove through the
camp on their mechanical vermin shooting off guns and cracking
bullwhips before Roselle and Foreman and Igor and the Goon Squad
ran them off. Nobody hurt. Then the next day a busload of Up With
People people from Provo drove in, uninvited, gave a free concert,
received a sitting ovation and the usual beer and flowers bit, cried a
lot and left quietly. Then came — what, Doc?"

"It's your bet."

"I check. Okay. Then one day there was a grand schism. Skism? The
Sparklers and the Twinklers demanded that Earth First! drop the
clenched fist as official symbol. Said it's too aggressive. Said it suggests
spiritual negativity, crystal imbalance, harmonic divergence."

"Quite right," said Doc. "Raise it two reds."

"What happened?"

"There was a discussion by the whole mob. Some thought the fist
should be holding a daisy. Some suggested a teacup. Some thought the
fist should have the middle finger rigidly extended. Others said make
it the little pinkie, more polite. Some guy from Australia said, Why not
whack off the bloody fist, give us a bleeding bloody stump? Italian guy
said, Cock and balls, cock and balls with wings, viva l'amore, viva la
Napoli. Women wouldn't go for that, they wanted something more
feminine, more Gaia-like. Cock and balls with, ah, vulva? No. Like
what? Like a bomb with burning fuse, Georgia Hayduchess said, or a
female monkey wrench. More yelling and screaming. Big argument
about plumbing, pipe fittings, pipe wrenches, male and female connections, suction valves, bolts, nuts, left-hand threads and right-hand
screws. Then the Twinklers and Sparklers got mad. As mad as Twinklers and Sparklers can get without releasing negative feelings. Their
official spokesperson made a nice little speech about how their pro-
posal was meant to be taken seriously but since it wasn't they felt the
time had come for them to leave Earth First!, no bad vibrations of
course, and return to their true spiritual group the Rainbow Gathering. Then they walked out. En masse. All thirty of them. What
happened next, Doc?"

"Don't remember. Raise her two bits."

"I'll stay. So they left. Then next day the naturists walked out. Said Earth First! was too strict and conservative, everybody but the nudists wearing pants or dresses, even some of the children. Made them feel self-conscious, they said, discriminated against. So they left, one dozen bareasses, all rosy red with indignation. Sunburned too — they forgot that North Rim is nearly eight thousand feet above sea level. That desert sun is hot. Some eco-femmes left because there was only one woman on the goon squad. After that, what? What'd she say? More speeches, parties, workshops, dances, sings, wolf-howl sing-alongs, full moon ceremonies, lost children, a few fights, usual fornication in the woods, two broken marriages, three weddings, one live birth, too much beer drinking and pot smoking, one midnight raid by the county sheriff and the Search and Rescue Team but they were too late, all the dope was gone by then, one last grand feast and final dance with music by the real Nitty Gritty Dirt Band — said they were, anyhow — and next day everybody went home. Or somewhere else. Or down into the canyon, never to return, who knows? So now what? What're we doing here?"

"Roll 'em back," the dealer said. "Roll 'em and bet 'em."

"I hate this game," Bonnie said. "It's too complicated. Worse than baseball. What's wild?"

"Nothing's wild," Doc said, matching Seldom's bet. "But remember, if you've got a wheel you can go either high or low. Or both ways. Your bet."

Bonnie peeked at her hand one last time. A-A-A-2-2! The full boat. She laid them down in what she thought would make a good betting sequence: A-2-A-2-A. Make 'em think I'm going low, bet the limit, scare out the Little Minnies. She rolled the first deuce and raised the bet. The others called. Nobody quit. This was not what you'd term a conservative game. Nor were the others conservative players, except Doc, of course, who always played as if he'd bet the family farm. As if poker was more than only a silly game. As if the game were another expression of life itself. He always played to win. Then threw away the winnings. My Doc. My crazy old man. My ball and chain. My hub.

"How long you think Earth will last?" said Kathy. "I mean Earth First! Sounds like they're breaking up already."

"Like the I.W.W.," Doc said, "they'll last until they become effective. Then the state moves in, railroads some of the leaders into prison, murders a few others for educational purposes, clubs and gasses and jails the followers and *voilà!* — peace and order are restored."

"We got no leaders," Susan cried. "We're all leaders."

"Lovely slogan. Therein lies your strength — if only it could be true. We'll see. But we all need leaders. Not masters, not bosses, not popes, not generals, but leaders. Someone able to say the right thing at the right time, willing to place himself up front when the enemy appears . . ."

"Or herself," Bonnie said.

"Exactly. Or herself. That Erika woman, a natural. Can't help herself, just naturally has to hurl her body into the forefront of the battle. Why? Brains, beauty, physical energy, ideas, emotions, idealism? Those help but there's something more in a case like that."

"She's not a case."

"Forgive me. In a woman like that. In a person, a personage, a human being like that. What is that extra quality? I would call it spiritual vitality. *Élan vital.* A great soul. There's no such thing, they told us in medical school. Show me this spirit, Doctor Zeitkopf used to say, and I'll show you a diseased pituitary gland. The brain secretes soul, he'd say, as the liver secretes bile. So we'd cut these bodies open, the living, the dead, humans, dogs, monkeys, rats, and what did we find? Glands. Nerves. Organs. Tissue. Gallstones. Tumors. Layers of yellow blubber. Bloated hearts, swollen spleens, necrotic muscle, intestinal polyps, brains swarming with dead-white tubercles. Ah hah! said Doctor Time-Head, you see? Iss nossing here but us chickens!"

The houseboat rocked in the midnight breeze. The children slumbered, dreamed, twitched their little limbs. The horses shuffled slowly, step by step, over the hard earth, ripping herbage from the ground. The great owl called. The stars burned like emeralds, like sapphires, like rubies and diamonds and opals across the black velvet sky, receding from us at near the speed of light, fleeing into space and time where neither space nor time can yet exist.

"Roll 'em again."

Bonnie revealed her third card, her second ace. Now they all knew she was going high. So what? She *felt* high, she felt supreme, she felt invincible. She called, she raised, she bet the home ranch, she showed her second deuce. For a moment it occurred to her that the full house, in this particular form of poker, was not a particularly powerful hand. Perish the thought.

"And what did you say to Doctor Time-Head, Doc?"

"Kathy my love, I said nothing. I was just another shy clumsy Midwestern intern, intimidated and overawed. But I suspected, even then, that Doctor Zeitkopf was overlooking something. Forgetting something. Something vital . . . like life. He knew everything about the parts but didn't consider the whole. These dead and dying bodies were not whole. A whole animal is a healthy animal and Doctor Zeitkopf never saw a healthy animal. Even the dogs and rats and monkeys in the research lab, though healthy when brought in, were half dead from fear when the men in the white coats came around. Sick with terror. Imagine, imagine, the *horror* of their situation. The unspeakable horror of it. Conrad himself, what did he know of the heart of darkness? Anyway — let's not get into that — anyway, a healthy young woman like Erika whatshername — what is her last name by the way, anybody know? — is a whole, a being complete, intact and compact, with a personality — no, wrong word, trivialized word — is a vital spirit, by God, in a way that no amount of analysis, psychoanalysis, chemical analysis, vivisectional analysis, tomographic analysis, computerized analysis could ever have predicted. A healthy active lively woman like your leader Erika is not a mere clever assembly of intricate parts, like say a computer, but something more like a . . . like a composition: a poem; a symphony; a dance. Some humans can be reduced to robots, to slavery, given the proper training, torture, genetic breeding. (Some cannot.) But no amount of robot could ever manufacture a human being. Or make a human out of a slave. Or make any other vital, happy, healthy, defiant animal. That is my belief, my conviction, I couldn't prove it on paper or on a blackboard or on a printout but I can prove it by showing you somebody like Erika. Erika and her friends, those vital spirits we saw out there in the woods, on the edge of the yawning abyss. If anyone can stop the megamachine they can. And if they can't . . . whose bet?"

They stared at him in wonder. Such words. Such talk. Such wild and wonderful imagination.

"You said a mouthful, Doc," said Seldom. "Took the words right outa my mouth."

"Then you're going to be on the Neck with her," Kathy said. "At the action, putting your body where your mouth is. Right?"

"Me?" Doc smiled in slight embarrassment. "No, as a matter of fact I can't be there that day. Got to . . . going to the, ah, the pediatrics convention in St. Louis. You?"

"We don't even know what day it will be. And yes," said Kathy, "I am going to be there. Whatever day it is."

"Me too," said Susan. She and Kathy looked at the others. The others looked at each other. A pause for reflection.

"I'll be there," Bonnie said, half lying through her teeth. A small white lie seemed necessary at this point, if she meant to reassure her husband. And she did. But who's he know in St. Louis? Never heard about this particular pediatrics convention before. Is that old man two-timing me? Impossible. No, it's possible, this is poker.

With observation swinging toward Smith, he endeavored to evade peer pressure by getting back to the game, the real game, the game of chance, the dance of life, poker. "Pot right? Let's roll 'em." He showed his fourth card: 4-3-2-6. All clubs. Possible straight flush. Possible wheel. "Read 'em and weep, folks, this here's no game for sodajerks."

Doc rolled his: three whores and a sodajerk.

Bonnie showed her second deuce. Two pair up. Possible boat. Likely bluff. Certain high.

Kathy showed hers: the rough seven. 2-4-5-7. Not much to bet your shirt on. But again, a possible low.

Susan rolled her second nine: two pair, nines and tens. Everybody going high? "Three queens bet," she said to Doc.

Doc bet the limit. Bonnie raised him. Kathy stayed. The dealer folded. Smith raised Bonnie. Doc raised Smith. Bonnie calculated.

"So what's it to me?"

"Twenty beans. Eight bits. One dollar. And no more raises."

"You're called." She bet her final dollar.

Kathy folded. "Too rich for me."

Seldom stayed, called, picked up some chips.

"Declaration," the dealer called. "Grab your chips. None if you're going low, one for high, two for acey-deucy."

The three remaining contenders held clenched fists above the table.

"Earth First!" cried Kathy.

"Declare!"

Three fists sprang open. Doc held one chip, Bonnie held one, Smith held zero. "We've been sandbagged," Doc said to Bonnie.

Smith grinned with smug satisfaction.

"Okay," the dealer said, "last chance: three queens still bet."

Again Doc bet the limit. Again Bonnie raised him. Again Smith raised her and Doc raised Smith and Bonnie called and Smith called. Showdown time. Smith showed his broken wheel, winning half the pot. Bonnie turned up her third ace. Full house. Doc turned up his fourth queen. High hand.

"I don't understand this game," she said.

"Nobody does," said Doc, watching carefully as Smith divided the pot. Dollar for you, dollar for me, dollar for you, dollar for me . . .

"Where'd you get that fourth lady?"

"God provides."

"And where is Seldom going to be when GOLIATH begins his march across the Neck?"

Fifty for you, fifty for me, fifty for you . . .

"I'm talking to you, Seldom Smith."

"Who, me?"

"Yeah, you. Where you gonna be, brother, on Saint Erika Day?"

Smith paused, thought, hesitated and said, "Well, Bonnie honey, reckon I'll be on the river again probly. Got a fourteen-day trip a-comin' up soon. Got to make a living. Got three wives, seven kids and about fifteen lazy fat no-good horses to support."

"From what I hear those three wives support you more than you support them."

He grinned. "True fact. But I help out some."

"So you won't be there."

He hesitated. A shadow of pain crossed his honest, wind-burned, leathery, homely, "incorrigibly bucolic" face. Only his upper forehead, always shielded by a hat when out-of-doors, revealed by its native pallor his membership in the "white," "flesh-colored," Caucasian or northern European race of man. That brow now wrinkled in perplexity; Smith found it difficult to commit even the simplest, most well-meaning, most innocent of lies. "Yes, ma'am."

"You won't?"

"No. Whose deal?"

The women looked accusingly at the men. "You're both chicken," Susan said. "All big talk and no action. You afraid we'll be licked? Afraid we might be arrested? Beat up? Have to go to jail? Well I'll tell you guys what I think: I think it's important to make a stand whether we win or lose. There's one thing worse than being defeated and that's not making any fight at all. Seems to me, Doc, I used to hear you say those very words."

He nodded, looking at his white strong clean physician's hands. "You're right, Susan." He went on, quietly, head down, as if talking to himself. "The megamachine means slavery. Submission to slavery is the ultimate moral disgrace. Live free or die. Death before dishonor. Code of the eco-warrior, creed of the free, motto of the noble in spirit. Quite true, Susan. It's nice to win — or so I've heard. But win or lose, the important thing is resistance. Defiance. Rebellion. Better to die on our feet than live on our knees. Quite so."

"So?"

"So I won't be there with Erika. Won't be at her side or even somewhere in the ranks behind her. Include me out."

"You big hairy silver-tongued coward."

"My heart will be with you."

"Yeah, your heart, seems to me we've heard that line before somewhere."

Doc bowed his head in shame. Seldom Seen Smith stared out the porthole into the darkness, wishing he were elsewhere. Bonnie felt embarrassed. All were embarrassed. Bareassed ignominy.

"One more game," Bonnie said, changing the subject.

"It's late," Kathy said. "I'm sleepy."

"Just one more. Potluck pot. Everything on the table and high card takes it all." Before anyone could object she gathered everybody's pile of chips, coins and bills to the center of the table. Not that anyone had much to donate but the good Doctor Sarvis. He watched glumly, saying nothing. Bonnie grabbed the deck, shuffled the cards briefly, prepared to deal. "One card is all you get and one card is all you need."

"Wait a second," Kathy warned. "Cut!"

"Right," growled Doc. "Don't forget to cut the fucking deck."

"So all right already." Smiling cheerfully, with *emphatic* cheerfulness, Bonnie slapped the deck down before Kathy on her left. No one objected. Kathy made a double cut. Bonnie restacked the deck — not meaning to — exactly as it was before. Everybody watched. Nobody said a word. "And here we go!"

She cracked the cards out one by one, each with a smart professional *snap!* of crisp and brilliant pasteboard. A ten of hearts for Kathy.

"Big ten!"

A two-eyed jack for Susan.

"Jack o'diamonds, jack o'diamonds, don't I know you of old? / You rob mah po' pockets of a-silver and gold. . . ."

A queen of spades for Seldom. "The black lady! We're moving right along, folks, moving right along and I think I see a pattern here and I think I like its looks."

She dealt the king of hearts to Doc. "Yeah! Big red cowboy! See what I mean, folks? Now watch this."

Holding the deck in her left palm, she rubbed the back of the top card with her right thumb, rubbing in the magic. Facing upward, eyes closed, she said, "Everybody watch close now. Don't want to hear any whining later. Got my mojo workin', got my mojo workin' . . ." She whipped off the top card — *"Voilà!"* — and slapped it down, face up. "Ace!"

She opened her eyes. Three of clubs.

Doc raked in the pot.

Smith watched with morose resignation. "Doggone that young J. Oral. Goldang useless FBI men. Ain't never around when you need them."

27

Behold GOLIATH!

We stand *for* what we stand *on*.

The flags rippled, the banners flapped, the placards rattled in the breeze.

EARTH — LOVE IT OR LEAVE IT!

No compromise in defense of Mother Earth.

The vultures watched from overhead, circling and soaring, dreaming and waiting, all the time in the world. The midday sun flared with plasmic hydrogen, joyous and fierce. A flock of pinyon jays swept across the Neck, one hundred feet from rim to rim, two thousand feet straight down on either side. Down, down, down and down, a vertical fall in spectacular relief, through the gulf of space before sandstone walls where only the nests of swallows clung, to the shattered rock below.

Getting even is the best revenge. (The only revenge.)

Love your Mother. Be true to the Earth. Be eco-centric not ego-centric. Bio-centric not homo-centric. *Terra primum. Wo ist die schrauben-schlussel Bande?* ONWARD TO THE PLEISTOCENE.

Recorder music floated on the air, thin and plaintive as the sound of a Japanese bamboo flute. Laughter, singing, nervous and excited talk, rose beyond the music.

The Earth First! warriors waited, more girls than boys, more women than men, more young than old. Indeed, many were children; some still babies in their mothers' arms; a few still curled in fetal slumber in the womb. Most except the unborn wore plain sturdy outdoors clothing, ready for scuffles, rough stuff, police arrest, dragging and clubbing and jailing.

IF WILDERNESS IS OUTLAWED . . .

Not yet visible but coming closer minute by minute were the bulldozers, the front-end loaders, the dump trucks, the road graders. Dim in the distance sounded the vast electrical uproar of the walking dragline: the G.E.M. of Arizona: GOLIATH.

Hearing that baleful roar — that scream full of bale — the affinity groups went into huddle, like high-school football teams confronting Michigan State. Heads bowed together, arms on shoulders, hips jostling hips, they shared and augmented their fragmented courage, broke the spiritual bread and drank the communion wine of love, reviewed tactics, recalled the nature of the ideal. Which is: not necessarily to be realized in our time but to serve, to serve forever, as a guide to the perplexed. The ideal not as goal but as reference, a steadfast Northern star for the human heart and mind.

. . . ONLY OUTLAWS CAN SAVE WILDERNESS.

The Syn-Fuels survey crew was present, three roosters and a chick, patiently hammering in stakes for the third time in the same place in three weeks. Fast as the crew drove them in the Earth First! commandos yanked them out and flung them over the rim: pink ribbons flying, the stakes vanished.

"You punks will pay for this," the crew chief howled, "you'll pay through the nose." A Syn-Fuels cameraman stood nearby with movie camera, recording the event, acquiring evidence. Or attempting to do so; his subjects were masked in bandannas and sun goggles and large hats with floppy brims; the boys wore Mother Hubbards over their T-shirts and bluejeans; the girls were dressed as Indians, feathers in their headbands, warpaint on their cheeks, black masks across the eyes. Another Boston Tea Party.

The police and police rangers had not yet arrived but even now the whock whock whock of approaching helicopters could be heard.

*   *   *

SYN-FUELS GO HOME. EURO-TRASH GO HOME. BACK TO BRUS-
SELS WITH GOLIATH. SAVE OUR GRAND CANYON. WHOSE
LAND IS THIS ANYHOW?

The banners flew, the flags rustled, the paper placards snapped and
popped and crackled, held aloft by proud little boys and pigtailed
bright-eyed brave little girls. The messages, however, would not appear on your home viewing screen. Why not? Because the "media,"
though invited, had once again failed to appear. Why? Such decisions
are made discreetly, quietly, by a few important people meeting on the
golf course, in the boardroom, at lunch in the Brown Palace in Denver,
at the Biltmore in Phoenix. A few brief phone calls to the appropriate
TV, radio and newspaper bureau chiefs settled the matter. After all,
some events make worthy news and some do not. Another orderly
protest demonstration against racial segregation in South Africa, for
example, comfortably carried out on the campus of Berkeley or Stan-
ford or Harvard or Yale ten thousand miles away, troubles no one,
causes no embarrassment to anybody, allows all involved to look
good, feel virtuous, risk nothing. But let a bunch of hairy redneck
rabble in some wasteland western American state interpose their
living bodies between the industrial megamachine and a little patch
of free country, open space, old-growth forest, natural nature, wild-
land and wildlife, and the horror runs deep through the hierarchy of
upper management. That kind of subversion (non-commercial) cannot be accepted; will not (anti-business) be tolerated; has to (pro-
populist) be most severely punished both legally and — in so far as
possible — illegally; and last but categorically imperative, shall not be
encouraged through the power of example by publicity in any form.
As in any well-ordered oligarchy, not only the event itself must be
suppressed but all news of it as well.

Therefore the "media" did not appear.

Except for one exception; the old gent, the buzzard-beaked free-
lancer from wherever he was from, that lean and hungry beatnik bard
with notebook and ballpoint pen (his "software"), he was there,
skulking among the sandstone boulders on a high point at the far west
end of the Neck where he felt safe from any danger of violence, flying
missiles, tear gas grenades, police apprehension, or harsh language.
Equipped with plenty of Brie, French bread, two golden apples and a
six-pack of Foster's Lager, he squatted at ease in the shade of a little
hackberry and waited for the action. Binoculars ready. Binoculars
already in use, in fact, as he surveyed the vast panorama before him,

watching the helicopters in the sky, the yellow machinery rumbling up the road, the police vans and police buses behind the machines, and of most interest to him, the centerpiece of the organized resistance. DEFEND YOUR MOTHER.

At the throat of the Neck, halfway from end to end and side to side, on the centerline of the projected roadway, stood a massive matriarch of Utah juniper, thick as an elephant's hind leg and tall as a giraffe, a shaggy splendor of a tree about nine hundred to a thousand years old. (The juniper is a hard, tough, dense, slow-growing and fine-textured plant, all-enduring and perdurable.) Before the bulldozers could pass through and the G.E.M. approach, this tree would have to go. The surveyor had already marked it for destruction with pink Day-Glo flagging and a red slash of spray paint.

NO PASARAN. VENCEREMOS. VIVA LA TIERRA.

Five women stood with their backs to the tree, facing the oncoming enemy. On the left stood Mary Sojourner, the handsome and gentle lady from Flagstaff, Arizona; she had a smile on her lips, a joint in her teeth, a fresh sunflower in her dark brown hair. On the right stood the Hayduchess, Georgia her name, a broad bulky powerful female from nobody knew where, chomping on a dead cigar. At Mary's side stood Kathy ("Mrs. Seldom Seen") Smith and beside the Hayduchess was Susan (the other "Mrs. Seldom Seen") Smith. Both looked brave, beautiful, frightened, vulnerable — that incomprehensible cryptog-amy of spirit and protoplasm, water and courage, electrified nerve endings with culturally inspired entelechy, the invisible and indivis-ible union of incompatible codependent symbiotics.

Where was Sheila — Mrs. Smith Number Three? Not present. She had remarried the old man after the ambiguity charges were dismissed (following Volume #1) but did not approve of public protest dem-onstrations, cared even less for going to jail. She had two small children to care for, a tree-nursery business to manage, a home to keep up in a respectable Bountiful neighborhood.

Nor was Bonnie Abbzug-Sarvis anywhere in view. She had betrayed her friends Kathy and Susan, despite promises, and her absence was duly noted. No Abbzug, said the former. I notice that, the latter replied. I can't believe she's not here, said Susan. But she's not, Kathy said. Maybe she's sick. Morning sickness? Maybe; or maybe she's late again. I can't believe that Bonnie'd let us down. Me neither — but looks like she done exactly that. Well . . . Doc's not here neither, not to mention you-know-who himself, the intrepid wild-water river guide, peak bagger, bronc rider, mule wrangler, dude handler, calf-roper, All-American cowboy he-man hero type. That's my husband you're a-puttin' down, Mizz Smith. Don't I know it — mine too. Yeah. Ain't he somethin' though. He's somethin' all right, but what? You know what I think, Kathy. What's that? I think when it comes right down to the nitty gritty that women are braver than men. You two are catchin' on, the Hayduchess said; men like to fight but only when they think they're gonna win. Men are great fighters, said Mary Sojourner, but lousy losers. They never was much good at this kind of thing, said Hayduchess, this passive resistance thing, I mean. That's right, said Mary; put a man on display, in public, friends watching, he thinks he has to get violent, make a fool of himself, clobber somebody, hurt people, make a bloody awful mess. Are we gonna go limp when they arrest us? Kathy asked; or walk to the bus on our own legs? It's up to you, honey, the Hayduchess said; they're gonna have to carry me — all two hundred pounds; I'm gonna tie up as much manpower as I can as long as I can. Me too, Mary said; make the bastards work, make 'em earn their overtime by God. Well, mused Kathy, I suppose you're right — but I think I'll walk; more dignified. Me too, Susan said; I don't want to be dragged by the heels over a mile of stones and blackbrush and prickly pear.

What do you say, Erika?

The young woman in the middle of the group smiled at the sky, showing her dazzling teeth. I sink I hug ziss tree so hard zay neffer make us part.

They'll break your fingers if they have to, the Hayduchess said. I know these cops. They get mad, they'll break your fingers one by one until you let go. And then charge you with resistin' arrest. Believe me, girls, I know these types. Christ, Erika, you forget already how that maniac Love tried to bury you with his bulldozer?

I no forget. But ziss time zay find zee Druid in zee juniper iss root to rock, eh? The Svenska maid smiled skyward like Saint Bernadette awaiting the holy visitation. Zay take me zay muss take tree also.

Brave words, dearie. But don't forget: no violence. No violence to them, no violence to ourselves. You understand?

I no forget. Like Saint Joan at the stake, Erika rattled her iron bonds and watched for the Visitant, listened for choral voices. But heard instead the clanking treads of the crawling Caterpillar tractors, saw the rising dust clouds. Mary Sojourner took a deep breath. Kathy and Susan glanced at each other for comfort, reassurance, courage and re-encouragement.

The Hayduchess spat out her soggy stub of a cigar. Gordon! she barked. Gordon! — get over here.

The young body builder, half naked as always, bronze as a California beach boy, gleaming with sweat like a shellacked gymnasium god, glanced their way. Wearing nothing but his ragged cutoffs, his golden beard, his running shoes, the mighty four-foot monkey wrench slung on his belt, he jogged toward the five women tow-chained to the juniper. His grotesque, exaggerated, redundant muscles rippled like pythons under the golden skin. Smelling of body grease, stale sunscreen oil, seminal fluids and decayed spermatozoa, he approached the martyrs, his triceps biceps pectorals writhing.

God, thought the Hayduchess, what a hunk of funk. And bunk.

Yeah? What's the matter, Georgia?

Chain's coming loose. Take it in another couple of links. We're sweating off a pound a minute here.

Do you good. But Gordon did as he was told. Picking up the steel chain tensioner that lay on the ground, he hooked its two ends to the long chain that bound the five women to the great tree. All right, ladies, everybody exhale. Suck in your tummies. The women pressed themselves still harder against the trunk of the juniper, drew in their stomachs, shut their eyes. Gordon pulled the lever to the closed position, cinching the chain tighter, and slipped a loop of wire over the end of the handle. Key, he said, who's got the key?

The Hayduchess gave him the key.

Gordon unlocked the padlock, where it sagged now on the chain, and relocked it three links to the right: three links tighter. Chained by the waist against the hairy-barked bole of the tree, the women were free to operate their arms and legs — to hug and embrace or to scratch and kick — but could not budge themselves to left or right; they felt and looked like excresence of juniper made human flesh.

Okay, said Gordon, now who wants the key?

Throw it over the rim, said Mary Sojourner; we're not leaving here till we all lose ten pounds.

Laughing, the naked body sculpture faked the toss.

Wait, screamed Susan.

Don't worry, the boy said. He tucked the key into the little watch pocket of his shorts.

Here they come, warned the Hayduchess.

A yellow pickup truck appeared at the far east end of the Neck and stopped. Beyond, two Mitsubishi bulldozers — Gog and Magog — uprooted trees and shoved them aside, pushed boulders off the right-of-way. Not far behind the bulldozers although out of sight below the rise of the land an infernal roar, the thumping of an iron tub, the clank and screech of cambered gears, announced the advance of the *G.E.M. of Arizona*, the Super-G.E.M., the 4200-W Walking Dragline earth-moving machine. Him. Her. It. The Thing. The Dragon. GOLIATH from GOLGOTHA, the giant from the place of skulls. Tyrannosaurus.

All right everybody! the Hayduchess shouted, anarchist taking charge, everybody join up. Link arms. Face the yellow Caterpillars. Have your flowers ready. Children, join your parents. Women, shield your men. Everybody smile. Hank, Willy, Maisie — get out those flags. Joey, load that camera.

DOWN WITH EMPIRE, UP WITH SPRING!

The crawler tractors moved out upon the Neck, following the survey crew as those four bedeviled workers marked the route with handheld flagging. Their stakes had long since been pitched over the cliff, each and every bundle, every single one. Not that the bulldozer operators actually needed guidance; the Neck was truly a neck, a narrow bridge of rock and sand connecting the plateau called Island in the Sky to the roadless mesa called Lost Eden. The surface of the Neck, though roughly level, was littered with boulders, embossed with humps of underlying rock, scattered with living trees and shrubs — not only juniper but a few pinyon pines, hackberrys, scrub oak thickets. Approaching side by side with little room to spare on either hand, the two tractor engineers stood in their cabs to gain a clear view. Twenty feet to their left, twenty feet to their right, lay the edge of the world, the verge, the brink, the terminus, the drop-off to utter ruin far below. The operators pulled bandannas from hip pockets, wiped dusty goggles, then still uncertain of their safety pulled down the goggles and let them hang on straps about their necks.

SUBVERT THE DOMINANT PARADIGM.

The Earth First! troops lined up across the narrowest portion of the land bridge, the stem of the wineglass, from the yawning abyss on the north to the dozing chasm on the south. For anchormen at either end of this human chain they had Gordon the Body and — yes! none other! — Oral the Moral, the spy, the snitch, the snoop, the spook, young handsome lowbrowed lovestruck broad-shouldered ex-virgin missionary Oral Hatch in person.

The aging journalist watched from his safe secure position on a shelf of rock above the west end of the Neck. He munched an apple, scribbled notes, lifted the glasses hanging from his neck and admired the Princess Erika in her chains, her flattened waist, her countervailing upthrust bosom, the defiant smile on her moist ruby-red beestung lips. Lordy lordy! he muttered, and groaned aloud like a man in pain. He *was* in pain, knowing feeling suffering that ache like a toothache where man has never yet found teeth. He forced himself to alter the direction of his observation, elevated the binoculars a half degree and studied the opposition at the far end of the Neck. He could not recognize the two shadowed, dusty figures on the bulldozers but beyond and above, on the high ground where the yellow pickup had halted, he saw Bishop Love in full beefgrower's costume — i.e., tight gabardine pants, the shiny Tony Lama boots, the belt with jeweled rodeo buckle, the belly-bulging shirt with its pearly snap fasteners, the leather vest, and surmounting all a silvergray Stetson with three-inch rolled brim and high tapering pinched crown. The Bishop's face, shaded by the hat, could not be seen except for one cleft chin jutting into sunlight and a whittled matchstick, for toothpick, stuck smartly into a wide and grinning mouth. J. Dudley Love, of course, rancher, miner, construction king, Bishop of Hotrocks, Landfill County, Utah — who else?

A shit-green government pickup appeared, pulled beside Love's truck and stopped. The BLM rangerette emerged, Virginia H. Dick in badge and gun, Mace and Mag-light, purple Vuarnet sunglasses and swollen nut-brown uniform. Staring at the scene below, she leaned on Love. His arm slipped around her midriff, hand cupping the ranger's portside mammary. She raised her face to his, he tipped back his hat in the traditional touching gesture of the Hollywood cowboy and kissed her full spang on the lips. Love, love, love; l'amour, l'amore, el amor, liebe liebe liebe; like anxious sheep the words bleated through the old journalist's balding head. He cringed with envy. Oh my, he thought, why ain't I doing that? With her? Well maybe not with her, but with *her*. That one wrapped in chains, the tree-hugger with her startling Viking eyes, her sweet *très elegant* fine-featured rosy face, that black mane of hair that hung from crown to croup — ! Jesus, Joseph, Mary and God!, the cruelty of life and desire. He fondled his manly organ, such as it was, and remembered the days of his youth.

NATURE: LOVE IT OR LEAVE IT ALONE.

A flashing strobe light rose above the eastern horizon, like a white star blinking. Then the black A-frame and little red spider lights, the mast and boom and high-slung dragline bucket came in view, rocking back and forth against a haze of dust, a maze of rattling chains, banging cables, clanking gears, crashing shoes, mad electrical pandemonium.

The largest mobile land machine on planet Earth was stomping forward, step by step, toward the Neck of Eden, a half-hundred terrified young eco-denders, the five helpless, idealistic, rebellious women strapped by linkages of cast iron to the ancient massive trunk of old Eden's arboreal matriarch. The ground resonated.

DEFEND YOUR MOTHER.

God, the reporter whispered to himself, as the flat yellow bulk of the G.E.M.'s engine room began to rise over the skyline, this is tremendous. This is terrible. This is magnificent. This is beyond the power of reportage to communicate, of photographs to limn, of newsprint to portray. Beyond the power of the heart to accept. For a moment he was tempted to rush down the slope, flinging his pen, notebook, cheese, lager to the ground, and lock elbows with Earth First! He considered and he thought better of it and remained where he was, safely out of the line of fire.

RESIST MUCH, OBEY LITTLE.

Walt Whitman said that.

Pinyon jays, brown towhees, a mountain bluebird and a sparrow hawk flew before the oncoming machines. Rabbits, horned lizards, king snakes, ground squirrels, a badger, a kit fox, a ringtail cat, emerged from their burrows in the trembling, shaken earth, perched upright for a moment on the edge of their homes and gaped in wonder at the iron dinosaurs bearing down upon their lives. Gaped for a moment and fled, scampering across the Neck, between the legs and through the line of the body chain, and on to the illusory safety of the mesa beyond. A few of the small furry creatures, blind with panic, slipped off the edge of the bridge, becoming airborne like angels, before disappearing into the embrace of eternity.

As you do unto the least of these, so do ye unto me.

God said that.

The women at the tree stared at the yellow monsters expanding before them. Standing tall as they could inside the taut chain, they waited, they braced themselves, they clenched each other's hands, they murmured words of power for one another's hearts.

Mary Sojourner said, Look at those tin bastards. They ain't got a chance against us, girls. Not a fuckin' chance.

The Hayduchess said, They's big but I seen bigger. You know the rule, ol' buddies: big machines, teensy-weensy wienies. The bigger the muscle machine the tinier the love muscle. Whoever's runnin' that walkin' dragline probly has a poodle's pecker. Dill pickle for a dong, I know the type, I seen 'em before many a time. Needledicks.

Kathy said, I'm sure glad Seldom's not here. He'd be looking for a skirt to hide under.

Susan said, Scared or not he's always doing that.

Ain't that the truth.

Erika the sea-captain's daughter said, Lad-eese, mein guten ka-merads, vat effer comes now to eat us up, I tell you ziss I luff you more zan any man I effer luff, even more zan I luff my Oral darlink. Kazzy, Soosin, Mary, Duchess, I luff you one and luff you all, my darlinks, my swede-hearts, my splendid hero lad-eese off Amerika, may Nephi and Moroni bless you one and all.

Well thank you, Erika honey, the Hayduchess said, that's spoken like a true princess. A true Mormon princess.

We love you too, Erika, said Mary Sojourner.

All for one and one for all! cried Susan Smith in a moment of adrenalized jubilation.

Amen! cried Kathy Smith.

The Mitsubishis came grumbling close, snorting through their blowholes, tracks clacking, 'dozer blades gleaming as they plowed the dirt, tore loose the living shrubs, crushed the homes and children of gopher, chipmunk, cottontail, vole, mole, bannertail mouse and kangaroo rat, ripped up the sod, scraped off the bunch grass and flowers, the wild buckwheat and the wild ricegrass. And then they came to the living juniper in the center of the Neck and its five living women obstructing the middle of the right-of-way (as they call it), and the tractors halted. Close; much too close. Engines panting. Stack lids bobbing. Fine red sand streaming down the concave sheen of the blades, projected above the women's heads.

Back that thing off! the Hayduchess shouted.

Grinning, the operator reversed his machine a couple of feet and lowered the blade to the ground. Letting the motor idle, he opened his dinner pail. His partner did the same. Neither bothered to descend from their leather thrones. Munching baloney sandwiches, each sipping hot coffee from a Thermos bottle, they waited. Waited for the "authorities" to appear and solve the situation.

GOD BLESS AMERICA LET'S SAVE SOME OF IT.

The flags flew in the desert air: the stars and stripes of the U.S.A., the red, white and green of Earth First!, the black banner of anarchy, the black and red of the Monkey Wrench Gang, the pink and gold of the Bonnie Abbzug Garden Club, the red on white of Hayduke Lives!, the Seldom Seen Marines, the Doc Sarvis Guerrillas.

But none of those celebrated personages was anywhere in sight. Earth First! was on its own.

The two pickup trucks descended onto the Neck and stopped behind the bulldozers. Bishop Love got out and approached the chain of bodies barring passage; Ranger Dick spoke a few more words into her radio and joined him. Knowing better than to ask for a leader, the ranger addressed the mob as a whole.

"Hi, kids. Nice to see you all again. I'll give you five minutes to disperse peacefully." She glanced at her wristwatch. "Then I'm calling the BLM police, the Coconino County sheriff's deputies, and the Arizona Department of Public Safety. This is an illegal assembly; you have no permit. Also —"

"Don't forget the Search and Rescue Team," the Bishop said. He grinned at the human chain from the deep dark shade of his cowperson's hat; only his sunglasses and the yellow carnotite gleam of his teeth were visible to his audience. "When my boys get here we'll have some action quick."

"No jurisdiction here," Ranger Dick said, softly and aside.

"Don't worry, Ginny, they all been deputized in Coconino County. Them boys mine got all the jurisdiction they want anywhere in Utah, Arizona, Nevada or Idaho. I seen to that personally."

"Also," the ranger went on, "you people are obstructing traffic. This —"

"Traffic?" asked the panpipe player. "Traffic? What traffic? There's not even a road here."

"Looks like a road to me," Bishop Love said, grinning his broad and genial County Commissioner's grin. "Sure looks like a mighty fine highway to me. 'We shall make straight in the desert a highway for the Lord,' " he quoted. "Whatcha mean, young fella? If this hain't a road it sure as hell is a road-*way*. This here's our legal authorized duly sanctioned mine access right-of-way road and by God —" His voice rose in pitch to a sterner level, the voice of a construction company executive and mining company board chairman. "— by God we mean to open this here roadway today. Now." Temper rising rapidly, the Bishop stepped forward. "Out of my way, punk. Move."

"No," the player replied. "We won't. We won't move."

"We shall not be moved," Mary Sojourner yelled.

The Hayduchess began to sing:

> We shall not be
> We shall not be moved

"Oh shut up!" Love bellowed, turning his attention to the women at the tree. For the first time he seemed to notice the heavy chain drawn around their waists. "Now what in the name of Holy Moroni you call this. You ladies out of your minds? Goldang green bigots again. Tree-huggers. Toadstool worshippers. Rock lovers. Fern feelers, posy sniffers, weed kissers, what the hell *is* this? Padlocked? What?" Bishop Love glared up and down the line of staring faces. "Where's the key to this lock? Huh? Who's got the key?"

No answer.

"Ginny, you got any bolt cutters in your truck?"

"Calm down, Dudley," the ranger said. "Remember your valves. You take your digitalis today?"

"Yes, Ginny, I took my digitalis today, goddamnit." The Bishop made an effort to ease his internal pressures. In a gentler tone he repeated his query.

"No," she said, "I don't carry bolt cutters."

"Hacksaw?"

"No hacksaw." She returned to her radio. "But I'll get them."

"Stop wavin' that flag in my face," the Bishop growled at a six-year-old girl waving an American flag in his face. The little girl began to cry. The girl's mother said something unkind to Bishop Love. The Bishop turned away, red with anger.

> We shall not be
> We shall not be moved

The Bishop glared at the singing women chained to the juniper. "Ought to get out my cannon and shoot that padlock off," he snarled. But he didn't dare do that; the padlock hung on the chain between the two Mrs. Smiths, only six inches or so from the hip of either. "Or take this here 'dozer, knock that tree over with you goldang Communist environ-meddler ladies still locked to it." He didn't dare do that either; if anyone got killed the Law would hear about it and maybe try to pin the blame on him.

The women grinned at Bishop Love, singing:

> We shall not be
> We shall not be moved

"Doggone morons." The Bishop glanced at *his* watch, then at the police. The two DPS helicopters had landed on a native pad of slickrock at the west end of the Neck, cutting off any retreat by the Earth First! demonstrators. A dozen men in S.W.A.T. team camouflage, armed with riot shotguns, tear gas launchers, helmets and face shields, emerged from the machines, stooping under the whirling rotors as they formed a skirmish line across the sandstone bridge. On the east end of the Neck appeared the county sheriff's four-by-four patrol units and prisoner-transport vans, and an assortment of Jeeps, Blazers, Rams and Broncos from Love's Search & Rescue Team. The men got out, loaded down with clubs, flashlights, ammo pouches and deadly semi-automatic firearms. Behind the deputies and search & rescuers, rising higher and higher into the dusty blue, advanced the Super-G.E.M. — that gadget so large, so outsize, it seemed to violate the proportions of the landscape. That is, it *loomed* above the horizon like a walking tower of yellow iron, a misplaced factory building seven stories high from Youngstown, Ohio, an invader from Mars reenacting the War of the Worlds. The strobe light flashed atop the 110-foot mast, diamond bright; the red eyes blinked on the summit of the 285-foot boom and A-frame, warning signals to low-flying aircraft. And it rocked as it walked, shaking from side to side on the irregular terrain; the powerhouse roared like a cannibal dynamo, Moloch the insatiable; and the 130-foot gigantic steel shoes — still unseen, still below the horizon — rose and fell, rose, cranked forward, descended with a crash, heaved mightily and hoisted twelve thousand tons of iron eighty inches above the surface and propelled the entire mass another fourteen feet forward. Fourteen feet at each step, onward and forward at maximum cruising speed of nine hundred feet per hour, or one good English mile about every six hours. Between the shoes, at each cycle, the round "tub" or base of the machine dropped upon the ground, leaving a series of overlapping circular imprints stamped into the desert earth. The trail resembled that of a dying dinosaur, unable to lift its butt from the ground, dragging itself toward extinction with awkward but heroic effort.

The Bishop staggered around the juniper on his high-heel cowperson boots, glaring in turn at each white ovaloid sunburned face and at the saddle-brown black-eyed moon-shaped Mongoloid face of the part-redskin Hayduchess.

"Don't know you, woman. Who're you?"

"The name's Georgia, Love, and I'm twice as mean as a wolverine.

Got the rag on and I'm touchy as a she-bear with cubs. Ought to floss your teeth, man, or keep your mouth shut, one or the other."

"Ain't we the sassy female though. Listen, lady, when I need advice from the likes of you I'll —"

"— Ask for it, sure. I know a good dentist at Navajo Mountain, Love. Her name is Horse. Mrs. Crazy Q. Horse. Uses vise-grips and a bumper jack, all work guaranteed. You been chewin' carnotite again?"

"What the hell you talkin' about, woman?"

"There's a funny blue glow on your gums. You got a mouth like a Gila monster's. Smells like it too."

The Bishop turned away in sullen fury. Glanced again at his watch. Nodded at Ranger Dick.

The ranger cleared her throat, addressed the line of arm-linked protesters. "All right, folks, time's up. Break it up now, I mean right now, or I'm calling in the riot squad." She waited for response.

The forty or fifty Earth First!ers shifted their feet uneasily, some casting a backward look over the shoulder at the DPS team behind them, others staring in wonder and horror at the advancing, growing, ever-advancing ever-growing figure of GOLIATH on the eastern skyline. The breeze slackened; the flags wilted, the placards sagged.

"No?" said Ranger Dick.

"No!" shouted Erika. "Vee shall not be moofed. Vee shall neffer be moofed. Eart' First! Last! Always!"

Ragged cheers rose from the barricade of bodies.

The ranger spoke quietly into the mike of her radio. The Special Weapons and Tactics team removed their nameplates and badges (sure sign of trouble), lowered face shields, drew skull-breaking batons from their belts, stepped forward onto the Neck of Lost Eden's mesa. The deputy sheriffs and deputized search and rescue team advanced from the other direction, smiling with pleasure. The survey crew stood looking on, holding hammers. The two bulldozer engineers closed their lunch buckets and revved their engines, spouting black smoke into the clear air. The motorized drill rigs, half-cab dump trucks and oversize road graders pulled up ahead of the Super-G.E.M., parked in the brush, and disgorged their crew of operators, oilers, blasters, swampers. Six-packs of Coors appeared, here and there a pint or quart of other potables. This looked like more fun than a Teamsters' picnic.

A murmur of discontent swept the line of obstructionists. Waving their flags, banners and placards, they shouted earthy slogans, referred to the Bill of Rights (always in questionable taste) and directed a number of personalized insults at Bishop Love, the Bureau of Land Management, the Syn-Fuels Corporation, the Federal government in general, the nuclear power and weapons industry in particular.

Ranger Dick pulled an electrical bullhorn from the front seat of her shit-green BLM pickup truck. "Take it easy, people, please. Please cooperate with the peace officers please and nobody will get hurt. You are going to be arrested but you will be treated fairly if you cooperate. Do not attempt to resist arrest, that is a felony, a very serious crime. Upon arrest you will be taken to the sheriff's buses for transport to Fredonia. If you refuse to walk to the buses you will be handcuffed and carried, so please cooperate with the police officers." She continued to speak into the mouthpiece of the bullhorn, reading from a slip of paper in her free hand. "Upon arrival in Fredonia you will be ar- raigned before a justice of the peace on various misdemeanor charges, at which time you will have the opportunity to post bond or in some cases be released on your own recog . . . recognizance. Mothers! please restrain your children, please!" she added in a sharper tone, as three kids about eight or nine years old broke ranks, ran to the Mitsubishi and slapped at the 'dozer blades with cardboard placards. Flies swatting a tank. "Mothers? Fathers? Whose children are those, please? They're going to get hurt. Take them away from the bulldoz- ers, please," she screamed, voice rising toward the soprano, "or we'll be forced to take action."

One tractor engineer, perhaps thinking to frighten the children away, elevated his dozer blade, canting it forward and back. Dirt and stones cascaded upon the nearest, smallest, slowest child. The child sat down on the ground and began to cry. A young woman broke from the body line and rushed upon the eighty-ton Mitsubishi, waving an American flag on a stout pole. She yanked her little boy to safety, then drove the brass spear-tip of her staff into the tractor's left eye, smashing it. Not satisfied, she drew back her weapon and thrust it at the other eye, barely missing as the driver reversed his machine and swung it aside on one locked tread.

Shouts of approval from the unruly mob; growls of anger from the duly authorized ruly personnel.

"Arrest that woman!" Ranger Dick commanded, pointing.

Two sheriff's deputies approached the spear-wielder. She faced them with her weapon drawn back over one shoulder, a seven-year-old boy clutching at her leg. "Don't touch us, you nuke pukes," she snarled, eyes glaring like those of a wildcat at bay. Her name in fact, as known in Earth First! circles, happened to be none other than Wildcat Annie, a Forest Service office clerk from Flagstaff, Arizona, divorced, mother of one, wife of two, mistress of three, lover of four: Miz Wildcat Annie, free woman.

The deputies circled cautiously. One crept behind her, made a lunge, got a chokehold on her neck. The little boy kicked him in the shins. The second deputy, club in one hand, handcuffs in the other, grabbed at her in front. Annie thrust viciously with her spear, jabbed the man behind on the backstroke, the one in front with her forestroke. Both men staggered, hands on their hurts. (The wildcat is a vicious animal; when attacked it defends itself.)

"Annie, Annie, don't!" yelled the Hayduchess, straining at the chain that bound her, longing to jump into the battle. "Go limp, Annie, go limp. . . ."

Two more men joined the attack, striking at Annie's pole with their heavy-duty Mag-lights. The spear broke; Annie sank down, covering her little boy with her body. One man struck her on the head with his club. She went limp — too late. Another manacled her hands behind her back, forcing the cuffs so tight her wrists turned white. They dragged Annie and the child away. The child wailed in fury and terror.

"Please do not resist arrest please," the ranger pleaded through the bullhorn, "and nobody will get hurt."

This scene was too much for Gordon the Muscleman. Leaving his anchorage at the north end of the line he rushed up to the center, pulling the mighty cast-iron monkey wrench from his belt. Samson unsheathing his sword.

"Gordon, sit down," the Hayduchess screamed.

Gordon ignored her. Charging at the nearest Mitsubishi, muscles rippling under oily bronze, he whacked it a mighty blow on the 'dozer blade. A tiny hairline crack appeared. The operator pulled his hydraulic levers, lifting the blade above Gordon's reach. Gordon stepped beneath it and swung his warclub into the radiator's protective grille. The grille caved in. (Nip-Ware: soybean metallurgics.) Gordon drew back and struck again. His monkey wrench sank into the fine leaden honeycomb of cooling fins. A stream of green Prestone gushed forth, like liquid from the Mosaic rock, and Gordon roared in triumph. As he struggled with his wrench, however, which was jammed in the depths of the radiator, the engineer lowered the 'dozer blade, trapping Gordon within its heavy arms. At once four burly cops surrounded him, batons descending again and again upon his hatless curly haired skull. Gordon went down, passed out, was shackled at the wrists and lugged away by the heels, his near-naked carcass scraping over sand, stone, the bristling little blackbrush, the prickly pear with its hairy spines, a stiff-bladed yucca, the mean and nasty hedgehog cactus, a few broken beer bottles and crumpled Pepsi cans left behind by the survey crew.

Blood on the rock. The tang of fresh blood in the air. A bleeding, unconscious, blood-smeared beautiful young male body flopping in the dust, fading away.

"Please," Ranger Dick begged through her amplifier, "please co-operate with the police officers. Resisting arrest is a very serious offense. These men are here to help you. Please . . ."

"Go limp," shouted Mary Sojourner, as the wave of deputies and DPS S.W.A.T. technicians closed in, "everybody just go limp. They won't club you if you're lying down." We hope, she muttered to herself. Police riot coming up.

"The policeman is your friend," bellowed Bishop Love, smiling, enjoying himself despite this latest assault upon his expensive im-ported equipment. "Try to remember that." His boys from the graders, trucks and drill rigs ambled near, also grinning, ready with wrenches of their own, ballpeen hammers, chainsaws, towing chains and tire irons, eager reinforcements when and if needed.

The bulldozer operator with the bleeding radiator, essaying a final service with his wounded machine, ground the treads of the tractor over the fallen monkey wrench, revolving half the weight of the Mitsubishi upon that one antiquated obsolete picturesque forever-symbolic Luddite appliance.

"Kill your engine!" the Bishop hollered, "afore it seizes up."

The operator obeyed, embarrassed, then attempted to save face by climbing down from his seat, picking up Gordon's monkey wrench — undamaged — and hurling it two-handed toward the rim of the Neck. Too heavy for him. His fling fell short by a yard, the tool sliding into a dense thicket (over-grazing) of assorted cactus.

"Fuckin' goddamn Sahara Club junk . . ." The operator glared at the disappearing Gordon, then at the women chained to the juniper.

The struggle was brief. Seeing the bloody fate of Wildcat Annie and golden-boy Gordon, the majority of the Earth First! demonstrators fell to the ground, hands over heads, hoping for a quick and non-violent arrest. The gesture did them little good. Enraged and inflamed by even token resistance, loyal to tradition, the police laid about with aban-don, cracking heads on every side, running down the few who tried to flee, collaring children and yanking them over the stony ground toward the waiting vans. Within ten minutes the opposition had collapsed and all prisoners had been dragged away.

All but the five young fanatics chained to the tree. Breathing hard, sweating like pigs, the lawmen clustered about this final knot of obstructionism and pondered the problem.

"Bolt cutters," a police Sergeant said. "Hacksaws."

"On the way," replied Ranger Dick.

"We got a chainsaw," another man said. "Why not cut down the tree and drag 'em away with a tractor, tree and all?"

"Not a bad idea," the Sergeant said.

"We'll wait," said the ranger.

"Burn the tree," the bulldozer engineer snarled, still miffed by his defeat. "Goddamn green-bigot witches, douse 'em with diesel, set the tree on fire. That'll learn 'em."

"Good idea," the Sergeant said, "but not legal. Where those tools?"

The tools arrived, one heavy-duty hacksaw with extra blades, and a heavy-duty bolt cutter with handles three feet long. The men tried the bolt cutter then the hacksaw but got nowhere; both chain and padlock were heavy-duty also, high carbon steel hardware especially designed (and selected) to resist such nibbling and gnawing attacks.

"*Plastique*," suggested another policeman. "A small shaped charge would do the trick."

"Not a bad idea," the Sergeant said. "Might have to take some casualties but that would do it. What do you say, girls?" They stared at him. "It's that or the key, girls. Tell us where the key is and we all go home in a jiffy. How about it?"

"Who you callin' girl, boy?" the Hayduchess said. "And where's your badge? What's your number, officer?"

"Yeah," said Mary Sojourner, "how about that, copper? What's your name?"

"Tough broads. Tough, tough broads." He slapped Mary, not gently, across the cheek. Her head bounced against the juniper's trunk. "Where's the key, woman?"

She kicked him in the shins with a heavy-duty hiking boot. "Don't know, man."

The Sergeant lurched back a step, rubbed his wound. "Hobble these ladies. All of them. Handcuff them too." Taking care, the men snapped cuffs on the women's ankles, then on their wrists. The police Sergeant, safe from kicks and claws, leaned his hard and mustached face into the delicate face of Erika the Nordska. "Now. You. Where's the key, miss?'' She did not — could not — immediately reply. The Sergeant grunted: ''Speak up. We're in a hurry.''

The Super-G.E.M. waited on the tapering east apron of the Neck, big shoes at rest for the moment but its electrical motors humming, buzzing, throbbing. The man at the control console of the air-conditioned cab peered out through his wall of glass, waiting. His assistant, the oiler, a young man in greasy coveralls, stood on the ground fifty feet below, ready to indicate by hand signals exactly where the monster might step next, safely, without tottering sideways over the brink. The drag bucket, big enough to hold four Greyhound buses in its iron maw, swung gently back and forth from the tip of the upraised boom. The red lights blinked, the strobe light flashed, high on the mast and A-frame, far above the seven-story powerhouse. The power cable lay in the dirt behind, an orange-colored serpent of copper, insulation and fabric, thick as a wrestler's thigh, leading up the slope and over the rise to the nearest mobile sub-station two miles away, the sub-station mounted on a sledge and linked in turn to the EHV (extra high voltage) powerline that looped across the desert between Page, Arizona and St. George, Utah. Time is money, said I. B. Watson, Henry Ford, Andrew Carnegie, Adam Smith, René Descartes, Francis Bacon, and the entire genealogy of logical positivists that began with Leviticus and achieved transcendent apotheosis in the figure of J. Dudley Love, Bishop of Ward One, Hotrocks, Landfill County, Utah. Even so trivial an interruption as this Earth First! farce — with motors running — was costing Syn-Fuels Corporation close to ten thousand dollars a minute.

''Speak up!'' the police Sergeant barked in Erika's face, spraying her with ungentlemanly spittle. ''Or we'll begin some *scientific* interrogation here, you know what I mean, young lady.'' He stuck a cigarette in his teeth, pulled a lighter from his pocket, thumbed it into flame, and waved it slowly back and forth in front of her pale, lovely, horrified face. ''Where's the key?''

She gulped. She licked her lips and swallowed again.

''Wait a minute,'' Ranger Dick said, ''what do you think you're doing? Put that thing away.''

''Yeah,'' the Hayduchess bellowed. ''Let her alone, you ugly pig. You're so fuckin' tough, try me.''

The Sergeant paused, grinned, lit his cigarette and looked around. ''Nervous, nervous ladies. What do you think I am, some kind of Nazi? I was only bluffing this kid. For godsake. Some people got no sense of humor.'' He spoke to his man on the other side of the juniper, still patiently grating away with hacksaw on chain. "How's it coming?"

"Slow, Sarge, slow. Take us another hour at least."

"Yeah? Well, keep at it. Somebody spell him off."

A pause.

"All right, wait, let's use our heads here." Smiling, Bishop Love came forward at last, after retiring to his truck for a bit of medical refreshment. The Bishop was a cough-syrup fiend; a dash of codeine could always get him through the most trying of afternoons, that end-of-the-day malaise. And indeed the shadows were getting lengthy. The black shape of GOLIATH had long since crept from base of tub over the eastern end of the land bridge to the top of the slope beyond. Quitting time was near for most of these machines and men, not to mention Ranger Dick and her beau J. Dudley. A very special occasion lay in view. Might as well call it quits for the day. Love looked at the man in the G.E.M.'s control cab, caught his eye, and made a throat-slashing gesture. Kill it. The man nodded, lowered the long boom safely among the junipers east of the Neck, setting the giant bucket down beyond the construction equipment parked up there. He then pushed the red button of the "Excitation" switch, shutting off power to the operating equipment. The main engine continued to throb; it had to be shut down by a throw switch on the interior wall of the powerhouse and fan vent room.

Love waited. When he heard the dragline motors die, he turned again to the crowd of impatient, irritated men in bloodstained uniforms.

"You got an idea, Bishop?"

"Yep." Grinning, Love advanced to the juniper, tugged at the massive log chain between the bodies of Erika and Susan Smith. Ranger Dick watched closely from her position apart; she despised this whole proceeding and earnestly longed to be through with it. "All we need," the Bishop said, "is a few inches slack in this here chain, right?" The others nodded. "So all we got to do," he went on, "is heist one of these here slim little female bodies out from behint this here goldang chain, right?"

"You must be talkin' about me," the Hayduchess said.

Love grinned at Georgia. "Not you, sweetheart." He surveyed the five women. "We best start with the skinniest one."

"You hear that, men?" the Hayduchess snorted. "You hear that? He's insultin' me. He thinks cause I'm half redskin he can insult me. I'm minority, man, I got rights. You pull anybody out of this chain you got to pull me first."

The Sergeant nodded to one of his men. The two took a firm stance before Erika the Svenska.

"Up or down, Sarge?"

"Up. We can get her hips through this thing a lot easier'n we can her . . . her, ah, chest. Don't want to damage this little sweetheart." The Sergeant put his hands under Erika's armpits. "Now you take ahold of her belt there, under the chain. Then lift."

At once the women began to howl. "Rape!" the Hayduchess bellowed, "rape! rape! rape!," and the others echoed her inflammatory cry. While Erika herself, in a voice loud and clear, called out, *"Noli me tangere!"* The kid knew her Latin. *"Noli me tangere!"* As best she could, with hands cuffed and ankles bound, waist chained to the tree, she wriggled free of the policemen's grasp. "Iss no touch zee body."

The Sergeant paused. Sweating and exasperated, he turned to Ranger Dick. "Ginny," he said, "are we raping this girl? I ask you."

"Sexual harassment," Mary Sojourner said. "Those two men are using her for sexual purposes while pretending to make an arrest."

"Right," the Hayduchess said, "it's sexism pure and simple."

The argument raged back and forth for another minute. When a pause came the ranger said, "You women are resisting arrest. Where's the key to that padlock? Give us the key, nobody will touch anybody for any sexual purpose while I'm here."

"That's absolutely right," the smiling Bishop said, slipping an arm around Ranger Dick's abundant hips. "We got no time for no hanky panky on duty, right, Ginny?"

She removed his arm. The key was not forthcoming. "Okay," the ranger said, "pull Miss Chickie-Poo out of that chain."

Again the two men took up position, bracing themselves for leverage. "And no touching any erogenous parts," Ranger Dick added. The men nodded, well aware at the same time that the supple lass beneath their hands was totally erogenous. She possessed no non-erogenous parts. None. But they would try. Hands supporting her armpits, tugging upward at the belt threaded through the copper-riveted loops of her bluejeans, they hoisted her an inch or two up from behind the chain.

Erika screamed: "No! No touch ziss body!"

The two men paused for breath and to readjust their awkward positions. At the same moment a large male figure came clambering over the south rim of the Neck, rose to full height and dashed toward the juniper tree.

"Hands off that girl!" cried Oral Hatch, R.M., hurling himself through the air and tackling the Sergeant around the knees. Both men crashed to the slickrock, fists and elbows flying. For a few seconds the battle was obscured by blurred, high-speed motion while the Sergeant's men stood by, batons upraised to strike. When Oral appeared on top, his head clear, the sticks descended — thunk! thunk, thunk! — and the issue was settled. ("Oral, Oral, my luff! my darlink!") Promptly and efficiently a couple of cops manacled young Hatch, yanked him to his feet and frog-marched him to the one van still waiting. The rest of Earth First!, singing and laughing, had been hauled off to bail or jail about half an hour earlier.

The old journalist, wedged like a lizard deep in a crevice under an overhanging boulder, watched and waited, fearful, trembling, snapping pictures when he could, scribbling notes and chuckling semi-hysterically: Ah splendid! splendid! Magnifique! Bellissima! Absolutely topping, topping!, I say. . . .

The contest was over. Hatch dispatched, the men dragged sweet Erika the Svenska maid from her place behind the chain, nearly stripping off her jeans in the process — that chain *was* taut — but not quite, since Ranger Dick did not for a moment allow her attention to be diverted from the arrest. With the chain now slackened, the police and deputies had no trouble pulling the remaining four women from their places and toting them off, shackled hand and foot, to the van.

After a bit of ceremonial handshaking and mutual congratulations, the DPS S.W.A.T. team ascended in their helicopters — one more miraculous assumption — and the sheriff's deputies drove off in their 4 x 4 entropy wagons. As the mutter of motors faded, a spontaneous chorus of cheers arose from the throats of the Search & Rescue Team and Love's construction workers — ten men, four women.

His arm once again around the waist of his smiling rangerette, Bishop Love saluted his employees with upraised can of Pepsi-Cola. "Yeah!" he shouted, grinning with pride, "I reckon we whupped *their* ass. I reckon them Earth Fist bigots ain't gonna give us no more trouble on this project. And afore we all go home, let's have a little victory celebration. Let's gather up all these goldang Earth Fist flags and rags and posters and make a bonfire. Now I just happen to have an icebox full of ribeye steaks in my little old truck, and two cases of Pepsi-Cola packed in ice. And also another thing — "

The boys interrupted with more cheers, not without a sardonic undertone, as the plugs from a few bottles of Wild Turkey flew through the air, and the snaptops from a number of canisters of Coors Lite clicked and clanked, aluminum on aluminum.

"— And the other thing is this, my friends, me and Ginny here, we're inviting each and ever' one of you, with your families and with your friends, those as have either, to come to a very special barn dance at the ranch tonight. Yep, folks, it's true, them rumors you been hearin' is absolutely true, me and Ginny Dick is a-gonna tie the knot tonight, Bishop J. Marvin Pratt presiding —"

Not again? Hooray for Love! Way to go, Dud! He old but he hain't dead! God bless our good ol' Bishop Love!

A fire began, ignited by the children's posters, the red and black and green and white banners of the defeated Earth First! Somebody topped the kindling with dead juniper and scrub oak, making a cheery blaze in the purple shadows of encroaching twilight. The men tossed their raw steaks directly on the flaming coals, aboriginal style. Love brought a small gridiron from his truck for those who preferred to grill their meat in a manner more ladylike.

The celebrants ate, drank, retold the stories of the day's battle, tossed their beer bottles and Pepsi cans off the rim and heard them fall, whistling away to nothing, into the darkening abyss.

The sun dropped below the mesas, buttes, domes and pinnacles, the plateaus and mountains on the far west — toward Nevada, the inland basin, the Great American Desert. The fat half moon soared overhead, pure and bright, safe for the moment from human greed, queen of the night, sweet as the desert stillness. Where coyotes howled, a kit fox barked, an airliner droned overhead, scoring the sky with vapor, and vanished.

"I tell you friends," the Bishop pronounced, "this here's a great day in American history. This is a day that will never be forgot. This is the day the people of Progress won out over the forces of Selfishness and Obstruction. Them Earth Fist wildmen and Ecological wildwomen made their last stand today and we smashed 'em. We flattened 'em. Extreme environmentalism and environmental extremism will never again raise its horrible head in the Arizona Strip country or maybe anywhere in the whole goldang American West, by God, ever again. They asked for a fight, we gave it to 'em, and we won. You mind my words, boys, ladies too, you come back here five years from now you're gonna see a Holiday Inn on this Neck, and a eighteen-hole golf course on Eden Mesa, and little blue lakes with real live ducks on them and a beautiful little city of fifty thousand retired folks and uranium miners and nucular engineers living here in their own homes and enjoying God's fresh air and God's own backyard and God's own scenery . . ." Inspired, waxily eloquent, Love raised his happy, fat, florid face to the new moon and rumbled, "I have a dream, my friends. I have a dream of America for Americans, where never again will a single square foot of our land be locked up for selfish elitist preservationists but where everything will be accessible to everybody in their own automobile and where industry can move in unhindered for the spirit of free enterprise that made America what it is today to provide jobs for everybody that's willing to work instead of wilderness playgrounds for greedy extreme elitist Sahara Clubbers and other wild dangerous animals. I have a dream, my friends, of America where people come first — up with people! — people and industry and jobs and unlimited opportunity for anybody with the guts and the glory to take advantage of America's glorious opportunity for everybody. That's my dream, my friends, and I dream someday that this here America will be the America we all enjoy, not just an elitist handful of greedy selfish wild preservatives and extreme crackpot ecologists with their pet mountain lions and pet grizzly bears trying to lock up America so the rest of us can't get in to enjoy it and maybe make a little honest profit too and that's my dream, my friends, my dream of the America I used to love and the America I expect to love again. That's my dream, my friends. What's yours?"

The night watchmen finally arrived, two sober men in Ace Detective Agency uniforms, armed and dangerous. But instead of beginning their patrol of the work area and its idle equipment they were dragged by the jubilant Bishop and his friends into the celebration. Which gave Love another idea: on C.B. He radioed J. Marvin Pratt back in town and invited him, urged him, *instructed* him to bring his Bible, his Mormon marriage manual, and all the friends and witnesses he could round up on short order and bring them all out to the Neck.

"Yeah," shouted Love into the mike, "we'll have the wedding out here, why the hell not, Marvin. Been a beautiful day, it's a wonderful evening, moon's up, we'll make an all-night goldang party of it. Bring more Pepsi, yeah, about ten cases. Yeah, okay, bring more booze for the boys, hell's fire I might even have a drink or two or three myself, why not, we got plenty to celebrate, Marvin, we had a great victory over the forces of Greed and Evil, we run off them green bigots forever, yep, that coward Hayduke and his Monkey Wrench hoods never even dared show their ugly faces, better bring more steaks, more chips, hotdogs and buns for the kids, we'll celebrate my second marriage in good old high country style, Marvin, bring Jake Lassiter and his fiddle, old man Wright and his gee-tar, that fella with the gut bucket what's his name, yeah we'll have music too, we'll have a big dance, don't forget the women, sure, bring my wife, she knows about this wedding, ain't no secret to her, we'll keep this here doggone shindig goin' till sun-up by God. Yeah, Marvin, I know it takes three hours to drive out here. So tell my gal Ellie to fly you out, she got nothin' better to do, she can bring eight at a time in that new Cessna, takes ten minutes. Land? You can land behind the G.E.M. That thing leaves a nice wide flat airstrip behind everywhere it goes and it's on the east of the Neck right now. . . ."

A vast grumbling rumble resounded through the night.

The Bishop paused for a moment, looking up from his radio toward the gigantic form of the walking dragline. He stared. "Now what the hell —?"

All conversation stopped. Every member of the party froze in position, staring toward the great machine. G O L I A T H was coming back to life. Its central searchlight, ablaze, came circling about and settled directly on Bishop Love, Ranger Dick, the S. & R. team, the construction crew, the jolly bonfire at their side.

"Rethlake!" the Bishop hollered. "Meeker!"

Two men rose slowly from their squatting position near the fire, the G.E.M.'s chief operator and his helper, each with a beercan clutched in fist.

"Rethlake!"

"Yeah . . ."

"Somebody's monkeyin' around with the G.E.M."

"I see it, Bishop."

"Who's up in there?"

The two men looked around, counting heads, studying faces. "One of the boys, Bishop. Ain't sure who."

Shielding his eyes from the violet glare of light, Love bellowed: "You up there, turn them goldarn lights off and get the hell out of that machine."

His answer was a roar of electrical turbines starting up as someone — or some *thing* — pushed the starter button. Above the roar of motors came the voice of the Super-G.E.M. itself, thundering from the exterior loudspeakers of the machine's public address system:

NOW HEAR THIS. NOW HEAR THIS. THIS HERE'S G O L I A T H SPEAKING, MEN, MASTER OF THE FUCKING WORLD AND FUCKING EMPEROR OF THE FUCKING UNIVERSE. WHEN RE-QUESTING PERMISSION TO SPEAK TO OUR IMPERIAL FUCK-ING MAJESTY, YOU WILL SINK TO YOUR FUCKING KNEES,

PLACE NOSE AGAINST GROUND THREE TIMES, LOWER PANTS,
AND REMAIN BOTTOMS UP UNTIL RECOGNIZED.

Love stared in amazement. The whole assembly stared in amazement. As they stared, the dragline's boom was activated by somebody
inside the control cabin, hoisted forty-five degrees and swung about
180 degrees from east to west on the Neck. Bull gears grinding, the
giant bucket bounced over the rock, smashing trees, flattening a drill
rig, knocking a road grader over the rim and completing the sweep by
clattering toward Bishop Love and his friends. They ran for their lives,
stumbling through the moonlight and shrubbery toward the far west
end of the Neck, beyond reach, they hoped, of the bucket and its iron
teeth. The bucket came to rest, awkwardly, on slack cables, about
twenty yards to the west of the two idle Mitsubishi bulldozers. There
it paused for the time being.

Panting hard, one hand on his chest, eyes bulging and his face a
florid purple, Bishop Love gaped at the machine towering in the
moonlight. The red lights oozed slowly off and on, off and on, like the
blinking eyes of a sleepy spider. The strobe light flashed atop the
A-frame, an intense blue-white pulse of lightning that could be seen
for twenty miles. The searchlight remained fixed on Love & Co.

Regaining his breath, the Bishop spoke to Rethlake, Meeker, the
two-man dragline crew. "You boys slip out there, unplug the trail
cable to that son of a bitch." They hesitated. "Go on now, he won't
see you. There's some drunk up in that cabin, he don't know what he's
doing, he's gonna damage that bucket if we don't get him outa there.
Go on now." Love patted the revolver on his hip. "We'll keep you
covered."

"You see that road grader go off the edge," somebody said. The
humans clustered together, in the midst of a clump of junipers, staring
up at the black outline of the G.E.M. against the stars, the unlit form
of the operator's cab far above the ground. "You see that thing go
over," the voice continued. "Like a toy. Sixty-ton grader. Like a
goddamn kid's toy . . ."

Ranger Dick, slipping an arm around Love's waist, whispered in his
ear. "Could be trouble, Dudley. You think maybe we ought to radio
the sheriff's office? The DPS? Get those helicopters headed this way
again?"

The Bishop snorted, half laughing. "Naw, naw, Ginny, what're you
talkin' about? I can handle this. That's my equipment, them's my men,
I'll take care of it."

". . . Yeah," another said, "never even heard it hit bottom neither. How's far's it down there anyhow?"

"Two thousand feet on the north side," a third man said. "About twenty-five hundred on the south. Straight down into Little Eden Canyon. Watched one of them crazy guys with a hang glider sail off here once. Never made it. Took them two days to recover the body. Carried it home in a black rubber sack. Squirrely winds got him, they said. What they found you could put easy into a one-bushel basket. Course they only picked up the main pieces. Like the head, pelvis, thigh bones, asshole and such."

"Don't want to hear about it, Melvin, for godsake."

"So what're you waiting for?"

"All right, all right, Bishop, we'll go. But if he comes after us with that bucket . . ."

"You can dodge it. Dodge the sucker. Keep runnin'."

"You too, Meeker."

"Sure, Bishop, sure." The two men started forward, out of the illusory shelter of the junipers toward the base of the machine, 13,500 tons of iron squatting like a frog on solid rock two hundred yards off at the far end of the Neck. The men had advanced no more than a few paces when a second spotlight on the A-frame blazed on, searched briefly to the right, to the left, caught them dead in the open.

HALT, MOTHERFUCKERS.

The men stopped, stiff as stone in the glare of Medusa's eye. The booming voice — basso profundo deus machina — continued:

YOU ASSHOLES TAKE ONE MORE STEP AND I'LL BRUSH YOU OVER THE SIDE LIKE TWO BUGS OFF A BOARD.

Reinforcing the threat, G O L I A T H raised his boom, reeled in the steel drag ropes and hoisted the mighty bucket to an upright position. Sparks flew as iron grated on sandstone. Clumsily, the bucket was dragged back toward the nearest Mitsubishi tractor — the crippled one with the dripping radiator. G O L I A T H slipped his prognathous jaw beneath the tracks and belly of the bulldozer, picked it up like a child (the tractor weighed only eighty tons) and lifted it tenderly, right side up within the bucket, about thirty feet above the ground. Tough — but oh so gentle.

One of the Ace security men nudged the Bishop. "We got plenty of firepower here, Bishop. Let's blast that clown in the control cab."

The Bishop considered. "Yeah . . . maybe. In a minute. Hard to see though. Don't want to damage the equipment."

"We could knock out those searchlights first. Blind the bastard, rush 'im, board that thing, find the guy in the cab and put him where he belongs for about six months."

"Well . . . hate to damage the equipment. Even one of them lights cost several thousand bucks. And you get all these half-drunk hard-hats firing away —"

GOLIATH again interrupted their deliberations:

ANYONE MAKE ANOTHER MOVE TOWARD THIS FUCKING
DRAGLINE I SWING THAT FUCKING CRAWLER OVER THE RIM
AND DROP IT LIKE SHIT OFF A SHOVEL INTO LOST EDEN
CANYON. . . .

"Afraid of that," the Bishop muttered. "We got a lunatic at work in that thing."

They hesitated. Again GOLIATH retracted, swung and lowered the bucket and picked up the second Mitsubishi bulldozer, holding both in his capacious maw and elevating them far above the monolithic stone of the Neck. And again he spoke, in that voice like the rumble of a volcanic and subterranean god: Vulcan speaking:

SAME GOES FOR ANY OTHER KIND OF FUCKING MONKEY
BUSINESS. WE'RE WORKING INSIDE TWO-AND-A-HALF-INCH
STEEL PLATE UP HERE. GOT REMOTE CONTROL HOOKUPS ON
ALL CONSOLE LEVERS. ANYONE TRY ANYTHING FUNNY AND
THESE TWO TRACTORS GO ASS OVER TINCUPS INTO DEEP
SPACE. I'M TALKING TO YOU, BISHOP J. DUDLEY LOVE. YOU
HEAR ME?

The Bishop flushed with anger. "Why you miserable wiseass . . ." he growled.

Ranger Dick tightened her embrace of his waist. "Easy, Dud, easy. I got an idea."

GOLIATH swung his bucket ninety degrees, extended the boom, and held the two bulldozers in suspension above the abyss on the north side of the Neck. One-half million dollars' worth of hostages, hanging above two thousand feet of moonlight and air.

YOU HEAR, LOVE? SPEAK UP. SPEAK UP OR I'M DROPPING
YOUR YELLOW TOYS INTO HELL. YOU HEAR?

The first spotlight remained fixed on Bishop Love and his intimates — the ranger, the two Ace security men, the group of hard-hats, the Search & Rescue team. At the same time, without waiting for reply, GOLIATH began another operation at the flanks of the machine. With a heavy clanking of cambered gears the monster's feet — the 130-foot-long steel walking shoes — began to rise.

"My God," the Bishop said, "what's he doing now?"

They stared in wonder. The shoes rose seven feet above the ground, rotated backward on the push cylinders for fifteen feet, then sank to the ground again, crushing three junipers, a clump of sagebrush, one hackberry tree, any number of beercans, oilcans and anthills. At this point, instead of coming to rest, the bellow of the 14,000-volt engines soared in intensity, straining with the tremendous effort of lifting the circular base tub — 105 feet in diameter — and with it the entire 4250-W walking-dragline Super-G.E.M., 27 million pounds (Fantastik Fackts!) of steel iron copper grease oil cable Plexiglas and also, apparently, a tiny microblob — somewhere within its intricate labyrinth of control cab, catwalks, gangways, bulkheads, corridors, engine room, fan house — a tiny living micro-organism of human flesh.

They watched. They gaped in amazement, mouths hanging open, as the whole gigantic impossible machine hoisted itself almost seven feet above the surface of the earth, tilted slightly, rocking a bit, and then slid backward, in reverse, for another fifteen feet before sinking once more, with a vibrant and resonant thud, down to solid rock. A cloud of dust and pulverized vegetation swirled about the foundations of the machine.

All present felt the ground tremble beneath their feet. GOLIATH walks. Five points on the Richter Scale. One small step for humankind, one giant step for GOLIATH.

"Holy Moroni," the Bishop murmured, "he's gonna hijack the G.E.M. of Arizona. He must be crazy as a . . . as a . . . a what?"

"Dudley," repeated Ranger Dick, "Dudley, listen to me, I've got a good idea."

"Hijack?" the Ace man said. "But where? Where's he think he's gonna take it? A baby can crawl as fast as that thing can walk. And anyhow for chrissake he's headed in the wrong direction. Can't go far the way he's headed . . . two, three, four more steps and . . . Sheet!" the man concluded in exasperation and disbelief.

"Why backwards?" asked one of the Search & Rescuers — a druggist by trade, not a construction worker. "Why's he walking it backwards?"

"Only way it goes," a hardhat explained. "It's a dragline walker, not a power shovel. Not a excavator."

"Suicide," the security guard went on, mumbling mostly to himself. "We got a kamikaze pilot running that thing."

"Will you listen to me, Dudley? Please? Stop worrying about your precious Mitsubishis and listen to me."

The Bishop blinked, turned his eyes away from the hypnosis of the spotlights, looked down upon the anxious and handsome face of his BLM lady-love. Looked down? Not much. Not more than two inches. She was nearly as tall as he, half his age, twice as good looking and maybe forty points higher on the Stanford-Binet I.Q. scale.

"Yeah, honey, yeah? What's your — " But again his attention was distracted by the grind and rumble of the walking gears. Squatting on his tub, grunting and groaning like a constipated fullback, GOLIATH was once again lifting up his two big feet.

"Shut off the power."

"What?"

"Shut off the goddamned power. It's all-electric, right? Get the power shut off."

"Honey, we — you saw what happened when — Jesus, Ginny, we can't even get *to* the power cable, let alone uncouple it. You heard what he'll do."

The shoes rose up, moved back, descended, planted themselves firmly on the bridge of stone. Again GOLIATH prepared to heave himself aloft. The ascending roar of his dynamo heart — that scream of fury — resounded through the desert.

"That's not what I mean," she said.

"What? Can't hear you."

"The sub-station," the woman shouted. "The sub-station. Radio the sub-station, tell them to shut down."

GOLIATH began to rise again — the tub, the seven-story power-house, the twelve-story A-frames, the fifteen-story twin masts, the twenty-two-story double-based convergent boom. The red lights squinted from the strain, the strobe light flashed like a neural synapse on the point of apoplexy, the independent spotlights roved and probed and peered about, dimming slightly as the lifting cylinders drew — with extravagant greed — upon the power supply. Again the mass of iron, of steel, of power, of howling majesty, shifted itself backward, another fourteen feet, toward the south edge of the Neck. Toward the brink.

"Ginny, Ginny! What happened to my brains?" Bishop Love

snatched the portable Motorola from the rangerette's outstretched hand. He pushed the microphone button. Holding the mike close to his mouth, shielding it with his free hand from the uproar to the east, he called his sub-station guard.

"Big Smoki, Big Smoki, calling Bunker Two. Come in, Bunker Two."

He released the button. They heard the crackle of static, then a fuzzy voice, androidal, in response. "Big Smoki, this is Bunker Two."

"That you, Henderson?"

"That's me, sir."

"Shut off the power."

"What? Can't read you, Bishop."

"Shut it off. Close it down. Quick, quick." The Bishop stared above the walkie-talkie toward the big machine in its suit of lights, setting itself down in a floating haze of sandstone molecules, shattered trees, glittering pink sparks of friction. Two more steps, maybe three — and the edge.

No immediate answer from Bunker Two.

"You read me, Bunker Two? Acknowledge, goddamnit."

A rasp of static. "Ten-four, Bishop, ten-four. Yes sir. We read you. But . . ."

"So shut off the power. Right now! Some lunatic's hijacked the Super-G.E.M. You read me?"

"We read you, Bishop, but . . ."

"No buts. This is urgent. Cut that master switch." The Bishop felt the sweat dripping from his brow, his neck, his eyebrows. He wiped his eyelids with a thick forefinger. "Bunker Two, I'm talkin' to you!"

"Sure'd like to oblige, Bishop, but I got a problem here. Two of 'em. A big one and a small one. Pointing guns at me."

"What?"

"Yep. Man and woman. Wearing Halloween masks. Some kind of A-rab robes. She calls him Yasser."

"*Yes sir?* What the hell you — who are they?"

"Yes, yeah, that's right. He calls her Golda, that's all I can tell you. In fact I better sign off right now, sir, that woman's giving me the cut-off sign. Bunker Two, ten-seven for now."

Dead air on the radio. Bishop Love stared at his sweetheart; she stared at him. Beyond, above, unapproachable, GOLIATH bellowed in pain and ecstasy, cranking up his big shoes for another playful, awkward lurch toward self-destruction. Such excess, such extreme, extravagant, exuberant, exhausting emotion.

"What do we do, Ginny? That machine cost Syn-Fuels thirty-seven million dollars. *Thirty-seven million!*"

The dazzling spotlight illuminated his drawn and sweating face, her softer, sweeter, far more human face. All brides are beautiful — even GS-7 career-track Bureau of Land Management government rangers.

She smiled. She opened both arms toward him. "Let it go, Dudley. It's only another piece of iron. Forget it. Let it go. Let's get married."

He glanced toward the machine — one more big step to make — then looked back at Ginny Dick, his darling, his sexpot, his second mate, his happiness, his woman, his affianced, his bride-to-be, his once and future, last and final, never-to-be-sundered absolute eternal and immortal other wife.

He stepped forward, took the strong young ranger in his arms, embraced and kissed her deep and long in the full glare of publicity, full in the eyes of friends and buddies, guards and employees, under the brazen eyes of mad GOLIATH.

Love, love, love. Sunk in their embrace, lips melting in one like Super Glue, eyes closed in a lingering swoon of joy, they even missed the high point of the show, the final push of GOLIATH's big feet, the fatal backward step upon the south edge of the Neck, the high rim of the canyon wall.

Yielding beneath the unendurable weight, the rim rock cracked. Slipped. Faulted. Spalled loose. Crumbled to a thousand falling boulders, each one a bomb. Sank into the moonlight and the darkness below. Dropping through space in silence.

The spotlights of the Super-G.E.M. swung wild toward the stars. The spider eyes blinked. The flashing strobe described a crazy intermittent arc across the blue of the night. The six-conductor 350 MCM trail cable slithered like a python out of nightmares over the stone, smashing through trees, and glided over the rim's edge in leashed pursuit of its master. Would the sub-station on its steel skids be yanked two miles to follow? Would the thousand-mile-long interstate EHV powerline be uprooted and pulled along with the sub-station? And what about the generating station at Page, Arizona (Shithead Capital of Coconino County), the cities of Saint George, Utah, Las Vegas, Nevada, Los Angeles, California, integral components of the spiderweb of power, tied by a million webs of fabric, copper and steel to powerline, sub-station, six-conductor trail cable — would they too, the entire great gross buzzing inferno of moronic trash, be dragged from its asphalt bases, would the whole absurd ephemeral system come bouncing over the mountains and skating across the desert to follow the leader, LORD GOLIATH, into the welcoming abyss of well-earned oblivion?

Not likely. No doubt some weak link would snap first. But it was possible. It is possible. It will be possible. If not today then tomorrow. If not tomorrow then, for sure, the day after.

Meanwhile,

GOLIATH fell.

He fell.

And as he fell he sang this song, in brutal pre-recorded basso-profundo carefree tones:

> HO-HO SAY CA-HAN YOU SEE
> BY THE DAWN'S EARLY LIGHT . . .

"Suicide, suicide," the Ace man marveled. "But what a way to go." Nevertheless: he kept his eyes peeled. He kept his eyeballs skinned, watching the moonlight and shadows on the rock, at the far east end of the Neck, where the *Super-G.E.M. of Arizona* had left its last track. Under the spectacular glory of ultimate mechanico-disaster, the Ace security guard looked for a tiny human figure, maybe two or three of them, hustling off to an imaginary safety. He was already on his feet, jogging forward, when in fact he saw them, and sounded the cry of pursuit.

> WHAT SO PROUDLY WE HAILED
> [Dopplerian *diminuendo* . . .]
> AT THE TWILIGHT'S —

"C'est splendide!" the journalist rejoiced, watching from his dark hole, scribbling, recording it all, *"c'est très* absolutely fucking *magnifique!"*

28

How They Done It

Only an hour earlier five figures on horseback were moving through the sagebrush at a brisk trot, headed for the Neck. Evening. Shadows long across the mesa plain. Nighthawks rising in the air, fluttering like bats in chase of bugs. A vast and forlorn sunset flared across the western sky, blood-red beyond a haze of windborne dust.

They rode in single file, following a primitive trail hardly better than a cowpath through the brush, between the pygmy trees of pinyon pine and juniper, brushing the open seedpods of *Yucca elata* on their five-foot stalks. The man in the lead, riding his favorite bay mare, was lank lean bright-eyed frightened beaknosed country boy of middle age wearing the filthy green coveralls of an auto mechanic, a black billed cap on his head, a big red bandanna around his neck. He was followed hard at heels by a stout broad burly brute with a black bandanna over nose and mouth, a greasy leather sombrero on his head, a giant Appaloosa gelding under his seat. This chap had small evil red eyes, in each of which burned the pinpoint fanatic fire of grim and resolute, unyielding happiness. *Getting even is the best revenge.*

The two in front set a hard pace, a brutal pace for anyone not accustomed to a long ride on stiff-legged dude horses jolting forward on alternating diagonal pairs of leg and foot. The third rider, bouncing in the saddle, lagging behind, voiced a bit of complaint now and then:

"You two bastards *have* to go so fast?"

No answer. The men in front ignored her. Actually the leader was concentrating on the path and route ahead and scarcely heard the words; while the second man, himself not much of a horseman and even less of a chevalier, didn't care. The woman continued to grumble. "We have all night, don't we? So what's the hurry? You want me to miscarry? If I ever tell my mother about this you two are going to be sorry you were born. What are we doing out here in this godforsaken wilderness anyhow? We could be home watching 'Wide Wonderful World of Nature' on Channel Six. If I weren't such a sweet lovable good-natured young woman I'd report all four of you to the BLM and let you rot in the Fredonia Village Jail for six months. This is a misdemeanor, isn't it? Conspiring to murder God? Or is it a Federal felony?" Nobody answered. Reins in one hand, cowgirl style, she held down her loose burnoose with the other, spurred her mount into a sudden canter and thus caught up with the surly silent man in front of her. The horses tossed their heads and tails, unused to such jostling proximity, disliking it.

Within a minute the woman was again falling behind. The two riders in front maintained their steady trotting gait, peering ahead at the bluish glow of a mercury-vapor security light, and — much farther beyond — at the dim red eyes, the bristling strobe, of lights that appeared to be stationary on the sky, like unmoved stars.

The woman continued to kvetch and bitch in her jocular, mocking fashion, neither expecting nor desiring any response. Straggling behind her came the fourth member of the party, even less of a rider than the woman. He clung to the horn of his saddle with both hands, trying to ease the jolt and jog, occasionally rising a bit in the stirrups to relieve his aching butt, and letting the tied reins simply hang on the neck of the docile, well-trained trail horse. Big as a bear but rather soft-bodied, awkward in the saddle, this man like the woman was shrouded in a flowing robe of moonlight blue; instead of a burnoose, however, he wore a floppy checkered dish towel on his head, bound in place with a rubber band. Dangling from his neck was a Halloween mask in the image of Yasser Arafat — that face that only an A-rab could love, surely the creepiest slimiest wormiest liberationist who ever crawled out of the sand pits, grease traps and cesspools of ancient Samaria.

"Why me?" the man had asked, days before, "why should I have to wear the ugly mask?"

"Because it fits," she said.

"While you are privileged to impersonate the lovely Mary Magdalene. Is that fair?"

"I always wanted to be a virgin."

"You're thinking of the wrong Mary, kid. Anyhow I'm going to call you Golda. Golda Meir. For the purposes of our bizarre nocturnal outing, I mean."

"Bizarre's the word. Sometimes I think you're crazy, Doc. Or senile. Letting that mad dog talk you into one more suicide trip."

"And you, my dear? Why then are *you* joining us?"

"Because somebody has to look after *you*, you fool."

Pause for thought. "True," he said. Scratching his bald dome. Removing and peering at the fogged-up lenses of his spectacles. "How true."

They lurched onward in the saddle, falling behind, then loping abruptly forward to regain their places. Jabbering away at each other among the grim silent *serious* environmental extremists trotting before and after.

Yes, the fifth horseman — riding easily, naturally — followed the pair from suburbia. This was the spectral old man in the Lone Ranger suit — comical ten-gallon white hat, black mask, pullover shirt with lace-up collar, gloves and gauntlets, tight blue cavalry pants, high boots, and around his waist the massive leather belt loaded with cartridges, two fine-tooled holsters, and in each holster the legendary silver-plated hand-engraved ivory-handled .44-caliber six-shot repeater. The shootist. The Masked Rider. Shane and Shinola, Tom Mix and Hopalong Cassidy, Sir Lancelot and El Cid, Gilgamesh, Jason, Siegfried and Luke Skywalker wrapped in one grubby Jungian package. This Lone Ranger and his outfit needed a visit to the Laundromat. He needed a shave. A shearing too. Probably a shit, shower, shampoo and shoeshine as well. Not to mention an eye transplant, a liver transplant and a sphincter implant. An old wreck, disintegrating organ by organ, like a worn-out Ford: now a fender falls off, now the shock absorbers go, the head gasket blows, the fuel pump falters, the differential dies, the clutch plate grabs. His horse, nearly as old as he is, stumbles now and then but recovers, regains its steady jogging gait, good for another thousand miles or two before the final burnout.

"Yasser, I'm gonna die."

"No you're not, my dear. Clench your gut. Use the stirrups. Lean on the horn like I do."

"I hate horses. If God meant us to ride horses why'd She invent the Mercedes-Benz?"

"Her ways are mysterious but the end is plain; a good laugh. The world was created to amuse a mind bored by the otherwise banal perfection of the absolute. Ask Hegel."

"Ask who?"

"Anybody."

The lead rider, slowing his horse, raised one hand in caution. He drew up and waited behind a juniper. The second rider, turning in his saddle, growled "Quiet back there."

"Quiet yourself," snapped Golda Meir. But she was happy to let her mount come to a stop with its nose browsing between the vast horsey buttocks of the Appaloosa. Yasser joined them, head to hindquarters. The fifth rider halted a short distance off, looking carefully to his rear, to all sides and above, mindful of helicopters and spotter planes.

"That's the sub-station right over there," Smith said, pointing. "See it, Doc? Quarter mile or so. Where the yard light is."

"We see it," Bonnie said.

Doc nodded in the deepening twilight, the spreading moonlight. He straightened the dishrag on his head, clearing his eyes and face. "Christ," he muttered. "No wonder they can't shoot straight."

"We'll tie up the horses here," Seldom went on, "walk the rest of the way." Addressing Bonnie: "All you and Doc got to do is creep over there, get the drop on that watchman. He's by himself. Young fella name of Henderson. Be sure to take his gun away and cuff his hands. Lock him to the light pole. Don't hurt him. Old Jack there, he'll back you up. Got your big iron, Bonnie?"

"My what?"

"Pistol, revolver, some kind of handgun?"

"Are you kidding, Smith? You know we don't own any guns. We belong to the American Civil *Liberties* Union, buster; we're against guns except in the hands of the duly constituted authorities. We say, Ban guns. Confiscate guns. What is this anyhow, a free country or not?"

Smith stared at Hayduke in helpless wonder. "They didn't bring a gun."

Hayduke growled, staring ahead. "Abbzug the wiseass. Show him your plaything, Bonnie."

"I *beg* your pardon, sir. My what? Here? On public land? In front of all these men?"

"You're wasting time, Abbzug."

She grinned, flashing fine white teeth in the moonlight. She reached into her capacious Bedouin robes and drew forth, with both hands, a sleek elegant precision-tooled Uzi 9mm machine pistol. She unfolded the stock, snapped it in place. Aiming the Uzi's muzzle at the sky she reached inside her robe again, pulled out a full ammo magazine and slammed it firmly into the breech. With practiced ease she slid the carriage back then forward, loading the firing chamber, set the action on semi-automatic and locked the safety. "Jewish," she said proudly, smiling at Smith. "This here's a Jew-gun, men. Israeli made and Israeli deployed. The gun that won the West. West Bank, that is." Turning her head, she smirked at Doc. "Eat your heart out, Arafat. Today Israel — tomorrow the world!" She tucked it out of sight.

Doc Sarvis and Seldom Seen Smith stared at Bonnie. "Holy smoke," said Smith. Doc nodded sadly.

Smith looked at Doc. "And where's yours, Doc?"

"Me? Mine?" The good doctor smiled. "I'm a pacifist, Seldom. You know that; I don't believe in violence. I've said it before and I'll say it again: Anarchy is not the answer."

"So what is the answer?"

Doc thought. "It's an unanswered question," he said after a moment. "Everything depends upon our interpretation of the silence." Brief pause for intellectual digestion.

"You fuckin' philosophers finished?" Hayduke asked. No immediate reply. He waited, frowning into the gloom, looking two miles west at the glinting strobe light of the Super-G.E.M. He heard no roar of motors. GOLIATH had paused. Was down, waiting. Waiting for him, Hayduke, George Washington Hayduke, father of his country. Not of the America that was — keep it like it was? — but of the America that will be. That will be like it was. Forward to anarchy. Don't tread on me. Death before dishonor. Live free or fucking die. Etc., etc.

"Let's get moving," he said. "Before all them cops and whirlybirds come back. Time for the swing shift."

All but the Lone Ranger, old one-eyed Jack, dismounted. They tied up the four horses. Doc and Bonnie put their masks in place, adjusted robes and hoods and dish towels, and slipped into the dark toward the electrical sub-station and the G.E.M.'s umbilicus to power, the two-mile extension cord. The Lone Ranger circled north and west to approach the same objective, slightly later, from a different direction. On horseback: he never walked. Never. Nowhere. Hayduke and

Smith, wearing dark coveralls, shod in running shoes, jogged forward on the dim trail that led to the new dirt freeway, the dusty smear of devastation, wide as a football field, that marked the track of the 4250-W. Each man carried a light field pack slung behind his shoulders. Hayduke also had a blunt .357 stuck in his belt at the small of his back; Smith wore his Granddaddy's old .44 in its stiff frazzled leather holster nestled at his groin.

Twenty minutes later they topped the gentle rise above the east end of the Neck, slunk a bit farther under the little desert trees, and stopped. Breathing hard, sweating, they studied the moonlit scene before them, Hayduke using field glasses.

GOLIATH squatted upon the near end of the Neck, occupying almost the entire width of that slender land bridge between plateau and island mesa. Except for the strobe and the red warning lights far above their heads, he was dark, silent, idle, apparently vacant of human life. No man sat in the operator's chair of the high, fore-projecting control cab. No one moved upon the decks and gangways of the engine house, the fan vent room, the catwalks of the lowered boom or the towering masts and A-frames.

"They shut her down," Smith whispered. "I thought they never shut that thing down."

Hayduke screwed night-vision lenses into the eyepieces of his big 7x50 Green Beret binoculars and looked beyond the dragline machine to the bonfire and mob of laughing humans at the far west end of the Neck. "Boys are having a party," he said. "About a dozen hardhats. Whole damn S and R Team's there too. That BLM rangerette what's-her-name."

"Dick. Ginny Dick. A nice woman. I like her."

"Dick. No kidding. Ranger Dick. Couple of those fucking gun-happy assholes from Ace. And by God there's ol' Bishop Love himself, in person, all meat, the great Horse's Ass in the flesh, wearing his Ralph Lauren cowperson costume, he's got one hand on the ranger's ass and a Pepsi in the . . . Pepsi? Pepsi hell, by God, Seldom, the Bishop is drinking a beer. A beer, I tell you."

"Coors Lite?"

"Let's see. Hard to tell. Old fart's got a big hand. But yeah, there's a case of that angel piss on the ground by the fire. They're grilling steaks. Sons of bitches are having a picnic while we work. Celebrating."

"I'm hungry, George."

"Yeah." Hayduke studied the tableau a bit longer, especially the

G.E.M., grinning his savage grin, muttering his harmless mantras. ''Fuckin' motherfucker . . . cocksuckin' son of a motherfuckin' cock- sucker . . .''

''Hungry, George.''

Hayduke snapped shut the binocs, rammed them in the case, case into pack. ''Work, m'fug. To work. First we work. Then we eat.'' He pulled on leather gloves. ''Come on.''

They half rose and slipped ahead through the shadows, down the gentle slope of bare stone and sand toward the monster, stopping every few seconds to look hard and listen harder.

''Should of brought satchel charges, George. Satchel charges. One hell of a lot easier.'' Now Smith drew on his gloves. ''Wouldn't it, George?''

Kneeling in the moonshade of a juniper, Hayduke peered up at the steel shoes, engine house deck, control cab. ''No glory in it that way. Too easy. And too hard — we'd need a ton of H.E. to demolish this fucker. Look at that thing — bigger'n the goddamn fuckin' state cap- itol . . .''

Hearing and seeing no sign of life, they padded to the ladder on the side of the near shoe, climbed from there up a steep gangway to the main deck and entered the dark interior of the powerhouse, sixty feet above the level of the ground. Hayduke paused, listening in the dark, then switched on a Mini-Mag-light, its intense little beam filtered through a blue lens for purposes of moonlight mischief.

''So?'' he says, ''how do we get to the control room?''

''Hain't sure, George.'' Smith opened a bulkhead door, flicked on his own Mini-Mag and played the light over a vast and complex warehouse-like interior, where dynamos and turbines under molded housings of battleship steel waited for the black button of excitation. ''Not that way, I don't reckon.''

''Thought you knew these machines.''

''George, I said I worked in that little one up near Craig, Colorado, about only half the size this here GOLIATH. And I was only the oiler: number-two nigger.''

''Maybe we follow that outside catwalk.''

''Yeah but there's gotta be a inside way through here to the cab too. Anyhow first we got to find the master switch to turn on power to the engine room.''

''Master switch?''

''Safety, George. In case control cab gets knocked off or something.'' Smith moved down the corridor between engine room and lockers,

looking for the wall-high circuit breaker closet. "Should be down here
... yep ..." He opened the box, checked a deep array of switches,
each about the size of a handbrake lever on a truck. He closed the
switch labeled MAIN, then the HOIST, DRAG, PROPEL, SWING, DUMP, P.A.,
LIGHTS, HEAT, A.C., CABLE and UTILITY switches.

"So ..." mused Hayduke. "Somebody gets in here they can stop us.
How we gonna watch this and outside too?"

"This'll help." Smith pulled a set of Master Padlocks from his pack,
selected one and locked the circuit breaker door.

They stepped out on the deck again, checking the party at the fading
then flaring bonfire. Sounds of music: somebody was playing a
battery-powered boombox. A few couples in black silhouette jerked
and jiggled, like spastic puppets, before the flames. Shrieks, shouts and
a bray of laughter rang through the night. Clash of breaking bottles.
Seldom Seen Smith gaped wistfully at the festive throng.

"There's wimmin there, George. We're missin' out on a good
party." Smith the wilderness lover always loved a party. Like most
solitary outdoorsmen he was a highly gregarious and incurably social
animal. "Wimmin, George," he repeated.

"Fuck 'em, m'fug, we got work to do."

"I love wimmin, George."

"Love women, do you? Female women? Smith, these days that
makes you some kind of queer. Come on."

"Well reckon that's the kind of queer I am. That queer kind of
queer."

"Anyhow you don't love women you just love women's bodies."
Hayduke tugged at Smith's sleeve. "Let's go."

"Hain't never seen a woman's body yet didn't have a woman inside
of it. Maybe you ain't noticed, George, but them female people come
in neat integrated little packages. I hain't complainin', you understand, but it's a true fact. Might be handier if they didn't but they do."

" 'Woman's ass and the whisky glass / Made a loser out of you.'
Seldom, you going to help me or do I have to do everything myself?"

"Ready."

"So which way?"

"We can get there from the outside but somebody might see us. Let's
try the long way." Smith re-entered the engine house, padlocked the
door on the inside, took the corridor past lockers and circuit breakers
to another high-pitched gangway aft. This brought them to an inner
catwalk with rails high inside the cavernous engine room. Ducts,
cables, steel rope, and a network of pipes hung suspended in huge

brackets from the overhead deck. Watching each step, following his pencil-beam of bluish light, Smith proceeded forward to another bulkhead opening. Hayduke followed hard on his heels, sweating with excitement, fear, joy, the lust for action. For heroic and noble action. The urge to destroy that which is evil, said the anarchist Prince Bakunin, is a creative urge. How true. How bloody awful true.

They passed through the bulkhead gangway and found themselves in the rear of the control cabin, cantilevered high above the ground. This part of the cab was like a small kitchen and bunkroom, with refrigerator, microwave oven, water cooler, coffee maker, work-bench, cabinets and table. One bunk with foam pad and blankets was folded against the wall. The walls were lined in genuine Formica pine paneling, the floor covered with authentic virgin linoleum tile.

"Hey," whispered Smith, "like a brakeman's caboose. Nice. Just like home." He opened a cabinet door and helped himself to a fistful of mixed nuts from an open can.

"What do you know about cabooses? Don't tell me you worked on the fucking trains too."

"Yes sir, one time on the Union Pacific out of Thompson Springs. About six months. Good job; I should've kept it, I'd be retired and drawing a fat ol' railroader's pension now."

"You'd be a fat old pile of retired shit. Get out of those peanuts. Where's the steering wheel on this fucker? Show me the starter, the gas pedal, the goddamn choke."

"This way." Smith turned off his flashlight; Hayduke did the same. The forward half of the cab was walled by sliding glass doors. Moonlight, starlight, night light provided sufficient illumination. In the soft gray gloom of the interior the men approached the operator's wide chair upholstered in leatherette. Jostling his friend not too gently aside, Hayduke enthroned himself in the seat of power. He placed his hands on the knobbed levers at either side of the operating console, put his feet on a pair of big pedals on the floor. Grinning with delight.

"Start up the mother, Seldom. I'll drive." He found himself facing eastward, the way they had come. "How do we turn it?"

"Hold your horses, George. Think. First we got to start up the motors. Big noise. When we do that Love and his team'll come charging across that there Neck like a herd of mustangs."

Hayduke drew his revolver and set it on the little steel table, with its dials and gauges, before him.

"Nope, that won't work. They got us outgunned about ten to one. And these glass walls won't stop bullets. Think, George, you're the sabotage expert."

Hayduke thought, recalling their plans. "Okay. Right. They're all bunched up now by that fire. So we turn on the spotlights first, keep 'em under strict surveillance. Then we pick up the hostages, let the fuckers know the terms. Where's the radio?"

"Keep your shirt on. Let's wire up the hand levers first so we can stay away from all this Plexiglas."

Hayduke nodded, becoming slightly more humble, opened his pack and pulled out a coil of wire and a fencing tool. Working quickly but pausing often to look and listen, they attached separate lengths of wire to each essential operating lever, including the horizontally moving foot pedals, and ran the wires back through the cab and onto the catwalk inside the engine room, shielded from outside gunfire by the bulkhead wall, plates of American-made A-36 carbon steel two and a half inches thick.

"Now what?"

"Escape route, George. Got your climbing ropes?"

They opened the cab's sliding door and checked out the catwalk that led to the great boom, 310 feet long from foot to head. When the dragline reached tipover point, they'd be far out on the boom (they hoped), beginning a couple of free rappels that should break all known world speed records. They doubled two carefully inspected 150-foot Perlon ropes around the steel webwork, leaving the running ends neatly coiled on the catwalk of the boom. They cinched up rappel slings, snapped on the braking carabiners, and returned to the operator's command post.

"We ready?"

"Reckon we are, George. Now let's see what we got here. . . ." Smith flicked on his tiny light, shielding it with one hand, and studied the switches on the control console. "Spotlights, searchlight, numbers one, two and three. Control handles on the ceiling there, George, right above the chair. Get set. Radio and mike on your left." He flicked on the radio switch. "Now you can talk to our ol' friends out there at the picnic. It'll sound like the voice of God Hisself. Scare the britches off ever' one of them. You about ready?"

"Ready." Hayduke plucked the radio microphone from its hook on the left control panel, depressed the button, cleared his throat. They heard, from the public address speakers high outside on the masts, a rumbling sound that rather resembled an avalanche of empty oil drums cascading down a steep pitch of broken cinderblock.

"Okay . . ."

"Do it, Seldom. Do it!"

Smith flicked on the searchlights. Hayduke swiveled the control handle on Number One, nailed Love & Co. with its blinding shaft of blue-white revelation. Smith turned on the black "Excitation" switch. Thirteen thousand eight hundred volts of electronic energy stirred the engines into life. Through the powerhouse walls came a rising vibrant roar equivalent, perhaps, to that of a hundred 747s revving up their turbo-jets. Hayduke, flushed red with triumphant exultation, spoke into the microphone, commencing his imperial monologue. "Now hear this," he said, firmly, clearly, but not shouting, "now hear this . . ." From somewhere above and outside, through the walls of steel and glass, came the grotesque mimicry of Hayduke's words amplified ten-thousandfold, reverberating across the desert wastes of northern Arizona. . . .

Standing at the main control console a little behind and to the right of the operator's throne, Smith flipped the SWING switch from "Set" to "Release." "Okay, George," he shouted above the general uproar, "swing that there bucket around, pick up them bulldozers."

But Hayduke, happily focusing his searchlight on Love and crew with one hand while bellowing god-like threats at the same time, did not or could not hear Seldom's instructions. Realizing this, Smith stooped and tugged at one of the wires they'd linked to the foot pedals. At once but slowly, ponderously, GOLIATH began to revolve upon his massive base, swinging to the right, that is, toward the south and east, the great boom nearly horizontal with the ground and the giant bucket, on slack cables, dragging and banging over the sandstone, smashing a little ten-ton Schramm self-propelled drill rig, crushing a Chevvy shit-green government pickup truck, and shoving a heavy-duty Caterpillar road-grading machine to the edge of the rim and over, out of sight out of mind. Smith released the HOIST brake, pulled the black knobbed lever on Hayduke's left, and elevated the bucket about fifty feet above the surface.

Hayduke kept on talking, adjusting the searchlight control as the machine came around 180 degrees, the operator's cab now projecting itself toward the abandoned bonfire, the defenseless Mitsubishi, the crowd of Searchers, Rescuers, construction workers and lovers scampering in a panicked herd into the sagebrush and junipers at the far west end of the Neck.

Smith released the right foot pedal, stopping the swing. He released the left HOIST lever, dropping the bucket to the stone on the farther side of the two bulldozers. Now what? Looking out through the front window, with its five-foot wiper dangling, he could see but not hear the huddled, gesticulating mob of celebrants staring up, their faces white under the glare, their little fists trembling above their little hardhat heads. Oh Jesus, he thought, they're a-gonna be mad. I mean real *pissed*. Sure glad they can't see us.

"Watch for guns," he shouted at Hayduke. "Get ready to duck." But Hayduke, enjoying the most glorious moments in his life since blowing up the Black Mesa coal train or rolling a boulder down on Bishop Love's truck or maybe — maybe — since that first night in the Shady Rest Motel with Bonnie Abbzug, Hayduke didn't seem to hear him. At any rate made no reply. Studying the console with his Mini-Mag Smith continued mechanical operations on his own.

He unlocked the drag brake, pulled the wire on the right-hand control lever, and draglined the mighty bucket toward the first Mitsubishi, cradled the tractor like a toy in the bucket's outlandish jaws, pulled the HOIST lever and raised the bulldozer aloft for all to see and contemplate. Hayduke thundered on, speaking proudly into the mike which he held, as customary, close to his lips. Smith lowered the bucket again and scooped up the second bulldozer, elevated both and swung them over the abyss. The boom reached well beyond the north rim of the Neck. One short yank on the DUMP lever and both would fall.

Oh hey, he thought, you know this really is kind of fun. But scary too. Watching Love and friends, Smith saw two men try to sneak forward, then stop transfixed by the beam of Hayduke's second searchlight. Any minute now they're gonna start shootin', Smith thought. Maybe rush us from behind too. He looked into the big rearview mirror on the right-hand side of the cab but could see only stars and moonlight in their rear. And then realized that the mirror faced south, that he was looking over the rimrock into the gulf of space. The void.

That way, he thought. The way we got to go. Bass ackwards over the edge, into the ditch two thousand five hundred feet below. Sure hope there ain't none of my horses down there. Be a hell of a note to drop this slab of iron onto my own livestock.

He released the PROPEL brake, placed SWING and HOIST and DRAG and DUMP into "Set" or locked position. Do it? Are we really gonna do it? Thirty-seven-million-dollar little ol' steam shovel we got here. Some folks won't be happy about this. Some folks won't understand. Won't even *try* to understand. Well — can't please everybody. He grasped the wire hitched to the PROPEL lever, looped it around the hard gloved and powerful middle fingers of his right hand. With his left hand he reached up and twisted the control handle of the third searchlight, performing a quick scan of the rocks, trees and shrubs on the eastward approach to the Neck. Nobody coming from that direction — yet. But above, in the sky, not far, he saw the twinkling wing lights of an oncoming airplane. Coming in low and slowly like a firefly, preparing to land on the Super-G.E.M.'s broad track. Of course. Sheriff's Dept.

"George!" Smith yelled. "George!" he yelled again, loud as he could. Hayduke finally looked around. Smith jerked his chin over his shoulder. "Get ready," he shouted. "We're goin' over."

Hayduke nodded. Smith had explained the necessary procedure beforehand. The G.E.M. could walk in any direction but only in a forward-facing, reverse-advancing attitude. Why? GOLIATH moved like a threatened crab, rearward only, because the cambered drive wheels of the two walking shoes rotated in one direction only, that is, away from the control cabin. The G.E.M. was a *drag*line excavator, after all, designed not for cross-country travel but for digging open pits, pits the size, if desired, of Lake Erie. Of Lake Titicaca. The Lake of Hell. Dis, where Satan lived, froze in ice to his bellybutton.

Smith pulled the PROPEL lever. Keeping the wire taut, he followed it through the cab through the bulkhead into the deafening clamor of the engine room. Quickly, efficiently, more by feel than sight, he dallied the line around a strut of the catwalk railing, secured it with a half hitch, and returned to Hayduke in the cabin. They listened to the thunderous grumble of the four hydraulic lifting cylinders, saw the shoes tilt, wobble, rise, reach apogee, and begin the backstroke under impulsion of the four hydraulic push cylinders, each cylinder driven by three 600-horsepower motors. Normal operating pressure: 2,500 pounds per square inch. Enough oil pressure to make a mere diesel locomotive engine explode like a fragmentation grenade.

They watched the shoes go down, press against the solid Navajo sandstone of the Neck. Loose boulders, crushed to powder by impaction, squirted from beneath the steel shoes in jets of fine pale dust. The shoes pushed downward. The engines strained, groaned, heaved. The entire machine, all but its two big flat jointed feet, rose eighty inches from the ground, rocking, banging, pitching slightly, like a ship on wavy water.

Hayduke and Smith put hands against the cab wall for balance. But they did not fail to keep the searchlights active, surveying the enemy for the first sign of a forward charge.

"What's the matter with them guys?" Hayduke yelled. He tucked his .357 in his belt, squinting at Bishop Love, Ranger Dick, Teammates and Crew, far below and two football fields away. "They going to let us do this without a fight?"

"They don't believe it, George. They don't know what we think we're a-doin'. Do you? Hain't too sure myself."

Feeling the machine slide backward now, toward the brink of the drop-off, Smith tried to see how far they had to go in that direction. Two more steps? Three? The rearview mirror was no help at all nor could he see any better by pressing his nose to the glass door. Ordinarily the swamper, the oiler, would be on the ground in this situation, directing the operator by hand signals.

GOLIATH sank down, six feet eight inches approximately, its circular fundament booming when it hit the ground. Clouds of dust flew up, swirled in eddies, floated eastward on the hot air rising from the canyon below. Grinding on, the shoes began another ascent.

"About time to get outa here, George." Smith slid open the door on the outer side of the cab and attempted to eyeball-estimate the distance to the rim. The powerhouse blocked direct view to the rear; he could see only off the starboard side in a quartering angle. In that direction the edge lay dramatically near — about twenty feet away. One more giant step for GOLIATH and he — she — it would be perched on the brink, teetering and tottering on the margin of eternity, so to speak. (Not exactly the manner in which Smith phrased the matter but encapsulating the mental image in his head.)

"About time to bail out, George. I'd say about one more cycle of them walkin' shoes and we crash. I mean take off, you might say, like ol' Butch Cassidy and the Bunch takin' that shortcut down off Black Box Point in that there San Rafael Reef country, recall what I'm talkin' about, George? Up in Emery County?" A pause. "George . . .?"

Each hand on a searchlight handle, Hayduke was forgetting his lookout duties. Instead he gaped at the vacancy of moonlit space coming closer and closer. Sweating with ecstasy, anxiety, succumbing to the euphoria of the depths, he muttered, "Parachute, Seldom. Goddamn, if only we had our fucking parachutes. What a jump. . . ."

"Never seen a parachute myself, George. Anyhow, let's bail off this here mechanical horse." Smith was also in a lather of sweat but ecstasy, of any sort, was far from his mind. He slid open the portside door of the cab, the opening to the inner catwalk that led to the boom and their escape route. Survival was what Smith had in his thoughts, survival with or without honor, he didn't actually care much at this point.

"Come on, George, for love of Christ come on!"

The walking shoes went down, they pressed, the engines strained, the dynamos at Glen Canyon Dam far to the east felt the pull of GOLIATH's need and greed, increased the tempo to provide the necessary peaking power. Lights dimmed for a few seconds in Saint George Utah as the Super-G.E.M. heaved its 13,500 tons six feet clear of the ground.

The G.E.M. tilted, yawed, pitched, rocking backward. Chains rattled, cables boomed. One hand on the doorframe for support, Smith reached in from the catwalk, clutched a handful of coverall sleeve, and yanked Hayduke free and clear, outside into the open air, the screech of machinery, the roar and uproar of power, the hot stink of oil and burning lights and straining pistons. But not before Hayduke, as a final gesture, pushed the PLAY bar on the P.A. system's recorded-message tape deck.

They saw the cluster of human figures facing them across the long slender peninsular bridge of the Neck. Saw two figures take tentative steps forward, bracing themselves to run. And then they felt, did not hear but *felt* the crumble and slippage of violated rock at the rear of GOLIATH's great feet. Saw the beams of the unmanned searchlights swing upward for a few rods, leaving their enemies in the relative obscurity of only moonlight. Felt the earth giving way, the deep resonance of an advancing earthquake, the meaning of Doom.

They leaped from the control cabin's catwalk — stung by terror into galvanic movement at last, vaulting the handrails — to the catwalk of the boom, raced up the filthy grease-slobbered steps to their rappeling point and the two trusted mountaineering ropes. Very quickly but not quite frantically, yet, they linked carabiners, diaper slings and themselves to the ropes.

The boom, locked in a nearly horizontal position, twitched beneath their feet. Clanged, clanked, clattered, began to rise, cantilevered skyward by the downward tilt of GOLIATH on his eroding fulcrum.

"Rappel," yelped Hayduke, "rappel!" Face greasy with sweat, he lowered himself through the open webwork of the boom and slid downward at reckless speed on the rope, grateful for the leather gloves on his hands. Smith followed at the side, not quite so fast, not quite so expertly. Looking down, Hayduke saw the end of his rope swinging free of the ground. "Oh no . . ." He increased speed, reached the terminus of the rope, let go and dropped. Ten feet. *Falling*, he thought, *fall* — and hit the blackbrush and mellow sandstone jump-school style, relaxed and limber, rolling with the shock. Unhurt, he jumped to his feet, hearing Seldom's plaintive bleat of fear. Where was that crazy cowboy? He heard another squeal and looked up: Smith dangled fifteen feet above, swinging in a short arc back and forth, arms outstretched, clinging desperately to the end of his rope. The Super-G.E.M., though canted backward at the rimrock's edge, was static for the moment, its shoes rotating backward in mid-cycle, off the ground.

"Let go, Seldom. Aim for the juniper. I'll break your fall." Hearing somehow, through the howling terror of GOLIATH, the thud and thump of running feet. They're coming. "Let go or you're a goner."

Smith let go at the end of his swing, falling toward a scrubby five-foot juniper. Hayduke arrived at the moment of impact and leaping forward, managed to get both arms under Smith's arched back, crashing with him into the midget tree. Scratched and bloody but unbowed, uninjured, they staggered free of the juniper's clutching branches. Wiping blood from his eyes, checking Granddaddy's revolver — family heirloom — and tugging down the bill of his cap, Smith looked for the right way to run. One man in uniform, far ahead of the others, was galloping toward them, shouting the alarm. Behind him came a dozen more. A quarter mile to the east, enveloped in a shroud of floury dust, five men and three women clambered out of Ellie Love's airplane, armed with Pepsi-Cola, Seven-Up, Jack Daniels, Wild Turkey, hotdogs, buns, relish, ketchup, flowers for the wedding, a couple of BLM bridesmaids, and the officiating magistrate J. Marvin Pratt.

"Let's go, George." Smith ran up the bare slickrock eastward, toward their friends, the hidden horses. But stopped when he became aware that Hayduke was not with him. He looked back.

George W. Hayduke stood petrified, gazing at GOLIATH on the verge, shoes descending for the final push, about to go over.

"George —!"

"Yeah." George waved back. "Keep going. Be with you in a minute." And George began to run, not after Smith however but toward the tilting G.E.M., the canyon rim. Smith watched him for a moment, clenched both hands in despair, and resumed his flight. Crazy bastard — am I spozed to do everything for him? Keep him outa jail? Wipe his goldang nose?

Can't miss this, was Hayduke's thought. A whole year's dream — he pounded over the stone, through the moonlight, leaping clumps of sage and prickly pear — and I don't even see it?

He raced toward the edge, watching the machine's bottomside come up, exposing not the smooth flat circular surface he'd imagined but a huge center pintle ringed with a series of concentric steel plates, the whole resembling the symmetric web of the orb weaver spider. Interesting.

He reached the rim, hearing as GOLIATH toppled, a vast medley of noises: crumbling and colliding rock, the screech of wrenching steel, the unabating bedlam of the electrical motors, the hiss of hydraulic pistons sheathed in oil, and above all, loud and clear, the opening strains of our fucking national anthem, blaring out of nowhere, everywhere, anywhere —

HO-HO SAY CA-HAN YOU SEE

He glanced back, feeling for his revolver. Gone. Shit. But his pursuers had halted for the moment, standing at attention, hats and hands on hearts, a lump in every throat, a tear in every fucking eye. Good men. He knelt on the extreme brink of the overhanging rim, sensing the shudder of bedrock beneath his bones, and he watched his enemy go down. That enemy he loved.

Going down, singing as he fell. Falling free the first three hundred feet past the Kayenta caprock, glancing lightly off a protruding ledge below — certain parts detached themselves in a spray of sparks — and floating farther out from the canyon wall, turning in graceful, relaxed, happy-go-lucky slow motion through the carefree medium of air. Beautiful. He saw the two Mitsubishi tractors ease clear of the inverted bucket, not far, sinking through space in precise congruence with the leisurely revolutions of the walking, now flying, 4250-W. Lovely. Accelerating too, of course, in unison, the heavyweight the flyweights, in thrall to the spell of gravity, exactly as Aristarchus, Epicurus, Galileo, Newton and others had calculated centuries before. Excellent. Newtonian mechanics, Hayduke reflected, was no longer adequate for sub-nuclear phenomena, perhaps, or for the ultra-galactic, but still good enough by God for regular fucking government work.

GOLIATH falling, falling, followed by the casual unlooping of his umbilicus, the thick trail cable, like an astronaut and his tether drifting off from Spacelab.

The dragline fell, cleared the base of the great Wingate cliff, struck the Chinle slopes a thousand feet below and bounced rolled skated to the lip of the Moenkopi wall and another free-fall. The bucket flew up and out in an arc of its own, the boom came half unjointed, the twin masts crumpled, the power cable snapped and the lights went out. GOLIATH soared outward again, pinwheeling into deep time, into geological history. The powerline, charged with energy, writhed and twisted like a tortured snake, smoking and sparking, and electrocuted a number of innocent desert shrubs, torched off a thicket of tangled sticks containing a family of pack rats and their guests the kissing bugs, burned up an eagles' nest. But not the eagles.

The G.E.M. dropped free for another five hundred feet and crashed in to the next talus down, barreling over and somersaulting down. One shoe fell off, breaking in half — then the other. The control cabin vanished in a puff of smoke and debris. Fires flickered in the fanhouse, the engine room. The boom, bent double, broke loose and continued its descent. Something exploded in the engine room and the plated steel swelled outward like a bubble, burst like a balloon. Disintegrating part by part, wrapped in flames, shriveling in magnitude, the 4250-W walking dragline Super-G.E.M. of Arizona, code name GOLIATH, sank down and down into the deep time of geologic history — from Jurassic into late Triassic, from late Triassic into early Triassic, ricochetting off the Hoskinnini Tongue and the Cutler Formation, shattering itself finally upon the floor of Lost Eden Canyon, the unyielding monolithic fine-grained rock of the Cedar Mesa Sandstone deep in the Permian Age, 250 million years ago.

Flames flickered far below among the mangled black ruins of the hulk. Smoke spiraled upward in sooty thermal columns. The rumble, clash and collision of falling rock would continue, slowly fading, for the next three days and nights.

Hayduke spat over the edge. Satisfied at last, he stood up, unbuttoned his coveralls and fondled it out into the open air, letting it breathe. Fully erect he staled like a stallion on the hard rimrock. Thank God I am a man.

"Freeze!" barked a strange voice. "Hands behind your head."

Oh shit *no*, groaned Hayduke in his heart. Not now. Not me. Not here. I can't stand a prison cell. That trapped feeling. Fucking claustrophobia. I'll die. The government will kill me quick, sure as shit. They know they got to do it, I know they got to do it, they know I know I know they know. But he obeyed instructions.

"Now turn around slow," the voice continued. "Let's see what we got here."

Hayduke obeyed. He found himself facing an oversize shadowy figure in dark uniform: half moon now far down the west, the face was hard to make out but it looked like, yes it was, that Ace security asshole

Jasper B. Bundy, six foot four and a room temp I.Q. of around 78. The guard held a short shotgun in his right hand, pointed at Hayduke's belly, and a snubnose revolver in his left. "You dropped something, buddy," he said, grinning. "Your Saturday night special." Craning his potshaped head forward, peering at Hayduke. "Goodwood? Casper Goodwood . . . ?"

Another man stepped out of the shrubbery, face masked in a bandanna, pointing Granddaddy's .44. "Drop the shotgun, mister."

The guard faced Smith. "You drop yours."

"No, you drop yours."

"I asked first."

"But I mean business. You don't. You wouldn't have the nerve to shoot a snake."

"I'd rather shoot you, mister, than any snake I ever seen."

More voices hollered in the distance, coming closer. Bundy, they cried, where are you? In the growing gloom it was getting harder and harder to see anything. Even horses.

The two gunmen faced each other, stymied by the general absurdity of the situation. Both well aware that guns are dangerous, ridiculous, capable of inflicting gruesome and painful even mortal wounds, and that one more moment of hesitation might be fatal for somebody. The Ace man lowered the .357 to his side, concealing it from Smith's view.

"Watch out," Hayduke said, "he's got —"

"Everybody!" snapped a fourth voice. "Drop them guns."

Startled, Seldom Seen dropped his antique. On his foot. It did not go off. Also startled, the Ace guard turned to face this new intruder, lifting the muzzle of the shotgun toward a man on a horse.

This time somebody pulled the trigger. Hayduke saw a blast of red flame in the dark, heard an explosion and saw the Ace man, Jasper Benson Bundy, stagger back a step and crumple like a sack of spilled meal, half his head blown away.

"Oh my gosh," murmured Smith, paralyzed by horror.

"Bundy!" someone yelled. "Where are they?"

Hayduke was first to react. "Quick," he said to Smith, "over the rim with it." He meant the body. Stepping forward, he grasped an arm and a leg. Sweat dripped from his face. "Hurry up."

Smith moved, doing the same. "You sure he's dead?"

"He's dead. Over the rim. They'll never find him."

Sound of running feet, coming this way. The Lone Ranger fired two rounds into the dark. That gave the feet pause. "Got to go, boys," he said to Smith and Hayduke. "Move fast."

"On the count of four," Hayduke ordered. With effort they lugged the large carcass to the edge of things. Sweating, they lifted it up. "One," said Hayduke, swinging it forward, letting it swing back. "Two. Three. Heave!"

The remains of Jasper Bundy sailed into space. He'd clear the first ledge three hundred feet below, judging from his excellent trajectory, but would probably splatter into a splotch of rags and pulp at the foot of the great Wingate cliff, far short of GOLIATH's splendid leap. Smith tossed the riot gun after its owner. "Hate guns," he mumbled. "In wrong hands."

"Grab your mounts, boys, and let's get the Christ by Jesus out of here," the Lone Ranger said. Holstering his dreadful cannon, he swung about on his silvergray, revealing two saddled horses — very spooky — on a short lead rope. Smith unlatched rope from halters and sprang onto his bay; Hayduke climbed aboard the tall Appaloosa; the three men galloped off. Into the dark. Down the rim of the Neck, up the slickrock dome on the east, into the juniper forest. (Overgrazing.) Gunfire rattled under the stars to their rear and on the right, a noisy but harmless outburst. Unseen, untouched, they raced on, Smith now in the lead, bearing toward the appointed rendezvous with Doc Sarvis and Bonnie Abbzug. A light airplane banked and circled overhead, searching, but the moon was down, the night complete, they were not seen. A number of motor vehicles raced along the G.E.M.'s broad track, spotlights beaming left and right, but the three horsemen, out on the big plateau, had by now swung far to the south of that particular route of pursuit.

Feeling safer, Smith slowed his horse to a trot, then a walk. The other two men pulled up to his side for talk, reining now left now right around the little trees, the dense clumps of sagebrush and prickly pear. (Cattle country: overgrazing.) In misty depths to their right lay the meandering course of Lost Eden Canyon, feeling the way by gravitational attraction and storm-sculptured erosion toward its confluence with Radium Canyon, thence to Kanab Canyon and the ultimate of canyons, the master canyon, the grandest of the grand.

"You killed that poor bastard, Jack."

"I know it. Was afraid somebody'd get hurt. Them overload hollowpoints do make a mess."

"Shot him dead."

"I know it, boys. The old one-eye hain't what it used to be. I don't feel too good about it. Nor too bad neither."

"What's that mean?"

"I was aimin' at that shotgun. Meant to shoot it out of his hand, like the Lone Ranger hisself always done in the funny papers."

"Good thing you missed. He had George's .357 mag in his other paw." Smith looked aside at Hayduke. "Get your shootin' iron back, George?" He touched his own for reassurance.

"Of course I got the fucker back." Hayduke grinned, the flash of teeth in the dark and hairy face. "You think I'd let a good old solid .357 go to rust? Sentimental value, Seldom: I stole that gun from a cop in Flagstaff long ago. Never been registered. Not in my name anyhow."

Falling again into single file and moving steadily on, they found Doc and Bonnie in their robes, waiting at the appointed spot where the Lone Ranger had left them only a brief time earlier.

Jubilant and frightened, wired up and exhausted, Doc and Bonnie began jabbering away, eager to hear the whole and complete story of GOLIATH's fall. They'd seen the lights go on, to be sure, heard the scream of power, the bellowing voice of Hayduke in authority, saw the searchlight beams stroke across the sky when the monster tipped over the brink, heard the snatch of song, the long ensuing silence, the deep-down echoes of destruction, but — what really happened? Tell us all about it, Seldom.

Hayduke swelled with pride. "Well," he began, "of course I didn't do exactly everything myself —"

The Lone Ranger interrupted. "Choppers," he announced, pointing southeast into the stars. "Choppers a-comin'."

They heard it then, the thumping throb of approaching helicopters, and looking where the old man pointed saw the blinking red signals, the blue shaft of high-intensity light aimed earthward, probing the area of the Neck. Coming their way. With a second behind it.

"Let's go," said Smith. He led, they trotted off, along the rimrock to a trailsign visible, in the dark, only to Smith and the Lone Ranger. Smith stopped, dismounted, began to uncinch his saddle girth. "Everybody down," he said quietly. "We'll unsaddle here, turn the horses loose, go down the trail afoot." He watched the helicopters as he worked.

Three obeyed, adrenalized again by fear. "Saddle first, bridle last," the Lone Ranger reminded Doc, who was fumbling at his horse's head.

"Yes sir."

Four horses stripped except for halters, Smith whacked his bay mare on the rump. She bolted off into the darkness, followed by the others. Headed north through the trees, bound for Susan's place, the home corral, the water trough and the mangers of alfalfa, they'd all be home by dawn, waiting.

One man remained mounted, a black silhouette against the stars. "So long, gang," he said. "You all done good. I'm mighty proud I knowed you folks."

"Jack," Bonnie said, "you're not coming with us?"

"Can't walk," he explained, lying. "Can't get a horse down Seldom's route. I'll see you all some other time, someday. Better get a move on."

Doc shook the Ranger's hand. "An honor to meet you, sir."

"Likewise, Doctor Sarvis."

Bonnie reached up, stretching, and grasped the masked man's gauntleted hand. "You're my hero, Jack."

"Thank you, ma'am. You're a princess."

Hayduke's turn. "Thanks for the help, dad."

"You're welcome, son." The Lone Ranger glanced at the sky, saw the helicopters still two miles off, and returned his steady one-eyed gaze to George Hayduke. "And here's some free advice for you, young fella: clear out of this country. Make yourself scarce for a while. Head for Old Mexico; you'll fit in good down there."

Hayduke grinned. "See you in Hell, Jack Burns."

"Let's go, let's go," cried Smith, hauling two saddles, blankets, bridles down the head of the footpath. Doc followed with the other two, making himself useful.

A final salute: the Ranger spurred his horse, at the same time yanking back on the reins. The old stud reared up on his hind legs and the old man doffed his floppy gigantic absurd white hat — one legendary gesture performed for one last time, always good for a laugh. The horse came down, hard, legs quivering slightly, probably the last time he'd let the Ranger play that trick. They turned together, man and horse, one animal, one centaur, one creation out of myth by history, and trotted away into the night. Taking their own route, no one else's, as always. Where might they be at sunrise, who could say?

Below the rim, Smith stacked the four saddles on their pommels deep beneath an overhanging ledge. Doc tried to help, handing him the bridles and saddle blankets one by one. "Goldang rats'll probly eat the belly bands afore I get back here. They love that salt. But can't be helped, we got to do it." He covered the saddles with the blankets, the blankets with a camouflage poncho, the poncho with an armful of sagebrush.

Bonnie and George came down. The four huddled tight together under the ledge as the first of the helicopters came overhead. They watched the searchlight's blue beam swing across the canyon walls, dancing forward, gliding back, going on, hunting for the trembling prey.

"They'll find Jack for sure," Bonnie moaned.

Smith squeezed her hand. "No they won't, honey. Not him. Can't figure out how he does it but that man and his old horse they can hide on a sand dune. In a stockpond. They can hide where there's nothing ever at all to hide in. You step on that ol' scarecrow before you see him. And then it's too late."

"You didn't even get to say goodbye."

Smith smiled. "He'll be around."

The second helicopter passed. The shuddering rotors dwindled off and faded out. The tumult of distant engines died away. A nightwind shivered through the juniper and pinyon pine. The stars reigned alone in the sky, constellations of radiant silence.

With slow and cautious steps old Seldom Seen led his friends down the falling, rocky path, into the secret hidden inner world of canyon and desert.

29
Loose Ends

"So where'd he go, Oral?"

Young Oral Hatch looked bad. His simple cleancut All-American Mormon face was a mass of purple bruises. One eye was swollen completely shut, leaking a dribble of yellowish matter at inner and outer corners. Head sunk between hunched shoulders, as if protecting himself from further blows, he seemed defenseless, beaten, without spirit. He held his feet together, pigeon-toed, like a little boy enduring a humiliating scold. He clasped his blueblack hands in humble contrition before his stomach, one hand inside the other, guarding his withdrawn belly. His hands exchanged position with each other frequently. Sweat glistened on his forehead, nose, upper lip. His bare head sagged forward, exposing to the powerful light his half-shaven skull, the pale gray skin, the inflamed wound with its rank of stitches. He wore no shirt. His shoes lacked shoestrings. The belt had been taken from his trousers. He sat on a hard steel desk chair, feet on a floor of cold gray concrete.

"How about it, Oral," said the second interrogator, "which way'd he go?" The second man, like the first, had a harsh and abrasive voice, larnyx chapped by too much Canadian Club, accent warped by the slums of Boston, outlook perverted and insight distorted by a life of crime. A life not *in* crime but as he would have proudly asserted, a life spent combatting crime. We tend to resemble what we most doggedly oppose. His name rhymed with the first man's name.

"Speak up, Oral," said Boyle. "You're not doing yourself any fuckin' good at all trying to act like a fuckin' hero."

"Yeah," Holye said. "You got no right to remain silent. You work for us. You're on the Company payroll. You're not a common criminal — you're one of us."

Staring at him from the darkness behind the hooded light, both men laughed. They never had liked him; had never pretended to like him; did not intend to like him. From their point of view, young J. Oral was a foreigner. An alien. Mormon, Utahn, small-town lad, product of an agrarian culture and a later generation that he was, they felt no more in common with him than they did for a punk pimp black from South Boston, a Puerto Rican welfare mother from San Juan living in Brooklyn, or an Ivy League fly fisherman casting his Wily Wizard upon the glittering stream of East Clear Creek, north fork, Arizona.

"You don't seem to understand the situation, Oral. You're in deep shit not only with us but with the law. Taking part in illegal demonstration, trespassing on government property, obstructing traffic on private right-of-way, conspiring to commit felonious destruction of property . . ." A sheet of paper crackled in Boyle's hand: the list. ". . . and worst of all, assault on police officer in line of duty. A S.W.A.T. team sergeant! Resisting arrest . . . Jesus Christ, Oral, these redneck boondock cops are gonna put you away for ten years at least. And I hear that state pen down in — where is it, Hoyle? Florence? *Florence*, Arizona? — I hear it ain't no comfy place, Oral. Attica's a clean decent civilized joint compared to Florence, that's what I hear."

Silence. A third man coughed in a distant corner of the cell, observing but taking no part in this routine interrogation. The Colonel, of course. In faltering health. Losing weight. Troubled by a dull ache in his lungs that would not subside. A fainting sensation when he rose too quickly from a sitting or lying position. Blood in his stool. He knew by inference what the problem was but only a blood test would confirm it, finally. The Colonel preferred to postpone that day of understanding.

"Where's Hayduke, Oral?"

Silence.

"We know you know. Where'd he go? And where's that Bundy, the security guard? What happened to him, Oral? Hayduke kidnap him? Kill him? Enlist him in the gang?"

No response.

"Where was Smith that night? His wife says he was in Green River but she could be lying. Wives do that. How about it, Oral?"

No answer.

"You like to see Erika again, Oral?"

A stir of interest. Young Hatch unclasped his cold hands, shifted his feet, looked up into the blazing lamp. "Where is she?"

"You want to see her?"

"Where is she?"

Chuckles of amusement. "Well now, our boy has come alive. Now he's talking."

"Answer our questions, Oral, and we'll answer yours."

The young man sighed, closed his eyes, lowered his head into his hands. "Can't," he mumbled. "Can't. Been telling you for three days, I don't know."

"Why, Oral, we've only been here about six hours. Three days, Oral? You're exaggerating things, Oral."

"Exaggerating? He's lying again. Where's Hayduke, Oral?"

"I don't know," he groaned, "I don't know, I don't know. I never saw him. I never heard anything about him. I don't even know if he's alive. They all said he was dead."

"Who did?"

"All of them: Doc, Bonnie, Smith, those Earth First! people. I never found anybody who knew a thing about him we don't already know. They all seem to think he's dead. And what's more . . ."

"What's more?"

Silence.

"What's more, Oral? What's that mean?"

"He's playing hero again, Boyle. He means what's more even if he did know he wouldn't tell mean nasty crude old naughty old things like us. Right, Oral?"

No response.

"Is that right, Oral? My feelings are hurt, Oral. Surely you don't mean that?"

No answer.

"All right, Oral, you had your chance. You blew it. Me and Hoyle and the Colonel we're off to Mexico now. We're not coming back to

Arizona for a long time. Maybe never. So we'll let you rot in maximum security for the next ten years. How's that grab you, punko?"

"Where's Erika?"

"Boy, you'll never see her again either. In fact the men from INS are packing her onto a BOAC jet right this very day; it's back to Norway for that little no-goodnik."

"Oh no!" cried young Hatch. "You can't do that. She has a passport and a visa. She's legal."

"She's a criminal anarchist, Oral. But she didn't admit it on her visa application. Anarchists aren't allowed to enter the U.S. And she has a whole list of criminal charges against her, just like you do. So out she goes. She's lucky we don't lock her up for ten years too."

Hatch curled up in his seat again, bruised face buried in his battered hands. His shoulders quivered. He sniffled. Half choking, he tried to suppress a spasm of sobs, then yielded to his grief, like a man, and let it come.

"Aw, gee," mocked Boyle, "the poor boy's crying."

"Poor little Oral. Mean old naughty mens make him cry."

Sniggering, they watched the young man weep. Mormon screwball, what more could you expect from a hick like him? From anybody named *Oral?*

The man in the corner stood up from his chair, slowly, painfully. "Get the jailer," he said quietly.

"What?"

"You heard me. You two have had your fun. Now we're taking him out of here."

"Then what?"

"Then we're releasing him. Without prejudice."

"But sir — "

"You heard me. Boyle: call the jailer."

"Yes sir."

Boyle departed the cell, vanished down a corridor of steel and concrete under uric-yellow lights. The banging and the clatter, the gabble and the rock, swelled up in volume as the other prisoners watched Boyle stride past.

Hoyle and the Colonel gazed on young Hatch. After a moment, heart softening a shade under the Colonel's stern eye, Hoyle said, "You hear that, Oral? You're still a special agent for about half an hour more. The Company's taking you out of here and turning you loose. How do you like that idea, Oral?"

Still sobbing, Hatch said nothing.

"A few more minutes and you're a free man, Oral. On your own. Free as a bird. Whatcha gonna do then? See your mother? Go to church? Follow Hayduke?"

At last young Oral raised his face from his hands. Cheeks moist and eyes red, he looked straight at the dim form of Hoyle seated behind the lamp, what he could see of it, and he said, "None of your goddamned business, Mister Hoyle."

Hoyle smirked. "Going to Norway, aren't you, Oral?"

"That's right."

"Like a young dog after a hot bitch, right Oral?"

J. Oral Hatch stood up. He turned the blazing floorlamp aside and looked down at the tough red smirking face of Agent Hoyle.

"Mister Hoyle?" Oral raised and closed his hands.

"Yeah?"

"Please stand up, Mister Hoyle."

Hoyle's grin widened, exposing his golden molars. "Stand up, huh? So you can knock me down, huh? Old man like me? That the idea, you Moroni-kissing chicken-eating geek?"

"Yes sir."

Hoyle stirred slightly, as if to rise, then lashed out with his right foot, shod in a copper's heavy steel-toed shoe. The sudden blow caught young Oral square in the knee. Gasping, he went down.

Hoyle stood up. "You still have a lot to learn, Oral. Too much to learn. You never would've made a real agent. You're not real smart, know what I mean, punko?"

The Colonel pulled on his topcoat and gloves. Flagstaff nights were cold, even in the summer. And no matter what the weather, anywhere, he never felt quite warm enough these days. He looked at Oral crouched on the floor, moaning, clutching at his knee, and at the bulky man standing over him, rubbing his hands and gazing down with satisfaction at his victim.

"You're not too smart yourself, Hoyle," the Colonel said. "Now you and Boyle are going to have to help him out of here."

"Yes sir. It's worth it."

Bishop Love and Mrs. Love the Second were married on the Neck, in the light of the rekindled bonfire, by J. Marvin Pratt, Justice of the Peace. The groom kissed the bride while those present (about a dozen, mostly women) smiled, cried, cheered, applauded. From the distance, at variant points of the compass, came the self-conscious barking of handguns, the harmless chatter of small-arms fire, the shouts of scattered anxious men lost in the dark. Helicopters disturbed the peace overhead but soon drifted eastward, circling and blinking like fireflies, idle and nonchalant, insouciant and small. Mrs. Pratt and Mrs. Love the First signed the marriage license as official witnesses. Someone popped a cork; toasts proposed and acclaimed, bubbly carbonated apple juice overflowed the clear plastic champagne glasses. Mrs. Love I took Mrs. Love II aside into the dark for consultation:

"Don't let him get you pregnant right away, Ginny darling. You stand up for your rights. You tell him no baby for at least six months."

Ranger Dick smiled, her arm draped around the other woman's neck. "Mabel, my dear, we'll keep that fat old fart under firm restraint from here on out."

"You said it. That's the way to talk."

They planned a two-week honeymoon in Honolulu. The Bishop and his Mrs. and his Mrs. And the eleven children? Couldn't hardly leave them behind. Them kids never did see a alligator or a monkey on a palm tree or a Beach Boy yet, Mrs. Love the First explained.

The Monkey Wrench Gang gathered for the last time — very tired but very excited — at the base of the canyon wall below Hayduke's Cave. While Doc, Bonnie and Seldom said their goodbyes, George scrambled up the rocky route in the dark to pick up a few things he'd need for his trip. Also, he explained, had to free his rattlesnake.

"I sure hope you two got an ironclad alibi for tonight," Smith said.

"We do," the doctor said, "if George gets us back in time."

"We're checked into the Bridal Suite at the Strater Hotel in Durango," Bonnie said. "We're celebrating our wedding anniversary."

"Southwest pediatrics conference," Doc explained. "Also."

"Durango? Durango, Colorado? You'll never get there tonight, Bonnie honey. It's too far."

"If we can sneak back into the room by morning we're okay. These robes will help. Got the DON'T DISTURB sign on the doorknob."

"That's still too far."

"Not by air. George is flying us."

"George? Our George?" Smith looked up into the darkness toward the cave. "Him? Where'd he get a pilot's license? Where's the airplane?"

Doc smiled wearily, sitting on a shelf of stone. Bonnie explained. No, George had no license. But he could fly anyway, sort of. Was learning fast. Liked to call himself the Green Barón. Beret? No, Barón.

And the plane was some kind of old two-seater with extra-long wings and huge fat tires. Could land and take off anywhere.

"There's three of you."

We sit on laps, she explained. I mean I do. I help him with the gas throttle, the fuel mix, compass readings and so on. We made it here, we'll make it back. I think. I hope.

Doc sighed heavily, thinking about it.

"And where you got this plane, Bonnie?"

Don't know exactly where he got it, she explained. You know George — probably borrowed it somewhere. You mean where is it now? Up there? She pointed to the top of the opposite canyon wall, about fifteen hundred feet above. It's up there. George discovered a route. Plane's parked on an old drilling site. That thing can land and stop in fifty yards.

"You'll need a lot more than that for a takeoff, honey. You sure you wanta do this?"

No problem, Bonnie explained. George worked out his own technique for a short-run takeoff. We drive the plane off the edge of the cliff, gain airspeed in the dive, climb up the other wall and away we go.

Doc looked worried.

"Bonnie, you sure you wanta do that?"

"We'll risk it. Better than ten years in prison. Besides, we promised Reuben we'd be home by tomorrow night."

Doc smiled faintly at the sound of his son's name.

Hayduke returned with a loaded backpack. He set it on the sand, unzipped the wide bottom pocket and coaxed out his rattlesnake. "Would starve in that cave. . . ." Buzzing like a maraca, the serpent at first objected to another disturbance but finally slithered away.

"So long, George. Don't suppose I need to know where you're a-goin' next."

Hayduke smiled happily. "No need, Seldom. But you could say I smell the sea in my hairy nostrils. A sea named Cortez. And you could say, in a few months, you might be getting a kangaroo-type postcard from a bloody bleedin' dinkum blighter name of Rudolf Herman. So long, Seldom Seen Smith."

"You be careful, George Washington Hayduke." They embraced. Neither man wept — both grateful to be free.

Seldom hugged his friends Doc and Bonnie. "See you at the houseboat, pardners. Don't forget. One week from today. Big party."

"Dealer's choice?"

"No, honey. No more poker. Just ain't fun without good ol' Oral no more. No, it's the end of our probation, you recollect? One more week and we all are good ordinary innocent law-abiding meek and humble U.S. of A. citizens like everybody else. Remember? Like a wedding anniversary, you might say."

Old Seldom Seen smiled at Bonnie Abbzug, at Doctor Sarvis, at the impatient and fidgeting George Hayduke. He winked at each, at one and all. "Now if you folks'll excuse me I think I better get outa this here playtime costume and get back into my regular rugged he-man cowperson suit. Burn these coveralls and gloves and sneakers, pull on my Wrangler *respectable* clothes and look like something cute."

"What's your alibi going to be?"

"Alibi? Hell, Doc, I don't need no alibi. I'm all alibi. Nobody ever knows where I am or even where I was including me. And I got three good wives who'll swear to it, anytime."

End of the Trail, White Man

Hayduke turned east from Punta "Rocky Point" Peñasco, a seashore colony belonging mostly to Phoenix, Arizona and drove for fifteen miles on the wet firm beach into the evening twilight. He seemed to do most of his traveling these days after sundown. He was alone. He drove the antique red convertible, top down as always, at optimum speed, forty miles per hour over the shining sand. Fast enough to keep the wheels from sinking, slow enough to avoid the driftwood, fishing nets, used tires, spiked lumber, whale vertebrae, poisoned sea lions, broken winejugs and other flotsam left ashore by the ebbing tide.

When he saw the ship's riding lights two miles offshore and a mile ahead flicker on then out four times, he turned on his headlights and responded with the same signal. The ship's lights blinked on then off twice more. Hayduke answered in the same code. Confirmation. The ship went dark. Hayduke drove ahead without lights, shifting into neutral and letting his automobile slow gradually, so that he'd have no need to use the brakes and flash red warning signals for a mile down the coast.

The ancient Cadillac coasted on and on, slower and slower. He meant to abandon the thing, here on the Sonoran beach, and leave the key in the ignition switch. Let some lucky beachcomber take it away without trouble, if he got here before the tide returned. Would be a small sentimental loss — Hayduke loved machines, even the silliest — but not much loss in a material sense. Until you've actually owned a Cadillac, he confessed to himself, you'll never know how badly designed they are, how shoddily made, how little difference it makes in love or life, in peace or war, in status or in state of mind.

The car rolled a little farther onward, leaving deeper and deeper tracks in the wet sand, and eased to a full stop near the high tide line. Hayduke trying to make things easier for the next thief. He climbed out over the door, pulled his entire supply of luggage from the back seat — a bulging Kelty backpack — and set it on the sand. He unwired and opened the trunk and removed a rolled-up inflatable dinghy, with oars, footpump, lifejacket, two waterjugs.

Hayduke looked out to sea, observed the small ship, black in outline against the pink evening sky, waiting. He unrolled the little neoprene boat, only six feet long, attached hose to valve, and pumped the thing full, taut and semi-rigid. He fastened oars to oarlocks, threw in his baggage, and picked up the bowline. The sea was only fifty feet away, a light surf rolling in and out, but he might have to wade and drag the boat another fifty feet before he reached knee-deep water.

A man shuffled over the dunes and onto the beach about a hundred yards to the southeast, a dark vague shape in the thickening twilight. Hayduke spotted him at once.

He looked inland and saw a second man, tall and thin in a wind-whipped coat, hands in pockets, approaching step by step, quite slowly but directly over the waves of sand, through the waving strands of sawgrass.

And the third man came from the third direction, precisely opposite the first, from up the beach, advancing cautiously on the wet sand, crouching, cradling in both arms a metallic object of indeterminate function but sinister intent. Hayduke saw that one too.

Oh shit. Not now. Not here. Not with my ship a-waiting only a mile offshore, my passage to freedom, a new world, a new life. No. Not fair. Absolutely unsporting. But even as he mumbled these phrases to himself, wallowing in self-pity, young Hayduke was unstrapping the top of his pack, fumbling for his new Uzi machine pistol. (Parting gift from an old friend.) But his .357 revolver came first to hand. He cocked the action and fired a single shot at the nearest enemy — the tall man in the coat with hands plunged deep in pockets. That man sank from sight. Completing the reflexive gesture, swinging left and dropping flat to his chest, Hayduke aimed with both hands at the second nearest man. At the same moment and in perfect unison the two gunmen on the beach fired at Hayduke, each from the hip with M-16 assault rifle, each triggering a sustained burst of fully automatic fire, each holding down the upward thrust of muzzle as he raked the sand from here to there, directing (not aiming) his spray of fiery dum-dums at the silhouette target turning and falling at the bow of the dinghy; one man shooting from the southeast, the other man from the northwest, in perfect Euclidean alignment. What the Colonel had called an enfilade and/or pincer movement.

A sweet stillness followed, without echoes, in which the only sounds were the murmur of the surf, the breeze at play in the sedges on the dunes, the hiss of escaping air from a fast-deflating rubber boat.

Half buried in the damp sand, Hayduke raised his head and looked about. Night was nearly here, assuming and subsuming rapidly, as typical of a Sonoran shore, the brief lavender fantasia of desert twilight. He looked down the beach and saw a human form, more or less, crumpled like abandoned kelp on the sand. Twisting his head, he looked in the opposite way and perceived, after a moment, the second gunman sprawled in similar disarray, comfortably dead. He looked for the tall slender man inland among the dunes: that man was gone. Apparently gone.

Feeling himself unhurt, not even touched, Hayduke did not hesitate any longer. He rose to his knees, slipped on the lifejacket, stood, ran in crouching position toward the water, expecting each moment the piercing heat of a bullet in his back. He splashed through the shallow surf, into the warm water, over the hard rippled sand of the sea bottom. Frightened little stingrays scuttled from his path, schools of sunfish fled before him. Sloshing into water more than knee-deep, he flopped forward and began to swim. He swam not fast but steadily, with firm powerful strokes, at a pace good for miles, toward the black figure of his darkened ship.

The full moon rose from beyond the mountains of a distant coast, glowing red as a blood-orange through the sea mist. Silent pelicans, a flapping frigate bird, a flock of gulls flew along the beach, wings weaving invisible patterns in the air. They vanished. Sympathetic dolphins, streamlined and glistening as submarines, swam in parallel with Hayduke toward the ship. The blood-red moon rose higher, clearing jagged peaks, and laid a blood-red track of hammered molten copper across the tranquil, shimmering, mysterious Sea of Cortez.

The Colonel stood on the topmost dune, hands in topcoat pockets,

and contemplated the idyll of the dead, the glowing sea, the doomed
Cadillac, the birds, the desert shore, and his own blood. The Colonel
too was wounded. He watched the slowly receding form of the
swimmer — easy target — and his wake upon the moonlight. The
man, the men, the birds, the dolphins, now here, now gone. That
lightless pirate ship out there would soon be gone as well. This very
shore and coast would slide, rise, fall, the sea itself become an enclosed
desert lake, turning to salt, shrinking century by century beneath the
glare of a pitiless desert sun. All in good time. The Colonel sighed with
satisfaction in his vision of time and transience. Of the way things are.
De rerum natura. With pleasure, despite the nausea in his bowels, he
recalled some favorite lines from a favorite poet. Murmuring, he
recited them aloud:

> Our terrors and our darknesses of mind
> Must be dispelled then not by sunlight. . . .
> But by insight into nature, and a scheme
> Of systematic contemplation. . . .

Very good, Titus. Well said. The Colonel advanced over the dry sand
and down to the beach, as close as he could get to the retreating prey
without getting his shoes wet. He kicked at the sagging, useless boat.
He gazed to left and right, at the bodies of his lieutenants dimly seen,
spreadeagled in pools of black blood. Poor fools, he thought in silence,
poor dumb loyal fools, how could mere hatred have brought you so
far, so terribly far, from the innocence of childhood and the sweetness
of youth? You have been terribly wronged; you shall be avenged.

The Colonel looked toward the distant swimmer, two hundred
yards away but plain to see on the moonlit red water, the converging
lines of his wake an infallible guide to his vulnerable, fragile, all-
too-human body. Unhurried, the Colonel opened his coat. He wore
an extra-long shoulder holster beneath. He drew out a gleaming,
chrome-plated, long-range pistol with extended barrel (for accuracy)
and telescopic sights mounted on the breech (for precision). He cocked
the hammer.

But paused again. The moon, the sea, the quiet surf. He smiled with
tragic resignation. The peace and splendor of this scene — his scene —
led him to remember another and much later poet, another and much
simpler poem:

> It is a beauteous evening, calm and free.
> The holy time is quiet as a nun. . . .

The Colonel inserted the barrel of the pistol between his lips and teeth, letting the muzzle come gently to rest against the roof of his mouth. He pulled the trigger.

Hayduke heard the shot, waited, felt no harm, continued stroking forward. He reached the shadow of the dark ship an easy half hour later. He read the name under the bow: *Sea Shepherd.*

"That you, George?" a voice called down from the rail above.

"It's me, Paul."

"About time." A rope ladder tumbled down the side, barely reaching the water as the ship rocked gently back and forth. "Grab that thing and come aboard. Had us worried, buddy. All that vulgar gunfire. You all right?"

"I'm all right, Captain."

Hayduke wrapped a hand around the ladder's bottom rung and rested for a moment. He stared back at the coast of Sonoran Mexico, the dark unpeopled desert, the rising brightening and triumphant moon. He unlatched the lifejacket and caressed his hairy chest. Scratched his belly. Felt the steady pumping of his heart. Alive. He was alive.

The captain's voice sang out in the night, joyous, jubilant. "Nancy M. — call back that landing party. Ed, Joey, haul in the anchors. . . ." More orders followed. Bare feet padded over the teakwood decks.

Hayduke smiled, turned, began climbing the ladder.

"And Nancy Z.," the captain hollered, waiting for his boarder, "run up the black flag."

"The black flag, Paul?"

"Yes. The black flag, Nancy. The black flag with the red monkey wrench. Party time! George Hayduke's here!"

31
Resurrection

The former deerpath is gone, obliterated by the hundred-foot-wide trail of the late Super-G.E.M. Where once the wild ricegrass grew, vibrant in the breeze, and bunchgrass, yucca, redbud, scarlet penstemon and purple lupine, is now the broad roadway of nothing but stone, sand, and compacted soil churned to a fine floury dust by the busy truck traffic that has ceased, on this route, only a few weeks before.

A little stream of murky water, dammed here and there by ruts of mud, zigzags this way and that, seeking and eventually always finding the way to lower ground. Where bedrock lies exposed the water oozes across ledges of bluegray limestone, streams through sculptured chutes and grooves, drops from convergent pouroffs into bubbling pools. At poolside the watercress, tules and sapling willow still survive, plotting a comeback. Pale frogs sun themselves on pale stone; dragonflies with emerald wings, with sapphire wings, with wings of ruby-red, dart hover hum above the water; tadpoles, minnows, boatmen bugs, fairy shrimp, mosquito larvae and horsehair worms (from the cattle) and liver flukes (from the sheep) squirm about below the surface, fucking friends and eating loved ones.

Away from the creek and the dusty triple-wide right-of-way, the canyon floor rises on each side toward talus slopes where juniper and a few pinyon pine grow among the scree and rubble of fallen rock. Above the talus stands a vertical, sheer, unscalable red wall of Wingate sandstone, soaring upward one two three four five hundred feet to the buff-white caprock on the rim.

A solitary horseman waits on the canyon's edge, man and horse dark in outline against the backdrop of a salmon-colored dawn. The rider gazes upon the empty road below. Sunrise, under way, can be seen in part from the depths of the canyon, above the purple mesas on the east.

Near the edge of GOLIATH's trail, not far from a certain half-dead half-alive juniper tree that lifts a twisted silvergray limb toward the sky — a gesture of static assertion, the affirmation of an embattled but undefeated existence — is a disk of impacted earth some twenty inches in diameter that differs somehow from the packed soil on either side. The difference, on close inspection, consists in this, that the circular area is rising, forming a slight but perceptible bulge. The rise is discontinuous: a stir from beneath, a bit of motion, then a prolonged pause. As if even the earth, in its most intimate and miniature crustal movements, must halt from time to time for rest. But only for a time; the tiny disturbance is resumed, the hard soil rises still further, shaping itself into a rough irregular dome, with cracks, that could serve as a geologist's toy model of a laccolith in process of formation.

The cracks grow longer, deeper, like the breaking of an egg. Another rest. Another stirring of activity under the surface and a tiny foot appears, a clawed scaly tiny foot at the end of a short limber scaly leg. Rest again. The emergent foot feels about in the open air, takes purchase on the earth, digs in, pulls. The second forefoot appears, dripping dust between its toenails, and with it a beaked ancient reptile head, small eyes humorous and wise, the slit of a mouth set in a tight grim resolute determined smile.

Rest. Dig. Climb.

Come forth.

Old man turtle emerges from his grave. The desert tortoise resurrects himself. Covered with dust but unbroken, uncrushed — uncrushable! — he clambers out, crawls forward, extends his four legs fully from his plated shell and stands erect. He squints to one side, to the other, then straight ahead, blinking. His dim old eyes reflect the gleam of the open sky, the growing light. He stares in wonder. He lifts his head high on its wrinkled neck and takes off, marching toward the invincible sunrise.

The horseman on the canyon rim, missing little that's alive and in motion, observes the rebirth of the desert turtle and doffs his big hat in salute. He replaces the hat and resumes his vigil, gazing toward the horizon for a sign of the enemy. Nothing this morning. After a while he blows his nose on the ground, wipes a finger on the horse's haunch, turns the horse and rides away.